PURPLE
HEARTS

PURPLE HEARTS

MICHAEL GRANT

First published in Great Britain in 2018
by Electric Monkey, an imprint of Egmont UK Limited
The Yellow Building, 1 Nicholas Road, London W11 4AN

Published by arrangement with HarperCollins Children's Books,
a division of HarperCollins Publishers, New York, New York, USA

Text copyright © 2018 by Michael Grant

ISBN 978 1 4052 7388 6

A CIP catalogue record for this title is available from the British Library

58384/1

Typeset by Avon DataSet Ltd, Bidford on Avon, Warwickshire
Printed and bound in Great Britain by CPI Group

Stay safe online. Any website addresses listed in this book are correct at the
time of going to print. However, Egmont is not responsible for content hosted by
third parties. Please be aware that online content can be subject to change
and websites can contain content that is unsuitable for children. We
advise that all children are supervised when using the internet.

MIX
Paper from
responsible sources
FSC® C020471

To all the real soldier girls.

"Today we rule Germany, tomorrow, the world!"

—*Adolf Hitler*

"And when we get to Berlin, I am personally going to shoot that paper-hanging son-of-a-bitch Hitler. Just like I'd shoot a snake!"

—*General George S. Patton*

1944.

World War II has raged in Europe for five long years, but the tide has turned decisively in favor of the Allies. France, Belgium, the Netherlands, Poland, Czechoslovakia, Denmark, Luxembourg, Yugoslavia, Greece, the western part of the Soviet Union and North Africa have all been occupied at one time, but now the edges of the Nazi Reich are being rolled up.

In Italy, Hitler's clownish Fascist henchman, Benito Mussolini, has been overthrown. Pro-Nazi governments in Hungary, Romania, Bulgaria and parts of Yugoslavia are looking for ways to make peace with the Allies. The Nazis are out of North Africa and southern Italy.

The Soviet Union is ruled by the paranoid monster Joseph Stalin. Having once made a treacherous peace with Hitler allowing the Soviets to stab Finland and Poland in the back, Stalin then found himself betrayed in turn by Hitler. Ignoring a peace agreement between them, the Germans invaded the Soviet Union, inflicting unspeakable brutality on Poles, Belorussians, Ukrainians, Russians and, of course, above all, the Jews.

But the Soviet Union has proven to be too big a meal for Hitler to swallow. The Nazis have been turned back at Stalingrad and Leningrad, forced to flee after the largest tank battle in history at Kursk, and are now retreating with a vengeful Soviet Red Army hot on their heels.

From June 25, 1940, and the surrender of France, to June 1941, when Hitler launched Operation Barbarossa against the

1

Soviet Union, Great Britain, her Commonwealth and her Empire stood alone against the Nazi tidal wave. With British cities being bombed by the Luftwaffe, and British shipping largely at the bottom of the Atlantic, cut off, hungry and alone, Britain still stood, the indomitable hero of the western world.

But after Hitler's ally, Japan, attacked Pearl Harbor on December 7, 1941, the great, sleeping giant across the sea finally awoke. The United States of America, which had till then limited itself to supplying material aid to Britain, was all at once, overnight, fully engaged in the war.

America's not-so-secret weapon was its productive capacity. By 1944 the USA was producing 96,000 warplanes per year, more than ten planes each *hour* in a twenty-four-hour day. In the total war effort, American industry produced 110 aircraft carriers, 41,000 cannon, 100,000 tanks, 310,000 aircraft, 12,500,000 rifles, and 41,000,000,000 rounds of ammunition.

It also raised, trained and equipped a military that by 1944 numbered nearly 12 million soldiers, sailors and marines.

The world waited as the Americans put on a poor show in North Africa and became bogged down in Italy under ineffectual generals. America's allies granted the genius of American war production, but they doubted the fighting spirit, grit, determination and competence of American soldiers, from Eisenhower down to the private in a foxhole.

The Americans faced the ultimate test: leading a fractious, suspicious coalition of British, Canadian, Australian, Free French and Free Polish forces to invade and liberate Europe, and to destroy Hitler's evil regime.

2

The Nazis were no longer advancing, but the Nazi empire was very far from beaten. New German weapons, the V1 cruise missile, the V2 ballistic missile, the world's first jet fighter, the Me 262, and the massive Tiger tank were coming online.

Now on the defensive, the superbly-equipped, experienced, well-trained, well-generaled and dug-in German army, the Wehrmacht, and its brutal and fanatical counterpart, the Waffen SS, were fighting to save the Nazi regime and their Fatherland.

The Nazi beast cornered was at its most dangerous.

Between D-Day, June 6, 1944, and the German surrender, on May 7, 1945, 125,000 American GIs—more than 350 per day—would die bringing freedom to western Europe and destroying the greatest evil humanity had ever faced.

PROLOGUE

There's a story going round, Gentle Reader, I don't know if it's true or not, but supposedly a guy heard it from a German POW. The story is that the first Allied bomb dropped on Berlin killed an elephant in the zoo.

I guess I'm sorry for the elephant, but that sort of sums up the way it goes in war. There's no moral sense to it. Sure, one side may be better than the other, I mean, I was at Buchenwald. No one needs to convince me the Nazis are evil. But what I mean is that in the day-to-day of it death and destruction do not rain down on the bad and spare the good. Death does not care whether you're a bright and sparkly hero or a yellow coward. Death doesn't know you, or care to know you. You're just the poor dumb bastard who happened to be in the wrong place at the wrong time. You're just that elephant.

The philosophy of the combat soldier in a nutshell: you're gonna die. Might be today, might be tomorrow, might be fifty years from now all safe and snug in your bed. But when your number is up, your number is up. And that might be in three . . . two . . . Bang!

Do I sound like a weary old veteran? A sweet young

slip of a girl like me? Shall I blush?

When this all started, when the US of A got into this war, and the Supreme Court decided what the hell, let's send women too, everyone wondered what effect it would have.

Could women fight? My girl Rio has a shiny Silver Star, a fistful of Purple Hearts, and a notched M1 that say yes.

Could the men fight alongside women or would the simple creatures be too distracted by feminine curves? Well, I once spent a long night in a hole with Luther Geer, who has never been a gentleman, but he is a good soldier, and he never even made a pass at me. Possibly he was distracted by the artillery barrage coming down on our heads. Possibly it was that I hadn't showered in . . . God only knows how long; you'd have to ask my fleas. We were not a man and a woman in that hole, we were two scared little babies screaming and cursing and so cold we were grateful for the warmth of our own piss running down our legs.

It was not a romantic evening.

And people wondered what it would do to us afterward, to us 'Soldier Girls.' Would we lose all our feminine attributes? Would we become mannish?

Stupid question. Women don't stop being women, and men don't stop being men. Both of us, men and women, become an entirely new creature: the combat soldier. You don't recognize combat soldiers by legs or breasts or the hidden bits; you recognize them by their eyes. Maybe a civilian wouldn't spot it, but we always will. We are our own separate tribe. We know things. And we are none of us, men or women, the people we started out being.

Sorry, Gentle Reader, I've been prosing on and I should be sticking to the story. It's just that as bad as North Africa and Sicily were, as miserable and brutal and pointless as Italy was, what comes next I am afraid will defeat my meager talents as a writer. I don't know quite how to explain Omaha Beach, or the bocage country, or the bloody goddamned forests they call the Hürtgen and the Eifel. And Shakespeare himself could not do justice to Buchenwald or Dachau.

Sorry.

I guess you can't tell, but for a minute there I couldn't type. Maybe it was more than a minute. I suppose it must have been a while longer because one of my pals here in the hospital came up and for no reason laid her hand on my shoulder and that's when I realized I'd been crying.

There are things in my head, pictures and sounds and smells . . . I did not need to know these things, Gentle Reader. I could have lived my life and never known, but now I do, and perhaps it's perverse of me, but I'm passing those terrible things along to you.

Not very nice of me, really.

Maybe that's why the old guys, the veterans from the first war, don't talk much. Maybe they don't want to inflict it all on unsuspecting civilians. Maybe they are kinder than I am. But I figure you deserve the truth.

Here's some truth: I once shot an SS prisoner in the throat. He was begging for his life, half dead from hunger and cold. He only had one boot and the other foot was black from some combination of trench foot and frostbite. And I put a carbine round right through his Nazi throat. I could have shot him in the head, but I wanted him to have a few seconds to reflect on the fact that he was going to die.

You don't approve, Gentle Reader? Are you tut-tutting and shaking your head? You would never do that? Oh? Were you there in the Hürtgen? Were you there on Elsenborn Ridge? No? Then with the greatest respect I have to tell you that your moral opinion means nothing to me. My judges are the filthy, freezing, starving men and women who were there with me. Come with me to the beach and the bocage and the forests, Gentle Reader, spend a few days, and then render your judgment.

Well, enough of that. Tell that story when it's time. Wipe your eyes and keep typing, old girl.

Time is short. They're shipping me out soon, back to the land of Coca-Cola and Cadillacs, and I need to finish this story. At night I read bits of it to some of the other guys and gals here. We drink the hooch smuggled in by our buddies outside, and we chain-smoke, and we don't say much because there isn't much to say.

This last part of my story begins with the most long-awaited battle ever.

For long years the Nazi bastards had been killing people in Europe. Doing things, and not just at the camps, things that . . . Well, you'll see. Let me just say that anyone who says G2 aren't real soldiers, I'll introduce you to Rainy Schulterman. She may be in intelligence, not combat, but she's a soldier that girl. She told me some things.

Where was I? Right, reminding you that we were still mostly new to this war. Everyone had been at it longer than we had, we were the new kids at school, but everyone knew we were the biggest new kid they'd ever seen. Before D-Day the war in the west had been mostly Britain and its Commonwealth.

After D-Day it was our war.

Every eye on the planet was turned toward us. From presidents and dictators, to car salesmen and apprentice shoe-makers, from Ike up in his plush HQ down to the lost little children with helmets on their heads and guns in their hands, the whole world held its breath.

D-Day. June 6, 1944. On that day many still doubted the American soldier.

By June 7, no one did.

PART ONE
D-DAY

SUPREME HEADQUARTERS
ALLIED EXPEDITIONARY FORCE

Soldiers, Sailors and Airmen of the Allied Expeditionary Force!

You are about to embark upon the Great Crusade, toward which we have striven these many months. The eyes of the world are upon you. The hopes and prayers of liberty-loving people everywhere march with you. In company with our brave Allies and brothers-in-arms on other Fronts, you will bring about the destruction of the German war machine, the elimination of Nazi tyranny over the oppressed peoples of Europe, and security for ourselves in a free world.

Your task will not be an easy one. Your enemy is well trained, well equipped and battle hardened. He will fight savagely.

But this is the year 1944! Much has happened since the Nazi triumphs of 1940–41. The United Nations have inflicted upon the Germans great defeats, in open battle, man-to-man. Our air offensive has seriously reduced their strength in the air and their capacity to wage war on the ground.

Our Home Fronts have given us a superiority in weapons and munitions of war, and placed at our disposal great reserves of trained fighting men. The tide has turned! The free men of the world marching together to Victory!

I have full confidence in your devotion to duty and skill in battle.

We will accept nothing less than full Victory!

Good Luck! And let us all beseech the blessing of Almighty God upon this great and noble undertaking.

—Dwight D. Eisenhower, Supreme Allied Commander of the Allied Expeditionary Force (SHAEF)

1

LUPÉ CAMACHO—CAMP WORTHING (SOUTH), HAMPSHIRE, UK

"Camacho comma Gooda ... Goo-ada ... Gooa-loopy?" Sergeant Fred "Bonemaker" Bonner does not speak Spanish.

Camacho comma Guadalupé, age nineteen, cringes and glances left and right down the line of soldiers as if one of them can tell her whether or not to attempt to correct the sergeant.

But there are no answers in the blank faces staring forward.

"It's Guadalupé, Sergeant!" she blurts suddenly. "But you can ..."

She had been about to say that he can call her Lupé. As in Loo-pay. And then it occurred to her that old, gray-haired, fat, bent, red-nosed sergeants with many stripes on their uniform sleeves do not always want to chat about nicknames with privates.

The Bonemaker turns his weary eyes on her and says, "This here is the American army, not the Messican army, honey. If I say it's Gooa-loopy, it's Gooa-loopy. Now, whatever the hell your name is, get on the truck and get the hell out of here."

Guadalupé starts to go but Bonemaker yells, "Take your paperwork. I didn't fill these forms out for nothing!"

Lupé takes the papers—there are several carbon sheets stapled together—and rushes to the truck. Or at least rushes as fast as she can with her duffel over one shoulder, her rucksack on her back with the straps cutting into her shoulders, a webbing belt festooned with canteen and ammo pouches, and her M1 Garand rifle.

She heaves her gear over the tailgate of an open deuce-and-a-half truck and struggles to get up and over the side herself until one of the half dozen soldiers already aboard offers her a hand.

She slumps heavily onto one of the two inward-facing benches. She nods politely and is met with faces that are not so much hostile as they are preoccupied by nervousness and uncertainty. That she understands perfectly.

She is only five foot five, tall enough she figures. She has black hair cut very short, the sort of dark eyes that seem always to be squinting to look into the distance, a broad face that no one would describe as pretty, and dark, sun-tanned hands and forearms marked with lighter-toned old scars from barbed wire, branding irons, horse bites and even a pair of tiny punctures from an irritable rattlesnake.

Guadalupé has had a mere thirteen weeks of basic training from an Arizonan sergeant who had precisely zero affection for 'wetbacks,' and who, as far as Lupé could tell, had no direct experience of anything war-related. Just the same, she was not a standout at basic, and to Lupé that was a victory. Lupé does not want to be here at this replacement depot, or in any other army facility, especially not in England getting ready for the invasion everyone says is finally coming.

Her only outstanding quality at basic had been her endurance. She had grown up on a ranch in southern Utah, a family-worked ranch. She started riding horses at age three, learned to accurately

14

throw a lasso by age five, and by age twelve was doing about ninety percent of a full-grown ranch hand's work. Plus showing up for school most if not all of the time.

But Lupé has another talent which did not come out during training. She'd shot an eight-point mule deer buck right through the heart when she was nine at a distance of three hundred yards. She'd killed a cougar with a shot her father advised her not to take because it was near-impossible.

Guadalupé Camacho could shoot.

In fact, she shot well enough to consistently fail to qualify with the M1 Garand rifle and the M1 carbine while making it look as if she were trying her best. She failed because she did not wish to go to war and shoot anyone, and she was worried that had she shown any ability she would be shipped off to the war. So on the firing range she amused herself by terrifying instructors with near-misses and general, but carefully-played incompetence.

It turned out not to matter. The pressure was on to move as many recruits as possible to the war in Europe, so Lupé was marked qualified with the M1 Garand, the M1 carbine, the Thompson submachine gun and the Browning automatic rifle— the light machine gun known as the BAR. She had in fact never even fired the Thompson, and with the BAR she legitimately could not hit much of anything—it was nothing like a hunting rifle—but various sergeants stamped various documents and thus she was qualified.

Stamp, stamp, staple, staple, and it was off to war for Guadalupé Camacho, Private, US Army.

Lupé had been drafted very much against her will. She was not a coward, nor lacking in patriotism, but she was needed at home. She had already missed the spring round-up, and if she didn't get out of the army and back to Utah she would miss the drive up to the Ogden railhead. It was to be an old-fashioned cattle drive this year—trucks, truck tires, truck spare parts and most of all truck fuel were hard to come by. You could buy everything on the black market, but Lupé's father simply did not do things like that. Besides, Lupé knew, he'd been pining for the days of his youth when cowboys still occasionally ran cattle the old-fashioned way. So her father, looking younger than he had in twenty years, had decided to do it with horses and ropes and camping out under the stars, bringing some extra hands up from below the border—Mexican citizens not being subject to the rapacious needs of the US military.

Lupé felt she was missing the opportunity of a lifetime.

She looks around her now, trying not to be obvious, sizing up the others in the truck. Five men, one woman. The woman draws her eye: she is an elegant-looking white woman with blonde hair and high cheekbones and an expression like a blank brick wall. Closed off. Shut up tight.

The only one who returns her gaze is a cheerful-looking man, or boy really, with red hair and a complexion that would have doomed him out under the pitiless sun of the prairie. He is gangly, with knees so knobby they look like softballs stuffed into his trousers. He has long, delicate fingers unmarked by scars or callouses.

Not the sort of man she's been raised around. The men she knows are Mexican or colored or Indian for the most part, compact, quiet, leathery men who can go days without speaking more than six words. Cowboys. Men whose list of personal possessions started with a well-worn saddle and ended with a sweat-stained hat. Some also owned a Bible and/or a Book of Mormon, because Guadalupé's father was a Latter-Day Saint and he tended to hire fellow Mormons on the theory that they were less likely to get rip-roaring drunk. They were also less likely to get ideas about his young daughter.

Guadalupé's mother had died of the fever shortly after her birth. Her father, Pedro, who everyone called either Pete or Boss or (behind his back) One-Eyed Pete, was determined to raise his daughter to be a proper lady.

A proper lady who could rope, throw and tie a two-hundred-pound calf in thirteen seconds. Not exactly rodeo time, but quick just the same. A proper lady who could cook beans and rice for twenty men and laugh along as they farted. A proper lady who could string wire, castrate a bull calf, cut a horn, or lay on a branding iron.

Now instead of putting her skills and talents to work, Lupé sits in the back of a truck beneath a threatening British sky being eyeballed by a city boy with red hair and a happy grin.

The truck lurches off, rattling through the hectic camp, weaving through disorganized gaggles of soldiers and daredevil jeeps before heading out into the English countryside.

"Hey," the redhead says.

"Me?"

"What are you, some kind of Injun?"

Lupé blinks. "No."

"What are you then?"

"My folks come from Mexico. I come from Utah."

"Utah, huh? Well, that beats all," he says and shakes his head. Then he leans forward and extends his hand. "Hank Hobart, from St. Paul, Minnesota. Pleased to meet you."

She's been expecting hostility—there are a lot of Texans in the army, and few of them are ready to be civil to Mexicans. So she is non-plussed by his open expression and the outstretched hand. She takes it and feels a softness she's never felt before in any hand, male or female.

"What do you do, Loopy?"

"Guadalupé," she corrects. Then, "Or Lupé."

"Loopy. That's what I said, isn't it?" He seems sincere, as though he hears no difference between his pronunciation and hers, which is more loo-*pay* than his loo-pee.

"Okay, Hank. I live on a cattle ranch."

His blue eyes go wide and his pale eyebrows rise to comic heights. "You're a cowgirl?"

"I guess so," she says, feeling uncomfortable since that title is generally earned by many long years of work. Where she comes from "cowboy" means a whole lot more than major or captain.

"Guess what I do?" Hank asks. He's tall, lanky, and so pale he's practically translucent, and he owns an almost comically large nose that belongs on a statue of some noble Roman.

Lupé shakes her head. "No idea."

"I play trombone in an orchestra." He mimes moving a trombone slide.

This is so far from anything Lupé might have guessed that for a moment she can only frown and stare.

"You like jazz?" Hobart asks.

Lupé shrugs. "Like Tommy Dorsey?" It's a lucky guess. There is no radio on the ranch, and what she knows of music is restricted to cowboy tunes and church hymns. But some of her school friends have radios, and she's heard a few of the big names.

He nods. "Best trombone player around, I guess. Man, if I ever got that good . . . If ever 'I'm Getting Sentimental Over You' comes on the radio, sit down and open your ears and, man, that is one cool T-bone." He has a look on his face that Lupé associates with religious ecstasy. Then he snaps back to reality. "So, where you figure we're going?"

Lupé shrugs. This is more conversation than she's had in a long time.

"Reckon we're going to France," Hank says. He looks concerned by the idea.

Lupé nods. "Reckon so."

"Hell, yes, we're going to France," another male GI, a big slab of beef with an incongruous baby face, sandy hair and tiny blue eyes interjects. "We're going to finish off the Krauts. They won't know what's hit 'em." He bounces his legs a bit, either nervousness or anticipation.

Neither Hank nor Lupé is excited at this prospect and conversation dies out. They ride for an hour on roads choked with trucks and jeeps, ammo wagons and half-tracks, 155 Long Tom artillery pieces towed behind trucks, and even Sherman tanks. All of it, everything, is heading southeast.

At last the truck pulls into a new camp with well-ordered tents in endless rows. It looks remarkably like the last camp, and the one before that. The army, Lupé notes, owns a lot of tents.

"Last stop! Everyone off," the driver yells.

They are met by a woman corporal who appears to be in a permanent state of irritation, rather like Sergeant Bonemaker. The corporal snatches paperwork, glances, and says, "All right, you three are going to Fifth Platoon. Report to Sergeant Sticklin." In response to their blank, sheepish stares the corporal points and says, "Go that way till you come to the company road, turn right. You know your rights from your lefts, don't you? Go right till you see a tent with a sign that says Fifth Platoon. Got it? Good. Now get lost."

The three detailed to Fifth Platoon are Lupé, Hank and the eager fellow with the baby face who is named Rudy J. Chester. He makes a point of the "J." He's from Main Line, Philadelphia, and he says that as if it's supposed to mean something special.

They find the company road, and after some questioning of busy noncoms they find the right tent. Sitting in a camp chair outside the tent are a male staff sergeant with a prominent widow's peak, pale skin and intelligent eyes, and a woman buck sergeant with her mud-caked boots up on an empty C-ration crate and a tin canteen cup of steaming coffee in her hand.

"Here they are," the staff sergeant says, at once weary and amused.

"Those are mine?" the woman buck sergeant asks. There is no attempt to disguise a critical, dubious look. "These are what I get in exchange for Cat Preeling?"

"Look at it this way, it's three for one."

"Except Cat can handle a BAR and won't wet herself the first time she hears an 88." The woman sergeant stands up and now Lupé sees that she has a long, curved knife strapped to her thigh—definitely not army issue.

"Line up," the woman sergeant says. "No, not at attention, do I look like an officer? Is this a parade ground? I'm Sergeant Richlin. You can call me Sarge or you can call me Sergeant Richlin."

Lupé looks closely and sees that amazingly the sergeant is quite young, probably no older than she is herself. Sergeant Richlin is a bit taller than Lupé, paled by weeks living with British weather, dark hair chopped man-short, blue eyes alert and probing.

"How about I call you sweetheart?"

This from the big boy from Philadelphia, Rudy J. Chester. He's grinning, and for a moment Lupé is convinced that Sergeant Richlin will let it go. Then she sees the way Sticklin draws a sharp breath, starts to grin, looks down to hide it, shakes his head slowly side-to-side and in a loud stage whisper says, "The replacements are here."

There's the sound of cots being overturned and a rush of feet. A pretty blonde corporal bursts through the tent flap, blinking at the gray light as if she's just woken up, glances around and says, "Uh oh." And then, "Geer! Beebee! Get out here. I believe one of the replacements just back-talked Richlin."

There's a second flurry of movement and a young man with shrewd eyes, and a big galoot with an impressive forehead come piling out, faces alight with anticipation.

"What's your name?" Sergeant Richlin asks.

"Rudy J. Chester. Sweetheart." He grins left, grins right, sees faces that are either appalled or giddy with expectation, and then slowly, slowly seems to guess that maybe, just maybe, he's said the wrong thing.

Rio Richlin steps up close to him, her face inches from his. He is at least four inches taller and outweighs her by better than fifty pounds. Which is why it's so surprising that in less time than it takes to blink twice he is on the ground, face down, with his right wrist in Richlin's grip, his arm stretched backward and twisted, and Richlin's weight on her knee pressed against his back-bent elbow.

"Oh, come on, Richlin!" the big galoot says. "Should of used the knife!"

The pretty blonde shakes her head in mock disgust. "She's gone soft, Geer. It's all this high living."

Richlin lets Rudy J. Chester writhe and struggle for a few seconds before explaining, "The average human elbow can be broken with just fourteen pounds of pressure, Private Sweetheart. How many pounds of pressure would you guess I can apply against your elbow?"

Chester struggles a bit more before finally saying, "More than fourteen pounds, I guess."

"More than fourteen pounds I guess, *Sergeant Richlin.*" She gives his arm a twist that threatens to pop his shoulder out of its socket.

"More than fourteen pounds I guess, Sergeant Richlin!"

Rio releases him. The blonde corporal mimes applause. The big corporal named Geer goes back under cover. Beebee shakes his head and mutters, "I missed the first part. Can we do it over?"

Private Rudy J. Chester gets to his feet.

"Now listen to me, the three of you," Richlin says. "This is Second Squad, Fifth Platoon, Able Company, 119th Division. This is a veteran division, a veteran platoon. Everyone in this squad has been in combat. You have not. Therefore everyone in this squad outranks you. Are we clear on that?"

Three voices say, "Yes, Sergeant."

"Okay." Now Richlin allows her voice to soften. "We have a few days, at best a week, to get you ready for the real thing. The real thing will be like nothing you learned at basic. Whatever ideas you have, get them out of your head, because you know nothing."

Three heads nod. Lupé thinks, *I should have mouthed off and maybe she'd break my arm and send me home.*

At the same time she thinks she's never before met any woman who could convincingly threaten to break a man's arm. Let alone a freckle-faced *gringa* who can't weigh more than a hundred and twenty pounds.

"This is Sergeant Sticklin, the platoon sergeant," Richlin goes on, explaining in a tone that suggests she's talking to the slow-witted. "Here's the way it goes: Franklin Delano Roosevelt gives an order to General Marshall who gives an order to General Eisenhower who gives an order to General O'Callaghan, who gives an order to Colonel Brace, who gives an order to Captain Passey, who gives an order to Lieutenant Horne who gives an order to Stick—Sergeant Sticklin—and then Sergeant Sticklin and I try to figure out how to carry out that order without getting you people killed. Is that about right, Stick?"

"It is," he allows, mock-solemn.

It might be funny, but it doesn't feel that way to Lupé. There's something specific in the way she says *killed*. It's not a word to Richlin, it's a *memory*.

"Keeping you from getting killed is the main job of a sergeant. When I was a green fool of a private fresh out of basic, I had Sergeant Jedron Cole to keep me from getting killed. He kept me and Stick both from getting killed in Tunisia, and in Sicily and in Italy."

"Many times," Stick agrees.

"Now it's our job to do the same for you. Maybe you don't care about staying alive to get home again someday, but I suspect you'd prefer to stay alive, so here's how you do that: you listen to Sergeant Sticklin. You listen to me. You listen to Corporal Geer there." She crooks a thumb toward the big galoot who has already disappeared back into the tent. "Corporal Geer is my ASL, my assistant squad leader. He and I are going to train the living sh— stuffing out of you in whatever time we have in hopes that you can stay alive long enough to carry Corporal Castain's extra gear."

Still not funny, Lupé thinks. Even Rudy J. Chester looks solemn. Hank Hobart looks positively petrified.

"Now get over to Company HQ to process in," Rio says. "When you're done, grab some chow and get back here and Corporal Castain will get you settled. And about eight seconds after that, Geer is going to march you over to the rifle range and make sure you know which end to point at the Krauts."

The three recruits turn and flee, not even bothering to ask where the Company HQ tent is.

But as they walk away, Lupé, who is in the rear, overhears Corporal Castain saying, "That was very good, Rio. Very Sergeant Mackie, if I may say."

And she hears a low chuckle from Dain Sticklin.

2

"Two packs of smokes and the gin," Rio Richlin says.

The corporal, a chubby young woman with a smiling face and cold eyes, leaning insolently against a jeep, sizes Rio up. "I can get gin anywhere. Give me your knife."

Rio makes a thin, compressed smile. "I have a sentimental attachment to my *koummya*," she says. "Besides, you wouldn't like it. I haven't cleaned all the blood from it yet."

The smile disappears from the corporal's face. She glances at the knife, then at Rio's chest, then back at the knife. "Four packs plus the gin."

"Done. I'll have it back in twenty-four hours tops."

Rio Richlin seldom wears her dress uniform, in fact, never recently, but there is one advantage in the remarkably uncomfortable get-up with its multiplicity of buttons, its impossible-to-keep-on cap and its khaki tie: in full dress one wears one's medals.

The three stripes of the buck sergeant will impress precisely no one in a Britain neck-deep in the soldiers, sailors, coastguardsmen and airmen of a dozen nationalities. But the red, white and blue ribbon, beneath which hangs a pale gold star, is the Silver Star, (despite the baffling color of the *actual* star) and is given for

Gallantry in Action. Quite a few Silver Stars have been handed out, but when Rio received hers it was the first time the medal had been awarded to a female combat soldier. Ever.

The star cuts down considerably on the number of leering, obnoxious, improper suggestions Rio has been on the receiving end of. Mostly you didn't get the Silver Star unless you'd made a fair number of German and Italian widows and orphans, and that realization causes some male soldiers to . . . well, reconsider making a crude pass at Rio.

Alongside the Silver Star is a second medal, a purple ribbon above a gold heart, which has within it a lacquered purple valentine, all framing a gold profile of George Washington himself.

This is the Purple Heart, given to soldiers wounded in battle. On the back in raised letters the citation reads *For Military Merit*, which is a bit silly since to Rio's mind there's no great "merit" in getting shot or sliced up by shrapnel. But resting as it does beside her Silver Star, the combination sends a clear message in the language of the US Army: this is the real deal.

This is a *combat* soldier.

And that separates Buck Sergeant Rio Richlin from ninety percent of the men and women in uniform swelling the trains and roads and villages and village pubs of Britain.

The transaction complete, Rio hops in the jeep and drives away, moving fast because that's how all the jeep drivers drive, fast, like gangsters trying to outrun the cops in a James Cagney movie.

It is forty-seven miles to the air base where Strand Braxton is based. It should be an hour's drive at most, but the road through the damp-lovely springtime English countryside is jammed with every manner of military vehicle from jeep to truck to tank. Military Police man crossroads and try to direct traffic, sometimes in loudly profane ways, and at one point Rio is told she cannot take a particular road but must go far out of her way. Here too her medals (plus two packs of smokes and a silk scarf) convince the MP that the restriction somehow does not apply to her.

The slowness of the drive eats up hours of time she doesn't have, and worse, leaves her free to think. Rio has a lot to think about—the imminent invasion and the role of her squad. It still seems strange to think of it as *her* squad. The squad, nominally twelve men and women led by a sergeant, in this case Rio, consists of her lifelong friend, Jenou Castain—*Corporal* Jenou Castain—as well as her long-time companions Luther Geer, Hansu Pang, Cat Preeling, Beebee, whose real name no one even remembered anymore, some replacements that didn't yet matter, and Jack Stafford.

Jack Stafford with whom she shared a foolish kiss long ago. Jack with whom she had spent a horrible night lying in a muddy minefield, huddling together for warmth. Jack, the Brit who'd ended up in the American army. Devilish, witty, fearless Jack.

Jack who is now her subordinate and about whom she was not to think of in that way. Not that she ever really had, well . . . occasionally. But that whole thing was utterly impossible now. Over. Done with.

Which is one of the reasons she was going to see Strand Braxton, because if Strand and she were . . . well, whatever you called it, engaged, she supposed, then she would have one more mental defense against stray thoughts of Jack.

Stafford, Rio chides herself, *not Jack*. Private Stafford.

She arrives at the air base to find more MPs, and these are not quite so easily dealt with. So she gives her name at the gate, and Strand's name, and after a phone call they decide she's not likely to be a German saboteur or spy, and wave her through.

The airfield is a vast expanse of torn up grass and mud distantly ringed by trees on two sides, farm fields on one side, and the road itself. Rio pulls over to look, taking it in. She can see a handful of low buildings, a stubby control tower with a fitful windsock, a bristling antiaircraft gun emplacement, the usual cluster of jeeps and trucks and low-slung tractors, and beyond them the great behemoth planes, the B-17s. She counts six, but suspects there are more out of view.

She pulls up to the parking area and spots a tall, young officer trotting toward her. He looks serious until he notices that she is watching him and then breaks out a big grin.

Strand Braxton throws his arms around Rio, lifts her off her feet and swings her around. They kiss once, quickly, then a second time more slowly.

Yes, Rio notes, *I do still like that.*

"Gosh, it's great to see you!" Strand says. "The MPs called me from the gate and I thought they were pulling my leg."

"Sorry I didn't give you any warning, but a pass came up and I grabbed it."

"How long can you stay?"

"Well, I have temporary possession of a major's jeep, so I've promised to have it back to his driver within twenty-four hours."

"Twenty-four hours! But . . . but we're *on*."

The phrase confuses Rio for a moment. "You've got a mission?"

He nods and for a moment his smile crumbles before being replaced with some effort by a less-convincing smile. "Probably a milk run. We haven't been briefed yet. Come on, I'll get you a cup of tea and you can meet some of the boys."

"I thought you fly-boys spent all your spare time drinking and carousing," Rio teases as they walk arm in arm, taking exaggeratedly long, synchronized strides.

"I don't know where that idea got started," Strand says, shaking his head. "No one would want to be hungover. Or even low on sleep. Now, once you get past the Channel and the Messerschmitts start coming up . . ." He laughs, but the laugh is as off as his smile. "Well, *then* you might want a drink."

Rio looks at his profile, but can't read anything in particular, beyond the fact that Strand looks tired. Tired and older.

I suppose I do too.

"Hey, are you taking me to officer country?" Rio asks, hesitating at the door to what is labeled "Officers' Dining Club and Dance Emporium." The sign is in official block letters, but is also obviously not the official army designation. Below it a second, smaller, hand-lettered sign: "God's Waiting Room."

Strand waves off her concern. "We don't stand on ceremony much. And we sure don't get enough pretty girls dropping by to push one away!"

Inside, Rio finds a long, rectangular room with a grab bag of chairs ranging from stern metal office chairs to plush parlor chairs and a scattering of low tables. The room smells of tea—a habit some flyers have picked up from the RAF, the Royal Air Force—as well as the usual coffee and the inevitable smoke. Perhaps two dozen flyers are present, sprawled or sitting upright, many with books in their hands and attentive expressions on their faces. A radio plays Glenn Miller's 'Sunrise Serenade.'

"We just came from briefing," Strand says apologetically. "We'll be heading off soon."

A very pretty redheaded pilot gives Rio a nod. Recognition? Comradeship?

Guilt?

"I know I should have waited till we had a time set, but you know how it is," Rio says. "Bad timing. But your letter did say as soon as possible."

"Well, I was hoping we'd have a few days in London," he says. Addressing the room in a loud voice he says, "Boys, this is Rio, my girl, so watch your language and keep the wolf whistles to yourselves."

Rio doubts that she is worth a wolf whistle. She hasn't worn makeup or fingernail polish in a very long time. She's dressed in a uniform that does not leave a lot of possibilities for showing leg, and her hair is the now-regulation two inches long.

And then there's her *koummya*, which she should certainly have left with Jenou. But the *koummya*, a curved ceremonial-but-quite-functional dagger she'd picked up in the Tunis bazaar, has become something more than just a knife; it has acquired the status of talisman. It is her lucky rabbit's foot. She knows it's superstitious, but without it she feels vulnerable. Even in camp, where she shares a tent with three other NCOs, she keeps it by her cot, always within reach.

Many eyes in the room go straight to the *koummya*, but then they move on, checking out her face and her figure, neither of which Rio thinks likely to please anyone, but smiles break out, and waves and nods.

And one wolf whistle.

"How long do you have?"

Strand glances at a wall clock and says, "If I trust my first officer and crew to handle loading and fueling, I've got four hours free."

Rio's heart sinks. Four *hours*? It's too long for a chat, too short a time for anything deeper. She has come here to reach a decision. To reach it with Strand, hopefully. To decide what *exactly* they are to each other.

No promises have been made, no proposal offered or accepted. But somehow Rio has felt that it was there, implied, assumed. An *understanding*. But she's not sure that's how Strand sees it. Maybe what he understands is different from what she thinks.

More importantly, Rio has changed.

When she first enlisted it had almost been a whim. Yes, her big sister Rachel had died fighting the Japanese in the Pacific, and yes, that formed part of her motivation, but when she is honest with herself Rio knows that she really joined because Jenou was joining, and because like Jenou she was bored with life in Gedwell Falls, California. And because she'd felt swept up. Like the great tide of history had risen around her and carried her off, a piece of flotsam in a flood.

She had never meant to be near the front. No one thought when the Supreme Court handed down its decision making women subject to the draft and eligible for enlistment that women and girls would end up in the thick of the action. But the army, with much internal fighting and several high-profile resignations, decided to treat female recruits just like the men. Some of that was male generals hoping to see women fail. Some of it was women (and some men) interested in equality of the sexes. Much of it was just a rigid bureaucracy not accustomed to dividing assignments by gender.

Rio had lied about her age and signed up in the autumn of 1942, at the same time as her . . . what to call it? Friendship? Her *friendship* with Strand Braxton? Autumn of 1942 was almost two years ago. She'd been an average, barely-seventeen-year-old girl, a girl with homework assignments and chores. Then had come basic training. And a brief sojourn in Britain for more training. Followed by Rio's first encounter with combat during the fiasco of Kasserine Pass in North Africa.

Since then she had been to Sicily and Italy and been shot at, shelled, strafed and bombed. She had marched many miles, carried many loads, dug many holes. She had used slit trenches and bushes, bathed in her helmet, changed sanitary pads in burning buildings.

Most profoundly she had gone from heart-stopping panic the first time she lined the sights of her M1 up on a human target and taken his life, to becoming a professional combat soldier. A professional killer.

And she had moved from a private, with no responsibility

but to obey orders, to a sergeant, with her own squad of eleven soldiers to look after.

Any baby fat she'd ever had was long gone. She was tall, lean and strong, with calloused hands and stubby, broken nails. When she moved it was with quick economy, efficient, wasting not a calorie of energy. And something had happened to her voice: it was still hers, but now it carried undertones that spoke of confidence, control and command.

She had also acquired several unladylike habits. She still smoked less than many, but smoke she did because when it was cold in a foxhole a cigarette was life's only small pleasure. And she drank on occasion, not usually to excess, but with enough devotion that there was now a flask of whiskey in her pack. When she ate it was like a starved wolf. When she spoke it was with less and less concern for curse words.

And then there was the fact that she had slept with Strand.

Yes.

That fact had never quite been . . . what? Figured out? Adjudicated? Processed?

The next time she'd seen Strand she had been leading a patrol that ended up rescuing a wounded Strand after his plane was shot down over Sicily.

And that too had not been processed.

War was hell on relationships.

"Four hours?" Rio says. "Well, let's make the most of them." Only when the words are out of her mouth does it occur to her that he may take this as a suggestion of sex. She blushes, but at the same time, would it be such a terrible way to spend the four

34

hours? It would distract them both from the weightier questions. A pleasant way to avoid . . . well, to avoid the very reason she had come here.

"Listen, there's a sort of gazebo behind the building, it's a place where couples sometimes go to be . . . to have privacy." He winces, obviously concerned that she is misreading his intentions just as she is concerned about him misreading hers.

The gazebo is more of a lean-to, a shelter enclosed on three sides but open to the airfield. Rio sees crew working on the planes, low tractors hauling trailers loaded with bombs, boxes of machine-gun ammunition being handed up through the belly hatches. Hoses crisscross the ground, pulsing with aviation fuel.

They sit side by side on a little bench, pastoral quiet contrasting with the feverish activity on the field.

"You know, Rio, I was quite proud of you when I heard about the Silver Star. Why didn't you tell me? I had to read about it in *Stars and Stripes*! One of the fellows showed it to me."

"It's not such an important thing," Rio says.

"Nonsense, it's a very important thing. It seems you are rather brave." He smiles. But again, it's not quite the right smile.

Rio shakes her head. "You know how it is. Everyone does their job as best they can, and one person gets singled out for a medal."

"You saved my life," he says flatly. He holds up a hand to silence her protest. "I won't deny that I've taken some ribbing over that. How I had to be rescued by my girl. How my girl has a Silver Star."

There is an awkward silence. Rio doesn't know what to say. Is she supposed to be ashamed of having carried off her mission? She glances at him and tries to read his mood from the set of his jaw. Yes, she realizes with amazement, he does actually seem to resent her, a little at least.

Or am I just imagining things?

"Should I have left you there?" Rio asks.

He shakes his head slowly. "No, sweetheart, of course not. It's just . . ."

"Just what?"

"Well, it's hard, that's all. See, I've missed the last two missions because of mechanical problems, all perfectly proper, I was following standing orders. But on top of, well, *you*, there's that, and some of the fellows take the joke a bit too far is all."

"I'm sorry, Strand. But there's nothing I can do about that."

"The story in *Stars and Stripes* even mentioned that I was delirious and singing Christmas carols."

True enough. When Rio's patrol had found Strand's plane, he had been wounded and out of his head. But the detail rankles Strand. His mouth twists at the memory.

"I should think people would find that funny and endearing," Rio says. She frowns at the sound of her own words. Is this how she speaks? In this diffident, apologetic tone? She has the sense that "endearing" may be the first three syllable word she's spoken in months. Her sergeant's vocabulary tends toward words of one syllable, generally either expressed in a low mutter or an irritated shout.

Jenou's right: I have changed.

"I'm a B-17 pilot," Strand says heatedly. "I'm not meant to be endearing or funny, Rio. I'm the youngest officer here, even my radioman is older, so, you can imagine."

"Well, I'm sorry."

"I never should have let you enlist," Strand mutters.

"It wasn't your decision."

"Oh, believe me, I know that! I let Jenou talk you into this madness. I can't imagine why they haven't sent you home to sell war bonds, you'd be a natural." He looks at her, forces a grin and adds, "Of course, they'd doll you up."

"They offered," Rio says.

He stares at her. "What? You mean they offered to send you home? Did you refuse?"

Rio shrugs. "I thought I'd be more useful here looking after my squad."

That's not quite the whole truth. She had been tempted to go stateside and had thought especially hard of refusing the promotion to sergeant, until an Army Intelligence sergeant named Rainy Schulterman, one of her fellow medal recipients, had guilted her into it. After painting a word picture of Nazi oppression, Schulterman had talked about green kids from Nebraska landing on French beaches and going up against the Wehrmacht.

"They'll need people who know how to fight and how to keep guys from getting killed. What do we call those people, Richlin? What do we call those people, Rio Richlin from Cow Paddy or Bugtussle or wherever the hell you're from?"

Schulterman had supplied her own answer.

"Honey, I hate to tell you, but they call those people sergeants."

Now here I am, Rio thinks, *Sergeant Rio Richlin, sitting awkwardly with her resentful . . . boyfriend? Beau?*

Fiancé?

Strand looks down and shakes his head. "Do you have any idea how many of the flyers here would go home tomorrow if they could? You don't . . . I mean, sure, I know you've been in the fighting, but you can't imagine what it's like for us."

"You're right," Rio snaps, turning more sergeantly by degrees. "I don't know what it's like to come back at the end of a patrol to find a comfy bed and a hot shower."

Strand waves a hand dismissively. "I didn't mean it that way. It's just . . . we lose men on almost every mission. You remember Lefty? You met him. Me 109, you know, Kraut fighter plane, caught him over Germany. Six of his crew were killed or injured in the first pass, two engines out. Lefty shot through the cheek but still trying to get his bird home. He went down in the Channel. Three of his crew bailed out and were picked up, but not Lefty."

Rio is on the point of retorting that she knows quite well what an Me 109 is, having been strafed more than once, and with a list of the deaths of her own friends, but that's nuts; surely, this is not some competition to see who is having the worst war?

"I'm sorry to hear about Lefty."

"You'll be sorry to hear about me soon," he says with surprising savagery. He clasps his hands together and Rio sees that he is trembling. "Sorry. I didn't mean . . . Never mind me. I'm usually in a foul mood before a mission."

"There's nothing wrong in being afraid," Rio says. "In fact—"

"Who says I'm afraid?" he snaps.

"Everyone is afraid, Strand."

He snorts derisively. "Everyone but you, Rio. Look at you. What would your mother have to say about that wicked knife?

Have you sent them a copy of your citation? You charged a squad of Wehrmacht by yourself!" His voice rises toward shrill. "You blew up my old plane and saved the Norden bomb sight and came near to being blown up yourself. My God, Rio, you've become the very model for all the rabble-rousers who support this whole crazy notion!"

"Crazy notion?" The strange thing is that as she speaks those two words, she recognizes the silky menace in her tone. It's pure Mackie, her sergeant during basic training. If things were not so tense she might laugh at the comparison. Mackie could terrify a recruit just by the way she *walked*.

"Yes!" Strand says. "Yes! I'll say it: crazy notion. Just because you've become a good soldier does not mean that it makes any sense for women to be in this war!"

"You have women pilots, women air crew. I saw a rather pretty redhead . . ."

"Sally? At least she would have the sense to go home if the opportunity came up. She agrees with me, with, well, everyone really. Women are meant to be the gentler sex. That's the grand design. Women aren't meant to . . . to . . ."

"Kill Germans?" The same Mackie menace.

"My God, Rio, listen to yourself. You positively sound as if you are threatening me!"

Rio jumps to her feet. "You're shouting at me, Strand."

His look is cold. His hands remain clasped, squeezing to stop the trembling. "You've made me a laughing stock. Fellows ask me when we're married whether I'll be doing the cooking and cleaning."

When we are married?

"I don't recall agreeing to marry you. For that matter, I don't recall you asking."

He frowns, puzzled. "It's understood, surely? You gave yourself to me; did you think I wouldn't do the right thing?"

"So . . . you would marry me from a sense of obligation? Duty?"

"No, no, of course I didn't mean that." He retreats quickly, but the resentment still comes through. "I love you. Of course I love you. I just sometimes wish . . ." He hangs his head. "I just wish sometimes you were still the sweet, innocent young beauty I gave a ride to in my uncle's old Jenny."

"That was a long time ago," Rio says. Her voice gentles at the memory. Strand's uncle had a Jenny, a Curtiss JN-4 biplane he used as a crop duster. Strand had already known how to fly and he took her up over Gedwell Falls in what was the most thrilling moment of her life. Up till then.

She had squeezed into a single cockpit with Strand, leaning back against him, feeling for the first time what a man's body felt like.

She wouldn't, couldn't lie to herself: many times she had wished she was back there, back *then*, being that version of herself. It wasn't her lost virginal naiveté that made her nostalgic, but rather the feeling that she had changed so much there was no longer any going back. The male soldiers would return home some day and would be seen as more than they had been, stronger, braver. But the women? No one knew how women who had been to war would be received.

Strand pictured her in an apron. So had she, once. And who knew, maybe she would see herself that way again.

Mrs. Strand Braxton?

Mommy?

Baking cupcakes for the PTA fundraiser? Wearing a nice summer dress to church? Excusing herself from men's conversation after dinner to go to the parlor with the other ladies to talk about hairstyles and movie stars and brag about little Strand Jr.'s A-plus in algebra?

That had been her mother's life, a life that had once been inevitable, but now felt very, very far away.

But even as she drifts toward those melancholy thoughts, a part of her mind is elsewhere, wondering if she could transfer Rudy J. Chester out of her squad; wondering if Lupé was as tough as she acted; wondering whether Geer is working them hard in her absence.

The silence stretches on too long.

"I guess we won't figure out what's what until it's all over," she says.

Strand snorts derisively. "There probably won't be an after, Rio. The Old Man says the Luftwaffe isn't what it used to be, but just about every mission a bird goes down. It's a matter of mathematics. Every mission . . . a Kraut fighter, ack-ack, mechanical breakdowns . . ."

"You can't think about that," Rio says. "You just have to focus on your objective." She very nearly pronounces it OB-jective, the way Sergeant Cole always did.

Suddenly Strand stands too. He turns cold eyes on Rio. "No, that's *you*, Rio. Not me. Me, I think about it. I'm not a machine." He makes an effort to end things pleasantly. "Speaking of

41

machines, I need to go and see to mine. It's good to see you, Rio."

"Yes. Take care of yourself, Strand. Goodbye."

That last word is to his back.

3

RAINY SCHULTERMAN—FOURAS, NAZI-OCCUPIED FRANCE

Rainy Schulterman—very recently commissioned *Second Lieutenant* Rainy Schulterman—parallels the shore in an inflatable boat paddled through the misty night by four American sailors, one of whom is seething and muttering to himself, while the other three stifle laughter beneath broad, conspiratorial grins.

Rainy is not laughing. Landing on French soil in the summer of 1944 is about as dangerous a thing as you can do short of actual combat. This is her second mission into enemy territory. The first one had been a fiasco—unqualified officers making foolish plans had landed her in the last place on earth she or any other member of Army Intelligence wished to be: a Gestapo jail.

Rainy had been afraid then. She is afraid now. Fear often speaks in her mother's voice, asking *why?* Why are you doing this, Rainy? You'll get hurt, Rainy. You'll die, Rainy.

But she has learned something about fear: you must always listen to it, but you need not give in to it.

Rainy grits her teeth and wishes the sailors would act a little less like, well, *boys.* Maybe they aren't worried about being picked up by the Gestapo or the Sicherheitsdienst (SD) or even the Abwehr, but she is. The Sicherheitsdienst, the intelligence arm of the SS, are animals like the Gestapo. From the Abwehr she would have expected firm but proper treatment—if she were wearing a uniform—the Abwehr are soldiers, after all. But Rainy is not wearing a uniform, she is dressed in widow's weeds, a worn old black dress shaped as stylishly as a potato sack, an obviously hand-knitted black sweater, a droopy, patched overcoat and chunky black oxfords. The Abwehr might hang her on the spot as a spy, while the Gestapo or the SD would torture her and then put her up against a wall.

That thought comes with vivid memories of men and women who she had not known, shoved against a wall she had not been able to see. She had heard their cries, their pleas for mercy, and their brave patriotic songs cut short by the crash of rifle fire. But all she had been able to see from her vantage point was their blood running down over the filthy window of her cell.

The remaining member of the little boat's crew is an older man. He's the one seething and, from time to time, shaking his head. Rainy shifts down the bench.

"Don't let it trouble you," she says in a barely audible whisper near the older rower's ear. "I don't."

"This new captain's a . . ." the sailor pauses, searching for the appropriate insult before coming up with, ". . . a landsman."

It amuses and even touches Rainy that the old petty officer is concerned for her feelings. The trip down from Southampton to this insignificant town on the Bay of Biscay has not been pleasant. An undisciplined and all-male crew had run through every version of leer, wolf whistle and mangled French proposition. The phrase "*voulez vous couchez avec moi ce soir,*"—would you sleep with me this evening—had been carefully learned by every serviceman with even a slight chance of reaching France, where the women were reputed to be plentiful and plenty ready. The line had been repeatedly tried out on Rainy.

There had also been a couple of unfunny practical jokes, the sort of pranks no one would have dreamed of playing on a male officer, not even a lowly second lieutenant. Not even a lowly *army* second lieutenant aboard a naval vessel.

Just before Rainy had gone over the side and climbed down to the waiting rubber boat, half a dozen sailors had said a cheery "farewell" by exposing themselves.

Yes. Definitely not the sort of thing enlisted men would have pulled on a male officer.

But then, Rainy reminds herself, they are boys, mostly. For most of them it is their first time at sea aside from training, the closest they have come to the war. In many cases it is their first time away from home, certainly their first time abroad.

Anyway, she has bigger worries.

They come to shallow water, with the waves piling up a bit, seizing and surging the boat forward. A single light shines in the dark village, perhaps over the church door. Off to the left Rainy sees the old Napoleonic-era Vauban fort, just like she's seen in the aerial photographs. It is a square with stumpy towers at the corners and a squat stone keep rising in the middle. It even has a moat according to the photos.

They are to pass the fort then turn toward shore. A smaller beach will be there and—she profoundly hopes—a member of the FFI, the French Forces of the Interior, which people mostly called the French Resistance, or the maquis.

If there is no one waiting for her, the orders say she is to abort the mission and return to the destroyer. This makes sense unless the ship you're returning to is like some disreputable fraternity house.

The contact had better be there.

The rowers are no longer thinking of giggling by the time the bow scrapes sand—it has been a long, hard row. The destroyer captain, in addition to being no disciplinarian and a landsman, is not overly brave and has kept his ship well out of sight of the shore.

To her left now a bluff blocks her view of the Vauban fort. To her right the beach curves in a perfect crescent. There are trees along the shore, but of the sort that shade homes, not of the sort that conceal machine-gun emplacements.

She hopes.

One of the sailors is panting far too loudly.

"Silence!" Rainy snaps in an urgent whisper.

"Who the fug do you think—" the sailor says in a nearly normal speaking voice which anyone—French or German—anyone within a hundred yards could hear.

Rainy puts the barrel of her Walther PPK—a German weapon, a souvenir—against the bridge of his nose. He goes cross-eyed to focus on it.

She puts a finger to her lips and says, "Shhh."

Silence. It extends. Nothing but the soft *shush shush s-i-i-i-g-h* of the waves and the flapping of a decorative flag on the short pole that marks the rendezvous.

Then comes the crunch of footsteps on sand. Rainy

strains to hear. Yes, just one set of feet. One person.

He appears as formless movement within shadow, then comes at last to where the fluorescence of the hissing surf illuminates his . . . no, her face.

In French Rainy says, "*Où est la tortue?*" Which in English means, "Where is the tortoise?"

A girl's voice, high-pitched despite her attempt to lower it to a husky whisper, says, "*Allée à la mer.*" Gone to sea.

"Is it the season for it?"

"Tortoise is always in season."

With the exchange of code phrases concluded, Rainy exhales. "All right, Navy. Put my gear ashore and you are free to go." There's some grumbling, but it's very, very quiet grumbling.

Rainy slips the automatic pistol into the leather holster sewn into the back lining of her formless black coat.

"I'm Lieutenant Jones. Alice Jones." She extends her hand.

The girl, a rather lovely young woman of maybe seventeen, shakes her hand firmly. "Marie DuPont."

This, like Alice Jones, is most likely an alias.

"I have some things to carry, if you don't mind helping," Rainy says.

"Of course!"

They divide the weight: a radio encased in a rubberized, waterproof container; a locked tin box containing five thousand dollars' worth of counterfeit Vichy French francs and German Reichsmarks; a satchel containing thirty-two pounds of TNT in half-pound blocks helpfully labeled, "High Explosive" and "TNT" in red block letters on tan cardboard, and, "Dangerous;"

47

a separate, smaller canvas pouch with thirty-two fuses; and a broken-down-for-easier-shipping Fusil Mitrailleur Modèle 1924 M29, the standard French infantry light machine gun, with two hundred rounds of ammunition.

All told it is something like a hundred and twenty-five pounds of gear and it is a struggle for the two of them to drag and haul most of it across the beach to the road. Waiting there is an aged Renault, still with wooden spoked wheels, which has been somewhat crudely remodeled as a panel truck.

Seeing them struggling, a man emerges from the Renault to help, gathering what they've left. A burning cigarette butt illuminates a craggy, whiskered face. They dispense with introductions and quickly load the gear into the back and drive off.

They go through town which takes very little time, Fouras being no metropolis, then they head east, keeping near to the north bank of the Charente River, and come at last to a small wood and tin shack beside a tiny jetty.

They unload the gear onto dirt and the Renault promptly drives away.

"Do not move, mademoiselle," Marie says. "They will wish to look at you."

Rainy nods. She raises her hands above her head and slowly turns a complete circle. She can't imagine what the unseen watchers will be looking for, but she generally applauds caution.

The door of the shed opens. It is dark within.

"After you," Marie says.

Rainy hesitates for a moment to let her senses take in the

scene, the area, the placement of a row boat at the jetty, a second shed a few dozen feet away. She notes deep tire tracks in the mud at her feet, too big to be the little Renault. Then, satisfied, she steps into the shack.

Hands grab her, twist her around to face the wall, and begin a rude examination of her body. The searching hand quickly finds her Walther and draws it out. Then they find the knife strapped to her thigh beneath the dress.

A match flares and a flame glows from an oil lamp set on a small table. The dim light reveals two people. One is an older man, short, dark complexion, pitted as if by smallpox or an adolescent bout of severe acne. He wears a shabby gray suit that looks as if it was cut for a man two sizes larger. His eyes are yellowed but alert, suspicious, cautious, skeptical.

Rainy is obscurely gratified to see that he is wearing a dark blue beret, just exactly what she expects of a maquis fighter.

The second man is younger, perhaps midtwenties, a bare inch taller than Rainy herself. He has an impressive pile of dark hair, clear dark eyes, an idealist's wide brow, and a nose that looks as if its lines were drawn by an artist. He's a good-looking fellow, or would be if not for the surly expression on his lips. He strikes Rainy as wishing to convey that he is not impressed by her. Which is fine, since she's not bowled over by him either.

Marie does introductions. The younger man is her big brother, Étienne. The older man is called Monsieur Faisan, literally Mr. Pheasant, yet another cover name presumably.

Faisan jerks his head at Étienne and Marie and they scuttle off to haul the boxes of weapons and explosives inside. Rainy keeps the box of currency with her. She eyes the Walther on the table, noting the way the butt is turned, rehearsing a desperate grab, should it be necessary. Passwords are all well and good, but many an agent has been picked up in this region. She can assume nothing.

No one has yet spoken directly to Rainy and she's content to leave it that way as Marie and Étienne unwind oilcloth and take out weapons and explosives and the precious radio.

Faisan when he speaks, speaks only French.

"*Des beaux cadeaux*," Faisan says. Nice presents.

Rainy's French is not as good as her German. Good enough to fool the average Wehrmacht soldier manning a checkpoint, but not a true Frenchman.

"You're welcome," she says in French.

"You're a woman," Faisan says, looking as though he'd like to spit.

"And you're a smuggler," Rainy says.

Faisan's brow rises. Étienne moves slightly forward as if he's going to do something, then subsides.

"Why do you say that?" Faisan asks.

Rainy shrugs. "Isolated shack by a river, a second shack with a padlocked door, tracks made by a heavy truck. And you seem cautious but not paranoid, meaning you feel fairly safe here. So you are a smuggler, and I'm guessing the Germans know it."

"Why would you guess that?"

Rainy shrugs. "You're not nervous enough. The Germans know you're a smuggler, and they don't mind because I'm guessing they get a cut."

Suddenly Faisan's face transforms. He smiles, revealing various nicotine-stained teeth interrupted by gaps. "A woman, but not a stupid woman. Welcome to France, madame . . ."

"Mademoiselle," Rainy corrects. "But more to the point, Lieutenant Alice Jones, US Army."

"Where is the rest of the invasion force, did you forget to bring them?" Étienne says.

"Never fear, monsieur, they are coming."

Faisan shrugs as if to say he hopes so, but will believe it when he sees it.

Marie fetches a bottle of cognac and four small glasses. She pours and hands them around.

"*La France libre*," Rainy says, and they drink a toast. To a free France.

"*Aux alliés*," Faisan counters. To the Allies.

Faisan sits in a rickety chair, suddenly looking tired. Rainy wonders if Faisan has been sick recently. He does not look well.

Étienne takes over the conversation. "And now, with all pleasantries aside, Lieutenant—"

"Alice will do," Rainy interrupts.

"As you wish. Mademoiselle Alice. We welcome you, and we welcome your gifts, but why are you come?"

"The Das Reich division."

None of the three French people are surprised. Waffen SS tank divisions often carry names as well as numbers, and the Das Reich, also known as the Second SS Panzer Division, is a name all-too familiar to the resistance as well as to Allied war planners.

"They aren't here," Étienne says.

"No, they're spread between Limoges and Valence D'Agen, three hundred kilometers from here," Rainy says.

"Then you know all that we know."

"The brass would like to know more: morale, the condition of their equipment, fuel supplies, ammunition on hand . . ."

"They wish to see how quickly the Das Reich can head north," Étienne says smugly.

Rainy shrugs a non-committal confirmation. It is no secret that the Allies are planning an invasion, the whole world knows it. And it's no secret that it will come somewhere in Brittany. When the invasion comes, the Das Reich division will be moved north to counterattack. Panzer divisions, tank divisions, are an obsession of Allied war planners, especially the well-equipped, well-indoctrinated Waffen SS panzer divisions. The Das Reich may have as many as 20,000 men and 200 tanks as well as artillery. The Das Reich is a big, strong, brutal weapon, a massive iron fist, and if it reaches the invasion beaches it could literally grind vulnerable Allied troops under its tank treads.

Étienne arrives at a decision after a quick glance at Faisan. "We cannot deliver you to Valence, we have no . . . connections . . . there. But we can get you to Limoges. The woods southwest of there are full of panzers under cover."

Rainy nods. One step at a time. "All right."

"We travel by boat up the river to Cognac. There we will meet a lorry that makes regular runs to Paris and can make a stop in Limoges. Do you have identity papers?"

Rainy produces a forged identity document naming her Madame Nicole Amadou, French war widow. Étienne looks at the document carefully. "This is good work."

"I'll pass that along to the SOE—they made it for us." The SOE, British Special Operations Executive, are far more experienced at forging French documents than US Army Intelligence.

"We will travel as fiancés, engaged to be married. Marie will accompany us as chaperone, so have no concern on that score." He waves her away, as if she had been hoping for a romantic interlude with him. "We will say that we are en route to Limoges where our mother lives and where the ceremony will be held."

"You're a little old to play my fiancé," Rainy says bluntly.

Étienne makes a rude noise. "We lost almost two million men in the first war, mademoiselle, and two hundred thousand plus more than a million prisoners in this war; most of the able-bodied men have been sent off to work in German factories as little better than slaves. There are not so many French men left that you can be choosy."

Rainy nods acceptance.

"It will be very dangerous," Étienne says. "If we are caught . . . well, you cannot imagine what the Gestapo do to prisoners."

Rainy doesn't like his superior tone at all. And she does not wish to spend the next week or more being condescended to— she's had quite enough of being treated like a second-class citizen because of her sex. She raises the little gas lantern from the table and holds it close to her face. The light picks out the small scar that bisects her lower lip, and the scar where surgeons went in to mend her broken jaw. She pulls back her hair to reveal a scar on the side of her neck. Then she unfastens the top buttons of her dress and pulls the collar aside to show the crooked collarbone beneath a mass of scar tissue. There's more, much more, but this much will do.

"I know exactly what the Gestapo does to prisoners," Rainy says.

Étienne falls silent and withdraws from the circle of light. Marie edges closer, fascinated and horrified. But it is Faison who rises, comes near, and with surprising tenderness touches the bump of her badly-healed collarbone.

He then raises his hand from her shoulder and turns it so she can see that there are no nails on his fingers. Tearing out fingernails is a favorite of Nazi torturers.

"Pour us two glasses," Faisan says and Marie complies. Faisan hands one to Rainy, takes the other himself. He makes no toast, says nothing at all, but their eyes meet, his old and sick, hers young and still vital. The old French smuggler and the young female US Army lieutenant have nothing to say to each other that can be turned into words.

They drink. He lifts the Walther from the table and hands it back to Rainy.

"*Et bien*," Faisan says with a sigh. "*Dépêchez vous.*"

Get going.

4

"You're killing me, Doc. You're killing me dead."

Sergeant Frangie Marr, frequently known as "Doc," stands before a tier of bunks six high. The lowest one is occupied by a black man with the extravagant name of Vanderbilt DeRay, who looks like someone who has crawled to hell, spent a week, and just got back.

Frangie Marr has seen many a combat wound in her time as an army medic, but even gut-shot GIs often looked better than a GI who'd been desperately seasick for forty-eight hours. Seasick without even leaving port, except for a false launch that had to be called back due to bad weather.

The air in the hold of the LST reeks of gasoline, engine fumes, human feces from a malfunctioning bathroom—called a "head" aboard ship—human sweat and human vomit, and it is so thick with cigarette smoke that Frangie doubts it contains enough oxygen to sustain human life. That is bad enough.

Worse, far worse, is the fact that no part of the big steel box designated Landing Ship Tank 86 is standing still. The flat-bottomed LST rises and falls on every swell, rocks and rolls on the wake of every passing ship. The floor is alive beneath her feet, a surging, heaving, sliding funhouse ride that has every single susceptible person aboard spewing seemingly endless buckets of vomit.

Some are blessedly immune, and are cordially hated by the sufferers. Some are in a sort of middle zone: queasy at times, maybe needing a relatively decorous and controlled vomit once or twice a day. Others . . . well, others lie prostrate in their own bodily fluids, weak, pathetic, fragrant, and a burden to themselves and everyone else.

"Did you take your pills?" Frangie demands in her Official Medical Voice.

"I did, Doc. You gotta get me a dose of that medical bourbon you got."

"It's rum, not bourbon, and—"

"Well, that's just foolish," Vanderbilt DeRay says, frowning and shaking his head. "You don't want rum if you got decent corn whiskey. Maybe something with some age on it, to mellow the flavor . . ."

"Sergeant DeRay," Frangie says sternly. "Alcohol is not a cure for seasickness. In fact, given your condition, and the fact that you stink of moonshine, I'd say you have been treating yourself with homemade hooch. And it does not seem to have worked, because you are the greenest black man I've ever seen."

This brings laughter from soldiers bunked above, and to the left, and the right, and behind. Of course only the immune can laugh, and since Frangie herself is Category Two: queasy and barely maintaining, she is not fond of soldiers who can ride this sluggish roller coaster night and day and still laugh.

She snarls at them over her shoulder, but while Frangie

commands respect for her skills, she is still the smallest person in the battalion, and known for being kind and easy-going besides, and her snarl scares no one.

Frangie has been assigned to an all-black tank battalion—all colored troops aside from some of the most senior officers. The battalion is comprised of seven Sherman M4 medium tanks, six Sherman DDs (the amphibious version of the Sherman fitted with a flotation skirt), five Stuart light tanks, an independent squad of assault guns (modified Shermans), four Tank Recovery Vehicles (Shermans with cranes welded on) and three half-tracks mounting 81-millimeter mortars and machine guns. In addition to all those killing tools, the battalion had a long trail of supply trucks and maintenance and repair squads with their own specialized gear, and a gaggle of jeeps, one of which will be Frangie's.

And of course two extra-nice Sherman M4s for the battalion commander and his operations chief.

Frangie is a medic, not a nurse, and definitely not a doctor, and she is not in any way specially qualified to treat seasickness (no one really is) but what sick GIs want most—aside from medical booze—is attention from someone with at least some medical standing, and Frangie is happy to play the part. However powerless she might be.

Frangie leaves the sickly sergeant and winds her way up on deck into lashing rain and blustery wind. The upper deck is covered with trucks and jeeps, with the much heavier tanks down below on the tank deck. Canvas covers on the trucks snap in the wind. Sailors haul ropes and push with rough geniality through gaggles of time-killing soldiers.

Frangie checks the wind, walks over to the lee side, and carefully vomits up her dinner. The next LST is moored just a few feet away, and over there, on that LST, Frangie sees a white sailor doing exactly what she's doing. They exchange grim nods.

LSTs are so thick in the harbor that Frangie could literally walk for half a mile just jumping from ship to ship. It's as if a rolling gray steel blanket has been drawn over the water. LST 86 has an unenviable position on the outer edge of one long row of LSTs, exposing it more directly to the bumptious sea.

This is no way to go to war.

"So you got it too, huh, Doc?"

Frangie wipes her mouth and reflects on the fact that once upon a time she would have been mortified to vomit in front of another person, let alone a man. But it's one of the funny things about war—it tends to force you to focus on what really matters: staying alive, doing your job, staying alive . . .

"Yes," she says, gritting her teeth. "I've got it too, though not so bad as many do."

"Reminds me of my wife when she was pregnant with our first."

This is safer territory for conversation. Better than talking about sickness when Frangie's stomach is still far from settled. But Frangie is not interested in conversation; she'd hoped to have a quick puke and then have time to reread a disturbing letter from home.

But politeness rules. "Boy or girl?"

"Boy," he says proudly. "Thomas Moore the Third, me being Thomas Moore Jr. He was our first. Then we had Elizabeth and Franklin. For FDR."

He's a staff sergeant, one of the tank commanders in "her" squad, Sergeant Tommy Moore of Ft. Walton Beach, Florida. He's in his mid-twenties, but looks older because his hairline is beating a fast and premature retreat. He's smaller than average, like a lot of tankers—the interior of a Sherman not being congenial to large folks—a garrulous, opinionated father of three who volunteered after Pearl Harbor but had been assigned to a maintenance battalion to be permanently in the rear. It had taken a fight for him to be reassigned to the battalion.

Frangie respects that. But she does not like Moore, having been on the receiving end of one too many slights or insults directed at her sex. Two years into the big change and the overwhelming majority of male soldiers still resent the presence of women as anything other than nurses or what might euphemistically be called "dance partners." And many of the women, some like Frangie with extensive combat experience, are becoming increasingly impatient with those attitudes. The pecking order is still painfully clear: white men, then colored men, who are more or less equal with white women, and at the very bottom, colored women.

Moore, despite never having fired a shot in anger or felt the concussion wave of a German 88, feels himself inherently superior to Sergeant Francine "Frangie" Marr, Purple Heart, Silver Star, campaign ribbons for North Africa, Sicily and Italy. And though Moore is a tank commander, a husband and father, and a man who fought for the right to fight, he is treated as inherently inferior to any random white draftee.

Overlaid on the structure of race and sex is the system of rank. A white draftee private with a sixth-grade education will salute a black lieutenant, but still consider that colored man his inferior, regardless of his accomplishments.

But there is also a deeper, less obvious dividing line. It runs between those who have been in 'the shit' and those who have not. Frangie Marr lives within a series of overlapping structures of race, sex, rank and the unnamable but undeniable awareness that marks those who have, from those who have not . . . yet.

"You reckon we're ever going to go?" Moore asks. There has been more than one false alarm on that score, and the eternal scuttlebutt comes up with a different D-Day and landing area every five minutes.

Frangie shrugs. "Not in this weather, but I hear the same latrine rumors you do, Moore." It's perhaps more curt than she intends—she is feeling better . . . better, but not exactly fresh as a daisy. Her mouth tastes like a dead squirrel. And while the rain has slowed, the wind is still whipping water off the deck to sting Frangie's cheeks.

"Yeah." Moore is silent for a long while. "Some of the boys are worried. Not scared, exactly, just worried. They've heard stories about panzers. How our 76s just bounce off their armor and their 88s go right through ours."

Frangie looks at him in surprise. Not because worry is unusual—a GI who doesn't worry about going into battle should be Section Eight, mustered out as crazy. No, it's the fact that he is confiding this to her. Is it because she's a woman, or because she's a medic?

Then it dawns on her: despite carrying a medical bag rather than a rifle, Frangie is a veteran. And Moore is not. He's seeking reassurance. And not just for "some of the boys."

"I suppose the air corps will have destroyed a lot of the panzers by the time we even get there," Frangie says.

Moore snorts derisively. "Air corps. We'll be lucky if they don't bomb *us.*" Another silence. "They're just nervous is all. Some of the boys. They don't know what it will be like."

Neither do you, Moore.

"I guess it's better to have all that armor plate around you than just be walking along like infantry," Frangie suggests.

Moore shakes his head. "Infantry can dig a hole. A tank? See, Doc, a tank is a big fat bull's-eye. A prize! No Kraut tank driver goes around bragging about how many infantry he killed; he wants to kill tanks. Heck, I want to kill tanks! I want to go home someday, prop Tom Trey—that's his nickname—up on my knee and tell him how Daddy wiped out all these panzers and saved the day! Problem is, old Fritz over in that panzer has better armor and a heavier gun than I do."

And more experience.

And his own children to whom he too would like to brag.

"They teach us that most wounds are superficial, and most fellows don't get hurt at all," Frangie says, squeegeeing rainwater from her eyes.

She doesn't know how to reassure Moore. In her first artillery barrage she had seen her friend, Doon Acey, a boy from back home, spill his intestines like fat sausages falling from a split grocery bag. She's seen traumatic amputations, chest wounds, head wounds, and the bullet to the left foot that is the signature of a soldier looking to escape the war by any means available. She knows the statistics and they're true enough, but she's held the hands of the dying, and she is all out of optimism.

"They say this new Tiger tank the Krauts have . . ." Moore makes a low whistle.

"They say lots of things."

"Yeah. I guess that's so. The only thing is, Doc, I'm . . . some of the boys are real scared of burning."

"Burning?"

Moore shrugs. "You know what the Limeys say? They call it a 'brew up.'"

"That's when they're making tea," Frangie says. "They call *that* a brew up."

Moore shakes his head. "Not when they're talking about a tank battle. Your tank catches fire, that's a brew up. Men trying to get out of the hatches. Maybe our own Willy Pete going off."

"Who's Willy Pete?"

"Willy Pete. WP. White phosphorous. We carry some white phosphorous rounds, you know, to make smoke. But if the Willy Pete gets on you, you can't put it out, see. It's like glue that just burns and burns and burns, all the way down to the bone."

Now Frangie definitely wants out of this conversation. She cannot reassure him because of all wounds it is burning that frightens her the most as well. The very thought of it makes her heart race with fear. She glances around, hoping for an easy escape.

"I wouldn't want to live if I got burned bad," Moore says.

And suddenly Frangie has the feeling the floor is slipping away for a whole different reason.

"We give you morphine and—"

"I don't want to burn in a tank, Doc. None of the boys do. I mean, if you find me in that, you know, *condition*, I wouldn't mind at all if maybe I got too much morphine. If you understand me." He laughs insincerely as if it's a joke.

"Sergeant Moore," Frangie says firmly, "I'm just a bedpan commando, I'm not God. My job is to keep you alive, not to kill you."

Moore stiffens and tilts his head back to look down his nose at her. "I wouldn't expect you to understand. You're a woman."

"Right. Goodbye, Moore," Frangie says and walks away.

The conversation is disturbing, but what strikes her now is how she had the nerve to just turn her back and walk away. That is definitely not typical of Frangie Marr. All her life she has been soft-spoken, kind to animals, deferential to older people, deferential to men, and above all, deferential to white folks. That's just common sense and decency, with that last bit being simple self-preservation—no colored girl growing up in Tulsa, Oklahoma talks back to a white person, not if she wants to reach old age.

Deference has in many ways defined Frangie's life. She has ambitions, but can't speak about them because it isn't her place to have high and mighty aspirations. All her life Frangie has given way to her parents, her pastor, her elders, her teachers, men and white people.

Moore is a colored man, not white, but he is older and he is a man. And yet, Frangie just turned her back and walked away. The realization adds a little swagger to her step, which causes her to trip and very nearly plunge down one of the many steel stairs.

She heads below to the main hold, the bright-lit steel cube at the heart of the LST, with its cargo of tanks. There are seven hulking Shermans, parked with trucks and half-tracks and jeeps between so as to distribute the weight.

Most of the tanks have slogans or names painted on the side or in some cases on the main gun. Harley's Harlots. GI Jane. Red Hot. One is named Nat Turner. Frangie wonders if the white generals know that Nat Turner launched a slave rebellion that ended up killing a whole bunch of white people. One of the tank commanders is being a smart aleck, and it brings a sneaky smile to Frangie's lips which, once upon a time, might have pursed in disapproval.

Weeks spent listening to her radical big brother Harder have not turned her into a Communist—they are atheists after all, and Frangie goes nowhere without her Bible — but it has forced her to see things a bit differently. All her life Frangie has moved to the back of the bus or trolley. All her life Frangie has known to look for the signs that say, "No Colored," or signs that designate special colored drinking fountains, colored bathrooms. This giving way, this automatic acceptance of white superiority, will have to resume when she goes home. The medic with the Silver Star for bravery, the young woman who time and again has run into the line of fire to save a life, will have to be . . . *meek.*

That meekness had always come naturally to Frangie. But meekness cannot be a part of what she does now, what she will soon have to do. There is no such creature as a meek combat medic.

On the LST are multiple holds on either side of the main deck, each a version of the puke-reeking box where she had made her rounds earlier. Her own niche is a small space that is the seagoing barracks of the medics, nurses and assorted medical technicians assigned to go ashore with the battalion and establish a field aid station, once the beach is secure.

Frangie has volunteered to move up with the advance elements rather than be stuck working with supercilious doctors and bossy nurses at an aid station or field hospital. It's more dangerous, but it's also more independent, and she's come to value independence. She will trail the advance in her own jeep with a driver, Corporal Rosemary Manning. Manning is nearly six feet tall, taller than most of the men, and makes an unlikely sight alongside the diminutive Frangie. The jeep has red crosses against white circles painted on the sides and the hood, a very different sort of armor that relies on the enemy to honor the sanctity of the medicos.

Since Frangie is small, young and reasonably agile she's been assigned a top bunk—just three high in this particular space. She unlaces and kicks off her boots, lies back on her wool blanket and runs a mental inventory through her supplies. Bandages, plasma, tourniquets, splints, salves, sulfa powder, tape, scalpel, scissors, needle and thread and yes, morphine.

She has never dealt with a serious burn injury. And now that Moore is no longer there to annoy her, his worries and questions persist.

What will it be like?

How will I do?

And just what exactly am I supposed to do to help a man inside a burning tank?

She draws out and unfolds her most recent letter from home. It's all the usual chit-chat, all but one paragraph:

Your father has been feeling poorly of late and has had to skip some work this week. But he's going to see Dr. Teller if he doesn't feel better.

It doesn't sound like much, but her dad generally has to be missing a limb to even consider going to the doctor. Frangie rolls onto her side, closes her eyes and prays fervently.

Please, Lord, if it is Your will, care for my father.

She then asks divine protection for Harder, for her little brother, Obal, and above all, and most fervently, for her mother.

She has too much to carry, Lord. Harder exiled from the family, me here, and . . . and the other things You know of, Lord.

The prayer brings terrible, sickening images to her mind. She was not born when it happened, and she grew up never knowing, but she knows now, and her imagination will not cease supplying lurid mental images of the great Tulsa riot, of colored men and women fleeing as white folk fired down at them from biplanes and threw gasoline bombs on black businesses.

But now, added to those images, come imagined scenes of Sergeant Moore burning alive.

Please, Lord, if it is Your will, care for Sergeant Moore.

For the last almost two days she's been dealing with seasickness, venereal disease and various psychosomatic illnesses, each accompanied by some version of, "I gotta go home, Doc! I can't be fighting Germans with this back pain!" This is not strictly her job, but the day-in, day-out of dealing with soldiers has kept her distracted from what is coming.

Coming eventually.

Coming soon.

The suspense is killing everyone. It's almost as bad for morale as the seasickness. Everyone wants to go, and everyone is afraid—anxious to get on with something that frightens them. In a hurry to discover whether they will live or die.

Though of course Frangie knows the majority of them simply do not believe in their own mortality. The men and the women, the average GIs, the ones who will soon be driving Shermans and being hunted by Tigers, just want to get it all over with.

And then, go home. Because if the American army has a single, unifying thought that runs through every division, every battalion, every platoon, white or black, it is: *Let's get this over with and go home.*

Frangie is not in a hurry, though she shares the general annoyance at the delays. She has been on the front line in Italy. She'd been badly wounded, though she has only hazy memories of being hurt. She had a long spell in recovery from her wounds, a pleasant spell once her pain was mostly gone, during which time she had worked in an unofficial capacity in the same hospital that treated her. There she spent some time with her brother, Harder Marr, now working as an army orderly.

She had also spent an unreal interlude with Rio Richlin and Rainy Schulterman, two women she knew as acquaintances, when the three of them were awarded the Silver Star. The three then had leave for a week and, joined by Richlin's friend Jenou

Castain, they had enjoyed themselves in London, going to shows and dining in restaurants like nothing Frangie had experienced.

The strangest experience for Frangie was simply being able to go into restaurants and pubs with three white girls, sit at the same table, and be served by white or brown waiters indifferent to her race. That was not the sort of thing that went on in Tulsa.

But that pleasant coffee break is now over. The war is coming back. Soon this LST will sail to meet it. Soon, very soon, the guns will erupt, the shells will fly, and men and women on both sides will be blown apart.

And some will burn.

Not that, Lord. Gentle Jesus, not that.

She should sleep. But sleep won't come.

A loudspeaker squawks, but she can't make out the words through steel bulkheads.

And then she hears the sound of running feet—sailors called to their stations. And the LST's engines come to life, sending vibrations reverberating through the deck.

Frangie checks her watch. Midnight has come and gone.

It is the morning of June 6, 1944.

5

The boat ride up the Charente had been pleasant and mostly problem-free. Rainy and her two French companions had been stopped and their boat boarded by the *milice*, the French police supposedly under the control of the treasonous Vichy regime, but effectively now under direct Nazi control. But this had been handled with some of the currency Rainy had brought with her.

At the dock in Cognac there had been another offer of currency and another cursory look around the boat before its cargo—mostly oysters, but some black market cigarettes as well—could be off-loaded.

The truck had been where the truck was supposed to be, already loaded with three big barrels of Cognac, the local brandy named for the town. It was just under a hundred miles from Cognac to Limoges, and the first part of that had been easy as well.

Rainy found herself almost relaxing, or relaxing to the extent she could, while crammed onto the narrow bench between Étienne and Marie. The seat had a loose spring that seemed determined to dig a hole into Rainy's tailbone.

The countryside outside the truck's dirty windows is beautiful, though bleakly empty to Rainy's New York City sensibilities. From time to time Rainy asks Marie what is growing in a particular field.

"Grapevines, of course."

"Ah. Right. I've seen grapevines before." She has, but not being very interested in agriculture Rainy has not quite made the connection between the stunted, misshapen vines and grapes. Or wine. "And what's this now?"

"That? Why that is *maïs*—corn—to feed the geese and the ducks and the pigs."

"Huh."

It is a boring drive. The only interesting bits come when the road winds through a village, but after a while all the villages look the same. Stone houses, tile roofs, small windows, narrow doors opening directly onto barely-there sidewalks; a baker, a butcher, a grocery store, a café, a shoe store, a dress store, all with small display windows, many with no sign to indicate their function because this area does not get many tourists, certainly not since war came.

"Okay, what's going on there?" Rainy sits forward, suddenly alert. The field beside the road has armed civilians slouching before it.

"Ah, that is tobacco. It must be guarded."

"We have a choice," Étienne says. "We are coming to La Rochefoucauld. There we have a split. We can go left which avoids the town and goes most directly to Limoges. Or we can go through the town and then pass through the forest, where we may come upon elements of our friends, the Das Reich. The Boche hide their tanks under the trees, fearing the RAF."

"That sounds good," Rainy says. But she senses something in the way Marie glances at her brother and makes a face.

Sure enough, as they enter the town, Étienne suddenly announces a need to stop off and check on a friend.

"A friend?"

Étienne shrugs. "A person I know."

"A woman," Marie says with sudden heat. "A woman who is a *collaboratrice horizontale*."

"A what?"

"A horizontal collaborator, a woman who sleeps with Germans." She spits dramatically out of the window and makes a gesture with her hand like she's trying to fling her chin at Étienne.

"She sometimes provides useful information," Étienne says defensively.

"Yes, but to whom?" Marie demands sourly.

Étienne shrugs. "Marianne is a patriot."

Marie's response is a snort.

"She may be able to give me information about the Das Reich. It is true that one of her . . . friends . . . is a *Sturmbannführer*, what you would call a major."

In the end the decision comes down to Rainy's need to use the toilet and her desire to stretch her legs. The stop is approved.

Étienne parks in a narrow street near a small, arched bridge over the River Tardoire. The street is walled by limestone and stucco homes built right to the edge of the road. Windows are mostly shuttered, though Rainy hears a child singing through one open second story window.

"There is a café just over the bridge," Marie says, leading the way as a somewhat embarrassed Étienne knocks on one of the doors. They cross the bridge and Rainy is delighted to see an impressive chateau looming over the town. It is like something from a fairy tale, something a princess might inhabit while pining for her Prince Charming.

So this is France, Rainy thinks. She'd always hoped to visit France, but not like this.

They find the café, a small, dark room smelling of damp limestone, garlic and red wine. There are six tables, only two occupied, and a small bar with no stools.

At the threshold Marie freezes for a moment and Rainy plows into her. It is immediately clear what has made Marie hesitate: one of the tables is occupied by a middle-aged French couple; the other is occupied by three German soldiers, junior officers by the look of their youthful faces, and confirmed by collar-boards with three silver pips. They are the equivalent of lieutenants, Rainy's own rank.

And they are Waffen SS, as clearly indicated by the twin lightning-flash insignia. They wear camouflage uniforms, not the formal black, and Rainy notes a grease stain on one man's trouser leg, evidence that they are not on leave or enjoying a day pass, but have managed to escape some sort of field maneuver for a quick bite in town. No doubt the food is better in the café than in the field kitchen.

Three Schmeisser submachine guns lean against the wall by the table.

One of the men, an *Untersturmführer* with prominent brows and a mangled left ear, looks up. He grins wolfishly at Marie. Then sees Rainy, sees the widow's black, and nods politely. He tears off a chunk of bread and goes back to his plate of langoustines.

Sitting too far from the SS men will be a signal. So will sitting too close. Marie guides them to the one table that is neither.

Rainy sees a hand-lettered sign pointing to "WC," the toilets, which are outside in an alley, a Turkish-style squat toilet with privacy provided only by a short, greasy draw curtain. Rainy does what is necessary, all the while in a sort of fugue state, half paralyzed with fear, half working through the odds.

Every part of Rainy resists going back into the café. Of course she knows she must, she can hardly abandon Marie, let alone her mission, but it will not be pleasant eating within a few feet of the Germans.

Back inside, Rainy listens while Marie orders a dozen oysters, two cheval steaks—horse meat, the only meat on the menu—and fried potatoes, as well as white wine and a bottle of mineral water. All perfectly normal and perfectly unremarkable.

Rainy has her back to the Germans and listens intently while seeming to carry on a sort of minimalist, whispered exchange with Marie.

Water, wine and a baguette arrive, and are plopped on the table by the proprietor, who is the only visible staff.

The Germans discuss prostitutes in ways that make Rainy glad Marie does not speak German. Though some notion of what they are so crudely talking about must have penetrated Marie's consciousness, because she blushes and bites her lip.

The oysters arrive.

The Germans move on to talking about someone named Burkhart, who is apparently a drunk, a loafer, and utterly useless, but knows all the best jokes. The Germans begin repeating jokes and laughing in a deliberately noisy, demonstrative way that makes the older French couple cringe.

The Germans call for another bottle of wine. Their second? Their third?

The atmosphere in the room, never exactly convivial, grows increasingly tense and menacing. Drunk German soldiers are never a good thing; drunk SS are worse. Drunk members of the Das Reich are worse still. Rainy has read the dossiers: the Das Reich fought on the Eastern Front against the Soviet Red Army, where even among the brutal forces in that pitiless fight, the Das Reich stood out for its monstrous treatment of prisoners, civilians, and especially Jews.

The *Untersturmführer* with the mangled ear is clearly looking at Marie, but also, increasingly, at Rainy.

The oysters are cleared away and the steaks arrive.

In ten minutes they can be finished and on their way. Ten minutes. Ten minutes in which Marie and Rainy must mimic an innocent pair of young Frenchwomen who have stopped for a quick lunch. Two women who are aware of the Germans, but not *overly* aware.

Suddenly Mangled Ear pushes back from the table, wobbles a bit to the hooting enjoyment of his compatriots, demands to know where the toilet is, and lurches right into Rainy and Marie's table.

Rainy glances at Marie and sees fear in her eyes.

"*Pardonnez moi*," the German says in barely-decipherable French.

"*Pas de quoi*," Marie says in a whisper. She looks down at her plate.

"*Untersturmführer Fritz Weiss, a votre service, mesdemoiselles. Zwei, er, deux jolies mademoiselles. Pourquoi toute seul?*"

It's mostly French, not grammatical, but comprehensible. He's asking why two pretty young women are there alone.

Marie offers their cover story. They are traveling to a wedding, the madame's wedding, in fact, in the company of Marie's brother, Étienne, who will be back at any moment.

At this the German grabs a chair, pulls it close and sits down with them. "You don't mind? More wine here! The ladies are parched!" He leers openly at Marie's chest and she pulls back. Then he turns shrewd eyes on Rainy and asks, "Where are you from?"

"Fouras," she lies in a hoarse whisper she hopes will disguise her accent.

The Walther is hard against her back. A suicide pill is sewn into the collar of her dress. She can feel the knife strapped to her leg.

The German waves that off. "I mean your family. You're not French."

Rainy offers a baffled smile. Marie steps in and says of course she is French, they are cousins.

The German tilts his head to the side. Then he reaches over, takes Rainy's chin and turns her face sideways in profile.

"No Frenchie ever had a nose like that," he says, and now the other two Germans are quiet and attentive, sensing their companion is up to something.

Rainy allows the hand, then, with disdain, pushes it away.

"I know a Jew when I see one," the *Untersturmführer* says, his voice silky but slurred with drink.

Rainy puts on a baffled look.

The German rests both his elbows on the table and leans close, his breath stinking of red wine and cigarettes. "I've seen many a Jew," he says, watching Rainy closely. "I know the look of a Jew. I know the smell of a Jew." He has a sudden idea. "Patron! Bring us ham!"

"Ham, monsieur?"

"Something pork. Ham. Bacon. A snout, a trotter, it doesn't matter."

As they wait, the air is so tense it vibrates. A small slice of ham appears on a plate. The German tears open a piece of the baguette and carefully folds the ham into it, making a sandwich.

"Eat it, Jew."

Rainy picks up the ham sandwich and takes a bite.

Jewish, but not kosher, you stupid Nazi asshole.

Rainy smiles and renders her hoarse whisper again. "*Merci.*" Thank you. And proceeds to eat the rest of the sandwich.

The other two Germans now erupt in guffaws, yelling good-natured taunts to their fellow, who smiles and nods a sort of apology to Rainy. He gets up unsteadily and heads for the back door, toward the toilet.

At that moment, Étienne comes rushing in the front door and in an agitated voice says, "We must go!" and only then spots the Germans.

Étienne freezes. The *Untersturmführer* with the mangled ear stops. Marie's eyes go wide. And from outside on the street comes the shrill sound of a furious Frenchwoman shouting, "Liar! Bastard!"

It all looks like a domestic row of some sort and the Germans are grinning again in anticipation. Until the woman bursts in through the door, still yelling curses at Étienne and then turns to the Germans and says, "*Il est maquis, lui, ce bâtard!*"

He's maquis, the bastard.

There is a frozen moment when the entire scene is an oil painting. Two Germans are seated. One German is turning back toward them. Étienne is blushing, already embarrassed and now appalled. Marie stares at her brother, her expression torn between rage and fear.

Rainy does the math.

Three Germans.

Truck down the street.

A long way still to go.

And then: no choice.

She pulls the Walther from her back, points it at the two seated Germans, *BANG!* shoots the one on the left, then *BANG!* the one on the right. Mangled ear is caught off-guard, but after a split second's hesitation, rushes at Rainy. She fires.

Jammed!

Marie pushes the German and he stumbles, but in the wrong

direction: toward the stacked submachine guns.

Rainy is up, knocking the table over. She slams the Walther down on the German's head, hitting him on the crown of his head, stunning but not killing him. He staggers to one knee. The cutlery and glasses and bottles have all fallen to the floor. She dives for a broken water glass, cutting her own palm, seizing the glass by its base and plunging a pointed shard into the German's neck.

But his collar-board turns the glass shard aside, and now, drunk or not, the German's training kicks in. He twists and drives a fist into Rainy's belly, doubling her over. The glass drops from her hand.

The German is bigger, stronger and more experienced at hand-to-hand combat. Rainy knows she will lose if she doesn't end this quickly. But how? With what?

But then a knife appears, one of the fallen steak knives. Rainy dives. The German dives atop her, hands scrabbling to grab hers. Rainy stabs the knife at his side, but the blade is too weak to penetrate his uniform and the tip breaks off. He shifts his grip, wrapping big hands around her neck. She stabs the broken blade into his neck, not a fatal cut, but enough to cause him to rear back, roaring curses.

Rainy kicks wildly, rolls away, uses a table to pull herself up, grabs a chair and slams it against him, like something out of a western barroom brawl. It does not break, rather it bounces away, having done no real damage.

Rainy grabs a wine bottle from the German's table and smashes it against his shoulder, meaning to go for his head. He kicks, hitting her shin. She swings again and this time catches the German on the bridge of his nose. Blood gushes, filling his mouth and spilling out.

He is stunned but still dangerous. Rainy takes her time with the next blow, bringing the bottle hard against his temple. He drops to his knees and Rainy pushes him onto his back, straddles him, fights past his flailing hands, finds the handle of the knife and begins sawing the short blade back and forth across his throat. Like she's trying to slice a tough roast.

The last of the cheap blade snaps off and she tosses the hilt across the room.

The German is bleeding profusely from several wounds, but he is not dead. He crawls across the floor now, trying to reach his Schmeisser, but his way is blocked by one of his companions, lying on his side and trying to get at the hole Rainy's bullet left in his chest.

Rainy smashes the bottle against the back of Mangled Ear's head, and this time it breaks, leaving the mouth of the bottle intact, and with a single long, pointed shard of heavy green glass.

Rainy straddles the German from behind, awkward in her bulky black dress, and stabs the shard into his jugular, then twists it back and forth, cutting deeper and deeper as warm blood flows over her hand.

She feels the way his muscles no longer seem to be acting under conscious control. Still she saws and digs and twists until she is sure, absolutely sure, that he is dead.

She stands back and tosses the bloody bottle aside.

The French couple, the *patron*, Marie, Étienne, and Étienne's prostitute, Marianne, all stare at her.

Rainy retrieves her Walther, works the slide to eject the jammed round, and in French says, "Messieurs, dames, I am going to tell you what happened here. These Germans got drunk and picked a fight with a truck driver who is heading west, toward Cognac. There was a fight, the truck driver had two friends, and they killed the Germans. Is that clear?"

No one answers.

"Is that clear?" Rainy demands. The *patron* and the French couple all nod yes. Étienne's friend is backing toward the door, looking very much as if she might scream.

Rainy aims the Walther and *BANG!* shoots her in the heart. Étienne lets loose a whinny of protest.

"Going west," Rainy says, her voice genuinely ragged now. "Truck drivers going west toward Cognac. Stick to that story and you'll be all right. This is maquis business, not yours. But if you betray the Resistance . . ." She lets the threat hang.

Three minutes later they are panting and gasping in the truck and driving at an average, unremarkable speed toward the east, toward the pleasant woods of the Périgord Limousin.

"We should have taken their guns," Étienne says, speaking for the first time.

"No, you imbecile," Marie rages. "We should not have stopped to see your mistress and you should not have found a way to make her angry!"

"If we took the guns it'd look like maquis to the Krauts for sure," Rainy says, her voice far calmer than her heart or brain. "Drunk truck drivers getting in a bar fight don't take Schmeissers."

Silence. Then Étienne says, "You didn't have to kill Marianne."

An even longer silence. Then in slow, measured but furious tones, like slow-motion violence, Rainy says, "Your arrogance ends right here, right now, Étienne. You screwed up. You could have gotten us all arrested or killed."

"You have no—"

"Shut up!" Rainy snaps. "This is my operation from here on in."

"We do not take orders from the American—"

"Stop it, Étienne." Marie's voice, like Rainy's, is tense and barely under control. "She's right. You were careless. That woman died because of you. And we all nearly ended up in an SD interrogation cell! Because of you and your . . . your *needs.*"

Étienne does not argue further. He continues driving and stares straight ahead.

Rainy uses the silence to put herself back together. The crisis is always easier than the aftermath, she has learned that. In a crisis it is all about speed and decisiveness. The aftermath, the sick feeling that comes with each obsessive mental replay of digging broken glass into a man's neck, feeling his blood, smelling it . . .

And the hole that appeared not quite perfectly centered in the mistress's chest.

Her hands tremble so she sticks them in her coat pockets. How long will it take the *milice* to show up on the scene? Would the SD get there first? Did the *patron* and the French couple have the nerve to lie to the SD?

No. But they might just repeat what she'd said about heading west. That very small ruse might just work.

But deep inside her a voice says, "No."

No, they would not convince the SD, not for five minutes. *So, make a plan, Rainy!* They had a good ten minutes' head start, but the SD could radio ahead, they could call in planes, they could mobilize the entire French police force as well.

Which meant the likelihood was they were not going to make it to Limoges. That was just the reality.

Time to hide.

And what better place than the middle of the Das Reich division?

"We've got a cargo of cognac," Rainy says, "and a bunch of thirsty Germans somewhere around here, right? So let's go make a sales call."

6

RAINY SCHULTERMAN—NEAR LIMOGES, NAZI-OCCUPIED FRANCE

They drive the truck-load of cognac and black market cigarettes around for a full day. Rainy's thought had been to use the cognac as proof of innocence, as proof that they were just smugglers, black marketeers. Surely, she figured, *surely* they would be stopped at a roadblock and then could negotiate a deal for the cargo. It had seemed so terribly clever when she'd thought of it.

They have three transport barrels of cognac, three hundred and fifty liters or roughly ninety gallons each, plus two hundred cartons of cigarettes of ten packs each. The Das Reich might be Nazi fanatics, but in war no one ever has enough alcohol or smokes, and Rainy is reasonably sure that an offer to sell and, crucially, a promise to return with more, will get the attention of any divisional quartermaster.

There is only one flaw in the plan: they encounter no roadblocks. Twice they pull off the road to avoid German staff cars racing by, perhaps in pursuit of them, perhaps not.

The first night after killing the soldiers Rainy, Étienne and Marie sleep rough, driving the truck down a dirt track deep into the Limousin forest. Étienne and Marie sleep cramped in the truck's cabin, and Rainy wedges herself into a place between two of the barrels in back. It is not comfortable, not even by army standards, and she sleeps very little. When she does sleep she is kneeling beside a river of blood, washing her hands in it.

The next morning, chilled, aching and frowzy, they stop at a small café for coffee and croissants.

"The croissants are good," Rainy observes, politely saying nothing about the coffee.

Marie says, "The coffee is *merde*. Chicory and roasted grain."

"It's hot," Étienne says. "Coffee is not the highest priority."

Rainy is not at all certain about that. She'd have paid a month's salary—a hundred and fifty dollars—for a decent cup. But Étienne has been distant and defensive since the incident with his mistress or girlfriend or prostitute, whatever she was—his stories varied—and Rainy does not want to argue with him. He has not yet chosen to share with them the reason Marianne ended up chasing him down the street yelling that he was maquis.

The people who join Resistance groups and risk death are a mixed bag, according to Colonel Herkemeier's briefing in London. Some are committed Communists. Some are followers of General DeGaulle's Free French. Most joined the maquis only after the Germans began shipping French citizens off to forced labor in Germany. There are dozens of groups under dozens of leaders, some quietly effective, some noisily useless. All are brave, that at least is clear: only a very brave person defies the Nazis.

But as Rainy watches Étienne fuss with the croissant crumbs he's scattered she knows that some are also informers working either for the Germans or the collaborationist traitors of the Vichy government.

"We should get going," Marie says.

"In a minute," Étienne answers. He has taken to overruling Marie on everything, asserting his now-questionable authority, though he has not yet challenged Rainy, who has carefully avoided antagonizing him. But his continued high-handedness is definitely getting on her nerves.

She tries to imagine a scenario in which Étienne is a traitor. Had he provoked Marianne into giving him up? Is she his contact with the Nazis? Had the two of them cooked up the little demonstration that had resulted in her death?

But why? Why not just walk in and tell the three SS men? Why the subterfuge?

Of course the answer is obvious: Marie. She is his sister after all, and he might not want her to know that he's a traitor. He could stand her thinking him a fool, but not a traitor.

You're talking yourself into it, Rainy, she chides herself, *and you have no proof.*

They spend the morning driving along a road that is the dividing line between the Limousin forest and farm fields, and again, despite seeing unmistakable evidence of tank tracks on the side of the road, they are not stopped.

"Any other time the Boche would have roadblocks every kilometer," Étienne grumbles.

"It's an unusual situation," Rainy allows. "Driving around and hoping to be—"

They hit a pothole in the road and the truck swerves. When Étienne wrestles the rickety vehicle back on the road they hear the unmistakable flapping sound of a popped tire. They pull off and sure enough the right front tire is blown, worn rubber mangled around the rim.

"Do you have a spare?" Rainy asks.

Étienne laughs bitterly. "Spare tire? Why not ask for a golden chariot?"

Rainy suppresses her irritation. Again. "Can you *find* a spare tire?"

Étienne shrugs. He rolls then lights a cigarette and stands thinking ostentatiously, as Marie and Rainy hike into the woods for a quick bathroom break. When they return Étienne has a map unfolded on the hood of the truck. "Tulle is not far. We have a contact there."

"Maquis?" Rainy asks.

"Communists." He spits on the ground. "But they may help us. In any case, we have no choice."

They drive the truck into the forest, shredding the last of the tire in the process, and cut branches to pile against the sides as camouflage.

"It's five kilometers," Étienne says. "You two wait here."

"I think I'd rather come with you," Rainy says.

Étienne is quick to understand her motive. "Do you, mademoiselle, propose to distrust me? This is not England, still less America. This is France!"

Marie, Rainy notes, remains silent, watching.

"It's not a question of trust," Rainy lies blandly. "I just don't like waiting in the forest and not knowing."

In the end the three of them are able to hitch a ride on a trailer being pulled by a tractor. It means sharing a ride with a load of farm implements and sacks of manure, which does nothing to improve Rainy's mood. They arrive at the outskirts of Tulle, wait until they are well past their destination, then jump off and double back to a small farm.

The farmer is a gnarled, whiskered old man with a total of three teeth. He sees them, says nothing, and jerks his head toward the barn before disappearing into the stone house.

In the barn they find two workmen: a thick-set middle-aged man, and a second man, this one in his early twenties, stripped to the waist and shoveling cow dung into a wheelbarrow held by the older man.

The older man sees them, glances at his companion, and without a word leaves the barn. The young man's dark eyes narrow at the sight of Étienne, but widen in happy recognition of Marie.

He starts toward her, grinning, then stops, abashed, and snatches up his shirt. He is ready to call her by name, but stops himself. "Mademoiselle, it is good to see you."

"Marie," she says, making a deprecating face.

"Marie, is it?" His laugh says he knows it's an alias. "Good choice, you could certainly be a Marie. And I suppose you must call me Philippe."

Hands are shaken, introductions made.

Rainy is wary of judging a book by its cover, but her instinctive reaction is that she likes Philippe. He's bright, alert, quick and not at all bad-looking, though he has eyes only for Marie. Still, she remembers Étienne's remark about Communists. The Communists, whose primary loyalty is to the party and its

Moscow overlords, is not technically an enemy of the United States. Quite the contrary, President Roosevelt bends over backward to excuse Stalin's brutality in the interests of maintaining a shaky alliance with the communist dictator. But that, Rainy knows, is not the opinion of the military who see the Communists as the likely next enemy, once Hitler is destroyed.

"What brings you to Tulle?" Philippe asks, buttoning his shirt while Marie blushes.

"Our truck blew a tire," Étienne says. "We hoped you might be able to help."

"Indeed?" Philippe says. "Well, that is not so easily done. Come with me, please."

He leads them out the back door of the barn to a crude lean-to with a piece of canvas for a door. The roof is low and slanted, there are no windows, and the candle that Philippe lights illuminates a collapsing cot, an empty crate used as a table, and one chair.

Philippe does not offer the chair. Instead he uses the side of his foot to scuff at the dirt floor and uncover a wooden trapdoor. He pries it up revealing rough-hewn wooden steps. They follow him down into a cool, damp-smelling, dirt-walled cellar. By the light of a single candle, Rainy sees two men.

And to her amazement, they are wearing uniforms. It takes her only a few seconds to realize that these are Royal Air Force uniforms, dirty, sweat-stained, and in one case blood-stained, but unmistakably RAF.

"Gentlemen," Philippe says, "I have the honor to introduce Mademoiselle Marie, her brother . . ." He hesitates, and Étienne says his name. "Étienne, of course. And this is Lieutenant Alice Jones, of the American army."

One of the Brits stands up and offers his hand. "Flight Lieutenant David Wickham, and this is my wireless operator, Sergeant Hooper. You'll have to forgive Hooper, his knee is a bit wobbly."

Rainy smiles at the inevitable British understatement: the 'wobbly' knee is clearly broken, and given the blood it's a serious fracture. Hooper is not wobbly, he's crippled.

Hands are shaken. Hooper remains lying on a duplicate of the cots above. Neither Wickham nor Hooper can be over twenty-one, maybe twenty-two years of age. The sergeant is a slight man, with a bent nose and nervous hands.

Flight Lieutenant Wickham looks like a recruiting poster model of an RAF flyer: tall for a pilot, with a wave of blond hair, blue eyes, a clear pale complexion, casual attitude, and an accent that speaks of good schools.

He reminds Rainy uncomfortably of her brother, Aryeh, a marine fighting in the South Pacific. Uncomfortable because any thought of Aryeh comes with anxiety. And uncomfortable too, because she finds herself attracted to Wickham, and that is not a thought that should occupy the same mental space as "reminds me of my brother."

"They were shot down near Strasbourg," Philippe says. "They have been brought this far, and now we await an opportunity to move them south into Spain, where they can be repatriated."

Wickham grins sheepishly and says, "I'm very much afraid that I strayed right into the path of German ack-ack." Then he frowns.

"Everyone jumped, but we became separated after coming down. Our French friends have been sheltering us ever since. Three weeks now. May I ask, Lieutenant: what news of the war?"

The cellar is little more than a hole in the ground, with a plank ceiling low enough to force the six-foot-tall Wickham to crouch slightly. There is a wine rack holding a dozen bottles. A quarter of the room is filled with a pile of charcoal.

Rainy sits on the end of Wickham's cot. Philippe gallantly brings a chair down from above for Marie. Étienne leans against a battered china cabinet that holds a radio on its top.

"I don't know anything about the war that you don't know," Rainy says. "The Russians are on the move. General Clark took Rome."

"And the invasion?" Wickham asks.

"We wait constantly on news of the war," Philippe says. "We expect the signal any day now. Any hour." He looks questioningly at Rainy.

Rainy shrugs. She has no specific information on the date or time of the invasion. But the fact that she has been sent to spy on the Das Reich, and that her operational plan involves exfiltrating in ten days, suggests strongly that it is coming very soon. "General Eisenhower seldom consults me for my advice," she says dryly, earning a laugh from Wickham and a nod from Philippe.

"Information must always be compartmentalized," Étienne says somewhat pompously. Rainy watches Philippe carefully for his reaction. He minimizes but cannot entirely conceal a dislike for Étienne. Is that because he does not trust Étienne? Is it because he simply does not like his tone of voice? Or is it perhaps that Étienne is a protective big brother to Marie in whom Philippe is clearly interested?

The old farmer who disappeared earlier now comes clumping down the steps to the cellar, carrying a mixed set of glasses. Behind him comes his wife, equally old but clearer of eye, carrying a tray of bread, cheese and a hunk of salami.

"*Merci, madame et monsieur,*" Wickham says in tortured French, obviously a phrase he has learned recently.

"*Je vous en prie,*" the old woman says.

The old couple leave. Philippe selects a dusty bottle from the rack and pops the cork.

"Who shall we drink to?" Hooper asks, sitting up, wincing in pain but trying gamely to be part of the conversation.

Wickham says, "To our American guest."

They drink to Rainy, or rather to "Alice."

Then Rainy raises her glass. "To the brave men and women who fight for the honor of France. And to the Royal Air Force."

With that out of the way they portion out the bread and cheese and Marie slices the salami. There is nowhere near enough to go around, but each is content with what they have, aware that what they eat comes from the meager supplies of the old couple. Then Philippe checks his watch. "It is time. Marie?"

Marie goes to the radio and switches it on. The channel selector is already tuned to the BBC. It takes a while for it to warm up, but then at last comes crackly music, the opening notes of Beethoven's Fifth Symphony. The clear beats of that

Beethoven opener have long since come to be represented by the Morse code:

Dit dit dit . . . dah.

Morse code for the letter *V. V* for victory.

"Your watch runs fast," Marie says to Philippe.

"Perhaps I am in a hurry," Philippe says.

"Yes, men are often in a hurry."

"Because pleasure delayed can become pleasure denied."

"Pleasure worth having is pleasure worth waiting for," Marie counters, with a small sniff of dismissal that earns a wry grin from Philippe.

There is subtext there, a flirtation, and Rainy conceals a smile, noting that Wickham too is charmed by young love.

Then . . . "*Ici Londres. Les Français parlent aux Français.*"

This is London. The French speak to the French.

"Two days ago we received the code to prepare. We await the final word," Philippe says.

But first, the radio voice says, "some personal messages."

He digs a slip of paper and a tiny pencil from his back pocket. Everyone—very much including the Nazis—knows that these "personal messages" are coded instructions to the Resistance. Owning an unauthorized radio, and especially tuning to the BBC, is forbidden and can be punished by deportation to camps in Germany, or forced labor more locally, or imprisonment or even death.

"*Demain la mélasse deviendra du cognac.*" Tomorrow, molasses will become Cognac.

Rainy looks at Philippe. Nothing.

"*Jean a une longue moustache.*" John has a long mustache.

And Philippe's eyes widen.

"*Les sanglots longs des violons de l'automne . . .*" The long sobs of the violins of autumn . . .

Philippe has stopped breathing.

"*Blessent mon cœur d'une langueur monotone.*" . . . wound my heart with a monotonous languor.

It is Philippe's utter stillness that cause chills to creep up Rainy's spine. No one breathes. Rainy has the feeling, at once frightening and thrilling, that the entire human race has just come to a fork in the road. The great battle for the future of human liberty has come at last.

A Communist Philippe might be, but he crosses himself in a way that Comrade Stalin would definitely not approve of.

"What is it?" Marie asks, and every eye in the room is on Philippe. He does not answer at first. He is stiff, staring. Then he blinks.

"The wait is over," Philippe says in an awed tone. "That is the final instruction to begin the uprising."

Rainy watches Étienne. What exactly is that expression? Philippe is distracted, mentally processing the difficult, dangerous steps ahead. Marie is excited and perhaps worried about Philippe. Wickham is uncomplicatedly joyful and slaps Hooper on the back. But Étienne? His first reaction is unreadable.

Then, almost peevishly, Étienne says, "And what about our tire? We still have to deliver Lieutenant Jones to observe the Das Reich. Those are my instructions."

Philippe grins. "Perhaps we can get you your tire. But first we must ask you for help. Two of my best men were arrested and deported last week. We are short-handed, and our assignment is . . . well, complicated."

"But we cannot—" Étienne begins.

Rainy cuts him off. "What do you need?" she asks Philippe.

"People who can use a gun," he says bluntly. Then, with a dubious shrug, he adds, "In a perfect world, someone who speaks German fluently. But that is . . ." He performs another Gallic shrug.

Rainy considers. Her objective is to find and shadow and report back on the Das Reich. On the other hand, she cannot do that without Philippe's help. And her orders do after all include language instructing her to render assistance where possible to local elements of the maquis.

"I speak German," Rainy says.

7

Rio Richlin—who does not suffer from seasickness, much—
is at a final company-level briefing delivered by Captain
Tom Passey. It is 3:25 a.m. Most hands hold mugs of
steaming coffee.

Captain Passey looks like a store clerk to Rio, a balding,
middle-aged man devoid of dash who was until two months
ago stationed stateside at a supply depot in New Jersey. He is
a dedicated officer, willing to learn, but in no way experienced.

Lieutenant Horne, Rio's platoon leader, sits in a folding chair
to one side praying he can keep his food down until the briefing
is over. Horne is of middling height, young like virtually all
second lieutenants, with a weak chin, brown hair and brown eyes.
He looks like a fellow determined to be important. But at the
moment he is trying not to puke.

Three other lieutenants stand in a knot to one side, splitting
their attention between Passey and their platoon NCOs, who
stand stolidly, looking on with the skepticism that seems to come
so naturally to those with stripes on their shoulders.

Three twelve-person rifle squads, plus a smaller headquarters
squad, make up a platoon. Four platoons make a company, and

Captain Passey is in charge of that company of roughly a hundred and ninety souls.

Each platoon has a lieutenant. Rio surveys the officers as Passey continues. She knows that Lieutenant Arch Manly has some combat experience, having been briefly at Salerno before earning a Purple Heart with a through-and-through bullet wound to his calf. But all told, the remaining lieutenants—Mary Gorski, Don Reynolds and Daniel Horne—average age maybe twenty-three years, have a total of zero combat experience.

Each of the three rifle platoons has, in addition to a lieutenant, a platoon sergeant, usually a tech or staff sergeant. These are Dain Sticklin, Drake Harwich and Francis "Frank" Lincoln.

Stick and Lincoln have seen combat, Harwich has not.

Below the platoon sergeants are the squad leaders, buck sergeants, sixteen of them in all, of which seven have been in the war, including Rio Richlin and Cat Preeling, two of the three females.

Not at the briefing are the assistant squad leaders (ASLs) who are babysitting their GIs, and are mostly corporals with a smattering of PFCs and buck sergeants. Of these sixteen men and woman, just seven—fewer than half—have seen combat.

The lower ranks, the privates, the body of the army, are also not present at the briefing, but less than twenty percent of the GIs in Passey's company have combat experience. And this in total, Rio knows, represents one of the more combat-tested companies in this relatively experienced division.

In short, most of the officers, most of the NCOs and most of the GIs have no real idea what is coming, a fact that Rio cannot quite put out of her mind as she listens to Passey rattle off recognition signals, assembly points, Day One objectives and so on.

Day One objectives.

Rio knows that phrase from Italy. It had quickly become a dark and unfunny joke. The Germans did not care about Day One objectives. In fact, they tended to object in the strongest possible terms to Day One objectives.

They stand around a sand table relief of the beach codenamed "Omaha," on a sheet of plywood, with water represented by blue paint. The beach is represented by sand glued in place. The tall bluff is glued sand on smoothed over papier mâché.

To Rio's knowledgeable eye it forms a series of conditions perfectly designed to kill her soldiers.

Passey says, "Now, I know I'm repeating a lot of stuff you already know. But this is a big day we have ahead of us. Field Marshal Rommel has been busy fortifying what the Nazi calls the Atlantic Wall." He pronounces Nazi as *Nazzee*, rhyming with snazzy.

Rio does not concern herself with the affairs of generals, but she knows that Erwin Rommel, nicknamed the Desert Fox, is no fool. Even as his troops were fleeing the British across North Africa, hungry, short of fuel and ammo, they'd had time to roll right over the green American army. And roll right over Rio Richlin, who can still remember the very mixed emotions of running away from German tanks.

As Passey speaks, Rio translates mentally from officer to sergeant.

"He has festooned the shallows with steel triangles we're calling hedgehogs, obstacles, many of them wired with anti-personnel mines. But the engineers will have seen to a lot of that."

Translation: *The hedgehogs will still be there, and many will still be mined.*

"The beach itself will have been prepared by naval gunfire and bombers to create holes and depressions you can use as fighting holes."

Translation: *Most likely there will be no holes, which in any case wouldn't be worth much because . . .*

"The heights are thick with pillboxes and reinforced machine-gun emplacements, so it will be your first priority to reach those and take them out. Word is that the flamethrowers are especially useful for this."

Translation: *The Krauts will have the height and the cover and can lay plunging fire down on the beach.*

As for flamethrowers, Rio does not like them. She can imagine that they may be useful, but she does not like the idea of any of her people walking around with a big tank of jellied gasoline on their backs when bullets are flying.

"Our landing spot is here." Passey taps the table with a pointer.

Translation: *Within a half mile of there, if we're lucky.*

"G2 doesn't think the Luftwaffe has much in the area, but don't neglect to look up from time to time, eh? A plane with the stripes painted on the wings is one of ours—anything else is Luftwaffe."

Translation: *Messerschmitts and Focke-Wulfs will add bombs to mortar and cannon fire.*

"As usual, the Nazi has defense in depth. Artillery here and here." Tap and tap. "Panzer units here and here." Tap, tap, tap and tap.

Translation: *It will be murder.*

"I won't lie to you men . . . and ladies . . . this will be a tough objective."

Translation: *Yep, it'll be murder.*

The briefing breaks up and Rio finds herself walking back to the hold with Stick, Cat and Frank Lincoln.

"Well, that was cheery," Stick says glumly.

"They couldn't find a damn beach that didn't have a damn cliff staring right down at it?" Frank Lincoln demands. "This is FUBAR. The beach is narrow, the bluff is high and steep, and the only comfort is that the air corps will supposedly have dug us some nice holes in the sand."

"Don't overlook the fact that a long, concave shape like that beach, plus the height, means Jerry will have both frontal and enfilade fire," Stick points out.

Cat shares a look with Rio. "My guys are as green as grass snakes. I got just three guys that never even fired a rifle in anger."

Rio is a bit luckier. Her squad consists of veterans Jack Stafford, Hansu Pang and Luther Geer, good experienced soldiers all; Jenou Castain, Rio's childhood friend, who could be useful when she felt like it; and Beebee, a genius of a scrounger, but a mediocre soldier generally found well back from the action. Counting herself, Rio has six reasonably capable soldiers. Then there are the three replacements who she's had for four days: Rudy J. Chester, Hank Hobart and Lupé Camacho. Of these, Camacho shows some potential, Hobart may settle down in time, and Rudy

J. Chester is likely to be killed, if not by the Germans then by Rio.

Last, and definitely least, there are the three other replacements she acquired through no fault of her own just last night: two women, one man, none of them able to dump sand out of a boot with the instructions printed on the heel, let alone do any damage to the enemy.

"If they can get the tanks ashore we may do okay," Stick says, straining for optimism. "And if the bombers have done their job."

"That's two ifs," Lincoln says darkly.

"I have more if you want," Rio mutters.

My first combat assignment as a squad leader is: invade France. Swell.

No sooner has Rio rejoined her squad in the hold than the order comes to stand by for embarkation. Numbers will be called, and units will advance to designated areas, all wonderfully planned out no doubt, but likely in Rio's somewhat cynical estimation to be the usual SNAFU. Situation Normal: All Fugged Up.

When did I get to be so negative?

Kasserine Pass, the Rapido River, Monte Cassino . . .

The troopship holds most of the division and they will be going ashore in LCVPs, also called Higgins boats, flat-bottomed, ramp-fronted boats just thirty-six feet long, ten feet wide and capable of carrying thirty-six soldiers, three squads: Rio's, Cat Preeling's, and the command squad, consisting of Lieutenant Horne, Sergeant Billy O'Banion, two runners, a radio operator, a two-man bazooka team, and a buck sergeant named Mercer whose precise function Rio has not figured out unless he is there as a replacement for . . . well, perhaps for *her* if things go badly.

A few rows down Rio spots Cat taking a pull from a flask. Cat sees Rio and holds the flask up in offer. Rio considers, but reluctantly shakes her head. Alcohol will soften the edges of her worry, and she *wants* to worry, she needs to feel the danger. One of the first times Rio had been in charge she had lost a man, Tilo Suarez, through nothing but carelessness. She is determined not to repeat that. No more carelessness. No more good people dead for no reason. She's heard some of the other squad leaders talking about taking pillboxes and maybe killing a tank, their excitement in inverse proportion to experience, but her measure of success is simpler: start the day with twelve, including herself, and end the day with twelve.

Into the boats, off the boats, up the beach, up the bluff . . . victory.

She smiles sourly at this private thought. Right. Victory. Because the Germans are known for giving up easily.

Rudy J. Chester is prosing away to Camacho and two of the newest squad members, a man and a woman whose names Rio has to struggle to recall, about his theory of combat.

"I figure the Krauts'll know they're licked when they see us coming," he says. "And with all the shells we're dropping on them, it'll be bim, bam, boom." He smacks his hands together, a dismissive gesture.

Rio steps to him, grabs his rifle, and points. "Your safety's off."

"I want to be ready," Chester says.

"Safeties on until you have something to shoot at," Rio snaps, resisting the urge to add, *you blithering idiot.*

One of the greenest of the greenhorns, a short, nervous, active man of twenty-two named Dick Ostrowiz, asks, "You've been in it, Sarge, how bad will it be?"

Too many eyes turn to await her answer.

"It will be bad," she says. There's no point lying. She has to establish from the start that she can be trusted to tell her soldiers the truth: bullshit is for officers. "It'll be loud and confusing and scary as hell. You'll be wet and loaded down. In fact . . ." She glances around to make sure Lieutenant Horne is nowhere near. She lowers her voice. "They've got some of you hauling fifty, seventy pounds of extra gear on top of your usual loads. We're probably just going to leave all that crap on the boat."

Geer, Stafford, Pang and Jenou all nod knowingly. Lupé Camacho speaks up. "Aren't we going to need all that extra ammo?"

"It won't be all that useful if you're dead," Rio says flatly. "A wet, scared, tired soldier hauling ammo boxes across the beach is the kind of bullshit some desk jockey comes up with. You're going to be lucky to manage yourselves and your rifle."

With a glance at Rudy J. Chester, Hobart says, "The Germans know they're licked, though. Right?"

Rio shakes her head. "The Kraut never gives up. If he ever looks like he's giving up, he's just moving back to the next line of fortification. If you think he's licked, he's getting ready for a counterattack. And if you think you're better, tougher, stronger or braver, you're wrong."

All conversation in the immediate vicinity stops.

"He's got better tanks and artillery. Better machine guns too. He's better trained and he's dead damned serious now, because he knows we're coming, and he knows we intend to kill him and take his country. He figures while we're at it we'll rape his wife and use his kids for target practice. See, the thing is? They don't know we're the good guys. They think they're the heroes. So they'll fight. They'll fight every inch of the way."

She lets that settle in for a minute. Then, seeing the wide eyes and nervous swallowing all around her, says, "On the other hand, we have the air, and we have the navy, and we have this." She smacks a hand down on the stock of Chester's M1 then shoves it back to him. "The M1 Garand is the best rifle in this war. Keep it dry and keep it clean. Keep the waterproof cover on until you are ashore. Be careful climbing down the nets. Listen to the crews, they'll tell you when to jump into the boat. We'll have a nice long wait as we circle around, and then when all the landing craft are loaded up, we'll head in. Most likely we'll take some artillery and some machine-gun fire on the way. Might as well relax during that because there's not a thing you can do about it. Once we get to the beach if you jump off into deep water, do not panic. Drop your belt and your pack, anything that weighs you down. Do that *before* you try to swim. Try to hold onto your weapon. But above all, do not panic. If you don't panic, you won't drown."

The possibility of drowning has clearly not occurred to most of the GIs. They exchange worried looks.

"Get to dry sand as quick as you can. They say there's a seawall, but it's low and poor cover. And the Krauts will have that wall registered, zeroed-in six ways from Sunday. As soon as we're ashore we go straight at the bluffs."

"The bluffs?" Camacho asks.

"They're fifty to a hundred feet high and the Kraut will be thick as sand fleas on top. But they can't shoot straight down, not

103

with MGs anyway, so you want to get out of the water, across that beach, to the base of the bluff as soon as your legs will carry you. If you freeze up or decide to take a break, you'll die."

"Cheery prospect, what?" Jack Stafford says, exaggerating his British accent for comedic effect.

Rio is the only one not to smile. She is being deliberately cool to Jack—any favoritism now, when she is in charge, would be disastrous. She will not play favorites, and more importantly, she will not be *seen* to play favorites. She is Jack's sergeant as surely as she is Geer's or Beebee's sergeant, and she cannot start down the road of protecting one at the expense of the others.

"You freshmen? You listen to the upperclassmen. If Geer, Pang, Stafford, Castain or Beebee tells you to drop, *drop*. They tell you to run, *run*. They tell you to shoot, *shoot*. Now get squared away, they'll be calling our number any minute."

"At least we'll be off this vomit barge," Geer says. This earns some nervous laughter and Rio is glad to hear it. Glad that Stafford can still amuse, glad that Geer can still be sardonic. There is a fine line between realistic fear and paralyzed terror and she wants her squad scared but not panicked.

"One last thing," Rio says. "Why are we here?"

Silence. Then, one of the newest recruits, a woman, says, "To kill Germans?"

"What's your name again?"

"Maria Molina, Sarge."

"Well, Molina, you are one hundred percent correct." Rio lifts her own rifle and holds it to her chest. "We are here to use this to kill Germans. You *will* kill Germans. You *will* kill every

Nazi son of a bitch on that beach, and you'll keep on killing them till we get to the crazy bastard in Berlin and shoot him in his little mustache!"

To her amazement, the squad cheers. Even Geer, who knows better than to think it will be that simple.

To one side she hears Cat giving her own version of the same speech. All over the ship sergeants are preparing their soldiers to kill and not to be killed.

Everyone is tense. Everyone is afraid, especially the ones who pretend not to be. But Rio sees some determination too. At least some of these men and women are itching to finally get into the war.

Luther Geer. Jack Stafford. Jenou Castain. Hansu Pang. Beebee, who has an actual name that no one calls him, and everyone (possibly including Beebee himself) has forgotten. Rudy J. "Private Sweetheart" Chester. Hank Hobart. Lupé Camacho. Jenny Dial. Dick Ostrowiz. Maria Molina. Five women, seven men: her squad. Her responsibility.

My people. My lives.

Rio recalls her father, the veteran of the Great War, telling her to find a sergeant she trusts and stick by him. That had turned out to be Sergeant Mackie during basic training, and then Jedron Cole.

And now *she* is the sergeant. And these are the eleven men and women whose best bet is to stick close to her.

Rio remembers Sergeant Cole talking to them as they landed on the beach in Tunisia as part of a doomed British commando raid. He'd offered stern, useful advice, but he had also worked to keep his squad loose. As loose as it could be. But that part does not come easily to Rio. She wants to reach these soldiers, especially the green ones, to impress on them all she knows, to imbue them with the fears that weigh so heavily on her. But the best she can manage is, "You'll all be fine if you do what you're told." It is almost certainly not true, but if there's one thing a US Army private needs it's hope. Hope and trust in their sergeant.

Which, God help us all, is me.

8

The LST powers on through the night.

At sea the LST pumps water into its ballast tanks to stabilize it for the trip, which would be good news but for the fact that the waves in the Channel are quite a bit taller than they'd been in port.

Keeping company to their left are two LCTs, like smaller versions of the LST but with an open hold and flat ramp at the front where the LST has swing-out gates. The LCTs carry the Sherman DDs, the duplex drives, the tanks with the bulky rings that, before inflation, make the tanks look like dainty ladies raising their skirts to step over mud.

There is only filtered moonlight coming through the few breaks in the clouds, so the more distant LCTs are more felt than seen. The nearest keeps station close by, bobbing and skittering over the waves. Frangie can see the skirts beginning to inflate. Crewmen buzz around tightening this and loosening that, manhandling the skirts into place as they inflate like four great air mattresses.

Frangie's driver, Corporal Rosemary Manning, and another medic— an older man, a conscientious objector nicknamed

Deacon for his presumed religiosity—stand on either side of her. It is still dark, but not quite darkest night, still an hour from the first assault, scheduled for 6:30 a.m., half an hour after sunrise.

"Think they'll swim?" Manning asks.

"What I know about tanks wouldn't fill a matchbox," Frangie says. "But I guess—"

An explosion cuts her short, a muffled boom, somewhere between Frangie's position and the still invisible coast of France.

"That's a ranging shot," Frangie says, feeling terribly knowledgeable with her two green companions, having spent time with an artillery battalion in North Africa. "You fire one to see where it lands. Then you adjust your aim and cut loose."

The cutting loose starts right on cue. Straining to listen, Frangie hears the distant popping sounds of the shore guns firing. Seconds later come deeper, muffled explosions that send up pillars of water like something summoned by an angry Neptune.

"Are they shooting at us?" Deacon asks.

"Not yet," Frangie says, glancing around to make sure no more experienced soldier is sneering at her presumed expertise. "Most likely we're still too far out at sea."

From a mile or more behind the LSTs comes an eruption of noise and fire and smoke, as the navy's big battleships and cruisers return fire, hurling far larger projectiles far further. The sound is like a loud bellyflop, a violent sound that bounces off the water, followed instantly by a deeper boom that extends out into a rumbling bass note.

The naval fire becomes general, fiery tulips wreathed in smoke, explosions that sometimes dwarf the ships themselves.

It's like a marching band made up of nothing but drummers, all pounding, pounding, firing ton after ton of high explosives toward shore. Lights like distant fireflies twinkle on the shore as the shells, each as heavy as a small automobile, land and blow apart men and machines.

There is no question that what's being thrown at France is greater than what the Germans are tossing back.

"I suppose it's wrong to think about the poor souls over there in France," Deacon says.

Manning snorts. "More the navy kills, the fewer left to shoot our boys. Or us. Fug the Krauts. They're worse than our own white people. That's a whole country full of KKK. Fug the Krauts."

Deacon shoots her a disapproving look, but says nothing. He's maybe as old as thirty, with hair already beating a retreat from his brow. Somewhat to her surprise, Deacon has given Frangie no trouble. He easily and automatically defers to her rank and title, works hard and conscientiously, and is good with the GIs. Frangie does not know either Manning or Deacon well, but she likes them both, though of course there's no way to know how they will behave later.

The naval shelling continues, endless explosions, endless bouts of fire, now joined by the destroyers so near that Frangie can smell the acrid smoke of their violent discharges.

Down in the LCT the Sherman DDs are inflated and squared away.

"They look like they're ready to go," Deacon points out.

"We're too far out, surely," Frangie says. The sea is still agitated, endless marching ranks of white-topped waves slap the sides of the LST, sometimes with enough force to send jets of freezing water up and over the gunwale.

"I suppose they know what's best," Manning says with a confidence Frangie does not share.

The sky is no longer black but a gloomy, steel gray, when the LCT slows and drifts away from the LST. The LCT's ramp begins to wind down. There comes the sound of the Sherman engines gunning. Exhaust smoke drifts.

Waves swarm over the lowered ramp of the LCT, surging up toward the tank deck. Cross seas roll the small ship with enough force to send one crewman staggering into a steel ladder.

"Head wound," Deacon mutters. "Sulfa, bandage, check his eyes to see if they're both pointed the same direction." He laughs.

"If they don't, send him to the aid station. If they do, send him back up."

Deacon sighs. "That's the part I don't like. I guess I feel like any GI that gets hurt should get a ticket home."

"Don't ever say that where an officer can hear you," Frangie says. "We aren't here to send them home, we're here to mend them just enough to get them back in the fight."

Deacon nods, but without agreement.

The first of the DD tanks rolls in ungainly, even rather comical ponderousness down the ramp. The very unboatlike skirt rises at the water's edge, coming up like a sleeve to all but conceal the tank which wallows in a sort of cereal bowl. The Sherman weighs just short of 67,000 pounds, and the skirt does not look adequate to the job of keeping it afloat. The tank commander sits with his upper body out of the top hatch, leather tank helmet on his head, goggles down over his eyes to ward off the spray.

"It floats!" Manning says.

"Huh," Frangie says.

The amphibious tank churns slowly away, an overly heavy, awkward boat, still more than a mile from a shoreline that is only now becoming visible in the growing light.

A second DD tank clanks down the ramp and splashes heavily into the water, then, like the first, begins to push its way through the waves.

At least, Frangie thinks, the rain has stopped. For now.

The third tank rolls but as it enters the water a big swell shoves the LCT sideways. The ramp swings left like a karate chop and crumples the flotation skirt of the DD tank. Green water rushes over the side, like a bucket being held down in a stream.

What happens next takes mere seconds.

The skirt on one side collapses completely. Water floods, rises quickly above the treads as crewmen pop up out of various hatches, all yelling. And then the entire thing, tank and skirts, seems to fall *through* the water. In seconds it disappears from view, leaving a swirling ring behind.

"Oh my God!" Frangie cries. Everyone on deck is yelling and pointing.

Flotation rings are thrown, a voice is heard on the public address system ordering rescue boats to be veered toward the doomed tank, but there are no bodies to be seen. The five-person crew is already at the bottom of the English Channel.

The deaths are too sudden. Five men dead without a shot coming close to them.

Deacon is whispering a prayer and Frangie joins in silently.

Those poor souls. How many will die with no one to send a prayer after them?

Frangie wonders if Sergeant Moore is watching, and whether he is suddenly thinking that drowning might be as bad as burning. At least it was quick, she thinks. But was it? Is one of those GIs in a tiny air pocket down there, straining to catch the last possible breath of air?

Then the lead DD tank, already a quarter mile ahead, suddenly goes nose down. The back of the skirt lifts, hangs in the air for a moment while voices on the LST cry out in renewed horror, and it goes down, disappearing beneath the waves.

Aboard the LCT, now some distance away, Frangie sees a pantomime of horror, crew and tankers watching, gesticulating, shouting inaudibly. The fourth and final Sherman DD does not move. Its commander sitting high in his hatch points with furious gestures toward the LCT's bridge.

"What kind of fool contraption are those things?" Manning demands, suddenly less sanguine about army planning.

The second tank still powers gamely on toward shore as the commander of the last tank, the one still aboard the LCT, can be seen climbing down on the deck, arguing with an officer as the flotation skirts deflate and sag.

But now, with the light growing, Frangie looks away from the tragedy aboard the LCT, and for the first time sees—really sees—what she is part of.

To left, to right, behind and ahead, the invasion fleet extends forever, literally beyond the range of her eyes. Great, smoke-wreathed battleships and swift, low-slung destroyers; corvettes practically like speedboats; mine sweepers, supply ships and oilers; squat and unlovely LSTs and swarms of DUKWs and Higgins boats. Not dozens, not even hundreds, but thousands of ships and boats. Thousands.

Now, overhead, Frangie sees hundreds of B-17s and B-24s drawing contrails like silk threads.

It's a giant hammer, an impossibly great sledgehammer ready to smash into France, ready to crush the Nazi Reich and roll it all the way back to Germany. Frangie's throat swells. She hasn't spent ten minutes really thinking about what is happening beyond her own duties. Her war has been saving lives and surviving, it has not been about great powers, great people or great deeds.

But now, for just a moment, she feels it, feels the hugeness of it, the superhuman effort it represents. The terrible danger, but more the astonishing courage of so many in such peril and yet so determined.

"Well, I'll be," Manning says in a voice she might use to whisper in church.

"There can't be that many ships in the world," Frangie says. "That's not an invasion fleet, that's a whole city floating on water."

Suddenly a voice is raised, a clear feminine voice.

"O beautiful for spacious skies,
For amber waves of grain,
For purple mountain majesties
Above the fruited plain!
America! America!

God shed His grace on thee
And crown thy good with brotherhood
From sea to shining sea!"

No one speaks until the last note dies out. For the first time Frangie really notices the Stars and Stripes flapping high on a mast. And despite Tulsa, and despite Harder's insistent voice in her memory, despite every injustice and horror that flag has so often meant to her race, her people, Frangie's throat swells and her heart feels very big in her chest.

"Maybe the Germans will just . . . give up," Deacon says wistfully.

"Double-check your supplies. You both have a pocket knife and scissors?"

Deacon and Manning both nod yes. Manning, in addition to being Frangie's driver, is a stretcher bearer and anything else Frangie needs her to be. Deacon is effectively her number two, a trained medic, but with far less experience.

Frangie realizes she's been brusque and says, "There's this soldier I met, a woman. She's G2." Seeing their blank looks she adds, "That's intelligence branch. Anyway, she was grabbed by the Gestapo in Italy. And she told us, me and the other girls with us, some of the things they did to her." Frangie shakes her head at the memory of a very drunk Rainy Schulterman talking in a running monotone, no emotion at all in her voice. But in her eyes there had been a dangerous light. "And now those same people," Frangie continues, "people like them anyway, the kind of people who torture and murder, they know we're coming for them. The wrath of Almighty God is about to come down on their heads."

"I don't know that God's involved," Manning says in her laconic way. "But sure as hell the wrath of the US of A is heading straight for them. They ought to give up if they had any sense."

"I imagine they'll look out and see all this and be good and scared," Frangie says. "But I don't think they'll quit. They've gone too far, done too much. So, like I said: quit gawping and check supplies."

She lets them go and stays behind for just a moment, needing to compose herself. The sight of the tanks foundering unsettled her. The odd emotion of hearing the song, the sudden realization that she, Francine Marr, little Frangie, was part of a moment on which the whole course of human history turned . . .

Injury and death on the beach, yes, she had prepared her mind for that. But to see human beings suddenly plunged beneath the waves . . . and to feel for a moment anyway that their deaths, and her life, and yes, her death if it came to that, were the stuff of history . . .

She is afraid. She knows what bullets and shrapnel do to a human body. She knows what pain does to people. She has seen tough old sergeants cry for their mothers.

But her job is not to show fear. Her job is not to cower. Her job is to run out into enemy fire, protected by nothing but some red and white paint on her helmet.

Frangie takes several deep breaths. She has managed to fill her days with work that was not hers, tending to patients, getting to know the soldiers in the platoon, keeping busy. In her off time she'd written letters home. And she'd read and reread the various manuals. Anything not to think about what is coming. Coming *now*.

Her hand goes to her stomach, feeling for the scar where the shrapnel went in and ripped through her intestines.

She has tried not to think about that day on a cobblestone street in an Italian village whose name she never knew. She has tried not to think of Doon Acey, or the nameless white officer in Tunisia, or of her own wounds.

After she won the Silver Star she could have gone home to tour Negro churches and theaters to sell war bonds. But she had chosen this, because *this* is what you were supposed to do if you are a Silver Star recipient.

Frangie's mouth makes a wry smile. No, she's being dishonest. She wasn't roped into this by the Star. She was roped in by thinking about colored boys and girls lying on beaches and in ditches, terrified, alone and in pain.

You're doing the right thing, for the right reason, Frangie, she chides herself. *It's not the sin of pride to give yourself* some *credit!*

That and a nickel will buy me a cup of coffee.

Thin porridge, good intentions are. So much less compelling than what she knows is coming, what is already making her heart race, her throat clench, her mouth go dry as dust: fear.

Fear is back.

She pictures a Sherman DD plunging down and down through the dark water. It would sink all the way to the bottom, fast, like a cinderblock. You sit cramped inside that metal shell, and suddenly green seawater pours in . . . She imagines their panic, their frenzy, their despair . . . Would they still be alive when the

116

tank landed on the seabed, disturbing the crabs and the fishes?

Would their bodies . . .

Fear is back.

She closes her eyes and prays for the fear to be replaced by faith. The Lord is her shepherd. He counts the sparrows that fall. He sees her. He hears her. He will watch over her.

But when she opens her eyes, the fear is back.

9

The ride to shore is much longer than Lupé Camacho expects. The Higgins boat turns tight circles for half an hour, breasting waves that rain chill spray down on the men and women of the platoon.

On and on and on, as seasickness claims one person after another.

Around and around in the dark, around and around while the assault forces form up. Hundreds of landing craft must all reach the beach at the same time, so around and around they go, a not-so-merry-go-round.

People try to smoke, but it's too wet. A couple of GIs try to get a dice game going, but no one wants to use up their luck on dice.

Some pray or count the rosary, but time wears them down, and most stop and just stare.

There is a brief distraction when hundreds of American bombers release their loads and massive columns of smoke rise from the direction of the beach. Some cheer and shout, "Get 'em, fly-boys! Plaster 'em!"

Lupé watches Richlin as Richlin watches the bombing. When it is over she sees a look of disgust on her sergeant's face, quickly concealed.

Soldiers are telling each other it'll be easy after what the air corps has done, but Richlin and Preeling must have seen something much less cheering. Glances between them reveal disappointment.

Lupé clutches her M1 to her chest, smoothing the stock down as if to quiet her heart and slow her breathing. Sergeant Richlin's instructions echo in her mind. Save your rifle. Abandon anything else, but not your rifle. Keep it dry. Keep it clean. Be ready.

Kill Germans.

Earlier the navy had served up an extra generous breakfast of ham and eggs, biscuits and gravy, toast and flapjacks and coffee. The swabbie cooks had gone all in. But most of that food had been hurled over the side by now, or else was sloshing in the chilly bilge water that seeps into her boots and numbs her toes.

She tells herself not to be afraid. She looks at Richlin. The sergeant's no older than she is, no bigger really, no stronger. But Rio Richlin stands there, leaning against the hull like she's waiting for a bus. She looks almost bored.

Across the water comes a sound of whistles, like a football coach summoning players. The public address speaker on the looming ship crackles to life wishing them, "Godspeed."

The first part of the wait is over: the boats finish their final circuit, then form into a rough line, and go straight for the beach, hundreds of Higgins boats and DUKWs, as the big naval guns fire over their heads.

There is no visible sun, but she knows that above the clouds it is rising. She sees pearly light silhouetting a town. The church steeple is a spike, an aiming point, a goal.

Between here and there is a mile of agitated water lacerated by

119

fire from the shore. The coxswain and his crew are on the lookout for mines, one crewman leaning out over the bow and peering forward. The hedgehogs are just becoming visible, looking like broken children's toys tossed by a giant into the surf.

"Okay, people," Richlin says in a voice pitched for her squad, the squad at the very front of the boat. "Remember what I told you. If they put us on dry land, grab your gear. If they land us in water, drop everything but your weapons. If you sink, do not panic."

Lupé glances back and sees Lieutenant Horne talking to Cat Preeling. Preeling, like Richlin, seems relaxed, as if this is a Sunday outing on a lake. Horne is far less calm. His face is frozen. Whatever he's saying to Preeling it seems to be just monosyllables.

Lupé turns to the remaining sergeant, Dain Sticklin. Stick is chewing gum. As she watches, he blows a pink bubble, then sucks it back in.

It's an act, Lupé realizes. *The sergeants, the veterans, they're putting on an act. Pretending nonchalance.*

The waves nearer to shore are taller and the Higgins boat is bucking, smacking waves that smack back, sending shockwaves up through Lupé's boots. Standing in the stubby superstructure at the back, the coxswain frowns intently at the sea before him. To the left a long line of boats, all bouncing along and—

Bah-whoosh!

An artillery shell lands near enough to spray Lupé. Fifty feet one way or the other and a boat would have gone up in—

Bah-whooosh!

A boat no more than two hundred yards down the line

120

explodes. Lupé sees a body twirling in the air, rising, arms flailing, and for a frozen moment Lupé has the mad thought that the soldier is flying away, escaping the war. But then gravity reasserts control and he falls back down into fire and smoke.

Lupé feels the coxswain back off on the engine, slowing momentarily, a reflex, then accelerating again.

Lupé is near the front with Rudy J. Chester and Hank Hobart and Dick Ostrowiz. There are six new members of Richlin's squad and she has put them all at the front.

Is this so the veterans can push them off if they freeze up?

Maybe, Lupé thinks. But she knows there's a harsher logic to it as well: they are untested. The veterans, Pang and Geer, Castain and Stafford and Beebee, they have all proven their value, and she and the other new additions have not. Her life is worth less to Rio Richlin than theirs.

Lupé's stomach rises in her throat and she has to swallow bile.

Nearer now, the beach. Nearer. Lupé's jaw aches from clenching. Her knees tremble.

The hedgehogs come thicker, closer together, steel beams welded together to form jagged steel pyramids, obstacles meant to tear the bottom out of any boat. Further in B a different sort of obstacle, wooden logs like telephone poles propped on triangular bases and pointed like pretend cannon, meant to stop any ship that gets past the hedgehogs.

Smoke rises behind the bluff, and with a sinking feeling Lupé now sees what Richlin and the others saw: the bombs all fell behind the bluff. They have not wiped out the Kraut positions, they have not even created craters on the beach.

Massive concrete pillboxes line the top of the cliff, especially around cuts in the cliff face, the draws, up which the Americans must necessarily go. Some of the pillboxes are so massive it seems they must collapse the cliff with their sheer weight. From within the pillboxes German machine guns and light artillery fire with impunity. German mortars are positioned behind the pillboxes, heavy artillery further back still.

Lupé glances at the gear at her feet. In addition to her usual load there's a musette bag filled with grenades. And a can of .30 caliber. Rudy J. Chester has been saddled with an additional BAR as well as his M1, either because he's big and capable of carrying the sixteen-pound hunk of steel and wood or because Richlin doesn't like him.

The other BAR leans against the gunwale, Luther Geer's hand steadying the barrel. With Pang and one of the newest squad members, Jenny Dial, they are the ones assigned the management of the light machine gun.

"Five minutes!" the coxswain yells over the thrum of the engines.

"Five minutes," Lieutenant Horne calls out. "Grab your gear!" He sounds like a scared child, his voice wobbly.

Lupé lifts the musette bag full of grenades, resting the strap on her shoulder where she can easily shrug it off.

Lieutenant Horne decides it's time for inspiration. "Remember, men, the American army has never been defeated. And we won't be today! This is when you prove your worth. This is the day you'll tell your children about!"

"Drop dead," Geer mutters under his breath.

Lupé catches sight of Cat Preeling making a wry, upside-down smile at Horne's exclusion of females.

The Higgins boat surges between hedgehogs and suddenly, without warning, the ramp drops.

Just as suddenly Lupé can now see the beach itself as well as the bluff. And she sees at least a hundred feet of water between her and the sand. She sloughs off the musette bag.

"Go, go, go!" Horne yells.

Hank Hobart and Dick Ostrowiz are first off the boat. Both plunge into the water and disappear from view.

A machine gun veers its fire toward them, *ping, ping* all around, holes appearing in the side of the boat, puckered like popped blisters. A soldier yells and falls down. Another seems surprised and says, "Hey, I think they shot me!" and plucks at her uniform trying to see the wound that spreads red across her chest.

Rudy J. Chester heaves the BAR in the general direction of the beach and it too sinks from view as Chester turns and tries to push back against the surge of soldiers as if his job is done now and he is quitting for the day.

Lupé pushes past, heart in her throat, breath coming in gasps that sound like sobs. She reaches the end of the ramp and—

Rio Richlin sees two of her soldiers, Hobart and Ostrowiz, disappear beneath the waves.

Rio sees Camacho stop like she's hit a brick wall, and fall, twisting to the side. The side of her throat is gone, a mass of blood and tattered flesh, draining blood like a cut water balloon.

"Geer! Keep 'em moving!" Rio yells.

"Go, goddammit!" Geer roars.

Rio strips off her gear, tosses her rifle to Jenou and jumps into the water.

It's dark under the surface, darker still in the shadow of the Higgins boat, with swirling sand everywhere and machine-gun bullets punching spirals in the water. She doesn't see either of her soldiers.

Then, a shape, a writhing form. She kicks herself toward it as the cold stuns her muscles. She grabs a handful of uniform shirt and pushes hard upward, forcing Hank Hobart into the air.

With her own lungs screaming, Rio fights through Hobart's panicked flailing, finds his belt buckle, drops the weight, and then releases Hobart so she can surface and suck a lungful of air. She dives again and finds Hobart floating, face turned toward her, blood billowing from his back.

Machine-gun bullets tear holes in the water all around, and Rio half swims, half walks up the shale incline, feet slipping and sliding, feeling as if with each step she's dragging the whole weight of the English Channel behind her.

Hobart. Camacho. Ostrowiz.

Three!

Rio's lungs find air and she pushes on, kicks something hard, takes a deep breath and plunges down to find the BAR where it sank. She lifts it, pushes it ahead of her, trips, swallows seawater, rises to one knee, and the retreating wave offers her the gift of oxygen once more.

Up and up, one foot after the other, she hauls herself and the BAR onto the sand, where she drops the machine gun, sits down behind the uncertain shelter of a hedgehog and looks back toward the boat.

The Higgins boat is riddled with holes. Bodies lie on the tilted ramp. Bodies float, face down. Bodies surge and retreat in the breaking surf.

Tsip, tsip, tsip!

Machine-gun rounds strike water all around. An explosion up the beach. Someone yelling in pain.

Ping! Ping! as bullets ricochet off the hedgehog.

"Medic! Medic!"

"Help me!"

Bullets ricochet off the hedgehog and now two soldiers are crowding Rio, desperate for cover, one screaming, "It's not fair! It's not fair!" until a round catches him in the stomach and he slides away, eyes staring until the light behind them goes out.

Rio spots Pang, walking bent and backward, hauling Jenou up the beach.

Is she hit? Is Jenou hit?

Jack Stafford is face down on the beach but she can see him crawling. He's alive.

Thank God!

One of the latest replacements, Maria Molina, is further out. She's got her arms around one of the hedgehogs, weapon gone. Beebee is with her, also scared to death, pale and shaking, but with his M1 still in one hand.

"Come on, second squad! Beebee! Molina! Move your asses!" Rio shouts.

Organize. She has to organize and move! This is her squad, these are her soldiers.

She hears Captain Passey's voice. "Get going! Get going! Stick, get these people moving!"

She has to get her people out of the surf, over the shale, and over the sand to the seawall.

Mortar rounds fall, quieter than artillery, sometimes preceded by a half second's whistle, then . . .

Boom!

Sand showers down on Rio. Something soft bounces off her shoulder. She does not look, does not want to see what it is.

Pang falls on his behind as Jenou suddenly starts yelling and stands up.

"Get down, Jenou!" Rio shouts.

Jenou looks stunned, and there's a bloody gash on her forehead dribbling blood into her eye, but she reacts by stooping low and running.

Beebee is wading ashore now, heavy with water and an overstuffed pack. Maria Molina still clings to the hedgehog like it's her only salvation.

Down the beach one of the hedgehogs explodes. The engineers are—somehow in the midst of chaos—going about the work of blowing up Rommel's fortifications, wading through the water with TNT and Primacord.

"Geer! Get Molina ashore!"

Geer doesn't look as if he thinks that's a good idea at all, but he runs, crouched low, back into the surf.

Jack Stafford lands beside Rio, grabbing his helmet as it rolls away, thrusting it back on his head with seawater rushing down his face.

"You okay?" Rio asks him.

He has no time for a smart aleck remark, just nods. He's so pale she can almost see his bones.

Geer reaches Molina and pries her hands from the steel even as a combat engineer begins placing packs of TNT. Geer half carries, half kicks Molina ashore, with machine-gun bullets making the water jump.

Lieutenant Horne is crawling across the sand, face red with effort.

"Richlin! Richlin!" he shouts, but seems to have nothing else to say.

Stick runs over and lands next to Horne. "Captain says we gotta get going, sir!" he yells.

But Horne has stopped and is now using his arms to scoop sand, like a turtle making a nest, perhaps imagining that six inches of loose dirt will stop a German machine-gun round.

Boom! Boom! Boom!

Mortars again, and one lands close enough to temporarily deafen Rio in one ear.

Rudy J. Chester, who Rio had begun to write off as dead, suddenly rises from the surf, and walks down the beach, fully upright, yelling, "No! No! No!" and waving his hands like a teacher trying to quiet a rowdy class of children.

"Chester! Get down!" Rio yells, but Rudy J. is beyond hearing.

She glances around, taking quick stock. Jack with her. Geer and Molina now crawling toward her. Jenou, face a streaked mess of bloody rivulets, is near and moving in the right direction. Beebee just a few yards away, hand holding his helmet down hard. Pang gasping for breath on his back, but unhurt. Jenny Dial shivering and cursing a blue streak face down to Rio's other side.

"If we sit here we die," Rio yells, voice breaking. "Get to the seawall! Second squad, let's go!"

She rises, stays bent low, and starts to run toward the seawall. She glances back and sees that only Jenou and Beebee are with her.

"Goddammit!" Rio cries. "Go, go, go!" she says to Jenou and Beebee. Then she runs back. She grabs Pang's collar and yanks hard. "Damn it, Pang, move!"

Geer grabs Molina and propels her to her feet and shoves her hard. She stumbles, hesitates, but then begins to run, shrieking wildly as she goes.

"Come back, come back, you'll all get killed!" It's Lieutenant Horne. Stick grabs the rim of his helmet and yanks the lieutenant sideways, shouting in his face, "Get hold of yourself, sir!"

Jenny Dial is yelling "fug, fug, fug!" and cursing like a drunk longshoreman, but she's running in the right direction, unlike Rudy J. Chester who is now walking along the beach like a demented holiday beachcomber.

Rio jumps to her feet and with machine-gun rounds *flit, flit, flitting* inches behind her heels she tackles Chester like a fullback, knocking him down.

He's still babbling, a mix of "no, no, no," and "let me go, let me go!" He writhes and kicks, hysterical. Rio lays on top of him, pulls out her *koummya* and holds the point an inch from his nose. "Get your shit together, Private Sweetheart, right the fug now!"

Whether it's the knife or Rio's snarling face that does it, Chester suddenly stops talking and stops writhing. And then he says, "Here I go!"

Rio rolls away. Chester stands up, and with a trailing scream, runs toward the seawall.

Rio, like a sheepdog, follows as her squad runs and staggers, weeping and cursing over the shale and sand.

BLAM!

A cannon round lands and tosses two soldiers from Cat's squad in the air. One is still alive when he lands, raising one hand to ward off further blows, but a machine gunner finds him and the hand falls.

Camacho. Hobart. Ostrowiz.

Rio's squad is already down from twelve to nine. Cat's in the same shape.

Ahead there is a low, concrete seawall topped with barbed wire. Rio lands hard against the concrete and sand of the seawall, panting, her heart a mad thing trying to kick its way out of her ribcage.

GIs are spread all up and down the seawall, wet, caked with sand, some bleeding, some shouting, some crying, some praying, most silently shivering. Dark shapes like piles of rags dot the sand. Soldiers lie floating face down or face up in shallow water, rising and falling sluggishly on the waves. The frantic, pitiful cries of "Medic! Medic!" come from every direction. Naval gunfire whistles overhead to land too far inland.

The Higgins boats are pulling away now, churning water, heading back to sea.

Leaving us, Rio thinks irrationally. *Leaving us here to die!*

There is only one thing to do.

"Geer! We gotta make a run for the base of the cliff."

"We'll get hung up in the wire," Geer yells. There are double coils of barbed wire ahead.

Every communication now is a shout or a scream. The noise from mortars, artillery, bullets and desperate soldiers is overwhelming. The air stinks of cordite and salt.

"Who's got wire cutters?" Rio yells.

Jack curses under his breath, fumbles in his pack, produces the wire cutters and starts to crawl up over the seawall.

"Stafford!" Rio yells. She'd meant to cut the wire herself, but it's too late and now the Englishman is on his back, under the wire, cutting one . . . two . . . crawl and reposition . . . three strands. The wire springs away in a coil.

"When I yell go, we go!" Rio shouts.

The soldiers looking to her are not all hers. Some are not even from the platoon. A bullet hits a man she doesn't know in the face and explodes out of the back of his head, carrying his helmet away on a geyser of blood and brain matter.

Rio yells. "Ready! Go!"

10

The disembarkation plan calls for Frangie and the rest of the tank battalion medicos to come last, once all the tanks and half-tracks are unloaded. Her jeep is on the upper deck and will have to be lowered by elevator to the tank deck once that space is clear of higher priority traffic.

The beach is close, coming slowly closer as the LST's skipper brings the ship in. Frangie feels contact, a slight lurch, as the hull touches ground. She hears a sound of steel grinding on sand, followed immediately by the whir of electric motors winching open the great bow doors.

From her high up vantage point Frangie can see much of the beach. Even to a noncombatant the problem is clear: a narrow beach and a tall cliff. Machine-gun fire from the top of the cliff is a symphony, with a loud zipper noise to the left answered by one from the right, volumes rising or falling on the breeze, sometimes five or six firing at once, their sounds joining and then separating.

The artillery fire is more sporadic, with shells dropping on the sand and in the surf and out to sea, sending up pillars of sand and smoke here, water there, a half-track, a jeep, a boat, a body.

The navy continues to launch its massive shells, but they cannot be used against the cliff, not at the distances involved, not without risking hitting the Americans on the beach.

There are bodies. Bodies in the sand. Bodies floating sluggishly in the water. And one man, quite near, near enough for Frangie to see the corporal's stripes on his shoulder, lies in the surf, on his back, helpless to move as the waves crash and foam covers his mouth and nose and then retreats.

"He'll drown," Frangie says to no one. Manning and Deacon are in the jeep, back toward the stern, patiently waiting to drive it onto the elevator.

Frangie scans left and right, searching for medical teams. There's a medic hunched over a man. Another crawling toward a woman with one leg blown off. Neither aware of, nor with time to do anything about the man slowly drowning.

The bow doors are open, the ramp sliding into place like an extended tongue. The first tanks will be rolling off soon. But it will be a long time yet before Frangie can disembark. Far too long for the corporal so close, so close, so doomed and yet so easily-saved.

Frangie does not decide to act, at least it doesn't feel that way to her. It feels as if her body simply starts moving all on its own, running to the hatch leading down, piling down the stairs with her musette bags banging against the rails.

On the tank deck it is a roar of engines, all the tanks and half-tracks revving as the ship's loadmasters rush about loosening the straps that had anchored the tanks to the decks. The commanders of each tank are visible, black men, black women, helmeted, ready, maybe even eager despite being afraid.

On a platform overlooking the scene Frangie hesitates for

a second, just a second, to take it in. Colored soldiers from the north, east, west and even the Deep South prepare to roll out and engage the white supremacist Nazis.

Someday I'll tell Obal all about this, she thinks. Then, *Someday maybe my own children too.*

She spots Sergeant Moore. He'll be the second tank off the boat. She weaves her way through preoccupied crew, jumping over a snaking hose being rapidly reeled in, and yells up at him.

"Sergeant Moore!"

He looks down in surprise. "Hey, Doc. I'm a bit busy here."

"Can I bum a ride?"

The question is so preposterous that Moore laughs despite the tension that has turned his face rigid.

"What the hell?"

"There's a man out there," Frangie says. "He's going to drown."

Moore shakes his head, but it's not a no. "You can climb up on the side," he says. His tone of voice carries an unspoken, *If you're fool enough to do it.*

Easier said than done. She finds a steel handhold and plants her foot on a bogie wheel. She bangs her knee painfully on unforgiving armor plate, heaves herself up and squats beside the turret.

"You need to jump right off soon as we're out," Moore says. "We'll be traversing the turret."

Frangie nods. Words feel hard now, like whatever part of her brain that makes words has run out of gas.

Before them the ramp completes its descent. The beach is there, right there! And the German gunners are already aiming at the LST's opening. Bullets ricochet off the bow doors and rattle through the hold, striking sparks.

The first tank revs its engines and clatters down the ramp. Moore's tank lurches hard and rolls after it, and Frangie has to scramble to keep her perch. Out and through. Out and down, the treads splashing through the last inches of boiling surf, throwing up a sandstorm as the treads spin and then bite.

"Thanks!" Frangie yells to Moore and leaps down to land hard on the sand. She stands up, immediately crouches, and searches for the drowning man. She spots him and dashes through the gap when the next tank rolls off. It's like running across railroad tracks between speeding express trains.

While being shot at.

She runs toward the wounded man, but as she does she suddenly realizes she's in a race. A Higgins boat is plowing toward the same spot. She trips, lands on hands and knees, and watches helplessly as the Higgins boat drops its heavy ramp, extinguishing whatever hope the injured soldier might have had.

Soldiers burst from the Higgins boat, too busy staying alive to concern themselves with the dead man under their feet.

The German gunners have loaded their armor-piercing rounds now and focus on the disembarking tanks. A shell bounces off one tank to explode inside the hold of the LST. A second round explodes in the very mouth of the ship and when the smoke clears Frangie can see that the ramp is twisted wildly. Three tanks have made it ashore. The rest will not be coming any time soon.

Neither will Frangie's jeep.

For a moment she dithers, confused, not knowing what to do.

Her place is with the tankers, but they are buttoned up and are already firing up at the bluff and drawing intense, focused fire down on themselves.

There are wounded everywhere, but the sand is almost alive with the tiny puffs of sand from bullets. Any move in almost any direction could cause her to intersect with one of those bullets.

There's a sudden smack on the side of her helmet. She drops, rolls onto her belly, pulls her helmet off and looks at it. There is a brand-new, shiny metallic crease, running right across her red cross.

A voice in the back of her mind yammers in panic that she should get back on the ship, get back on, she isn't supposed to be here, she isn't even responsible for these other wounded, she isn't made of steel, she's going to die, to die, to die.

But again her body decides. She slaps her helmet back on and starts to half-crawl, half-run, like a four-legged animal, toward a woman moaning in pain.

"I'm here, soldier," she says. "Where are you hit?"

A thigh wound. Sulfa, compress, wrap, morphine.

A man runs past, his legs buckle and he falls. She's seen the bullet, a tracer round. It's gone through his belly and come out the back. Stomach wound.

"I'm here, soldier. Lie down and don't move."

She cuts open the uniform to expose the wound. It's seeping not spurting. She rolls him partly over and removes his webbing belt to get at the exit wound. A round hits and makes the soldier jerk. Where? Where was he hit? A jet of blood from his shoulder, a lengthwise hit, the bullet digging a tunnel from his collarbone down into the meat of him, ripping arteries and tendons and organs.

Beyond help.

She stabs morphine into his neck, says, "You'll be okay, just stay down." He will not be okay, she knows it, he does not. She does her half-crawl, half-run toward a voice crying, "Medic! Medic!"

She finds a sergeant sheltering a lieutenant with his body, his back to the gunners.

"Get down, you fool!" she shouts and swarms over the lieutenant, searching for the wound. But then the lieutenant's eyes flutter open. He looks around wildly, frowns up at Frangie and begins to sit up. He's only suffered a concussion. The sergeant who'd been sheltering him lurches forward, cursing a blue streak as his pants leg turns red.

Expose the wound, apply a tourniquet to slow the bleeding, which is serious but not arterial, sulfa, bandage.

"You want a shot, Sarge?"

"Hell, no," he says. "I'm gonna go kill the sombitch who shot me!"

Frangie crawls away toward a body like a pile of rags. She feels the neck. No pulse. Move on.

A wounded man in the surf, like the man she'd jumped off the boat to save. This story ends more happily. He's been shot in the back, legs paralyzed, but he'll most likely live. Might not walk, but he should live, and at least he won't drown. She lights him a cigarette and puts it between his lips.

She finds a woman sitting hunched over, rocking back and forth. Not injured. Frangie pushes her onto her back.

"Here, soldier. Take these. They'll give you courage." She digs a half dozen M&Ms from her pocket and places one in the panicked soldier's mouth. Blank eyes come suddenly alive. Frangie pours a few more into the GI's hands.

A man wanders down the beach, his entire uniform below the chest is drenched with blood. She can do nothing for him, he's moving too fast and there are nearer cases.

A woman sergeant is dragging herself along, using the butt of her M1 as a stick, digging it in, dragging herself toward the too-near, too-distant bluff. As she advances at a snail's pace she leaves one leg behind. Her thigh is tattered uniform, shredded flesh and blood.

"I'm here, soldier," Frangie says, crawling to her.

"Don't need no help," the woman says doggedly. Then focuses on Frangie and says, "You're a Nigra!"

"I'm a medic," Frangie snaps. "And if I don't tie off that leg you'll bleed to death in two minutes!"

The woman seems baffled by this, then like someone in a horror movie who slowly senses the presence of a vampire, she turns her head and sees. "My leg! Where's my leg? Where's my leg?"

Frangie peels back the trouser leg revealing a tangled mess of pulsing veins and whitish tendons and the mangled white bones of the knee. She whips a tourniquet around the stump and begins feeling through the bloody mess for arteries amid the veins. She finds one and with slippery fingers ties it off. The stump is still bleeding heavily and Frangie cannot locate the artery.

She needs plasma, but all of that is in her jeep. She wipes her brow, she's sweating, and goes back to the gruesome job of feeling for pulsing blood. She finds the artery but it's split lengthwise, and too much of it is buried in muscle.

The woman says, "Aw shit," and dies.

A machine-gun bullet hits Frangie's musette back, blowing open packages of gauze. She glances left: more boats coming in, more soldiers running down ramps into water, too many disappearing below the churning surf. She glances right and sees the twinkle of a German machine gun firing, firing as if it is aiming right at Frangie Marr.

"Who the fug are you?" It's a white captain, running past with a half dozen soldiers.

"Sergeant Marr, sir!" she cries.

"You a medic?"

Frangie nods and taps her helmet with its red crosses.

"Come with me!"

"But . . ."

"Get your lazy black ass up off the sand and come with me!"

It's an order from an officer and she has no choice but to obey. She runs after the little squad as machine-gun fire plucks at the sand and their uniforms.

They run past a young lieutenant carrying a severed arm. "I found this," the lieutenant yells. "I don't know whose it is!"

Suddenly they are at the seawall and they collapse against it, squeezing in between soldiers already huddled there. A metallic *ping* and Frangie sees a neat hole in the helmet of the man to her right. Blood gushes down his face.

"All right, you sons of whores," the captain roars, "we're going for the bluff!" He makes a chopping motion with his hand, then jumps up, but no one jumps with him. He stops, turns and says, "Goddammit, get up! Get up! You want to stay here and die?"

A handful of soldiers rise. One falls. The others go running after the captain and Frangie finds herself running too, no longer crawling, no longer crouching, just running, running as if she can outrun the bullets.

Boom!

A mortar round lands a few feet away and knocks Frangie over. Her mind screams *stay down*, but her body is already up again, up and running, running until she stumbles right into a lump that trips her at the very base of the cliff.

Soldiers on both sides, all white, all extra white with fear, clutch their rifles as if the M1 is salvation itself.

A German potato masher grenade comes skittering down the cliff, bouncing, then is stopped by a tiny brush outcropping and explodes, showering dirt down on Frangie.

"Anyone here hit?" Frangie yells. Yells left. Yells right.

A voice answers, "Fug! I'm hit!"

It turns out to be a grazing wound in the shoulder—lots of blood, but no danger. Sulfa and bandage.

Frangie pushes her back against the cliff and closes her eyes, praying more fervently, and with more jumbled words than she has ever prayed before.

When she opens her eyes she sees her LST, smoke billowing from the open bow doors. Hoses spray salt water on a raging fire, sending up clouds of steam to mingle with the oily black smoke.

Only one of the battalion's DD tanks made it to shore, and it is now running parallel with the beach, offering a rolling shelter to soldiers who run hunched over in its lee.

Another tank still pumps rounds into the bluff, but it's a losing proposition: the German gunners are in hardened emplacements or pillboxes, and from the angle the tank has its shells either slam into dirt or go skimming off into the air.

The entire length of Omaha Beach seems to be burning vehicles and burning boats or ships, smoke and flame, soldiers face down or on their backs, flailing weakly.

"Marr?"

Frangie twists and sees a familiar, freckled face. "Rio?"

"Fancy meeting you here," Rio says. Her friend Jenou is bleeding from a superficial wound.

"It's a popular beach," Frangie says through chattering teeth. Then, "Castain, put a bandage on that. Get it from your med kit," Frangie says. It's not a wound that needs a medic.

"Got any spare morphine?" Jenou asks. "I'll take all you got, I want to just go to sleep!"

"You got blood all over you," Rio says to Frangie. "You sure you aren't hit yourself?"

Frangie shakes her head. "Not my blood."

In the space of a few very, very long minutes, Omaha Beach has become populated with a strange sort of beachgoer: bodies lie where sunbathers might have spread blankets.

It is a disaster. A disaster. There is no way off this beach, and they are all going to die here.

Yea, though I walk through the valley of the shadow of death . . .

A man falls, a red flower blooming on his belly.

"Take care of yourself, Rio," Frangie says.

And then she crawls out from the shelter of the bluff and with machine guns chasing her, runs to the fallen soldier.

"I'm here, soldier."

11

Rio watches Frangie Marr running back out, leaving the relative safety of the cliff base, armed with nothing but gauze and morphine. She does not expect to see the medic alive again.

"Little Nigra's got balls," Geer mutters.

Rio looks around her. Jenou is alive and well and sporting a tan and red bandage peeking out from below the visor of her helmet. Jack Stafford is also alive and unhurt. She does not see Pang or Beebee. But two of the replacements, Jenny Dial and Rudy J. Chester, are within shouting range.

Three dead. Two missing. Her squad is down to seven soldiers, including herself, and two of them are raw recruits. Then she sees Maria Molina running up from the beach. Bullets ping all around her, but at last she flops down atop Geer who curses then shifts to make room for her.

The situation on the beach is clear in only one respect: no one, but no one, can climb the bluff in the face of deadly German fire. The only way up is through one of the several draws, like river channels, that cut into the cliff. The nearest one is just twenty yards to Rio's left, where she sees Stick huddled with some of his soldiers, as well as a number of men and women from other platoons who, like some of those around Rio, just sort of ended up here.

The draws are the only path off the beach, but the draws are covered by German pillboxes with more hardened emplacements behind. Tanks would help greatly, but only once the cliff is topped. A tank trying to force the draw would be knocked out and become an obstacle. In the end it will be infantry work.

But it is not work that Rio can do with her squad alone. She steps away from cover long enough to spot Cat Preeling. Captain Passey is with her. Lieutenant Horne's location is unknown.

Then she sees a man, a colonel, walking right down the line of huddled soldiers. It is not her colonel, nor anyone she's ever seen before. A mortar shell lands too close and the colonel runs, bent over, hand on his helmet, and squats halfway between Rio and Stick.

"Who's in charge of this outfit?" he demands.

"Captain Passey," Rio says. She makes a chopping motion in his direction.

"You come with me," the colonel says, and sets off at a lope toward Passey and Stick.

"You heard him," Rio says. She and her squad and half a dozen soldiers from other units follow her, running crouched along the base of the cliff.

They bunch up around Passey and Stick.

"All right," the colonel says. "I got some Bangalores off the engineers, and we are getting ready to blow the wire in that draw. We need to charge that draw, cut the wire and take out those pillboxes."

"The draw is enfiladed six ways from Sunday," Passey says.

"I am aware of that," the colonel says. "But there are just two

143

kinds of people staying on this beach: those who are dead and those who are going to die."

Passey nods.

"All right then," the colonel says. "Now—"

His words are drowned by an explosion. The Bangalores have gone off. The unknown colonel, Passey, and Stick turn the corner into the draw.

"Let's go!" Rio says. She blends into a stream of soldiers all following the colonel's lead. The wire has been blown, but in the back of Rio's mind is the likelihood of mines. The colonel and Captain Passey must also have thought of it and they're leading the way, so . . .

Not all officers are useless.

The draw is like a steep-sided gully. A huge concrete pillbox with sinister firing slots looms on the left. A smaller one is planted on the right. Bullets fall like a hailstorm. A man just in front of Rio is hit. She leaps over his falling body, accidentally kicking him, tripping, keeping her balance and . . . *run, run, run!*

Only now does it occur to Rio that she has no weapon. She tossed aside her rifle to dive after Hobart and Ostrowiz, and the BAR she'd rescued lies back on the shale.

A man screams, twists and falls back against the dirt wall.

Rio says, "You sit tight and give me your rifle!"

"I think they done killed me!" the soldier cries, pawing at his uniform to find the wound.

"Medic!" Rio shouts.

She grabs the wounded man's M1 and fumbles two clips from his ammo pouch, then rushes to catch up. Geer is just ahead with Maria Molina and a couple of soldiers from a whole different outfit.

The draw narrows ahead and soldiers are bunched dangerously. A single mortar round could take out a dozen people. The two big pillboxes can no longer bring their machine guns to bear, but German soldiers atop the rise now hurl grenades down.

Cat Preeling catches one in midair, looks confused as to what to do next, then at the last second throws it like a professional outfielder aiming for home plate. It explodes up above them, scattering dirt, but harming no one. A second grenade blows both a man's legs off and within seconds all ten pints of blood in his body have made mud out of the sand.

The colonel huddles with Passey and Stick. Stick waves Rio over and she plows toward them, stepping on the legs of soldiers now clinging in panic to the side of the draw.

"We have to take out those MGs," the colonel says.

Passey looks at Rio. "Sticklin says he'll try it, but he can't go it alone."

"Yep," Rio says, trying not to sound as terrified as she is. It's flattering that Stick wants her, but on the other hand, it may be a suicide mission. "How do you see it, Stick?"

Stick squints, peeks around a piece of fallen concrete, ducks back as machine-gun rounds bounce where his face had been and says, "See that crack there?"

Rio sees the crack. It looks like a washout from recent rains, just wide enough for a single soldier. It runs all the way to the top of the draw where it is blocked by a thicket of barbed wire.

"Maybe get us one of those Bangalores?" Rio says. Without

waiting for an answer she yells, "Bangalores! Bring up a Bangalore!"

After a few minutes during which another man is hit, though not fatally, the Bangalores are handed forward. They are five-foot-long steel tubes painted olive drab with yellow lettering and packed with explosive. They can be joined together to form a longer torpedo by use of a metal sleeve, with the leading tube capped by a steel nose to allow the torpedo to be shoved through sand and under the wire.

Stick has one Bangalore, Rio the other. Stick also carries the five-inch sleeve used to connect the two segments.

"Ready?" Stick asks.

"Yep."

They kick loose of their wedged positions, jump and run, feet plowing loose sand. It is thirty feet to the crack, thirty feet of being chased by machine-gun fire.

They drop beside each other at the base of the crack and look up. It's a twenty-foot climb into coils of wire.

"Kind of have to wedge ourselves in," Stick says. Rio nods. Her mouth is full of sand, making speech difficult.

Stick pushes into the crack, leans against one side, plants his feet on the other side, and begins to ascend. It is slow and not at all easy. When he is halfway up he calls down, "Hand me one!"

Rio balances the Bangalore and heaves it up to where he can grab it. He's found a ledge and he precariously balances the torpedo there before calling for Rio to send up the next section.

Then Rio starts to climb, mimicking Stick's moves till she is just below his boots and eye-level with the balanced torpedo.

Stick climbs some more, peeks over the lip and in a relieved voice says, "I got a little defilade up here. Send me the bangers!"

Again she hands the explosives up, and he shoves them over the lip. She shimmies until she is face to face with him, and peeks over the edge. The barbed wire is thick here, multiple coiled strands. Beyond the wire she sees a gun emplacement, side-on, just a long rectangular slit maybe thirty or forty feet away.

She crouches back down. "What do you think, Stick?"

"I don't think it's an enclosed pillbox. I think it's a reinforced trench. Figure a squad of Krauts, maybe two, maybe three embrasures connected by an open trench."

Rio looks at him in surprise and shakes her head. "Well, you've been paying attention during briefings."

"I happened to talk to one of the Canadians who was in on the Dieppe raid . . ."

Rio says, "Once we blow the banger the Krauts will send infantry out to get us."

Stick nods. "Yeah. Be better if we could follow up strong before the smoke clears. Call some people up here with grenades. I want smoke and frag. And have someone grab my Thompson."

"Yep." Rio can see her soldiers down below, a huddled bunch of scared faces peeking out from behind rocks, fallen dirt and scraps of concrete. This is not a job for one of the new soldiers. With a churning, sick feeling in her stomach she quickly does the math: not Geer, he'll have to take the squad if she doesn't make it.

Planning for my own death.

"Castain! Stafford!" She relays Sticks instructions. Then she and Stick wait, face to face, both breathing hard, faces coated with sand and dust and congealed smoke.

Stafford is first. He hands up Stick's Thompson and Rio's newly-acquired M1. Then he hands up a musette bag containing a dozen grenades of mixed type.

Jenou comes behind him, carrying her own carbine and a bag of ammo clips for the Thompson and the M1. Jenou and Jack are squeezed in the place just below the two sergeants. Ammo and grenades are parceled out.

Stick says, "When we blow the wire I want smoke up there. And we go right behind it. Right?"

Heads nod. Jaws clench.

Stick attaches the nose piece to one of the Bangalores, shoves it a few feet away, then with support from Rio manages to get the connecting sleeve in place. He pushes the long assembly forward. Then he sets the fuse and yells, "Fire in the hole!"

Boomf!

Dirt erupts upward and falls in a hard rain, clattering down the crack, sliding into collars and shirt fronts, mouths, ears and eyes.

Jenou and Jack both pull the pins on stubby cylindrical smoke grenades and throw them overhand with a looping move.

"We'll give the grenades five," Stick says. Smoke grenades take a few seconds to really get going.

There's a muted pop as the smoke grenades ignite.

"One . . . two . . . three . . . four . . . five!"

Stick surges up and over. Rio slips, catches herself and drags herself up and after Stick, clawing her way over the rim of the gully. The air is still full of falling dirt and swirling smoke from the explosion, now augmented by the white smoke of the two grenades.

Stick and Rio run through the smoke, staying low as Rio hears shouted orders in German.

Barbed-wire fragments tear at Rio's boots and trouser leg. The ground is sand and chunks of concrete, leftovers dumped during the construction of the pillboxes. She cannot see the gun emplacement but charges in the direction she last saw it.

A swirl of movement in the smoke. Rio stops, shoulders her rifle and fires. There is a cry of pain.

Stick's Thompson opens up, a half dozen rounds that earn a German curse.

Suddenly a gust of breeze parts the smoke and Rio is close, very close to the German position. She dashes up a short slope and there it is right at her feet. As Stick predicted, it is a trench, with two main branches, one leading to their target machine-gun position, the other branch ending in a similar embrasure no doubt overlooking some other gully. The firing positions are concrete frames around the long rectangular slits, open to the sky. She sees three Germans with their backs to her, working two machine guns, the brass flying. She senses rather than sees Jenou and Jack behind her.

In both machine-gun nests the Germans fire on, pouring lead on the troops below, but other Germans are grabbing their weapons and running for the exits, some pausing to fire up at the looming Americans above them.

"Grenades," Rio says to Jack and Jenou.

Jack opens the musette bag of grenades and he and Jenou pull pins and toss, pull pins and toss.

Bam! Bam! Bam!

Rio stands at the edge of the trench and picks her targets. The old guy grabbing a Schmeisser. *Bang!* Through the chest. The young kid, scared, running and nearing the exit. *Bang!* Through the side and a second *Bang!* in the back. He falls and blocks the exit with his body.

Stick's Thompson spits fat .45 caliber rounds into the backs of the nearest German gunners. One machine gun falls silent.

A German peeks up over the side of the trench, leveling his rifle. Rio shoots him in the head.

But she has been too preoccupied with the slaughter in the trench, with grenades exploding and targets presenting themselves in her sights, to look behind her. Neither has Stick.

Rio senses rapid movement behind her just as she fires the last round in her clip. The clip pings out. Her hand goes automatically to her ammo pouch, even as she turns, turns . . . way too slowly.

The German's Schmeisser is leveled. His finger is on the trigger.

And then he seems to trip, takes a big step to steady himself, falls to his knees, and then to his face. Behind him Maria Molina's carbine smokes.

The young woman who practically had to be kicked ashore by Geer has come up on her own initiative to join the fight.

Having killed everyone at this end of the trenchworks, Rio and Stick walk cautiously around the trench, looking for an angle on the remaining German machine gunner who still, despite everything, fires down at the beach. Stick tosses a grenade and the machine gun is silenced.

A dust-caked German comes running, firing his rifle wildly. But Rio and Stick are above him. Both shoot the German.

A voice yells, "*Kamerad! Kamerad! Nicht schiessen!*"

"Come on out of there!" Stick yells.

"*Nicht schiessen!*"

Rio speaks no German, but she can guess what it means: *Don't shoot.*

Another German comes staggering along the trench, passing directly below Rio, holding his arm and dragging one leg. He is unarmed. He walks up the ramp and of his own accord drops to his knees and laces his fingers behind his neck.

Rio stares. The German has a wrinkled face, the wrinkles made more prominent by dust. He's lost his helmet, and his head is mostly bald.

The German must be in his fifties. An old man!

"That's what's been killing us?" Stick demands. "Richlin, secure the trench."

"Trade me your Thompson," she says.

Rio hops down into the trench with the submachine gun, followed by Molina. Beebee too has now materialized.

The emplacement is more developed than it looked from above. There is extensive use of concrete to strengthen the sides of the trenches, and there are side chambers—none deep, but still covered—where ammo crates or rations are stacked. The grenades have burst most of the crates, spilling ammo. The ammo is of no use as salvage since it is of the wrong caliber, but Beebee drops into the trench and now begins digging through the rations, stuffing sausages and cans into a musette bag. On the body of a dead German officer he finds the ultimate war souvenir: a Luger pistol. He winks at Rio and stuffs it in his belt.

The two machine guns are still mounted, one tilted skyward since the gunner died still gripping his weapon. He grips it still, though the back of his uniform looks like it has been attacked by furious badgers. Two German soldiers lie atop each other. A third German has been blown against a concrete wall and now looks as if he's sitting down, legs out, unblinking eyes staring at nothing. A fourth German is in two pieces, feet pointed up, face pointed down.

"All clear!" Rio shouts.

Below in the draw, the colonel orders the rest of the platoon to advance.

Rio grabs one of the German's canteens, smells the contents and upends it, drinking deep: better to save her own water supply. Molina stands a respectful few paces away. Rio searches the young woman's face for signs of the complete and abject cowardice she displayed on the beach. But Molina looks undisturbed. In fact, she seems to be nodding to herself, as if approving of what she's done.

Maria Molina looks like nothing special, a wide brown face, brown eyes, brown hair. She's of average height and average weight. Nothing special, but Rio breathes because of her.

"Thanks, Molina. Good shooting."

"Any time, Sarge." Molina's eyes keep flitting back to the German who'd been cut in half.

Rio nods. "Yep. Welcome to the war, Molina. How you liking it so far?"

Molina looks alarmed until she realizes that this is as close to an official ceremony of acceptance as she is likely to get. Richlin is talking to her like she would talk to Geer or Castain. As if she is an actual adult. She has, in a phrase she recalls from a detective novel, "made her bones."

"I like it a whole lot better when I can shoot back," Molina says.

Rio laughs. "Castain, Stafford, and you too, Molina, let's take a walk ahead and see what we find. Maybe kill some more Krauts."

12

When handed a weapon the first thing to do is check the safety—
on—and then rack the slide to see if there is a round chambered.
But this weapon is unfamiliar to Rainy.

"Why that's a Sten," Sergeant Hooper says, seeming revived by
the sight of something familiar and British.

Philippe is handing out weapons: Sten guns for Rainy, Marie,
Wickham and himself; a German Luger pistol and four grenades
for Étienne.

Perhaps Philippe knows that Étienne prefers handguns.

But maybe, Rainy thinks, he has given Étienne the weapon
least likely to allow him to shoot them all in the back.

Paranoia, Rainy chides herself. But then a different word: *caution*.

"I want a Sten," Étienne says.

"You carry the grenades," Philippe says. "I've seen you play at
boules—you have an accurate throw."

True? Or a weak excuse?

Étienne frowns but does not argue. This is Philippe's territory.

Rainy sits beside Sergeant Hooper who walks her through the
gun. It looks small and cheaply-made to Rainy, who is accustomed
to the larger, heavier, more complicated Thompson used by US

forces. The Stens are weapons favored by the British SOE, which has been financing and arming the maquis. It's little more than a steel pipe, with a stubby barrel at one end, a magazine sticking awkwardly sideways, and a metal pistol grip at the back.

"Safety here. This button is the selector," Hooper explains. "In for semi-automatic, out for full automatic. Of course this is the commando version with the pistol grip. It normally comes with a short metal stock."

"Rate of fire?"

"Five hundred rounds per minute. Of course you've only got a thirty-two round clip, so short bursts, eh?"

"Does it climb?"

Hooper shakes his head and gazes admiringly at the crude weapon. "It doesn't look like much, the old Sten, but there's not much climb and she won't wander either. Of course beyond a hundred feet you couldn't hit a London coach at high noon, but up close she'll do the job. Nine millimeter, meaning you can use German ammunition at a pinch."

"That's what it's loaded with," Philippe says. He's busy showing Marie how to use the gun, though Rainy has the distinct impression that the demonstration is unnecessary. Unnecessary, but given the flush in Marie's cheeks, not unwelcome.

"If she jams," Hooper goes on, "you just pull the magazine, give 'er a tap on the ground, stick 'er back in, cock, and Bob's your uncle."

The plan is straightforward, but not easy. The target is a German fuel depot supposedly containing hundreds if not thousands of fifty-five-gallon drums of gasoline. This is part of the fuel supply for the Das Reich, and Rainy can see definite advantages in knocking it out. In fact, she is rehearsing explanations in the back of her mind for her boss, Colonel Herkemeier.

They will arrive at the fuel dump from two directions. Étienne, Marie and Wickham will walk up the railroad tracks and provide a diversion at exactly 1:05 a.m.

Philippe and Rainy will take a horse-drawn cart with one barrel of the cognac taken from their disabled truck. They will go right up to the gate of the dump and see if they find a willing buyer. But whether they are stopped at the gate or allowed inside, the 1:05 diversion will give them an opportunity to make their play.

A smaller detachment of freedom fighters, older men and some children, has been detailed to set up an ambush to slow any German reinforcements. The Germans won't take long to get past the ambush, but every minute will help.

Simple. Simple and extremely dangerous. They could be stopped en route. They could be shot on sight at the gate. Étienne could fail to start a diversion. If he did start a diversion, the Germans may not be fooled. If Rainy and Philippe do make their way into the facility, they may still be shot, or be burned in the explosion they hope to start.

There are, Rainy thinks as she sways along in the wooden seat of the cart, many ways to fail or die on this mission. And few ways to explain her decisions to Herkemeier.

The horse's hooves make a pleasant clip-clop as they set off into the chilly night.

If they are stopped by French *milice* Philippe will do the talking; if stopped by Germans it will be up to Rainy to talk their way through. Philippe is dressed like an older man in a voluminous and oft-patched coat and a beret. He sits hunched over as he holds the reins. He will look to a casual observer like an old man out with his sister or wife.

At one in the morning.

"How do we start the fire?" Rainy asks as they roll slowly past a graveyard on one side of the road and a vineyard on the other.

"Shoot up the barrels and toss a Molotov cocktail," he says. He points to his coat pocket. A damp rag protrudes from the mouth of a wine bottle.

"How far can you throw that?" she asks pointedly.

He hesitates. "Maybe not far enough," he admits.

"Thousands of gallons—sorry, liters—of gasoline could make a hell of a big explosion."

"I hope so," he says. Then lightly, as if he doesn't really need to ask, "What would your intelligence people say is the best way?"

"Something with a fuse if we had it."

"We do not."

Rainy shrugs. "Shoot holes then send a burning truck into it?"

"So . . . We figure it out when we get there?"

Rainy says nothing. She has a personal and professional dislike of half-baked plans. But she sees no alternative to improvising.

"I suppose Marie does not speak of me?" Philippe says, trying with no success at all to sound casual.

Rainy deflects. "How do you know her?"

"Oh, we knew each other before the war as children. Étienne as well. We are all from the same small town, though we moved away."

"Why move away?"

He hands her the reins and begins to roll himself a cigarette. "Étienne got a job as a school teacher in Fouras. Their mother died, their father was taken away to Germany. Forced labor. So Marie went with Étienne."

"And you?"

"I left when the war started. Oradour is a small town, full of friends and relatives. I knew I would resist, and I feared German reprisals."

"Oradour." Rainy's French is good, but she struggles with the soft, throaty French 'r' sounds.

"Oradour-sur-Glane," he clarifies. "There's a completely separate Oradour-sur-Vayres, just thirty-five kilometers away."

"What, you're short of names so you used that one twice?"

He smiles.

"She likes you," Rainy says.

He turns so abruptly that the makings of his cigarette go flying. "Did she say that?"

Rainy shakes her head. "Didn't need to. It's obvious. Obvious to Étienne as well."

"Étienne."

She waits. It's an interrogator's trick the army taught her: most people find a long silence intolerable and will say more. Philippe is not most people.

A truck full of French *milice* drives past, going the other way. They stiffen, but the truck rolls on until its tail lights can no longer be seen.

They come to an intersection. The woods press close on one

side, with fallow fields on the others. Philippe snaps the reins and they plod on through. The wagon is the sum total of traffic at this time of night.

"That's the ambush point," Philippe says when they are through. "Our people are in the woods. If the Boche comes this way . . . The gate is just around that bend."

Rainy reaches under her coat to snap the safety off on her concealed Sten gun. Three magazines are in her left coat pocket. One will have to be snapped into place before she can use the Sten. She reaches behind and draws out her Walther, sticking it in her right pocket.

Slowly, slowly they come around the bend, and slowly, slowly the gate comes into view, barbed wire over wooden posts, with a tall wooden gate. The gate is locked from the inside with a chain. A bored German soldier in an ill-fitting uniform stands with rifle hanging, chafing his hands and blowing into them to warm his fingers. A few feet behind him is an ugly, squat, concrete blockhouse with a wooden door, and beside it a firing slot, presumably housing a machine gun. Smoke curls from a pipe chimney.

"Not SS," Rainy says.

"No," Philippe agrees. "SS men don't guard fuel dumps. He'll most likely be some poor Pole or Ukrainian pressed into service. A lot of the less-than-frontline units have German officers and NCOs, but pressed men from the east."

The guard spots them and yells something over his shoulder while unlimbering his rifle. He holds the rifle at his waist. Rainy has not seen him touch the safety, but she cannot be sure.

Philippe waves his hand in a big arc and rattles off a quick stream of friendly-sounding French, the most prominent words being *cognac*, and *officiers*, officers.

The guard orders them to halt and they do at a distance of a hundred yards. Too far. A helmetless sergeant comes out of the cement bloc hut, pushing his uniform into place and smoothing his hair, looking very much like a man who has been catching forty winks.

The NCO yells, "*Was willst du hier?*" What do you want here?

Rainy glances at her watch. 12:59 a.m. In six minutes Étienne is to provide a distraction.

Philippe offers an eloquent shrug of incomprehension. In French he explains that he and his sister are here to see whether the German officers are thirsty. Then he adds, "My sister speaks German."

Rainy translates into German, and this seems to reassure the NCO. He waves them closer. But he also ducks back inside and re-emerges with a helmet on his head and a Schmeisser in his hand.

Clop, clop, clop, the wagon advances.

They stop a second time, just before the gate. The German sergeant orders them to get down and come forward, hands in the air.

Step. Step. Step.

Two minutes.

They stop when they reach the gate. The NCO asks again for an explanation. Rainy takes her time about it, launching into a long tale of how she and her brother just happened to find a barrel of cognac. This part of the story is clearly a lie and is meant to be understood as such by the German. He will of course assume that they have stolen the barrel. The sleepy NCO gets a shrewd look on his face, the kind of look people get when dealing with possibly useful criminals.

After a while the German impatiently silences Rainy with a raised hand. In response, as though trust has been established, Rainy lowers her hands.

The German does not like this. He orders her to open her coat. If she does he cannot fail to see the Sten gun hanging low on its strap over her belly where the coat is at its blousiest.

She protests that she is not a whore! She has not come here to be insulted! Is she to undress for the amusement of this lowly sergeant?

It's a convincing display of feminine modesty and French emotionalism—at least that's how the German sees it. He grins and says something rude along the lines of not needing to rape some old widow woman in . . .

But then something triggers in the German's mind. He frowns. *Old woman?* He leans forward to peer closely at her.

From out of the night comes a burst of automatic fire. The German jerks his head left, realizes what is happening, snaps back, raises his Schmeisser, stops, stares, and claws at his chest where the bullet from Rainy's Walther has entered.

Bang!

She aims again, shoots the young guard as he fumbles with his gun, once, twice, then shoots the staggering sergeant carefully in the head.

"I'll get the bolt cutters!" Philippe says, but before he can move Rainy has shot the lock on the gate. She draws the gate open.

Philippe, ever the maquis fighter, grabs the Schmeisser and a spare clip from the dead sergeant. German voices shout. From the woods beside the dump comes another burst of Sten gun fire. A hand-cranked alarm starts to whine.

No grenades. A weak and only partly-effective distraction, and no guarantee that the small garrison of Germans will run that way rather than toward the sound of a handgun at the gate.

"Do we go?" Rainy demands.

"We go," Philippe says.

Rainy draws out her Sten gun and snaps in a magazine, while Philippe checks his purloined Schmeisser. They are through the gate and now Rainy sees the fuel dump proper. There are two massive pyramids of fifty-five-gallon drums, stacked as much as nine barrels high. A loader sits parked. Two trucks are parked to the right. To the left a low wooden barracks spews German soldiers, uniforms askew, rifles being hurriedly loaded on the run.

The Germans are more than a hundred feet away, too far for accuracy, but Philippe and Rainy both pivot and spray automatic fire that may hit no one, but succeeds in causing the Germans to dive to the ground.

Where the hell are Étienne and Marie and Wickham?

Rainy and Philippe leap to cover behind a parked forklift.

"Go!" Philippe orders. "I'll hold them off!"

Rainy knows better than to argue. There is no saving Philippe by standing at his side; the only salvation will come from making a very big fire.

Rainy shrugs off her coat and runs. The shoes, chosen to look like typical footwear for a working-class Frenchwoman well into an era of shortages, begin to come apart, one sole loose and flapping absurdly as she runs toward the closest pyramid of fuel.

She spots cover of a sort, a low stack of empty jerry cans, the familiar five-gallon steel containers. She drops to her knees behind them, pushes the selector switch to fully automatic and sprays the pyramid of barrels with the rest of her first clip, pauses to reload, and empties the second thirty-two rounds into the barrels, bullets punching holes with heavy metallic *thunk* sounds. A bright light on a wire strung between poles snaps on and blinds her a little so she cannot see the streams of gasoline, but she can smell them.

Behind her Philippe fires in careful three-round bursts, keeping the Germans pinned down. It won't last long. These may not be front line troops, but if there's a single living officer or NCO he'll have them organized for a flanking counterattack within minutes.

And now . . . only now . . . does it occur to Rainy that she has no lighter. No matches. No way to make a flame.

She looks around her frantically. Empty jerry cans. Leaking barrels. A pump. Nothing!

She feels a wetness in the foot with the disintegrating shoe. Gasoline is pooling around her.

Philippe! He'll have matches or a lighter. He'd have to, he smokes. She dashes back to him.

"I need a match!"

He reaches inside his shirt and pulls out a small box of matches. Then the Molotov cocktail in his coat.

Rainy grabs them and races back, but now a file of German soldiers appears, creeping cautiously between the two barrel pyramids. Surely, Rainy thinks, they smell the gas, they must be splashing through it!

But this is not the time to worry about these Germans who may not all be Germans; these men in gray who may be unwilling cannon fodder for the Third Reich.

She looks down, finds the edge of the advancing wave of gasoline, makes sure she is outside of it, flicks a match which, amazingly, catches on the first try. She lights the rag wick, steps back and smashes the bottle hard against the nearest barrel.

There is a small *whoosh* as the Molotov cocktail catches. Flames race along the ground, leap up to the still-draining barrels, and . . . *whoooosh!* A small fireball sucks air toward it, feeds itself on this fuel, heats the gasoline around it forming a vapor mist which explodes with a noise like a million matches struck at once.

Bah-WHOOOOSH!

Then a second explosion, a flat smacking sound like a big piece of dropped plywood, and a flaming barrel flies through the air like an out-of-control Roman candle, spraying burning fuel. Flame spreads quickly across the spilled gasoline. And it spreads to the half dozen soldiers who shout in fear, crying out in words that are not German.

Rainy does not want to see what comes next. She pivots, races back to Philippe, fires a few rounds over his shoulder at the Germans beyond and yells, "We need to get out of here!"

Philippe nods. Their horse-drawn wagon is still where they left it, but that fact is overwhelmed in importance by the sudden, sharp crackle of gunfire coming from down the road.

"The ambush!" Philippe says.

Somehow German forces have already been sent, triggering the ambush.

Impossible! Not even the Germans react that quickly!

But that's beside the point, because what matters is that the road is closed to them. The only option left is the railroad tracks, which are beyond the now-towering wall of furious flames and boiling smoke.

Flames lick at the tires of the forklift, their only cover. The heat is intense and mounting by the second. Rainy's skin feels stretched as tight as a drum skin. She smells her hair crisping.

"We take this!" Philippe yells, smacking a hand against the forklift.

"You drive," Rainy says.

Philippe jumps into the single seat. Rainy climbs on the back. Two Germans rush toward them, one spraying his Schmeisser, the second is on fire and screaming as he runs in panic, trying to outrun the flames burning his flesh. Rainy shoots them both, finishing her last clip. She grabs Philippe's gun as the forklift engine catches and the vehicle jerks forward.

They veer away from what is now a mountain of flame, jetting hundreds of feet in the air, turning night into an orange-lit nightmare of eerie shadows.

"Hang on!" Philippe yells, and Rainy sees that he means to crash right through the chain-link fence separating the dump from the railroad tracks. She grabs a handhold, but the sudden crunch of impact stops the loader and knocks Rainy off. She rolls on the ground, quickly pops up and fires a burst through the smoke toward whoever might still be pursuing them.

Philippe backs up, then rams the loader forward again, aiming for one of the poles, which this time tilts away. The fence is down but the loader is stalled in place, hung up on the fence, so Philippe and Rainy both race on foot through a narrow band of woods, toward the train tracks, where they turn north, running flat out along the ties until they spot a body ahead. A body with blonde hair.

"Marie!" Philippe cries.

She is alive. Hair a mess, clothing dirty, but alive. There is a red mark on the side of her face. A bump swells beneath the flesh of her temple. Her Sten gun lies beside her and Rainy scoops it up.

"Can you move?" Rainy demands.

Marie nods.

Philippe and Rainy haul Marie to her feet and as they run, Rainy pops the clip on Marie's Sten as Marie gasps out her story.

"Étienne! My own brother," she says. "A traitor! He was calling to a German patrol. Wickham shot Étienne, but before he died Étienne shot the Englishman. Both are dead!"

At least a dozen rounds are gone from Marie's clip.

Rainy does not relax her helpful grip on Marie's arm, but as they run a terrible sadness wells within Rainy.

There is a traitor, but that traitor is not Étienne.

13

"Dig in," Rio says.

They may be the two hardest words she's ever spoken. Ordering her squad to dig in means she too must dig a fighting hole, and she, like every one of them, is exhausted to the point of sleepwalking.

They have gained the heights. They've moved a few hundred yards inland. To the amazed relief of everyone on or near Omaha Beach, the dreaded Luftwaffe, Germany's air force, has been nearly invisible. But word has come down to expect a counterattack at any moment. The Germans will certainly counterattack, the only question is whether it will come in the form of small probing attacks, or full panzer divisions.

Night is falling on the longest day in any of their young lives. The platoon is lined up fairly tightly with a massive hedge to their rear and an open field ahead. They sit slumped forward or lying on their backs, legs extended, a row of men and women so destroyed they don't look any livelier than the dead soldiers on the beach.

The field, perhaps an acre in size, is bordered by the same hedges. Rio's squad is positioned closest to a wooden-gated gap. In the field are three cows taking turns moaning loudly. Rio knows the sound well—it's the distress cry of cows who have not been milked so their udders are painfully distended. For years Rio had the chore of milking her mother's small herd before leaving for school. Since she was twelve, she'd been waking up an hour earlier and stumbling out into misty darkness to fill buckets with milk. And on the one or two occasions where she petulantly avoided her chores, the cows would be making just this sound when she came home from school. She had faced her mother's raised eyebrow and irritated expression.

"I can't dig," Rudy J. Chester says. "I am all worn out."

Normally this kind of statement would earn sneers and taunts from the others, but the truth is Rudy J. speaks for all of them.

"Let me ask you something," Rio says. "If the Krauts suddenly opened up on us, would you have the energy to dig then? Yeah? Then get up off the ground and dig!"

For emphasis she kicks the sole of Rudy J.'s boot. He looks as if he's about to argue, but in the end he rises ponderously and unlimbers his entrenching tool.

"Geer!"

"Yeah?"

"I'm going to reconnoiter."

"You want company?"

Rio shakes her head. "Make sure they dig in. I'll get . . ." Her eye stops at Jack Stafford. Jack is a cheerful fellow normally, but he looks now to have had all the cheer drained out of him.

If anyone has to get shot . . . well, Jack is a veteran. Jack kills Germans. Whereas Molina has potential that might benefit from experience.

"Molina, you're with me. Leave your pack. Dial and Chester will dig for you."

Molina stands up, using her carbine as a stick, wobbles a bit, but does not complain.

"We're going to recon that hedgerow," Rio explains. "No talking, no bumbling around making noise. And don't fire unless I tell you to."

"Right, Sarge."

They walk down the length of the platoon, passing Cat Preeling who looks up and says, "Off to find another medal, Richlin?"

"Going for a little stroll, see what's in that hedgerow."

"Want company?"

"Nah, Cat, you rest up, you look like crap warmed over."

That earns a genial raised middle finger from Cat, and Rio laughs. For the benefit of any watching Germans she makes as if she's leaving the field, but instead she creeps along in the deep shadow of the right-hand hedge, the one separating the field from the road.

"Safety off," Rio whispers to Molina. "But do not shoot me in the back, I will resent it."

That last comment brings a smile to Rio's lips. It is one of Sergeant Cole's phrases. *I will resent it.* It occurs to her, not for the first time, just how much her job as sergeant involves mimicking Cole or Mackie. Perhaps that's the way it always goes, she thinks. The art of war is learned in the doing, and the new and the untested learn from those who've gone before.

Just as Molina is now copying her moves.

Well . . . good. Molina had a bad start, but she recovered, and now she's showing a willingness to learn. Probably because she embarrassed herself so badly on the beach.

They creep along, stopping to listen every few seconds when Rio raises a fist. There is distant artillery banging away somewhere. Bombers way, way up in the sky, a barely audible buzz. Is that Strand up there? She can't help but wonder, though she is not sure she should care anymore.

Mrs. Strand Braxton, cooking and cleaning house and making sure the children wash behind their ears.

Is that even possible? Even if he still wants her?

Two pictures: herself here, now, with her Thompson at the ready, sneaking around in the dark night of Normandy; and herself in some future life, apron around her waist, face and hair made up, pulling cookies from the oven.

Her father had gone to the Great War while her mother stayed home.

I've become my father rather than my mother.

No wonder Strand is troubled. What man would want to marry a woman who had cut nine notches into the stock of her now-lost rifle? What kind of housewife walked around with a *koummya* strapped to her leg? Was she going to have children and tell them bedtime stories of the time she spent the night shivering in a minefield with Jack Stafford? Would she tell them about Kerwin Cassel and how she had tried to hold the blood inside him and his last word was a simple, "Oh."

Did Mommy kill Germans? Yes, Mommy did.

They reach the far hedgerow and now Rio moves a few steps at a time, stopping to listen, sniffing the breeze for the smell of men hiding. But the only smells are leaves and grass and the oh-so-familiar scent of cows. And the mournful groaning of those beasts is the only sound.

After half an hour she stops and signals to Molina to come closer. "Hedgerow is clear. For now at least."

Molina exhales as if for the first time in a long while.

"Let me ask you, Molina, where are you from?"

"Me? I'm from a little town in northern California, you wouldn't know it."

"Try me."

"It's called Petaluma. We—"

"Petaluma! Hah. Well, I'll be," Rio says fondly. "I know Petaluma well. I'm from Gedwell Falls!"

The two hometowns are just an hour's drive apart.

"Well, gosh, we're practically neighbors," Molina says. Then, feeling she's being overly-familiar, she adds, "Sarge."

"What do your folks do?"

"My father is a farmhand, my mother, well, she takes in wash and bakes pies for a diner."

"Is that so?" Rio says. "I don't suppose you've ever milked a cow? Because those cows are in a bad way. I was thinking, maybe . . . since the hedgerow is clear . . ."

She sees Molina's smile in the dark.

Most of the milk is squirted onto the grass as Rio and Molina squat beneath the cows and perform the job so familiar to both women. But both also fill their helmets with the fresh liquid, and carry the warm, cream-rich goodness back to the squad.

The helmets are passed around like a communion chalice,

and what's left Rio gives to Cat. Molina immediately acquires a nickname: *Milkmaid.* The name could as easily be applied to Rio, but there are some things you don't call your sergeant with the big, scary knife. At least not in her hearing.

And then, the artillery barrage comes, and Rio's squad cringes at the bottom of their freshly-dug holes, praying to their various gods for deliverance, licking cream mustaches from their faces, and thinking of home.

14

"Hey there, short stuff!"

Frangie sits on dry sand with knees raised, head hanging down. Daylight has come in the form of filtered sunlight and intermittent soft rain. She is surrounded by the detritus of battlefield medicine: torn paper packaging from bandages, bloody gauze, syringes, and the discarded weapons and gear of those men and women who had no further use for them.

The field aid station has been set up. Doctors and nurses are ashore. And newer, fresher medics have followed the infantry breakout and are now up past the bluff.

Frangie looks up wearily, wondering who is calling to her and at the same time feeling the vague sense that she knows this voice. Then she breaks out in a wide smile.

"Well, if it isn't Sergeant Walter Green of Iowa," she says.

"Don't get up," he says. "I'll sit."

He's a bit taller than Frangie and quite a bit broader, a young black man with an older face and spectacles that have earned him the nickname Professor. And some new stripes as well.

"They made you a master sergeant?" Frangie wonders.

He flops beside her, turning toward her with unmistakable pleasure, though she's pretty sure she's never looked more of a mess. Her sleeves, lower trouser legs and chest are stiff with dried blood. Her boots are crusted with human excrement. She is covered in sand and dust. There is sand in her socks, her underpants, her bra, her ears, her nose and her mouth.

"You are a sight for sore eyes," Walter says.

"Your eyes must not be working right."

She has the oddest feeling that she should lean forward and hug him. But that is not done, not in the army, not amid the fresh proof of carnage, and in any event not with the restrained, churchgoing Sergeant Green.

"You've been busy," he says, soberly surveying her surroundings.

"I didn't even know you were landing here," Frangie says.

"We weren't. We were supposed to be about half a klick east of here, and instead they landed us two klicks west. We've been pinned down until now." He shakes his head. "What a foul-up."

That is the kindest thing Frangie's heard anyone say about Omaha Beach. Graves registration teams are hauling bodies out of the surf, taking notes, attaching identity tags, lining the bodies up in neat rows for the trucks that will follow. The dead will be sent back out to the ships as space becomes available. And that might be a while because the beach has gone from a scene of battle to a great snorting, rumbling, clanking circus of men and matériel and vehicles. More LSTs and Higgins boats arrive with fresh soldiers, fresh tanks, food, fuel and ammunition.

Out to sea the battle wagons still fire salvos that roar overhead like runaway subway trains, to explode on targets beyond the beach. But the imposing bluff has been taken, the pillboxes flushed out with grenades and bazookas, and the German guns at both ends of the beach have been taken. A gaggle of German prisoners marches past, disarmed and unhappy, guarded by a swaggering, gum-chewing PFC.

Frangie's own LST has been jerry-rigged to allow the battalion's tanks to come ashore. Soon they will form up and head inland and Frangie will follow. Her jeep has survived, as have Manning and Deacon.

"Omaha is FUBAR," Frangie mutters, then winces because within that mordant acronym is a word she can't imagine Walter ever saying.

But Green nods silent agreement. "I'm happy to see you're okay." Then, in a lower voice, like he's saying something improper, adds, "Miss Frangie."

"Likewise. Walter."

Silence falls, and Frangie wonders if it is as comfortable for Walter as it is for her. She has no desire to go anywhere, that will come soon enough. She has no desire to be with anyone at this moment other than Sergeant Walter "Professor" Green.

Of Iowa.

"Wonder how long it'll take for mail to get to us?" Walter wonders.

"You expecting something?"

He dips his head, bashful. "My mother will be sending me her homemade fudge, and some socks." He looks away. "For my birthday."

Frangie laughs. "Birthday boy, huh?"

"June fourth, actually, couple days ago."

"I don't have a gift. Unless you'd like some sulfa powder."

He grins and shakes his head. "Oh, that's okay, Miss Frangie."

She wants to ask him how old he is. He might be a year or two older than she is, but he might also be in his late twenties, or even early thirties. Which really doesn't matter at all, him being just another soldier. Not even slightly her business.

How old is too old?

Too old for what, Francine Marr? Too old for what?

"I reckon mail will catch up in a week or two," Frangie says.

"Mmmm. Yeah, that'd be about right. Do you hear anything from Tulsa?"

He remembers where she's from? Okay, maybe that's not a big deal, maybe he just has a good memory.

"I guess it's all still there where I left it. Obal—my baby brother—has a summer job collecting metal scrap. My dad's still not all-the-way healthy, but I guess he's in less pain. My mother . . ." Her mind goes to her mother and inevitably to what Harder, her big brother, told her about the conditions of his own birth. Images of her mother, practically a child at the time, a newlywed, being held down and raped by white men amid the flames of Tulsa's black neighborhood rise unbidden but hard to dismiss.

Walter waits patiently. Frangie smiles crookedly. "I guess they're all fine. And how is Iowa?"

"A long way away," Green says softly. He jerks his chin. "That's my lieutenant coming. I best stand up and look soldierly."

"A colored officer?"

Green heaves himself up. "Yep. Unfortunately he figures he

176

needs to win the war all by himself. Whatever color, an officer's an officer."

He offers his hand and helps Frangie to her feet.

"Well, I hear there's a war on," Walter says.

"That's the rumor," Frangie says.

For a long, awkward moment they look at each other, and then with a frustrated snort Walter walks away to intercept his lieutenant.

The tank battalion forms up and begins to rattle toward the draw. Rosemary Manning pulls up in the jeep. Deacon is perched on the back, legs dangling.

"You get more two-inch compresses?" Frangie asks.

Manning is a cheerful beanpole, one of those people who through no fault of their own make one think of a fish. Her eyes bulge from a narrow face. "Got it all, Doc."

Frangie swings herself into the passenger seat, twists and surveys her goods as Manning steers in the tracks of the tanks.

White soldiers line the draw, many asleep hunched over, some playing cards or rereading old letters. Frangie is used to hearing at least a few slurs and insults, but these soldiers are exhausted and shaken up, and anyway, it doesn't take a foot soldier long to develop a deep appreciation for any tank with a big white American star, regardless of who is driving it.

Then someone does call out. "Hey, Marr!"

It's Rio's friend, Jenou Castain. She's leaning against a piece of broken concrete and writing in a tattered journal.

Frangie waves. "How you doing?"

"Time of my life," Jenou calls back.

Frangie laughs and they drive on.

"Who's that white girl?" Manning asks.

"Friend of a friend," Frangie says.

Manning glances at her. "You got white friends?"

"One or two."

"On account of you being a medic and all."

"Nah, I met her best friend, Richlin, when we were at basic side by side." She smiles. "We hid in a tree from a wild boar."

Manning clearly finds this hard to believe. "You must be from the north."

"Tulsa, Oklahoma."

"Tulsa! Well, I'll be." Manning frequently says "I'll be," but she has yet to say what she'll be. "You fixing to be a nurse after the war, Doc?" There's a distinct tone of disbelief.

Frangie is not in the mood to have anyone tell her she can't be a doctor. It might be a pipe dream, but it's part of what keeps her going. She deflects. "How about you?"

"Me?" Manning sighs and shifts gears with a grinding sound. "I haven't thought about it. I suppose I'll get married, have maybe three . . . no, four . . . little ones."

"Are you engaged?"

Manning laughs as if this is the funniest question ever. She laughs till tears fill her eyes and she's in danger of driving off the side of the road they have now reached. Finally she says, "Me, engaged?" She shifts gears and the transmission sounds like it's full of gravel. "No. No, no, no. Not yet. Maybe never. I'd like to be, but boys don't like girls taller than them. See, that's your advantage, Doc, if you don't mind me saying so.

There aren't many menfolk shorter than you."

"True enough," Frangie allows, and thinks of Walter who has a few inches on her, but would have to tilt his head back to make eye contact with Manning.

"What you might ought to do is marry that sergeant with the spectacles. Men with glasses are smart, and smart men don't beat on their women."

Has Manning read her mind? "Sergeant Green is just an acquaintance."

Manning is silent for a full minute before finally saying, "If you say so." It comes out singsong.

The column is moving uphill away from the beach and Frangie looks back, seeing just a wedge of Omaha Beach framed by hedges. From this distance she does not see bodies, just a confused mess of trucks and boats and ships. Overhead P-47s, their wings heavy with racks of missiles, zoom by, the whine of their engines a counterpoint to the rumble and clank of the tanks.

The road is paved here, but narrow, made to feel narrower still when they pass through hedges that rise ten feet or more on either side, nearly turning the road into a tunnel. The column stops and starts every few minutes, but they are off the beach, and definitely in France.

"I suspect we are part of history," Frangie says, meaning it as a self-deprecating remark.

"Oh, I don't have to suspect," Manning says. "This is the biggest thing this old girl has ever been even close to. Before this the biggest thing I ever did was come in second in the third grade spelling bee."

"What tripped you up?"

Manning's long fingers tighten on the steering wheel, and she glares. "Prestidigitation. It means something like a magic trick." She looks sharply at Frangie. "Can you spell it?"

"I don't think I'll try," Frangie says. She's wondering how much conversation she can manage with Manning. Wondering if she should cut it off. But Frangie does not have the capacity to ignore someone, and Manning is looking at her instead of the road, so Frangie says, "P-r-e-s-d—"

"Hah! It's 't.' P-r-e-s-t-i-d-i-g-i-t-a-t-i-o-n. You'd have missed it too. Well, I'll be. How about you, Deacon?"

"All I can spell is tired," Deacon says. "T-i-r-e-d. I can use it in a sentence if you want."

Up ahead, far up the column, an explosion. Frangie fidgets, not sure what to do, not sure what her duty is. But no call comes for a medic, and after a few minutes the column begins clanking forward again. They come to an area where the narrow path between hedges opens up into a low-lying field. And there she sees the Sherman with its left tread spooled off and a smoke scar up the side.

"Anyone hurt?" she asks a sergeant.

"Nah. Fool went driving off into a minefield. Just lost a tread."

The column moves on and whatever slight relaxation Frangie had begun to feel is gone now. Mines. This innocent, late spring landscape is not innocent at all.

They rattle on for ten more minutes when louder explosions, and more, one after another, *boom! boom! boom!* echo back from the front of the column.

Frangie's jeep is trapped between overbearing hedges on either side, the rear end of a belching Sherman ahead, and the press of men and vehicles coming off the beach behind. They are boxed in.

Machine guns ahead, speaking two different languages, the zipper of a German MG 42 spitting twelve hundred rounds per minute, and the answering American Browning .50 calibers, firing at half the rate. Smoke rises into the sky.

There's more artillery, then a big, metallic *CLANG!* as something hits steel plate armor. Frangie's view is almost completely blocked but she sees fire and flying debris. Then a Sherman fires, reminding Frangie of a tobacco-chewer spitting angrily. A second later the tank shell explodes on its target.

A file of GIs comes running past, infantry, their rifles held at port arms. Soon she hears machine gun and rifle fire.

It's half an hour of sitting in her hedge-and-steel enclosure before the column moves again, and this time they pass a destroyed Sherman. Its turret lies in a hedge, trapped by the tight-woven branches. The rest of the tank burns and smokes.

There's a medic tending a wounded man in a ditch and Frangie calls to him. "Need a hand?"

The medic waves her on. "Superficial."

"What about that crew?" she asks, indicating the burning tank.

"No help for those boys," the medic says darkly.

Again the column advances between the hedges, the hedges so thick, so dense, that they somehow were only partly crushed by the full weight of a tank turret.

At a wide spot in the road the Shermans squeeze aside to let a jeep with a white major rush past. Ahead Frangie can just glimpse a church tower indicating a village.

The column lurches back to life and motors on.

"When do we get out of these hedges?" Manning wonders aloud.

P-38s are in the air, three of them arcing toward the barely-glimpsed village. More sounds of explosions, more columns of smoke.

They come to a crossroads, where the hedges retreat a little, allowing Frangie to breathe. She'd been almost holding her breath in the claustrophobic confines. Four tanks now peel off from the main column and head down a side road, racing along at speed in the open.

A battalion runner comes back along the line, his jeep dipping into ditches to squeeze by. The driver spots Frangie and pulls up. "Captain says maybe a medico ought to go with Sergeant Washington's detail and—"

The next part is obliterated by the shriek of falling artillery.

"Fug!" the runner yells and leaps from his car. Frangie, Manning and Deacon are right behind him, as are the men who've been riding on the outside of the tanks. She lands in a wet ditch and hugs weeds as shells explode all around the intersection.

The tanks break for cover, some veering down one road, some down the other, some powering straight ahead.

Shells rain down for five minutes—a very long five minutes.

The cries of "Medic!" rise in the ensuing silence. Frangie grabs her bags and runs.

15

They follow the train tracks, Philippe in the lead, Marie close behind him, Rainy bringing up the rear.

Rainy goes over the facts again in her head. Étienne, Wickham and Marie had been together, tasked with creating a diversion. Wickham and Étienne are apparently dead, Marie alive and only slightly hurt. Rainy had heard two bursts of Sten gun fire. There had been no sound of German weapons.

Étienne, Wickham and Marie. But only two, Wickham and Marie, had Sten guns, Étienne had a pistol and grenades. So the shooting was either from Wickham or Marie. It is extremely unlikely—unlikely to the point of absurdity—that the British flyer would have been the traitor.

A burst of Sten gun fire, a pause, a second burst.

The first would have killed Wickham. Then a pause as Marie pleaded with Étienne to join her. And, when he refused or perhaps even drew his pistol, the second burst.

There was no escaping the obvious conclusion: Marie had killed both men.

Marie was a traitor.

Now what do I do?

The sensible if ruthless thing would be to draw her Walther and shoot Marie in the back of the head. Philippe was obviously sweet on her, maybe even in love, and she couldn't count on him to do the job. Or even be certain that he would understand.

It would be an act of charity for her to do it.

Right now.

But the rational part of Rainy is having trouble with every other part of her. She is jazzed, keyed-up, jumpy and nervous. The gun battle, the massive explosions that still rock the night, it all leaves her feeling unreal, feeling a little bit crazy. She thinks she's right, but she isn't sure her brain is working right.

And she isn't sure that she is an assassin.

How the hell has it come to this? She is meant to be sneaking around and reporting on movements of the Das Reich, and instead she's very likely to be picked up by the Gestapo or the SD, even as she debates executing one of their collaborators.

Her hand reaches beneath her coat, touches the butt of her pistol, and suddenly Philippe calls a halt. There's a railway signalman's shed where the track splits. Philippe pushes in, fumbles and finds a lantern, and strikes a light.

"Let's have a rest, eh?" Philippe says. In the harsh light his face looks grim. "What do you think, Marie, shall we rest?"

Rainy does not think it is time to rest. Not at all. In fact, it's insane. They are still on the railroad tracks. The Germans will follow the tracks as soon as they can get a handful of men together. They have maybe twenty minutes.

But Marie agrees with Philippe. "Yes, let's rest here."

Marie takes the only chair, lays her Sten gun aside, puts her hands over her face and cries quietly.

"I am very sorry for Étienne," Philippe says.

Marie nods.

"It must have been very hard," Philippe says quietly.

Marie starts to answer, but hears something in his tone. Rainy hears the same thing.

Philippe goes to Marie and touches her cheek. "Tell me," he says. "Tell me how they turned you."

"Turned . . . what are you . . ."

Philippe says, "Lieutenant Jones, do you believe we should stop here for a rest?"

"No."

"Why?"

"Because the tracks lead straight to us."

Philippe points at Rainy. "You see? It is obvious. And yet, Marie, you go along."

Whap!

Philippe slaps Marie hard across the cheek, hard enough to start blood dribbling from her nose. "Traitor! Collaborator! Tell me how they got to you."

Marie tries innocence. "I don't know what you're talking about! Why have you struck me?"

Philippe, overcome by emotion, turns away. Rainy says, "You killed them both, Marie. You shot Wickham, and when you couldn't convince Étienne, you shot him. Your own brother."

"He was a bastard!" Marie cries with shocking venom. "My

brother! Hah! If you knew . . . Forever sneaking around to look at me in the bathtub!"

It is a confession, however much Marie wishes to cloud things with accusations.

Marie makes a quick grab for the Sten, but Philippe knocks it to the floor, and now the Walther is in Rainy's hand.

Rainy looks at Philippe. He has recovered somewhat. Now the maquis fighter is back. Now he wants and needs to know how Marie was recruited, by whom, and how many others in the organization are also turned.

"He is going to marry me," Marie says defiantly.

"Marry you? Who?"

"My *Sturmbannführer*," Marie says, spitting it defiantly. "He owns a castle in Germany, his family is very rich! When the war is over we will be married."

"A *Sturmbannführer*?" Philippe demands. His voice cracks. "That's an SS rank. You've been sleeping with an SS officer?"

Marie, desperate, tries to turn things around. "This one." She stabs a finger at Rainy. "Do you know what she is? She is a Jew! Look at her, she is a dirty Jew! Her true name is probably Cohen or Silberstein. She does the bidding of the English Zionists, a Jew bitch bringing war and destruction to our countrymen, Philippe!"

Philippe looks helplessly at Rainy. Their eyes meet, and both know what must happen. They are on the run, easily-exposed, and after blowing up the fuel dump there will be no mercy from the Germans.

And no more time.

"I cannot," Philippe whispers, pleading with Rainy.

Marie's eyes go wide. "What are you talking about? Do you . . . are you proposing to murder me? My God, Philippe, have you lost your mind? The invasion will fail! Dieter told me himself, the Atlantic Wall cannot be breached. And what then, Philippe. What then when the English and the Americans have been thrown into the sea? The Germans will come for your family, my family . . ."

"I . . ." Philippe's eyes are filled with tears. "I cannot . . ."

Rainy nods. She feels as if her body has been replaced by a cold, marble statue. She can barely force the words out through a jaw clenched so tightly her teeth might crack. She wants to throw up. She wants to yell, *It's all a mistake, all a terrible joke, I'm going home to New York, to my room, to my things, to my mother and father, to my brother, to the world where people do not kill each other.* In a choked, grating voice she says, "Why don't you take a look outside and have a smoke, Philippe."

"What? What are you talking about, you fools? Are you mad?"

"No," Philippe says dully, a man trapped in a nightmare. "I am French."

He rushes to the door and disappears into the night.

Marie turns her lovely face, now streaked with tears, to Rainy. "I can save you. I can tell Dieter you helped me to escape!"

"And will you tell him also that I am a dirty Jew?"

"You cannot hurt me, you . . . You cannot . . . No! No!" She rises from her chair, hands like claws ready to scratch at Rainy.

Rainy says, "Don't worry, I'm not going to kill you. Relax."

Marie relaxes back into her chair and sighs heavily. There is even the slight curl of a smile at the corner of her lips.

Rainy says, "It's not Cohen or Silberstein, mademoiselle. It's Schulterman."

She raises the Walther and fires once. *Bang!* A neat round hole appears as if by magic in the center of Marie's forehead. She slumps to the floor.

Rainy stands trembling over the body. The sound of the shot, magnified by the close quarters, seems to echo on and on. But the sound of the shot will not carry to the Germans, not from within the shed.

"No other way," Rainy whispers to herself. At her feet the body of the pretty young Frenchwoman releases its urine and feces. Blood forms a pool in the shape of a leaf.

No other way.

She finds Philippe outside, smoking and weeping silently. "I loved her," he says.

"Let's get out of here."

She leads the way, following the tracks that Philippe has assured her will take them close to his old home town where he can hope to find shelter for them.

They hear the German patrol long before it reaches them. But the voices are not speaking German—more pressed, unmotivated eastern Europeans who dutifully follow the tracks through the forest but do not bother to patrol through the trees where Rainy and Philippe silently watch them pass. Had they been SS the search would have been far more efficient.

Dawn shows pink before Philippe speaks again.

"It had to be done," he says.

"Yes."

"This war is cruel."

"Yes."

"We cannot reach Oradour during daylight," he says. "We will have to sleep rough."

Rainy nods, though she is not at all sure she can sleep. The image of a small round hole in a girl's forehead will follow her for many days. Perhaps for the rest of her life.

This war is cruel.

"Is it true that you are a Jew?"

Rainy nods.

Philippe looks pained. "I am sorry for . . . Well. You understand. Some people listen to the voices of the Church or Vichy when they speak of Jews."

Rainy is about to say that she isn't much of a Jew, that she does not attend shul, rarely goes to temple, and does not keep kosher. But the words won't come. There are times to draw distinctions between the Orthodox true believers and the more liberal, more secular Jews. But Nazi-occupied France is not the place, and mere hours after she has executed a Jew-hating collaborator is not the time. In the world of the Nazis and their allies, there is no distinction between this sort of Jew and that sort of Jew.

It is as simple to the Nazis as black and white: Jew or not Jew.

How terrible, Rainy thinks, that her religion, her tribe, had never been as meaningful to her as it is now. She'd never denied her background; she just didn't really care. She'd seen herself as above ancient tribalism. She'd seen herself as perhaps part of, but not defined by, her nominal faith. All her grandmother's stories of pogroms in Poland, all the casual antiSemitism to be encountered in America, all the Stars of David given to her at birthdays, the rituals of Yom Kippur and Passover, the eye-rolling repetition of, "Next year in Jerusalem," none of it had made her really care, none of it had made her lock her fate to that of her people, or even to think of Jews as 'her people.'

But that was done. That was over. Jew or not Jew?

Jew.

"I never was much of a Jew," she says at last. "The war . . . the Nazis . . ."

Philippe sighs. "I never was much of a Frenchman. But the war . . . the Nazis . . ."

Tears come to blur Rainy's sight. She's not a person who cries, and doesn't want to be seen to cry, so she stays behind him, choking off sobs that threaten to worsen, to get out of control.

The grisly killings at the café, the cold-blooded execution of Marie, the terrible memories of captivity . . . She knows now, deep down in her bones, that there is no going back, no erasing or forgetting. These things will be with her as long as she lives, and they are so huge, so overpoweringly sad and wrong and yet necessary that she knows her mind will be chewing over each act forever. She knows that she will never again be who she once was.

Rainy Schulterman, clever young girl with lots of ideas, Rest In Peace.

So much lost.

They walk deeper into the woods. The leaves drip and the pine needles squish under their feet but heat is rising and with it humidity. It's going to be a long, hot day.

Rainy is in no way an outdoorsy type and instinctively dislikes the woods. But Philippe finds a fallen log and they stretch out on it, and exhaustion carries Rainy quickly to sleep. She wakes after only a few hours when her stomach rumbles. Her mouth and throat are parched. She manages a few hours of on-and-off sleep until Philippe also wakes.

"I don't suppose you brought us breakfast?" Philippe says.

"No, and I'm starving. A glass of water would be nice too."

"That at least I can provide. The river is just . . ." He looks around, peers up at the sun for direction, and points.

Sure enough the river is only a ten-minute walk. It's a narrow stream, no more than a dozen feet across, the banks thick with trees and bushes crowding in to reach the water. Rainy pushes through and kneels by the river, drinking her fill.

"We can follow the river if you don't mind brambles." Philippe glances skeptically at her shoes.

"I never thought I'd miss combat boots," Rainy says. "Where's this river go?"

"Why to Oradour, of course. This is the River Glane."

They follow the Glane as Rainy's shoes slowly come apart. She tears her coat—a burden anyway in the stifling heat—into strips and binds them around shoes and feet, which helps somewhat, but makes stepping over branches and pushing through thickets even harder.

After a very long walk, a break to eat a few berries they pick along the way, and more walking, Philippe ducks down and motions Rainy to do the same. He points and she sees a thin filament snaking from an unseen bank out into the river.

"Someone is fishing."

They creep closer and then Philippe says, "It's Bernard! He's a boy from my village."

"Can you trust him?"

"I trust no one anymore," he says sharply. Then, softening, "But Bernard is playing hooky from school, it seems. He will find us food for fear I will tell his mother, who is a holy terror. And, who knows, he may have fish. *Holà!* Bernard!"

Bernard turns out to be an eleven-year-old boy with a round head and close-cropped mouse-brown hair. And yes, he has fish. And he has cleverly brought along a ham sandwich, which Philippe appropriates in the name of the maquis.

Bernard mourns the loss of two of his fish, and the sandwich, but he's a lively boy with a conspiratorial air about him, and clearly hiding in the woods with fugitive maquis is more fun than doing multiplication tables in school.

"How far are we from the village?" Philippe asks him. "It's been a long time since I wandered this river."

"Oh, it's just there," Bernard says, waving vaguely.

"Have you happened to see Monsieur *et* Madame Gilles?" Philippe winces a little, recognizing that he has just revealed his true last name to Rainy.

"Your maman and papa? Of course! How can I not see the headmaster? Or his wife?"

"It seems you do quite a good job of not seeing the headmaster when you prefer to go fishing," Philippe says. "But tell me: are they well?"

"Of course, monsieur. Only . . . well, everyone is afraid of what the Boche will do. Because of the invasion. They must be very angry. And . . ." He lowers his voice. "You heard what happened in Tulle?"

"No, what?"

Bernard makes a throat-cutting gesture. "The SS. They hanged a hundred men. They say it was because of the maquis."

"Retaliation? My God, are you sure? A hundred men? There are no hundred maquis in Tulle, there are not a hundred maquis in the Limousin!"

Bernard gives a worldly shrug. "I don't think the Germans care. They are simply angry."

Philippe shakes his head. "We cannot go into the village, it would give the Germans an excuse."

Rainy sags. She'd been hoping for sleep and a meal. She'd been hoping to join up with more *maquisards*, to get back to her uncompleted mission. Her legs are a network of fine scratches. Her shoes are bundles of rags. Every muscle aches. And there is a deeper weariness of the spirit.

Bernard snaps his fingers. "You know old Brun's cabin?"

"Is it still standing?"

"Of course! They took Brun for the forced labor, so he is gone, but the cabin is still there as he left it." The boy grins. "You know old Brun. No one wants to anger him! He has a shotgun!"

"You must tell no one, Bernard," Philippe says. "No one at all. Not your parents, not your friends. No one. Not a word!"

Bernard makes a cross over his mouth.

And Rainy realizes that her life is now in the hands of a mischievous boy. But at least he isn't sleeping with a German officer.

"Show us," she says.

The cabin is nicer than Rainy expects. To start with it has furniture, an actual table and chairs, a mildewed sofa, and one low bed, also mildewed. There is a small kitchen area that seemingly relies on a wood-burning fireplace. And there is an outhouse. No hot shower, but joy of joys, there is a day's worth of canned food. The cabin is dry enough, as long as you don't count the corner where a leaky roof has caused the floor to discolor and buckle. And it is just up a wooded slope from the River Glane, so there is plenty of drinking water.

"Maybe we should just sit out the war here," Rainy says.

Bernard flops contentedly on the sofa, reveling in his role as fixer for Philippe and Rainy. Philippe goes out to gather firewood.

"You're a clever boy," Rainy says. "So you know that if you say anything to anyone, there is a very good chance your friend Philippe would be arrested, perhaps shot?"

Bernard nods solemnly. "Why are you here? Are you a spy? I didn't know women could be spies."

Rainy hesitates. Her life is already in Bernard's hands. He surely knows she is not French, and he seems bright enough to guess that she is either British or American.

"I'm here looking for German tanks."

"I don't know where they are," Bernard says. "I only know where they *were*."

Rainy blinks. "I'm sorry, did you just . . ."

"I have seen many tank tread marks. Not far from here."

"Can you show us?"

"Tomorrow, in the morning before school?"

"Okay," Rainy says, thinking it can't be this easy. Then again, this mission could hardly be described as easy so far. "Tomorrow, *before* school."

After Bernard leaves, Rainy warms canned soup for herself and Philippe. It is a glum meal, interrupted twice, once when they hear a dog barking, and a second time when they hear loud engines, which turn out to be Luftwaffe planes overhead.

Rainy takes the sofa—she's smaller than Philippe—but has a hard time sleeping.

It is the endless replays that keep her awake. Again and again she runs through the events at the café. What could she have done differently? What mistakes were made? Why had she not suspected earlier that Marie was a problem? Had she missed clues? Had it all been inevitable? Had there not been a way to avoid that small round hole?

Philippe's voice comes from the dark. "You should sleep."

"I know."

After a pause, he adds, "It was necessary. You did what was necessary."

"I know."

Another long pause, then, "You are a soldier, as I am."

"Soldiers do not kill unarmed girls in cold blood. I was an executioner."

He sighs. "Tomorrow you will be a soldier again. And some day when this is all over you will be a woman. You will be married and have children."

"And you'll be a man with a wife and children," Rainy says. "And neither of us will ever speak to them about this day."

"No," Philippe admits. "We will not."

Bernard is true to his word . . . mostly. He reappears early, but very definitely during what should have been the school day, unless French children went to school in midmorning. Philippe chides him, but it is clear from the way he goes about it that a young Philippe Gilles had once ditched the exact same school to run in these same woods.

Bernard brings a whole baguette broken in two for easier carrying, and a wedge of cow's milk cheese with a wrinkly, chalky rind. They wolf this meal down and then set out with Bernard. The boy moves through the woods like an animal born and bred in the forest, dodging brambles, leaping fallen logs and tiny streams. Even city-bred Rainy has to smile at the leggy kid in the gray smock and short shorts, who snatches berries and pops them in his mouth, chatting all the while about his friends, about a hunting trip with his uncle, about how much he despises girls—though not mademoiselle (meaning Rainy) because she is not a girl, she is a spy.

Philippe's talk of marriage and children has Rainy watching the boy through different eyes. Her big brother Aryeh, a marine, has a child, not that Rainy (or Aryeh) has seen much of her. But Rainy can imagine, just barely, a world with a Manhattan version of Bernard, a smart kid who knows his way around the subway and alleyways, and looks a little like Rainy.

It's easier than trying to picture a husband for herself. She's only ever been on one real date, and that was with a boy named Halev, who she barely knew. And she has to laugh at the notion that the son of an Orthodox tailor would be interested in settling down with the sort of woman who kills people.

In her imagination now she is being questioned by her future, imaginary Bernard, her son or daughter.

Couldn't you have just tied her up, Mom?

Couldn't you have convinced her . . .

In her imagination this unformed, faceless child, *her* child, looks at her with a solemn expression. Rainy imagines a sense of betrayal. She imagines the pitiless eyes of a child judging her, trying to absorb the fact that *Mommy shot a girl.*

My life will be either lonely or a series of lies.

Some day if she finds her way back to safety she will be debriefed by Colonel Herkemeier. He will understand. He may even approve. But even he will never see Rainy the same way again.

The scarlet letter, like the book she'd read in high school. A scarlet letter *A*, but not for adulterer.

A for assassin.

They reach a clearing, which upon closer inspection is a firebreak, an unpaved path cut through the woods. There Bernard points triumphantly at the ground.

There is only one thing that leaves tracks like this: a tank. Many tanks, in fact, because the ground is chewed up all the way along the firebreak.

"Go home now," Philippe tells Bernard. But Bernard is not so easily gotten rid of. So they decide to pass as a family out hunting for berries and mushrooms, father, mother, and son. Of course Rainy would have had to be a very, very young mother, but the ruse is the best they can do. And at a distance they might look innocent enough.

They follow the tracks for a mile, and it is early afternoon when they begin to see signs of more activity, stacks of jerry cans, discarded empty crates, cigarette butts. They stop and duck into the woods upon spotting a German half-track, obviously broken down, with two shirtless German soldiers working on the engine.

They take a long detour around the half-track and come to a road. They rest by the side of the road, well back in the trees, and try to ignore rumbling stomachs and the fact that they have picked up fleas along the way. Rainy scratches her legs leaving tiny blood trails from fleabites.

Philippe says, "They must have a company based nearby. I can guess where. There's a—"

He falls silent at the sound of engines. Engines and clanking treads.

The first vehicles to appear are two motorcycles with sidecars, followed by a line of half-tracks and trucks. Rainy watches from her concealment, dutifully noting details: the stenciled numbers on the sides of half-tracks, the condition of the vehicles, the mood—insofar as it is possible to guess based on smiling versus worried faces.

Definitely Waffen SS, she notes with satisfaction. She has found part of the Das Reich division. Just a column, but it may yield greater finds.

Coming up last, trailing the column, comes an open staff car. An SS *Sturmbannführer*, the equivalent of a major (Marie's alleged castle-owning Nazi?) is the main occupant. He's a whippet-thin, good-looking, youngish man with a wide grin who wears his cap at a rakish angle.

Philippe breathes, "That is Adolf Diekmann, ambitious and vicious."

Rainy stares intently at the SS officer. The enemy. What goes on inside a mind like that? What turns a handsome man, a man who by the look of him had every privilege, into a Nazi? The question seems to have new urgency now.

Moving through the woods they keep pace with the column which is moving in fits and starts, thanks to an overturned hay wagon blocking a small bridge. Just beyond the bridge is an intersection. And that is when Philippe urgently grabs Rainy's arm.

"What is it?"

"The road they're taking . . ."

"Yes?"

"It goes to my village. It goes to Oradour."

16

They run through the woods, tripping, faces whipped by low branches, gasping for air, Bernard leading the way. The path through the woods is shorter than the road, but they are not half-tracks, they cannot run at thirty or forty miles an hour. By the time they arrive, panting like racehorses, the Germans are drawn up at the edge of town.

Bernard, without a word of explanation, ducks through a bush, and disappears out the other side.

"He's going to see the excitement," Philippe says. "Most likely the Germans are conducting a search. Perhaps for maquis, but there are no maquis in Oradour, there never have been!"

Philippe leads them to a spot in the woods just beside the river which in this area is thickly overgrown on both banks. "Are you afraid of heights?"

Rainy shakes her head, no, and Philippe begins climbing a tree with the ease of familiarity. Rainy joins him thirty feet up, resting in a crotch between branches, with Philippe standing on the branch and shading his eyes. The sun is high and very hot.

Oradour looks like any number of villages Rainy saw in Italy, a village of stone houses beside matching stone shops, all intermingled so the school for girls is beside a garage, and a café might be cheek-by-jowl with a barrel-maker. Most of the town extends just a few blocks along a single street. Newish tram tracks glow in the sun. An ancient church anchors the end of town nearest the river, furthest from where the Germans are forming up.

There are people in the street, children playing, mothers carrying babies, an old woman scolding a little girl, a young couple walking arm in arm, an old man pushing a wheelbarrow, a line of mostly men at the tobacconist.

"It's tobacco ration day," Philippe observes. "This may be an advantage. After the Boche search and go away we will be safe going into town to buy food. And I can visit my parents."

"Shouldn't a search be done by the *milice*? Or at least garrison troops? Those are Waffen SS *Panzergrenadiers*."

Philippe has no answer. Then, voice dropping in worry, he says, "They're sending out flankers. I think . . . they're encircling the village."

Rainy's heart sinks. If the SS throw up a cordon around the town they may well come right through this spot. They stay silent, hugging the tree trunk, grateful for the spring foliage that is their camouflage. Soon they hear spoken German, laughing and loud tramping. The SS cordon is forming behind them, at least five hundred feet back. They relax their postures slightly, but keep to the lowest of whispers.

"Do you see them?" Rainy says. She rises cautiously, turns carefully, holding onto branches lest her rag-shoes slip. She catches a glimpse of a uniform. Maybe it's more like three hundred feet.

"Look!" Philippe hisses, pointing.

Rainy sees a file of German troops now advancing at a quick walk into town, jaunty on the downhill slope. The residents stop and stare, but don't seem overly-afraid. One of the soldiers ducks into a pastry shop and emerges with a fistful of brioches. A playful tussle breaks out as fellow soldiers try to grab one.

Now come the sounds of Germans shouting orders, some in the German tongue, some in hard-edged French. They are ordering the residents to gather on the fairground so they can search the village. The term *fairground* is perhaps a bit grand for the space involved, which Rainy can see only as a bright, narrow wedge between rooftops.

"Normal when a village is searched," Philippe says, but he sounds as if he's trying to make himself believe it.

Time passes. The heat is stifling now in midafternoon, though it is surely more bearable up amid the leaves of the tree than down on the fairground. Rainy's legs begin to cramp. A bicycle comes rolling down the main street of Oradour, passing into and out of shadows, the cyclist seemingly unaware.

"My God, it's my father!" Philippe says a bit too loudly for Rainy's taste. She glances in the direction of the German encirclement and sees nothing but a wisp of cigarette smoke.

In the town a German soldier grabs the arm of Philippe's father and hauls him off his bike. He appears to be protesting, but the German gives him a shove toward the assembly and he is lost to view. His bike is left in the road, and it is that fact that causes Rainy's heart to pound faster. Germans are orderly people, not the sort to leave a bicycle in the middle of the street.

Not normally.

German soldiers can be seen pushing in doors and often emerging with booty—women's dresses, bottles of wine, a small, intricately-carved wooden end table. These they stack in the street or carry away to the trucks.

A group of people comes into view, a hundred, maybe two hundred, all men, all being driven away from the fairground. They are hurried along by soldiers who still laugh and saunter as if this is nothing but a rather dull way to spend a brilliant Saturday afternoon.

A second group emerges heading in the other direction. These are all women and children. They are shepherded toward the church.

A half dozen soldiers come from the direction of the trucks, carrying two machine guns, chatting as they go.

On the main street the group of men is divided into smaller groups of twenty or thirty each, and marched away by soldiers. It is then that Rainy spots Bernard being furtively pushed away by an older man who keeps pointing toward the church. A German intervenes, pulls Bernard by the collar and kicks him in the backside. Bernard slinks toward the church.

"Thank God," Rainy whispers.

The older man—perhaps Bernard's father—watches the boy leave and makes the sign of the cross over his chest. Rainy sees others doing the same. She quickly loses sight of most of the groups of men, but she sees the group with Bernard's father and ... yes, Philippe's father as well ... as they are directed into a barn.

"No," Philippe whispers.

Three German soldiers begin to set up a machine gun.

"But why?" Philippe cries.

The machine gun opens up. Cries of pain and outrage float on the air between bursts. The firing goes on and on, and now from other parts of the village come answering machine guns, firing and firing.

B-r-r-r-r-r-t! B-r-r-r-r-r-t! B-r-r-r-r-r-t!

The men of Oradour are being murdered.

Philippe is listening to the sounds of his own father being killed. He is as still as if he were a painting, a handsome young Frenchman standing in a tree while his father is gunned down within hearing.

And he can do nothing.

B-r-r-r-r-r-t! B-r-r-r-r-r-t! B-r-r-r-r-r-t!

At least, Rainy thinks, Bernard is safe with the women and children in the great stone church. Even the SS wouldn't murder women and children. Certainly not in a church.

On and on the machine guns fire and Philippe weeps openly, sagging to his knees on the hard branch. Rainy grabs his shoulder, afraid he will fall.

The church is much nearer, right in plain sight though they have a side-on view of the front door. From within the church Rainy hears cries of anguish, questions, *Why, why?* Wailing voices, crying babies, women crying, *My Pierre. My Joseph. My Thomas. My Charles.*

They know, the women, they know even if the children do not yet understand, the women know their husbands and fathers and brothers, their uncles and cousins, their friends, their neighbors are being massacred.

B-r-r-r-r-t! B-r-r-r-r-r-t! B-r-r-r-r-r-t!

The Germans have set up a machine gun outside the church door, in the middle of the small plaza where no doubt the congregation gathers to exchange news on Sunday mornings after mass.

Then Rainy sees two Germans carry a box with cords dangling from it into the church, and now the cries of fear come louder, more frantic, *Pourquoi, pourquoi?*

Why? Why?

The four Germans come rushing back out of the church and just behind them comes the first black smoke.

"They're burning them," Philippe says. "My God, they're going to burn them!"

Cries become screams, louder when those inside the smoke-choked church push open the door.

And when the church door opens, and the first women, many with children in their arms, or held by the hand, come rushing out of the smoke, the Germans open fire.

B-r-r-r-r-r-t! B-r-r-r-r-r-t! B-r-r-r-r-r-t!

Smoke rolls out of the church door, skimming above a rapidly growing pile of dead. Dead women. Dead children. Babies, crying, screeching, suddenly silenced as a machine-gun bullet finds them and ends their lives.

Dead in a pile of dead at the door of God's house.

The windows of the church blow out, glass tinkling on stones, as the fire grows and the women and children climb over the bodies of their neighbors only to be ripped apart and join the pile themselves. Flames lick upward through the door, through windows.

And still the Germans fire, and reload, and fire again, pouring lead into women and children choking on smoke.

It is a long time before the firing stops and the last screams are silenced. A long time until the German soldiers, some looking down and rushing as though in a hurry to put the day's massacre behind them, others sauntering, laughing, carrying stolen goods, set about the job of annihilating the village itself, tossing incendiary grenades through windows and doors. And as the last of them piles aboard their trucks, the village is engulfed in smoke and flame.

From their treetop perch Rainy and Philippe watch, hoping somehow to see life, to see a man or a woman or a child emerge.

Roofs collapse in showers of sparks.

"I must see," Philippe says.

Rainy knows it's a bad idea. She also knows there is nothing she can say to stop him. They climb down together, and Philippe leads the way to a small footbridge. They dip scarves in the water and tie them over their mouths and noses against the smoke, like bandits. They cross the river into a scene of manmade hell. The village is aflame. Smoke is thick, penetrating their damp scarves and making them choke and cough. The smell of burning wood, burning fabric, burning furniture, burning bodies is sickening. Fire and smoke are everywhere.

"My father," Philippe says as if explanation is needed, as he races up the slope to the barn. Here the roof has collapsed, spreading broken tiles over a mass of perhaps two dozen bodies. The clothing of the dead singes and catches fire, and quickly burns out. It is the flesh, the human fat, that burns longer.

Rainy puts a hand on Philippe's shoulder. He shakes it off. He wishes no comfort. No comfort is possible.

Half blind from smoke, eyes swimming with tears, they walk back with dread-slowed steps to the church. Here the roof still burns, but has not yet fallen. They kick their way through machine-gun brass that tinkles merrily on the cobblestones. They cannot enter without climbing over dead bodies, bodies not yet stiff, bodies that sag and slide and force Rainy to her knees, steadying herself with a hand pressed down on a bloody face.

They see inside.

"Oh, God," Rainy cries. "Oh, God. Oh, God."

Here there is no pile of two dozen. Here are hundreds. Hundreds of women and children. A baby, less than a year old stares up at Rainy, its blue eyes open, its body pierced and torn apart by bullets, like a rag doll a mad dog has taken as a plaything. An old woman lies atop a child of six, her arms frozen in a futile attempt to protect him. A woman sits against one wall, her dress burned away to reveal flesh that is red and black.

Somewhere in the gruesome tangle of bodies lies Bernard. Rainy searches for his face, but soon gives up. What is she hoping for? Does she want to see the lively little boy dead? Does she want to see those mischievous eyes staring blankly up at her?

Philippe calls out, "Is anyone alive? Does anyone still live?"

His answer comes when the roof begins to collapse in sections. No. No one still lives in the church at Oradour-sur-Glane.

Their faces black with smoke they retreat to the river's edge. Philippe collapses on the ground, head in his hands, weeping.

"I have to leave," Rainy says dully.

"Why? For what? What is the point anymore?"

"I have to track the division. I have to report back on their movements."

"I cannot." He shrugs helplessly and looks with devastated eyes back toward his home town.

"I know," she says.

"I must . . . someone must . . ."

"I know."

He nods acceptance. "You have your duty."

"Yes," she says.

My duty to track the Das Reich. My duty to report back. My duties as a soldier.

And my duty: to find Adolf Diekmann, the smiling SS monster in the command car, and kill him.

Assassin?

She will wear the word easily if she finds him.

17

"It's like we're back in Italy, Cap'n," Stick says to Captain Passey. He and the rest of the sergeants, along with the lieutenant platoon leaders of Passey's company, have been called together for what Passey called a "skull session."

"How so, Stick?"

"Well, there we'd take a German defensive line, and there was another right behind it. Here it's the hedgerows. We take one and in the next field we're starting all over from scratch."

Passey nods. It is clear to Rio that the captain puts more stock in Dain Sticklin than in most of his officers which, in her opinion, speaks highly of Passey's good sense. The lieutenants are mostly ninety-day wonders, young men and women of little to no experience and not all that much book-learning either.

Rio's division, the 119th, has been spared the protracted battles for Cherbourg and the Cotentin peninsula. And the British forces are taking on Caen. Which leaves the 119th slogging through the bocage, as the French call this countryside.

After days of fighting in the bocage, Rio has learned some lessons, and she hasn't lost any more soldiers. Cat has had two killed, one by friendly fire from a P-38 Lightning, and she's in a very un-Cat-like funk, saying nothing, just scowling.

"That may be," Passey says. "But I want to know how we're going to advance. We're taking too many casualties and going way too slow."

Rio knows—as everyone now does—that while the landing is a success and the beachhead is secure for now, forward progress is slow, very slow, with her platoon often doing nothing in the course of a day but fighting its way across a single field to take a single hedgerow. At this rate they'll be in Berlin about the time Rio is ready for a rocking chair.

Stick says, "The people are behaving well, for the most part. But they still can't get the idea of marching fire. And they will still hit the ground every time they hear a loud noise."

"The Kraut is counting on it," Lieutenant Horne says, perhaps feeling that his platoon sergeant is taking up too much of Passey's attention. "They fire a shot, everyone yells 'sniper!' they all hit the dirt, and once they're laid out flat, in come the mortars or the 88s."

"Yep." A lieutenant from another platoon agrees, nodding vigorously. "They got MGs at the corners of every field, antitank guns, riflemen in the hedges, artillery support and when all else fails they roll a Tiger up on us."

"We need—" Rio starts, before quickly silencing herself because none of the other three-stripers are speaking up.

"Go ahead, Richlin," Passey says. She's acquired some standing with Passey since the breakout from the beach. Passey had shown skepticism about the women under his command, but he's more interested in winning than in playing favorites.

"Well, sir, the best thing I've seen so far is this Sherman with a bulldozer blade on the front," Rio says, feeling like the only child in a room of adults. "It can push straight through a hedgerow, which means we don't have to come in through gaps the Krauts have zeroed in on. But that was just once, I haven't seen anymore since."

"What about antitank fire?" Passey asks. "What about mines?"

Rio says, "The mines in those fields are Bouncing Bettys and the like, mostly antipersonnel, not antitank. The 88s, as you know, sir, are usually on high ground a distance away, so unless the air corps can take them out . . ."

Passey says, "The fly-boys are scared because they say we're shooting at them."

Cat looks like she's building up a head of steam to say a few things about the air corps, so Rio jumps in. "Those 88s have the roads and the entrances to fields ranged, they don't have the center of a hedgerow zeroed in, they've got MGs and mortars for that. The tank-dozer I saw in action broke through in about three minutes. I'm not saying the Krauts can't aim and shoot in three minutes, but it wouldn't be easy and it wouldn't be as accurate."

Passey nods. "The only tanks in this sector are a colored battalion of Shermans. I'll talk to their colonel and see whether we can get some help from them."

The meeting breaks up and Stick, Cat and Rio walk the few feet to the field kitchen. After days of C rations the stew and biscuits are a wonderful luxury.

The camp is a chaos of vehicles and soldiers and sad-looking tents. They find an unoccupied spot upwind from the latrines and sit on crates and stuff their faces, feeling guilty about their people up at the front who are opening yet another can of cold hash.

"It's good you spoke up, Richlin," Stick says.

"Captain's all right," Rio says through a mouthful of burning hot apple cobbler.

What is unsaid is that Lieutenant Horne is *not* okay. His panic on the beach has left him tarnished in the eyes of the platoon. And since then he has been taking risks with himself and his soldiers, trying to prove himself.

"I'm wondering about some NCO-to-NCO outreach," Stick says.

"What's that mean?" Cat asks.

"Look, we have a push on tomorrow. Captain's got to talk to his colonel, who has to think it over and then maybe get hold of the colonel of that colored tank battalion, and in this army nothing gets done in twenty-four hours."

"You're saying we go talk to some of the tank drivers?" Cat asks. "Captain will blow his top if it goes bad."

But in the end the three of them take a detour on their way back to the front line, a detour that takes them to the motor pool—two tents and a jumble of treads, bogie wheels, carburetors steeping in cans of gasoline—of the tank battalion. There they find a furiously angry master sergeant puffing intensely on a huge Meerschaum pipe who begins by telling them that he (puff) does not take orders (puff) from some staff sergeant just because he's white. (Puff puff.)

Stick, being an educated fellow, turns to logical argument.

But Rio has had experience with men whose lives are spent with machines. She knows their language. She grabs a piece of wrapping paper and sketches the tank-dozer, and sure enough the pipe-puffer cannot resist looking.

"It wasn't like an actual bulldozer blade," Rio explains. "It was more like this, see. Like teeth, kind of."

The master sergeant stares and puffs. He takes the pencil and begins drawing. Stick starts to speak but is stopped dead by a raised hand and an angry puff.

"We could bring up some of the scrap metal off the beach . . . (puff) cut at a bias (puff) . . . weld it here . . . (puff puff.) Hmmm."

(Puff.)

"I might get my captain to let me try it out. (Puff.)" Then a crafty look comes into his eye. "Of course that's a lot of work. I don't have men to spare bringing scrap up off the beach. And you know, all that welding (puff) would take a lot of my energies." He sucks on nothing, takes out his pipe and knocks the ashes against his boot. "A man can't plan right without a little pipe tobacco. Sure can't work without it. No, not even if he had a mind to."

A year earlier Rio and Stick and Cat might have missed the implications of that speech. But they are veterans now and understand that the army runs on favors.

"How much pipe tobacco would it take to focus on a job like that?" Cat asks.

"Oh, I'd say a full two pouches. And it's thirsty work besides."

"I had a premonition it might be," Cat says.

In the end they agree on a single pouch of pipe tobacco and two bottles of liquor (or four of wine) for two modified tanks.

"I can get my hands on the scrap metal," Stick says. "The other stuff . . ."

"I have a guy," Rio says.

Back with her squad Rio calls Beebee over. "I need a pouch of pipe tobacco and some booze."

Beebee considers. "It'll take me two hours . . . if I can get a jeep."

It takes him three hours, but in addition to the bribes he comes back with a complete ham, a part of which is sent along to encourage progress at the motor pool.

The next morning two Shermans with dramatic dentures at the front come rattling up. One is assigned to Rio's objective.

"Okay, here's how we do this," Rio explains to her squad as the tank commander sits in his turret listening in. They are in a cleared field facing a secured hedgerow. "Tank goes through this hedgerow. We follow. Marching fire, people. Marching fire, walk and shoot, walk and shoot. Don't make me have to yell at you when I should be shooting Krauts. We cross the field, with us behind it, figuring the tank will pop any mines. The tank goes right ahead, bang into the facing hedgerow. Right? And we go through the gap, split left, Preeling's people go right, we roll the Krauts up and the tank skedaddles before the Kraut spotters can zero in. We dig in. And listen up: I mean dig in. Half the time we get somewhere they come right back at us while we're draining our canteens and boiling coffee. Through the safe hedge, follow the tank, through the next hedge, left and right and shoot anyone you see. Right?"

"Right, Sarge," a few voices mutter.

Well, Rio thinks, I'd be more worried if they were cocky. Better scared. "We jump off in ten minutes."

Heads nod. Geer says, "You sure these colored boys know how to drive a tank?"

"You have a white tank unit you can call up?" Rio asks.

The tank sits idling, exhaust fumes rising. The tank commander and the bow gunner are both poking up from their respective hatches. The Germans will hear them. They'll know tanks are coming. Hopefully they won't know from where and they'll have all their *Panzerfausts* at the corners of the field.

If this doesn't work, I'll be in the doghouse.

Rio looks down the line at her squad. Her solid soldiers, Geer, Pang, Jenou, and Jack; the risen-from-the-dead Dick Ostrowiz, who reappeared three days after the landing, having been given up as drowned; the enthusiastic and overly-eager Jenny Dial; the goldbrick Rudy J. Chester; Beebee, indispensable as a scrounger, but not the most eager-beaver of fighting men; and Maria Milkmaid Molina, who was shaping up to be a decent soldier.

Two short of a full complement, not that she wishes for more green replacements, God forbid. But someone who could handle a BAR, or remember to throw a grenade after pulling the pin, would be nice. Despite the tension, or perhaps because of it, her thoughts go to the soldiers who have not made it this far. Cassel. Suarez. Even Magraff. And the new ones, Hobart and Camacho.

"Ready?"

They nod or grunt.

The signal comes. Rio yells up to the tank commander who

waves her off and says, "Don't you worry, honey, we will tear up that little old hedge."

He guns the engine and the Sherman gathers speed. It's going maybe fifteen miles an hour when the welded teeth bite into the base of the hedgerow. The bushes tilt away and wave wildly, a clear-as-day signal to the Germans.

The tank backs up, hits it again, and this time sits grinding its gears, treads kicking up clods of dirt and grass as the squad stands close by.

It takes a third and then a fourth rush by the Sherman and suddenly the front of the tank tilts up and it plows right over the hedgerow into the field beyond, tilting like a playground seesaw.

Now the squad competes for space behind the tank, and no one but Jack, Jenou, Pang and Geer is employing marching fire, firing from the hip even without specific targets to keep the Krauts pinned down.

Machine guns open up from the far corners and Chester and Ostrowiz promptly fall on their faces as the tank pulls away.

"Get up! Get up!" Rio yells. "How many times do I have to tell you? Move!"

Now comes the whistle of artillery and a dirt flower erupts in the middle of the field, showering the GIs and the tank with dirt and debris. The tank buttons up, closing the hatches, relying now on inadequate periscopes for steering.

"Move, move, move!" Rio shouts and reaches down to grab the collar of Chester's uniform and haul him to his feet. The German gunners must be careful not to hit their own position so the safest reaction to mortar fire is to advance. "Ostrowiz! Move!"

The tank is ahead of the infantry racing toward the far hedgerow in the knowledge that the German artillery will have to stop firing or risk hitting their own men. The tank hits the second hedgerow like it did the first, but the tank commander has learned, and this time it takes only three charges from the Sherman to knock a hole in the hedgerow.

Rio is at the rear, pushing Chester and Ostrowiz. Geer leads the way through with Dial and Pang beside him. They pivot left out of Rio's sight and she hears frantic rifle fire.

The tank commander, no longer worried about the mortars that rain down on the now-empty field behind them, is up out of his hatch and swiveling the big machine gun toward the tree line. The tank is behind the German line now, behind gray-clad soldiers rushing up with their *Panzerfausts* at the ready.

This Sherman has a .50 caliber for the tank commander, and a .30 caliber bow gun. Both lacerate the hedgerow, cutting through the Germans like a scythe going through wheat.

Rio pushes through the gap, pivots, sees Jack trip and for a heart-stopping moment thinks he's been shot. But he's up, cursing, and firing at German troops who now retreat in both directions along the hedgerow.

"Dig in, dig in!" Rio shouts. She grabs the entrenching tool from the back of Chester's pack and shoves it in his hands. "Soon as those Krauts are clear the arty's coming!"

Shovels out, the dirt clods start flying as the tank continues spraying deadly fire, now into the next hedgerow. Then the tank fires its big cannon and the center of the next hedgerow explodes. The Germans over there are firing back, but only sporadically in the presence of the Sherman's annihilating fire.

A *Panzerfaust*, the German counterpart to the American bazooka, flies, trailing sparks. It misses the Sherman and the Sherman chases the track of *Panzerfaust* smoke with lacerating machine-gun fire.

Then the tank turns and roars back through the hole it has made.

Rio checks her watch. Eleven minutes start to finish and another square of Normandy's endless checkerboard belongs to the Americans.

Berlin is closer.

18

It is the refugees who make it possible for Rainy.

They are everywhere, on roads, in fields, running away south and east from Norman villages annihilated by Allied bombs or naval gunfire or artillery. Normandy, not Brittany after all, old Ike has fooled everyone. The American military is devoted to the idea of cutting US casualties by the use of overwhelming destructive power—destructive power that falls on the Germans, but also anyone close by.

Towns, villages and farms burn. Retreating Germans loot whatever they can carry away, and what they don't loot the Americans and Allies do. The French people are caught between an American hammer and a German anvil, between bitter German soldiers and jumpy, suspicious Americans.

Rainy has broken the refugees down into types. Women predominate because many young men have been sent away for forced labor, or else are Vichy-collaborating *milice*, or with the maquis, or lying in a French military cemetery. The women wear layers of clothing despite the heat, knowing that they will be seeing cold nights and rain. They carry all they can—bags and suitcases, sausages and cheeses stuffed into pockets.

Then there are the children, some solemn and holding their mother's coat or sleeve, some skylarking because after all they are children. Babies cry. Toddlers sniffle. Siblings break out in squabbles, but fall silent when the oppressive air of fear wears them down.

The men are mostly old. This war and the previous war and forced labor have killed or imprisoned most of the younger men, and many younger women as well. The men carry small chests on their backs, or push a wheelbarrow piled with household possessions.

Women, children and old men, all plodding down roads and ditches, through fields and woods, a great moving mass of downcast, frightened people, all heading away.

Rainy is moving in the other direction. No one seems to care, including the Germans. She has a big, bloody bandage wrapped around her head. It covers one eye, which is bad if she has to aim a weapon, but has the effect of showing only the right side of her face. On her head she wears a filthy cloche she took from a dead woman. It is pulled low to hide her military-short hair. What shows of her face she has dirtied.

But it's the blood that is the master stroke. She'd had to cut the back of her arm to get the blood and saturate the torn fabric she used as gauze. People don't make eye contact with wounded folks. People don't want to think about the eye beneath the bandage, the eye that seems to have bled quite a bit.

She has her forged papers, but over the course of three days she has been challenged only once when a Wehrmacht corporal decided to take her into the woods and use her. She'd started to undress as if complying, then wrapped her ragged, much-torn coat around the Walther to muffle the sound of the shot.

It made a smoky mess of the left side of her coat, with a bullet hole and a big smear of gunpowder residue, but with each day the roads are more jammed with refugees, and she is more invisible.

She is on foot wearing a decent if overlarge pair of boots. She is not proud of how she came to have the boots, because she looted them from a shoe store that had just been looted by Germans. They'd taken all the fancy shoes, the high heels, the men's dress shoes, but left the ugly, practical footwear. She thought of leaving a bit of her hoarded currency behind, but a crisp twenty-Reichsmarks note might attract attention. Instead she makes a mental note to come back some day and pay the proprietor.

I may be an assassin, but I'm no thief.

The thought brings with it a droll smile.

It is midday, hot, the sun steaming the clouds. Rainy's feet are blistered. She is hungry and thirsty, and the villages she passes through are either thoroughly looted, or burned, or both. Food is on the minds of every refugee. Already Rainy has seen women and children bending over to drink muddy water from ditches and puddles.

The sound of machine guns precedes the sound of engines. She looks up, shades her eyes, and sees two planes coming low and slow, crossing the road left to right. The planes are firing toward a stand of woods well back from the road across a field.

They zoom overhead, guns blazing, and Rainy sees the black-and-white invasion stripes on the wings and relaxes: they are either USAAF or RAF, not Luftwaffe. P-38 Lightnings, easily identified by the twin tails.

The two P-38s take a tight turn over the woods and come tearing back, parallel with the road this time. They each drop a bomb, with one landing in the woods and the other landing in the field, killing a horse.

The refugees—all but Rainy—have leapt into the ditch running beside the road, but now a dozen or more leap from cover and go racing across the field to the dead horse. A dead horse is food, and many run with knives already drawn for butchery.

The P-38s are not done. They come arcing around for another pass, good, conscientious pilots ensuring that they have destroyed whatever was hiding in the woods.

What happens next is terribly clear. Rainy has spent many hours poring over aerial reconnaissance maps. She knows what the world looks like to a fighter pilot buzzing low at two hundred miles an hour. Tanks look like trucks and half-tracks. And humans are dark smears, blurry shadows. At two hundred mph no one is able to spot a uniform vs. a civilian coat. Anything, a broom or a hoe, can look like a rifle.

The P-38s come in at treetop level, engines roaring, and begin firing .50 caliber machine guns and cannon, strafing what the pilots must have thought were fleeing Germans, but are in reality hungry refugees.

"No!" Rainy cries, a futile protest, unheard in the cacophony of exploding cannon shells and screams.

The planes fly off and now more screams, more cries, a blood-drenched child wandering in the field, a woman crawling, a man dragging a foot attached by nothing but torn meat.

Rainy runs toward them, half her mind afraid that the P-38s might come around one more time, the other half grappling with her utter inability to do anything. She is not a medic. She is not a nurse. And when she reaches the dozen men and women, three dead, three more wounded, she finds she can do nothing. Nothing at all but stare in horror.

A man shoves her aside and mutters something about knowing what he's doing. He has a long, curved knife and sets about butchering the horse with quick, efficient cuts. A butcher, plying his trade with his feet planted in the blood of a dying woman.

More refugees now pour into the field, some to gather their lost or frightened loved ones, most to get some of the steaming red meat now being doled out by the butcher.

A woman with children in tow walks back across the field, all of them carrying chunks of horse meat in their hands. Rainy knows that this image will join many other horrors in her nightmares. Mothers ignoring mothers keening over their lost children, focusing on keeping their own fed and alive.

Rainy moves on, foot following foot, ashamed of the scrap of raw horse's haunch in her pocket. The blood of the meat will seep into the breech of her Walther and she thinks, *I'll need to clean that.*

Mile after mile, a salmon swimming upstream, she moves opposite to the refugee flow, trying not to see the fear in faces, trying not to hear the cries of hunger from children, trying not to see a legless old war veteran hauling himself along on a board resting on wheels taken from an office chair.

All this suffering because of one mad bastard in Berlin.

After a while she creeps off the road into the woods and makes a small fire. She spears the hunk of horse meat on a stick and cooks the meat until it sizzles and drips fat. She eats it while it is still so hot it burns her hands and mouth.

It is better, tastier, than the horse meat from the café she'd been at with Marie. Hunger makes flavor.

Revived, she drinks from a small stream, cleans her pistol, and rejoins the road. Closer to the battle lines now the refugees carry less and less. These are the ones who held out, who thought they might tough it out, but have been driven out by German military police and *milice*.

Go, leave now, you have five minutes to pack.

And now, closer to the battle, the roads are jammed by Germans going in both directions, beaten units fleeing toward the rear, fresh units going toward the fight. Rainy begins to see wounded Germans now, men in dusty gray with bandaged limbs and bellies and heads. Some still carry their Mausers or Schmeissers, their *Panzerfausts* and mortar tubes; others have abandoned their weapons and shuffle along staring blankly at nothing, faces haggard.

German ambulances try to force their way through soldiers, refugees and farm animals, and all spill into ditches and fields. Some of the fields are mined and single refugees, or groups, are blown apart when they wander into them.

It is the full chaotic misery of war: wounded soldiers, terrified civilians, men on their way to battle, hunger, thirst, worry, fear, degradation.

At a crossroads all traffic stops so an SS tank unit can push through. Rainy finds herself in a ditch with other refugees, listening to grumbling from regular Wehrmacht troops about the SS, their special treatment, their nice new uniforms, their updated weapons.

This is interesting, but not new. The Allied intelligence services have long known of the tensions between SS and regular army divisions.

Rainy's pulse quickens. She has found the Das Reich again, though too late. The Das Reich is obviously already committed to battle and she has been able to do nothing to warn Allied planners.

Then, purely by chance, she spots a chubby sergeant. He is the man who took brioches from the bakery in Oradour.

The Das Reich division is nominally nineteen thousand men, though it is surely under that strength now. Like any American division it is broken into companies and platoons. This sergeant, this one chubby Nazi, is a link to the company that gunned down the residents of Oradour. Rainy will never get this chance again. She waits by the side of the road, face down like a frightened civilian, eyes raised to watch.

Adolf Diekmann does not travel by car this time. This time he rides in a tank. Rainy almost does not recognize the *Sturmbannführer* without the broad grin and the happy-go-lucky air. He seems downcast, eyes hollowed by weariness and . . . and guilt?

No, Rainy tells herself, not guilt. The SS do not feel guilt.

She waits until they are past, then follows. She cannot hope to keep up, but if she just keeps walking she will, sooner or later, come to wherever the smiling *Sturmbannführer*'s unit is based.

Rainy walks as night falls. Walks as the heat of the day dissipates. Walks on increasingly empty roads as the refugees flop exhausted by the side of the road. Soon there are only military vehicles. She notes with grim amusement that they ride with lights off, feeling their way through the black night in fear of the romping Allied planes.

Finally she can walk no more and passes a miserable night in the woods, with refugee families snoring all around. The next morning she pushes on and things have changed. She can hear distant explosions. Sometimes she hears the rattle of machine guns. The air smells of smoke, and great pillars of it rise in the north.

She walks now through an increasingly chaotic scene. The roads are narrow with tall, imposing hedges on either side. German artillery can be seen in fields, their long tubes aiming north, belching fire and smoke. She passes masses of German trucks pulled up in fields reduced to churned mud. She passes a German field hospital, with huge red crosses painted on tents in hopes of being spared by the marauding Allied planes.

She comes to a bend in the road and upon turning stops suddenly, face to face with a column of German tanks and trucks, all blackened by fire, many extravagantly dismembered. They look as if they were fashioned out of clay, their armor twisted, their cannon barrels curled. Some still burn sullenly. A team of *Osttruppen*, Poles and Russians and Ukrainians forced to fight for their oppressor, works as graves registration teams, pulling charred, stiff bodies from the wreckage. The bodies lie by the side of the road, men missing hands or feet, men with faces turned into fright masks, others seemingly unhurt but still dead. Some of the bodies are burned. The aroma of cooked meat mixes with the stink of decaying flesh to turn Rainy's stomach.

She notes that one of the *Osttruppen* is stripping the bodies of watches, cigarettes, war souvenirs and packs of crackers or lengths of dry sausages.

She pries a twenty-Reichsmarks note from her box of currency, crumples it in her fist and tentatively approaches the man who is busy trying to work a ring off the finger of a dead German. He is not happy to be observed.

"Go away!" he says in heavily-accented German.

"I want food," she says.

"Everyone wants food. Fug off!"

"I have money."

That stops the thief in midtwist. He drops the hand with the ring, but the dead man is well into rigor mortis and the hand stays elevated, like a macabre Nazi salute.

"What money?"

"Reichsmarks. I have twenty marks. Cash." She holds it out for him to see. He moves toward it and she backs away.

"Food," she says. "That sausage." She points at the brown cylinder protruding from his pocket.

The soldier glances toward his rifle, leaning against a fence post. Rainy carefully draws her Walther, keeping it low so only he will see it. "I can pay you twenty marks, or I can shoot you and take the sausage and keep the money," she says.

Am I a thief if I steal what a thief has stolen?

A worldly smile appears on the man's features. "I'm a

Ukrainian, I won't die for German honor." He spits out the words *German honor*. "Give me your money."

They carefully, suspiciously, trade money for sausage.

"You are hungry, and I have not had a woman in a long time," the soldier says, leering.

"I am trying to find my lover," Rainy says. "He is an SS *Sturmbannführer* with the Das Reich."

The man shrugs and jerks his head toward the north. "Up there. Maybe your man is there. But you had better watch out for the maquis, they are killing whores who sleep with Germans."

Rainy moves on, gnawing on the sausage, no longer acting the part of a dirty, scared, starving refugee, but living it. Soon she is forced off the road by a rush of German tanks rolling forward. She watches them until they are almost out of sight and then sees them turn right off the road into trees.

It is another hour's walk, pushing always against the incessant flow of refugees, till she reaches the spot where the tanks have turned off. She stops. It is not a road to anywhere, the tanks have made their own road, crushing fences and crops to disappear beneath trees they hope will hide them from the eager P-38s and P-47s and Spitfires.

The deception fails. Three P-47s, their wings heavy with missile pods, lacerate the stand of trees with pass after pass, firing missiles, blazing away with machine guns. As soon as they are gone, Rainy moves closer. The German encampment is in a fury of activity, with medics hauling men from tanks, soldiers spraying fire extinguishers on burning trucks, repair crews already assessing damaged treads and twisted gun barrels.

Veterans, Rainy figures. The chaos is too controlled: this is not their first air raid. Rainy hides behind a fallen log and peeks over the edge just in time to spot the fat German from Oradour, the one person she recognizes, aside from her prey.

It is the right company. She has found them. Now to wait for him, for the smiling *Sturmbannführer*. Though how she is to take him on in the midst of a company of SS she cannot imagine.

Are you an assassin now, Rainy Schulterman?

She watches intently, hour after hour as the light declines and shadows lengthen, but she does not see him. Nevertheless, she has an idea where he may be: there is a concrete German pillbox at the edge of the wood, well situated to cover the road.

In there. He must be in there, no doubt laughing happily again, no doubt imagining himself at risk only from the sky.

She falls asleep, propped against her log. When she awakes it is in sudden panic when the log bounces hard and all the noise in the world descends with a massive series of crashes.

At first she thinks the planes are back, but no, this is artillery, big 105 and 155 millimeter shells exploding. And she is in the middle of it, cringing beneath her log, hands pressed against her ears to dim the crashing noise. The ground beneath her bounces and shakes. The air is stifling with the smell of powder and smoke.

The barrage ends. Sudden silence. Clods of dirt rattle down through the leaves. Rainy hears shouts and cries of pain. Can she get away with walking straight into the chaos and pretending to be a shell-shocked refugee?

No, they'll peg her as an informer who gave the location to the Americans. But she can creep closer. She crawls on hands and knees through fallen pine needles, sliding beneath bushes, sometimes crawling on her belly. She reaches a crater, still smoking. A dead German is being hauled out.

Rainy slides down into the crater, taking the dead man's place. From this vantage point she is much closer. She can see more and hear a great deal more. A gaggle of officers is at the entrance to the pillbox, smoking and occasionally barking orders. The pillbox has been hit but not damaged beyond a smoke mark.

Three officers. One with his back to her. She cannot see his face, cannot tell the color of his hair beneath his hat.

No closer, Rainy: wait.

She listens. Talk of moving to a different map grid. Discussion of whether they'll find cover there. Names mentioned in low voices, the dead. Then a laugh and someone mentions that the damned Americans have blown up the officers' latrine and a joke about not defecating until they are back in Berlin.

One of the officers, perhaps prodded by this, walks a few paces, and urinates against a tree. The man with his back to Rainy laughs and goes in pursuit of his own tree.

For a brief moment, only a moment, she sees his face.

Can she? Not without being caught. A single pistol round will have the whole camp racing here, guns blazing.

Is it worth dying to kill this one Nazi butcher?

The decision is physical as much as mental, as if her own body has decided, as if she is being moved against her will. She stands up and in German says, "Don't be alarmed, *Herr Sturmbannführer*, I have only come to make you an offer."

The German jerks, caught off-guard, and says, "Run away, you dirty woman. I don't want your body."

"I have American cigarettes."

This stops the German in midstride. He glances back toward the camp, toward the pillbox just twenty or thirty feet away. Reassured, he finishes rebuttoning his trousers and says, "How would you come to have American cigarettes? Where did you get them? There are no Americans near here." Then, under his breath, "Not yet, anyway."

"I have them here," Rainy says, and levels the barrel of the Walther at him.

"Ah, a Walther. You have good taste in handguns."

"Follow me or die."

"Follow you?" He laughs. "You think your little popgun frightens me? Do you think I fear death?"

"I wasn't thinking of killing you. I was thinking of shooting you in the legs."

"The legs?" He's baffled.

"Yes. Like your men did in Oradour. You shot the men in the legs so they couldn't run. Then you burned them."

The tanks are all revving up now, getting ready to move out fast, before the American artillery or planes come after them again. Is it enough noise to cover the sound of her pistol? No. But it is enough to stop him calling for help.

"I played no part in that," he says.

"No? Hand me your identity papers."

He hesitates, glances wistfully at the oh-so-near safety of the pillbox, then with a show of amusement he hands over a small, well-worn buff folder. She flips it open. His picture is there, smiling at the camera.

"Adolf Otto Diekmann," Rainy reads.

"That is my name," he says. "But you must understand, mademoiselle, I was shocked at what happened at Oradour. Why . . ." He laughs. "We later learned it was the wrong Oradour! We were meant to . . . to search Oradour-sur-Vayres. A silly mistake."

"Lie down on the ground," Rainy says.

"So you can shoot me?"

"I won't shoot you. I'd prefer not to die. I just want you face down so I can run away."

It's not the most convincing story, but Diekmann has no good alternative. Sighing as though he's being asked to do something ridiculous but he's playing along, he drops to his knees, says something about making a perfect mess of his uniform, and lies down.

There's a piece of concrete nearby, leftover spillage from the construction of the pillbox. Rainy lifts a big piece, a foot across, triangular shape, heavy, and slams it down with all her force on the back of Diekmann's head.

The blows sound like a heavyweight's punches. Not loud enough to carry over the sound of revving tanks. She waits, panting, until his breathing stops.

"For Bernard," Rainy says. "I liked that kid."

LETTERS SENT

Hi Mom and Dad and Obal,

Well, we are all done with D-Day. I imagine you've heard about it, and yes, I was there. Right on Omaha Beach.

And Obal? Guess what I'm assigned to? A colored tank battalion! And since I can practically hear you asking, yes, I have been inside a Sherman tank and I've ridden on one. In fact, I'm sitting on a log right now and not fifty feet away is one of our tanks having a bogie wheel replaced.

We are off the front line right now so I am helping to set up the aid station—mostly paperwork and unpacking boxes. I find it very boring, but dullness is welcome given the alternative. Anyway, the brass will probably move us up again soon, but please don't worry. The Germans have been pretty decent about honoring the red cross, just like we do with their aid people.

I was so sorry to hear that Daddy is unwell. I hope it's nothing serious. Get better soon, Dad!

Since you asked, Mom, I could use some things from home, but only if it's easy, and only if it doesn't strain the family finances. I would love a couple extra pairs of socks, for myself. Also, if you happen to have any old, torn or run stockings, those make excellent tourniquets. And this will sound crazy, but M&Ms, you know, the candy? I sometimes give a few to soldiers who are hurt. It calms them down and makes them think of home.

Well, that's it for now. Daddy, get well!!
Love to you all,
Frangie

Dear Colonel Herkemeier,

I am writing to you as the mother of a soldier. My daughter Elisheva (Rainy) Schulterman works for you, I believe. We have not had a letter from her in some time. I'm sure I'm just being silly, but could you ask her to write so I know she's all right?

Thank you,
Ethel Schulterman

Dearest Rio,

I feel that our last meeting went badly and I am sure I'm entirely at fault. I'm afraid I get a bit keyed up before a mission, especially as the previous two had gone badly with my plane having to return for repairs. I apologize if I was beastly.

Yesterday we had one of our socials, a sort of drinks-and-dancing evening in the village. All the guys were there and there were a lot of nurses and Red Cross ladies, but yours truly behaved like a perfect gentleman. I only danced with the old battle-ax who is in charge of the nurses, and I drank very little. You would have been proud.

Even if I had been tempted to stray or let my eye wander I'd have had no chance because all the fellows have decided that you're the sort of girl who might come after me with that knife of yours. It's become a regular thing to tease me about you.

I don't mind much because any time they say your name I still see you not as you are now but as the girl I knew from back home in Gedwell Falls.

Someday, hopefully soon, this will all be over and life can go back to normal. Maybe then we can get back to being regular old Strand and regular old Rio. I'd like to put all this behind me and I know you must feel the same. We will need to put all this out of our minds and just be a man and his girl again.

I guess we haven't really talked much about after, have we? I suppose I don't feel I have the right until the war is over. I don't want to try and tie you down when anything could happen to me. But if we can turn the clock back some day, back to before, I think we'll be fine. I sometimes daydream about it and picture heading off to work in the morning with your pancakes in my belly and your kiss on my lips. You can make pancakes, I hope? That's a joke!

Anyway, I love you and miss you.

Strand

XXX

Dearest Lupé,

I don't know why I'm writing to you. We got the notice today. They sent an army chaplain to tell us since we don't have anyone carrying telegrams out here.

I guess you wouldn't figure your old dad for the kind to cry. But I can't seem to stop. I love you so much and I am so proud of you. I guess I never told you that, but you know, I'm old-fashioned. My father, well you never knew him, but he was tough and I guess I thought I had to be tough too. But my heart is broken, that's the truth of it.

I don't know what to do, sweetheart. Everything is just all wrong now. I can't bring myself to believe it. I still expect to see you come up the drive and I would rush out to greet you and we would throw the biggest barbecue ever with all the neighbors and the hands. That's been the picture I've kept in my mind ever since you left.

Now they tell me you won't be coming home at all. There's talk of a graveyard there in France. It feels wrong to me. I want you here. You should be with Gran Martinez and Pops and your mom.

Baby. My baby. My little girl. I keep going over every time we ever disagreed or argued. I can't help it. I just wish so many things had not been said, and so many other things had been said. I love you, Lupé.

I know you are in the loving arms of Jesus, that's what your mother would say if she were here. I'm writing this because I hope somehow you can read this letter from heaven. Someday I will be with you again. In my Father's house are many mansions: if it were not so, I would have told you. That's what it says in the Book. I go to prepare a place for you. That's what Jesus said and I have to believe it or go nuts. So baby, my darling, my sweetest Guadalupé, you're with your mother now, so the two of you just wait for me in that mansion. Leave a light on.

All of my love,
Daddy

Jenou,

I know you have other things on your mind, but I simply had to tell you. Your father and I have separated. I won't go into the sordid reasons, but we have agreed to sell the house. I have rented a small apartment, just one bedroom, I'm afraid, from Mrs. Brannigan's brother. Your father has moved to Oakland. I know nothing of his situation there. Perhaps he'll write to you, but just remember this was not my choice. He's the one who strayed. I just felt you should know, because when you get out of the army you'll have to think about where to live.

Mother

Dear Maria,

So your sergeant's a terror, is she? That makes me laugh. What did I tell you? Man or woman, a sergeant is a sergeant is a sergeant. My old sergeant could curse the paint off a barn door, spit tobacco juice thirty feet, and keep us running until we all dropped dead on the ground and he was still running in place. Backward!

Mother and Poppa are fine and so am I. Poppa and I got the old Ford running finally and the weather has been glorious.

Well, as you know I'm not a writer, so I best keep this short. Anyway, it's pretty boring here and much more exciting where you are.

Take care, Meemo, we all miss you here. And we are very proud, even Grandpa, though he won't admit it and still mutters about it being unnatural and so on.

Keep your head down. Come home in one piece.
Your loving brother,
Tommy

Dear Mother and Father,

I don't have much time, I'm only in the rear to pick up replacements and give Beebee an opportunity to scrounge us up some smokes and booze and necessary items. But I wanted at least to get a note to you to say that I am all right. The landing was tough. And the fighting afterward has been tough. But the word is the Krauts are retreating and we should be in Paris soon. Maybe I can send you a bottle of perfume from there! Something alluring and foreign. (That's for Mother, of course.)

Father, I still remember you telling me to find a good sergeant and stick to him. And now I am the sergeant, though I don't know that I'm a good one. To say it isn't easy isn't half of it. I don't like it much to tell the truth. My people still treat me in a friendly way, but it's different. There are times when they don't want me around because I'm "Sarge" now not just "Richlin." Even Jenou! No one warns you, but the higher up you go the more lonely it gets. It's almost enough to make me feel sorry for Ike.

I do have a quick funny story though. The other day while we were on a hike we came across some very full cows and no one to milk them. So me and one of my new privates did the job. I believe we set a speed record for milking! The smell really took me back and made me feel a little sad. And the taste was great too, though I happen to think our cows give a sweeter—

Damn. Okay, my ride is here and I think Beebee is anxious to make his getaway. I suspect the two big cans of peaches in his arms came from the officers' mess and I know for sure that whatever that is clinking in his rucksack did.

Bye for now. Love,

Rio

PART TWO
PARIS

19

"I thought French men were supposed to be romantic," Jenou says. "But they all look a bit, you know . . . small."

Rio sits with Cat and Jenou at a minuscule round table at the outer edge of a sidewalk café in Paris, at the corner of tiny Rue Saint-Benoît and the larger, grander Boulevard Saint-Germain. They each have a beer. They have a demolished tray of salamis and cheeses. They wear clean, pressed uniforms, with polished boots and tightly knotted ties.

And they get looks from the locals. The looks are baffled or reproachful or sneering. Paris, it seems, does not quite know what to make of women soldiers.

Rio's division did not take part in the triumphant march through liberated Paris, a fact for which Rio is grateful. The division that marched through Paris to an enthusiastic crowd kept right on marching up to the front, which is now rapidly approaching the German border.

Instead, Rio's division is quartered outside the city and profits from a generous policy on passes.

"Jenou likes them over six feet," Rio says, and Jenou nods agreement.

"I like them over six feet *away*," Cat says, smiling her upside-down smile so she doesn't sound too hostile.

"It's fine for the men," Jenou says. "Paris has plenty of whores. But what about us? Where's my six-foot-two Frenchman ready to fulfill my every wish for a pack of smokes and a chocolate bar?"

"No boy back home, Castain?" Cat asks.

Jenou leans toward her, nearly knocking over her beer. Her fourth beer. "Can I ask you both something very, very, very important?"

Cat withdraws, her mouth tightening. Almost as if she dreads the question.

"Can we not stop this bullshit of calling each other by last names? I mean, when it's just us, when we aren't around the rest of the platoon?"

Cat relaxes. "Okay, *Jenou*, no boy back home?"

"No boy, *Cat*," Jenou says. "And no home." She pulls out a short letter and smooths it on the table for the other two to read.

"Gosh, Jenou. That's a kick in the teeth," Cat says sincerely.

Rio looks at her inebriated friend. She knows that Jenou's home life has never been happy. She knows Jenou despises her father and holds her mother in cynical contempt. But she's never known all the reasons. And on occasion when she has pressed, Jenou has always retreated into sour private smiles and a shaking head.

"You can stay with us, you know that," Rio says.

"Us as in you and your folks? Or us as in you and Strand?"

"Ha ha," Rio says. "My folks, of course." She blushes and tries to hide that fact by taking a drink.

A Frenchwoman with two little girls in tow comes by. The girls stop to stare and Jenou says, "*Bonjour.*" The mother pulls the girls sharply away.

"How is old tall, dark and handsome?" Jenou asks.

Rio shrugs. "Haven't seen him since we landed."

"That's what's called being evasive," Jenou informs Cat.

"Can't we just be tourists?" Rio complains. "All we've seen so far is one big church."

"Notre-Dame?" Cat says. "That's what you're calling 'one big church?'" She shrugs. "Well, I guess it was big. Anyway we've seen the Eiffel Tower, we drove right by it!"

"Shit. Look!" Jenou jerks her head toward a man across the street. It's Lieutenant Horne and two other officers, and they are walking down the street in a state of serious inebriation.

"He's not setting a very good example," Rio says.

Cat says, "Nonsense, he's setting the perfect example." She raps the table top with her knuckles. "*Garçon!* We need something more than beer. What have you got? Anything but Applejack, we drank our fill of that in Normandy."

The waiter brings three small glasses of Armagnac, which they dutifully down in a single swig.

"Doesn't look like the Frenchies have had too hard a time of it," Cat notes sourly. "If even a single bomb has fallen on Paris, I'd be surprised."

"That's the advantage of surrendering early," Rio says with equal cynicism.

Despite mostly warm welcomes in Normandy—despite the catastrophic suffering of locals caught in the crossfire—American soldiers are not quite happy with the Parisians, who they suspect of being collaborators with the Nazis. A rumor has been going around about Frenchwomen acting as snipers, defending their German boyfriends. Rio has seen no evidence of this, and she knows well that rumors are wrong most of the time, but it has created a chill between the Americans and the Parisians.

Of course, drunk soldiers making crude approaches to decent Frenchwomen have not helped either. But the general mood is that the French have not been properly appreciative.

"So, we going to the big museum?" Jenou asks.

"Jen, you don't have to keep me company, you know," Rio says, her tongue distinctly looser after the Armagnac.

"Are you trying to ditch me because I'm not a sergeant?" Jenou asks.

"No. No, no, just the opposite. I'm sure Dial and Camacho are off having fun, probably with Cat's two girls. Fun you can't have with your sergeant lurking around."

"Ah, it's lonely at the top, isn't it?" Jenou mocks. "Come on, Rio, everyone knows we're friends. They already won't do anything with me because they figure I'll tell you."

Rio frowns. This has never occurred to her. She is a drag on Jenou's social life. She decides to try harder for cheerfulness. "Well, Cat, what is it we sergeants do for fun in the big city?"

Cat considers for a moment, then she stands up abruptly. "Ladies, we are in Paris, France: let's go look at paintings. Not because we want to, but because when we get home—touch wood—everyone will ask us about it."

*

Frangie Marr is looking at paintings, but not in a museum. She is just a fifteen-minute walk away from Rio, Cat and Jenou, standing with Manning and Deacon and craning their necks up in silent awe in the hushed interior of the Sainte-Chapelle.

The church is not vast like Notre-Dame; it is Notre-Dame's smaller, more modest, much more beautiful little sister. Stained-glass windows rise fifty feet, all around them, separated only by graceful stone pillars. The arched ceiling is deep blue and decorated with stars so it seems to be a majestic, star-strewn night sky.

The stained glass is stunning, each tall window a story told in bits of colored glass. The colored light dazzles on the tile floor. Statues of solemn saints occupy alcoves, with Mother Mary holding pride of place.

"It's like being inside a kaleidoscope," Deacon says.

"Well, I'll be. I ain't the most churchgoing person ever," Manning says. "But if I was ever to feel the Holy Ghost I reckon it would be here."

Frangie doesn't say what's on her mind: that she *does* feel the Holy Ghost. That she feels the presence of God renewed, intensified with each turn of her head. She contents herself with saying, "Sure does beat Pastor M'Dale's church. Though I don't guess it's as homey."

She spots a small line of women sitting in an empty pew near a sort of ornate, carved phone booth. From time to time a woman emerges from one side of the phone booth and another goes in.

"That's the confessional," Deacon says. "See, in the papist church you confess your sins every week to a priest. Otherwise you can't take the sacrament."

"Confess?" Manning wonders with a laugh. "Who'd want to do that?"

A group of GIs erupts in loud laughter on the other side of the church. The old ladies, and some of the other tourists, mostly military, look askance, but no one says anything.

"Disrespectful," Deacon grumbles. "I have half a mind to go over there . . ."

"Those are white soldiers, Deacon," Frangie points out.

"They still should show some reverence for a house of the Lord. Even a papist house of the Lord."

Frangie makes eye contact with a marble saint whose eyes are blank but somehow reproachful. "What denomination are you, Deac?"

Deacon smiles fondly. "Church of the Brethren in Marion, Indiana. It isn't much more than a cinderblock building by the side of the road. Even on Easter Sunday it's never more than seventy, eighty souls. But I sure do miss it."

"You church folk," Manning says tolerantly, shaking her head. "Me, I sleep late on a Sunday morning. I have a late night on Saturday at the café."

"You're a waitress?"

Manning makes a dismissive noise. "Hell, no . . ." She stops and covers her mouth and shoots a guilty look toward the altar. "I mean, gosh, no. I'm a short-order cook, a grill man except for being a woman."

Frangie has been long enough in the war to turn her mind briefly at least to ways in which she can benefit from Manning's cooking skill. But nothing comes to mind—she doubts even a great grill woman can do much with C rations and a spirit stove.

"How come they didn't make you a cook?" Deacon asks.

"Because every other colored person who gets drafted they make him a cook or a bottle-washer, or an orderly, or else send 'em to a support battalion digging latrines for white folks. I didn't tell them I could cook, I told them I could drive." She laughs happily at the thought. "I didn't want to spend the war digging shitters—sorry, slit trenches—for ofay officers."

Deacon doesn't smile much, but he smiles at this. "You don't have to love the Lord, Manning, He loves you. Must have. He made so much of you." Manning has a clear four inches on Deacon.

She pats him on the head.

They fall silent as the sheer splendor of the place weighs on them again. It is impossible not to be awestruck at the artistry, the skill, the incredible hard work and dedication that made the Sainte-Chapelle possible.

But it is that very nearness to God, combined with the alienness of the place, that makes Frangie want to question Him. *Why?*

That is her question. *Why?*

Two months have passed since D-Day. Frangie can't begin to guess how many men and women she has treated, saving some, losing others and, she hopes, comforting even the doomed ones. She has seen the human body inside and out in every detail. She has seen intestines and stomachs, esophaguses and brains. She's seen stumps where arms or legs had been. She's seen faces destroyed beyond any hope of repair. She's seen tankers burned to charcoal over half their body while the other half screams,

screams in agony no matter how much morphine she gives them.

She's heard too many scared, childlike voices calling for Mama, Mom, Mother, Mommy . . . Too many begging her to help . . . too many begging her to let them die . . .

Tell me why, Lord. Why? I would usually add, if it is Your will, but I've seen too many things and now I need to know.

"Why?"

"Are you asking the Lord or me?" Deacon says.

"Whoever has an answer," Frangie says. "You look around this place and you have to think, wow, look what human beings can make. Look at all this beauty. And that same creature builds Tiger tanks."

"War is sin," Deacon says.

"Tell that to Adolf," Manning says, wandering back from examining an alcove.

"*Ye have heard that it hath been said, An eye for an eye, and a tooth for a tooth: But I say unto you, That ye resist not evil: but whosoever shall smite thee on thy right cheek, turn to him the other also*," Deacon recites. "That's what Jesus had to say."

"Uh-huh," Manning says. "I got a quotation too. It's like this: mess with me and I will pay it back tenfold. If you start trouble I will sure as hell finish it. That's not the Bible, that's me."

Deacon tilts his head to look up at her. "Would you shoot a German, Manning?"

"Yes. I would," Manning says.

"And you, Doc?"

Frangie has no quick answer to that question, so Deacon reframes it. "Let's say you got a soldier, wounded, and a Kraut soldier pops up and he's going to kill that man. Would you shoot the German dead?"

Frangie squirms under the close examination of her two companions. Both of them are so sure of their answers. She is not.

"I don't know, Deac. I guess if that ever happens, I'll just have to see."

"It's all in my report, Colonel," Rainy says to Herkemeier.

Herkemeier has her report. She's spent two days preparing it and typing it out. They look at each other from across a metal desk that has been stuffed into a corner of a room in one of the government buildings taken over by the US Army in Paris. Behind them is cheerful chaos: civilian employees carry boxes of folders and wheel filing cabinets into place; Signal Corps soldiers string phone lines; military and civilian typists clack away at their machines; officers rush to and fro looking down at clipboards.

There is, Rainy thinks, a lot more chaos in war than a civilian might imagine. No one writes histories of the men and women who organized this moveable feast of mayhem, but somehow those anonymous folks eventually create order.

"I've read your report, Lieutenant," Herkemeier says, not concealing his irritation. He calls her "Lieutenant" the way an annoyed parent might use a child's full name. "I am asking now about you. Rainy Schulterman. The woman. *You*."

"Me?" Rainy shrugs. "I'm feeling fine, sir."

Herkemeier sighs. "Come on, Rainy. You don't have to do that with me."

It's Rainy now, not Lieutenant, she observes. He wants her to

251

open up and, she concedes, he has that right. He is her superior officer and he has a valid interest in knowing her state of mind. But Rainy is not merely a keeper of secrets because she's in intelligence, it is her core nature to give up as little as possible.

Give him something.

"I failed in my primary mission," she says. "I feel . . . disappointed . . . by that."

For a minute she half believes Herkemeier is going to throw her report at her. Then his expression softens and he shakes his head in a mix of irritation and amusement. "When this is all over you should look to a permanent career in intelligence, Rainy. You are the most close-mouthed person I've ever met."

Rainy's eyebrows rise. "But surely when the war is over we won't be . . ." Her words peter out as she begins to sense the truth.

Herkemeier snorts. "This war isn't going to end, Rainy, not really. Things have changed for good. Or ill. But changed. The USA isn't going to retreat back behind the oceans this time. There will be spies. Believe me, there will be spies."

Rainy nods. "I suppose a knowledge of Russian would be helpful."

Herkemeier points a finger at her. "You didn't hear me imply any such thing. Patton was nearly fired for slighting our gallant Soviet allies. But . . ." He shrugs. "It's never a bad thing to pick up a language."

Rainy nods slowly. It's a new thought. She'd always assumed after the war she would return home, go to college and become . . . well, something worthwhile. A lawyer? A teacher? A . . . what?

A spy?

"I'm fine, Jon," she says, relenting a little. "It was bad. What I saw in Oradour, that was very bad."

He plays the professional interrogator and remains silent.

"Look," she says, leaning forward, "do you want me to say it bothered me? Of course it bothered me. I spent some time with that little boy Bernard and . . ." And suddenly her voice betrays her and for a moment she cannot go on. Her next words come out in a lower register. "A terrible, terrible place. There, are you happy? You got me to admit that I'm a woman and I have emotions."

"A human being, not a woman," Herkemeier corrects gently. "Do you think because I'm a man I read your report without feeling anything? Do you think I didn't feel some of the horror behind your very cool, detached, professional report?"

"I didn't mean to imply . . ." She lets it trail off, embarrassed.

"Listen to me, Rainy, you're one of the best field agents I've ever seen. You failed to get us information on the Das Reich, but you took out a fuel dump that slowed them down and saved American GIs. You also . . . eliminated . . . a maquis traitor. And you killed the Nazi bastard responsible."

"Not yet," Rainy says, and an almost dreamy look calms her features. "The bastard responsible is about five hundred miles east of here in Berlin."

"Rio."

The voice is familiar, and Rio suspects that if she'd refused that last drink she'd recognize it immediately. But as it is her brain is foggy and her step is unsteady. Cat is sleeping it off on the bench in the Tuileries Garden where Rio plopped her after Cat went face-down.

Jenou has accepted an invitation to go dancing with a rather dashing young Polish officer. Personal friendships between enlisted and officer are extremely out-of-bounds, but that only applies to officers wearing the US uniform. Poles are—at least to Jenou's mind—fair game.

Rio turns toward the voice and blinks. Blinks again.

"Strand?"

He comes to her, places hands on her upper arms and draws her close for a kiss. A rather sloppy kiss, Rio thinks, possibly because her lips are numb. Also because his face won't quite stay still.

"What are you doing here? Have they moved you guys up?"

Strand glances furtively over his shoulder. And only now does Rio realize he's not in uniform. He's dressed in slacks and a white shirt with an Ike jacket, his only concession to military appearance.

"I need to talk to you, Rio," he says, and even drunk she feels the urgency.

"Sure. What's . . . I mean, what . . ."

He is looking around for a place to go and spots a café. One thing liberated Paris is not short of is cafés. He leads them to a table in the far, back corner, to a booth hidden from sight each time the kitchen door swings open.

"Coffee," Rio says. Strand orders a beer. She's about to warn him that beer leads to staggering through the streets of Paris, but his expression is too serious for jokes. And not just serious, but heightened, alert. Nervous.

Afraid.

Their drinks come and Rio downs the bitter espresso in a single gulp. Then she drinks half a bottle of mineral water.

"Okay, what is going on, Strand?"

"I guess there's no good way to . . ." He stops, reaches across to take her hands and says, "You love me, don't you?"

"Of course," she blurts, then frowns, not quite sure . . .

"And I love you. I want to marry you."

Rio laughs. "Are you proposing?"

"Oh, I know it's not right, I should be on one knee, and there should be a ring . . . but all that matters is we're going to still be together, no matter what."

Rio may be drunk, but not so drunk her brain doesn't raise the hairs on the back of her neck at the phrase *no matter what.*

"Strand. What's happened?"

He sits back. He tries out a jaunty smile which evaporates instantly. He fidgets with his glass. Then, in a rush, "I'm AWOL."

AWOL. Absent without leave.

Rio waves a dismissive hand. "Half of Paris is AWOL," she says. "The city is neck-deep in AWOLs and outright deserters. I had some fellow from New Jersey offer to sell me nylons and a Luger. Right on the street! Black marketeer, not that I'm saying you're . . . I mean, AWOL is one thing, some company punishment, clean latrines for a day . . . deserters are a whole different thing."

"Rio. I'm not going back."

"Back where?"

"Back. I'm not going back to my unit. I'm done. I'm done with this war, I just want to go home. I want to go home with you."

"I'm sorry, Strand, but I'm confused."

He calls the waiter and motions for another beer. Rio orders more coffee. This is clearly a coffee situation.

"I can't do it anymore," Strand says. "Everyone's getting killed. Our last raid we lost three planes! Thirty people. I watched them get hit, I watched them go down, and you know, you watch and you wait to count the chutes. And no one jumped, Rio. They all augured in."

"We've lost some people too."

"Of course you have. But you don't understand. Eighth Air Force keeps increasing the number of missions we have to fly before rotating out. I mean, it's math, Rio, it's math! Of the guys I started out with, only one is alive. They just keep sending us out till we're all dead!"

He has become worked up, voice rising in pitch, cheeks red.

Rio struggles to comprehend what Strand is saying. He's gone AWOL? He's deserted? Strand? Strand Braxton is a *deserter*?

"No one wants to die," she says. It's meaningless, really, but she feels the need to say something as her head keeps spinning around and around.

"I'm not a coward!" Strand says sharply, as though she had just accused him of it. She hadn't. Hadn't even formed the thought. But now . . . well now, there it is.

Is Strand a coward?

"You have to go back," Rio says. "We get GIs walking off the

256

line all the time. Sometimes it gets to be too much and they need a few hours to—"

"Go back? You want me to go back?" He stares at her as if seeing her for the first time. "My God, Rio. I expected you to understand. I could die. Me! I could die. I *will* die if I go back, I know it. I feel it inside."

"Strand, if you desert they'll look for you. They'll find you, eventually, and arrest you. Especially you being an officer!"

"I'll change my name," he says. "I've never liked my name that much, it's strange and slightly pompous, I think. I could be a Tom or a George or a Jack."

Instantly an unbidden thought: *You are no Jack.*

It's an unworthy thought. Rio wishes it had never come up, because now she is thinking of them in contrast, Strand and Jack. Strand the dashing pilot, the boy next door, the good son, the one she'd been supposed to marry. And Jack who was less dashing than witty, was from some town south of London, and was her subordinate.

A completely foolish comparison.

And foolish to compare their courage too. It is true, she does not know what a B-17 pilot endures on a bombing run over Germany. It had to be terrifying, holding the stick, working the pedals, struggling to keep your plane flying in a straight line as ack-ack exploded all around and Luftwaffe fighters sprayed machine guns at you.

Of course, it was no picnic advancing over an open field with mortars dropping all around you either, and Rio had seen Jack do just that many times.

"This is nuts," Rio mutters to herself more than Strand.

"I know it would be hard being married to me under a different name, but you'd get—"

"Jesus, Strand!"

Her outburst makes him recoil. He drops her hands.

Rio says, "It's not a question of what you call yourself, Strand, it's . . . I mean, it's just not possible. What do we tell my parents? Or your parents?"

"I don't know," Strand says, suddenly savage. "But at least whatever it is I'll be alive to tell them. I guess I was a fool to think you'd understand."

"Understand? That you're a deserter? A *deserter*? Every day I'm on the line I have to send someone out on patrol, or tell them to run straight at a machine gun, and they don't desert."

"You think I'm a coward."

"No, Strand I—"

"You think I am a coward. Admit it!"

"Strand, I'm—"

"Admit it!"

"Yes, you're being a coward! Yes! You have to go back, Strand, right away, before it gets worse."

He sits all the way back now, hands dropped to his sides. He looks smaller, narrower, as if his shoulders have shrunk. "You'd rather I die." He shakes his head bitterly. "You're not a woman anymore, Rio, not a woman or a girl. No woman sends her man to die. A *sergeant* does that, not a woman. You're unnatural, you know that? You're a freak in a freak show! Gaze upon the warrior woman with her bloody fugging knife and her Silver fugging Star!"

The switch from pleading to hectoring is sudden and shocks Rio. Strand isn't just angry at her for doubting his plan or even for doubting his courage. This goes deeper. This has been festering for a while.

Since I rescued him in Sicily.

He has no doubt taken a lot of ribbing over that. He'd been saved by his girlfriend, and his girlfriend had won a medal for saving him. But so what? Military life came with a heaped helping of teasing, challenging, ridiculing, but if you delivered, if you came through in the crunch, all of that faded away.

Anyway, does Strand imagine that life as a woman in the army had been easy?

He had lost friends? So had she. He'd been scared? So had she. His life was at risk? So was hers.

My God, I'm stronger than he is.

The thought is so unexpected that it elicits a short laugh which Strand takes as ridicule.

"I tell you you're no woman and you laugh at me," Strand says, dripping bitterness from each word. "I guess that proves my point."

Rio sits, silent, head down, slowly metabolizing this new and startling information. Big, tall Strand Braxton has found his limit. His courage is used up. His self-respect is shattered. And even if she could help him, any help would be rejected and seen as still more proof that she was "no woman."

She is now quite sober. Quite completely sober.

Rio stands up. "I'm still a woman," she says coldly. "It's just that I'm a better woman than you are a man."

She turns and walks away, pursued by a wave of conflicting emotions. Sadness. Anger. Self-pity. But most revealing of all to her is one single dominant emotion.

Relief.

PART THREE
HÜRTGEN FOREST

"In the Hürtgen forest proper, our gains came inch by inch and foot by foot, delivered by men with rifles—bayonets on one end and grim, resolute courage on the other. There was no battle of Europe more devastating, frustrating, or gory."

—Maj. Gen. William G. Weaver, Commanding General,
Eighth Infantry Division

"We are taking three trees a day, yet they cost a hundred men apiece."

—Anonymous army captain

20

Joe Pastor climbs down from the truck. He is in a forest, has been in a forest for an hour now, bumping along in the back of the deuce-and-a-half. The truck is jammed with men and women, almost all young, all white, none capable of looking tough.

Joe notices things like that, like the looks in people's eyes. He's a watcher, one of those people happiest on the sidelines observing. He observes a woman trying persistently to write a letter despite the jerkiness of the transport. She struggles over each word, puzzling it out before putting pencil to paper, more often than not tearing the paper in the process.

He observes a man who has rolled the sleeves of his uniform up to reveal a lurid tattoo on his forearm of a scantily-clad woman entwined around the word *Texas*.

He observes a man who chews gum, snapping it, blowing bubbles, looking around constantly as if anxious for conversation and finding none in this taciturn group.

They are all wet through to the bone having been left standing for an hour and a half, waiting on the truck to arrive at what had come to be called the Repple Depple, a torturing of the words Replacement Depot.

Joe wonders if these are the men and women he'll be fighting alongside. And he wonders if he shouldn't force himself out of his shell and actually engage some of them. Try to make friends for once.

But Joe Pastor comes from quiet folk in Boston, his father a newspaper editor and his mother active in causes and charities. His father is the shy, quiet one, and Joe's mother rolls her eyes in mock despair at how much her "two boys" are alike. Fortunately, Joe's little sister Barb is practically a carbon copy of their mother, so there is balance in the home.

The home that Joe suddenly misses with a pang so intense it almost doubles him over.

I didn't know homesickness could hurt so bad.

The truck rattles to a stop. Joe leans out of the back, peering around the canvas cover. He sees no special reason to stop here, except for a tiny sign stenciled by engineers with some incomprehensible numbers. A female corporal stands with an M1 carbine hiked on her hip, a cigarette dangling from her full lips, and an expression of weariness bordering on catatonic.

The driver clambers down with his clipboard held importantly and says, "Pastor. Joe Pastor."

"That's me!"

"Swell. Grab your gear and get off. This is your new home. Lucky you."

Joe does as instructed. He jumps down and the truck quickly lurches away to deliver the rest of its replacements.

"I'm Castain," the corporal says. "Let's go. We've got a little rumble scheduled for—"

Suddenly they hear the crash and pound of artillery. It's not on them, but it's near enough for Joe to think he should get into the ditch. Which he does. And then notices Castain looking down at him with a puzzled look.

"Hey. Pal. That arty's a good mile away, and it's dropping on Germans. That's *ours*." She waves a hand. "You'll get so you know which is which, not that we may not get an accidental shellacking by our own artillery, but in this case it's just a little wake-up call for Fritz."

"Fritz?"

Her answer is a slow drawl. "Yeah. You know, the Germans? They're this bunch of assholes who keep shooting at us. We don't know why. I think they don't like us."

He clambers up out of the ditch.

"You smoke?" Castain asks.

"No."

Castain nods. "Then give me your issue. Otherwise you might be tempted, and it's a bad habit."

Joe dutifully digs out his army-issued tobacco ration and hands it to Castain, who favors him with the kind of smile you reserve for dealing with the not-quite-all-there.

"Green as a whole field of new alfalfa," Castain says. "A little suggestion? See how you got your grenades hanging? You don't hang them by the fugging pin. See, because when you're running around the weight of the grenade could pull the pin and you blow yourself up and me, and I will not be happy. I will resent it!"

For some reason that phrase brings a crooked smile to the corporal's face and for the first time it occurs to Joe that she is actually quite pretty. Which does not help, because if there's one thing that intimidates Joe more than a foul-mouthed veteran, it's a pretty girl.

He quickly rearranges his grenades.

"Okay, let's go," Castain says. "Listen up, because we are going right into the shit when that barrage stops."

He falls into step behind her, confident that he can easily keep up with the young woman. He is quickly disabused of this notion because Castain moves through the dense forest like a monkey, stepping narrow, sliding through gaps, jumping fallen logs, and using close-packed trunks like a gymnast. Joe is soon panting. And all the while Castain keeps up a stream of words that is at once laconic, constant, and sometimes incomprehensible.

"See this path we're on? See how it's marked out with tape? That means engineers have cleared it. That way and that way? Mines and booby traps. Bang! And suddenly you don't have to worry about ever having babies."

Joe instinctively reaches for his crotch. He looks left, looks right, peers intently for sight of a stretched booby-trap wire, and falling behind in the process so he has to jog to catch up.

"Richlin is your squad sergeant, Stick—what the hell is his real name? Sticklin. Yeah, Dain Sticklin, he's the platoon sergeant. Both rock solid. Captain Passey's all right for an officer, not big on chickenshit. And Lieutenant Horne, well . . ."

He's about to prompt her when he notices the shrug and correctly decides that he's being given information that is not to be spoken of openly.

"There's a battalion of colored tanks going to make a run and we're going along to keep them from getting lonely," Castain says.

"Job number one when working with tanks? Don't get run over! They can't see much through their little portholes, and they will absolutely run right the hell over you."

Wait a minute, is she saying I'm going into actual combat? Now?

"Here's the way your day is planned out: you're gonna fall in with the rest of us, and we're going to walk along beside the tanks, then we're all going to turn and go blazing into the woods and the Krauts will panic and flee!"

Joe feels he may need to throw up.

"Here's how it's actually going to happen: you're gonna fall in with the rest of us, and we're going to walk along beside the tanks, and the Krauts will be raining mortars on our heads and getting their MG42s nice and warm, and then a tank's gonna blow up and everyone's going to be screaming and yelling and running around like chickens with their heads cut off."

"I think I need to—"

"Puke? Go ahead. Better to get it over with now."

He pauses, leans against a tree and empties his stomach.

"There are two schools of thought on stomachs," Castain proses on as artillery pounds and Joe retches. "Your optimist says it's best to have a nice, big breakfast so you have energy for a long fight where you might not get a chance to eat. Your pessimist on the other hand says better to have an empty stomach, and bowels too, though no one can take a shit anyway, if they've been living off C rations, without shoving a grenade up your rear. Or unless you've got the trots, and if you don't, you will." Then, realizing she hasn't finished the thought, she adds, "Empty stomach in case, you know, in case you're gut-shot. You don't want your half-digested Ham and Lima Beans bubbling out of the hole."

Joe had thought he was done puking. No. He had more.

Usually after throwing up he felt better. He does not feel better.

"You're gonna think mortars, hey, I better hit the dirt! Uh-uh. Mortars you keep moving forward. First of all, Fritz is careful not to shell his own people, unlike the idiots in our artillery, not to mention the goddamned air corps shooting anything that moves. So the closer you are to their lines the safer you are from shelling. Also, the way shells hit, see, the shrapnel keeps flying mostly in the same direction the shell lands." She makes an exploding motion with her hands to illustrate. "So you want an 88 or a mortar to go off behind you, not in front."

"But . . ."

"But?"

"But if you get closer to the Germans, don't they, you know . . . shoot at you?"

They're moving again, but Castain pauses a beat to look him over as if examining a rare but hideous new life form. "Why yes, I'm very much afraid that they will shoot at you, Private Dumbass. The Germans are very fond of shooting, and their favorite thing to shoot at is dumbass greenhorns."

She takes his shoulder and pulls him close. "Here's the secret not many people know: our job is to go and kill the sons-of-bitches Krauts before they can kill us. Shhhh! That's a secret known only to Ike and Patton and me."

They move on and now Castain switches from glib mockery to a more intense and hurried tone. The artillery barrage goes on and it sounds—and feels—horribly close. It's like a long, slow earthquake, wobbling and shaking under his boots.

"In the woods you can't see shit. So you do what's called marching fire, right? You shoot even when you don't have a target because the Kraut doesn't know you're just shooting trees, he thinks he better keep his head down. Right?"

"Yes, ma'am. I mean, yes."

"I don't mean just fire away till you run dry, but don't just carry your rifle, use it. And if you do see a Kraut, what do you do?"

"I . . ."

"Shoot him. You shoot him right then, no thinking about it, you aim and you shoot the bastard."

Is it possible to throw up with an empty stomach?

Better empty if you're gut-shot.

"If you see dead Krauts fire a round into their heads to make sure. And do not loot the bodies because—"

"I wouldn't do that!"

"Shut up, Private Dumbass. Don't touch dead Krauts because sometimes the bodies are booby-trapped. Same with their dugouts. We got a guy with the squad, name of Beebee, he's our scrounger. He knows his way around Fritz's little wires and such, and he's fair with dividing up the booty."

"The artillery stopped," Joe observes. "Maybe we're not—"

"Kid, listen to me: shut up. Shut. Up. You know nothing about *nothing*. Do what you're told and *only* what you're told."

Joe has not until this minute noticed that the tapes marking the path are gone. Instead he's noticed that there are very few leaves or branches on tree trunks that are often scorched black.

And suddenly he realizes they are walking through a thin line of foxholes. He sees helmeted heads peering cautiously out.

A young female sergeant spots Castain and gives her a brief wave. Castain leads the way to the sergeant who, on closer inspection, must be even younger than Joe himself.

"This is . . ." Castain pauses, holding a hand toward Joe. "What's your name?"

"Joe. Joe Pastor."

"Yep. Pastor, Richlin; Richlin, another idiot who doesn't know how to carry a grenade or which end of the gun to point."

A woman? His sergeant is a woman?

"Right," Richlin says, not even looking up from loading loose .45 caliber rounds into a Thompson clip. "As usual we're giving the Krauts time to reset the table." Then she glances at Joe and says, "Put him with Pang."

Pang, to Joe's shock, is a Jap. Or something pretty darn close to being a Jap. But he's polite—for a Jap—and makes space in his foxhole for Joe to climb down in with him.

"Got a name?" Pang asks.

"Joe Pastor."

"Welcome to World War Two," Pang says. "And yeah, I look like a Jap. I am one, partly, so you can either get used to that, or go dig your own hole."

Joe does not want to dig. He wants to vomit and defecate simultaneously. Water fills his boots. He looks down, and sees that Pang is standing on a piece of wooden crate, keeping his boots dry. There is no room on the crate for Joe.

"We'll be jumping off here, pretty quick. Make sure to take

the safety off. It's hard to shoot with the safety on. No, not yet! I didn't live this long letting greenhorns run around loose shooting me in the behind."

"What do we do when we . . . when we jump off?"

"We get up out of this hole and go where Richlin points. Then we shoot and we get shot at." Seeing the distress on Joe's face, Pang softens a little. "Look, kid, on the bright side maybe you get a million dollar wound? A nice through-and-through in the meat of your calf, let's say. Just stay next to me."

A big man drops into the foxhole and curses on finding Joe.

"What's this, Pang, you making friends?"

"New guy, Geer."

"Hmmm," Geer says. "What are the odds you figure?"

Pang shrugs. "Beebee says any new guy is five-to-one in the first twenty-four hours. Odds will change after the first fight."

"Yeah, he'll be dead or crying, one or the other," Geer says, and only slowly does it penetrate Joe's nearly-paralyzed brain that they are talking about him. Betting on him.

Betting on his life.

"I'll go ten bucks at five-to-one," Pang says, eyeing Pastor like a racing tout checking out a horse.

For the first time Geer looks at Pastor. It's an up-and-down appraisal that takes in Joe's uniform, his weapon, the contents of his webbing belt, his face and ends with an intent stare into his eyes. "Nah. You're wrong this time, Pang. I'm going to take that bet, and you're gonna give me back what you won on Dial."

They are. They are openly betting on his death! Right in front of him!

Something changes, some scent on the breeze perhaps, because both Pang and Geer check their weapons, ratcheting back the slides to check for rounds in the chamber and look for any grit that might cause a jam. Joe follows suit, fingers trembling as they travel over his M1.

Pang and Geer take deep swigs from their canteens, and Joe copies them.

Suddenly, without warning, they are clambering up and out of their foxholes. From off to the left comes the sound of Sherman tanks revving and treads grinding over foliage.

"Where are they?" Joe asks frantically, walking at a steady if shaky pace alongside Pang and Geer. Geer has a BAR hanging from a strap, leveled at waist height, with an ammo belt looped over his shoulder.

Geer pauses. "Pang! Give me a scratch, I can't reach with this damned BAR!"

"I am not scratching your crotch, Geer!"

"It's my back, come on, Pang!" As they walk Pang scratches Geer's back vigorously while Geer mutters, "Fugging lice."

Ahead Joe sees a clearing, a space between these woods and identical woods further away. It's like a road cut through . . . no, of course, it's a firebreak. Joe's seen firebreaks hiking in Vermont.

Through stumps of blasted trees Joe sees Sherman tanks veering right, heading on an intercept path with the infantry. To his amazement he spots a Negro head beneath the leather tanker's helmet of the first tank's commander.

"They're colored!" Joe says.

"Yeah," Geer mutters. "This war's gone all to hell. Women, Japs,

Nigras, hell, see that fellow over there? He's a goddamn limey!"

Joe glances and sees a handsome-looking fellow with a ginger beard darkened by soot and grime. He's walking a pace ahead of Richlin. Joe spots a wicked knife on Richlin's leg and it does not reassure him. It is obviously not regulation.

Brrrrrrrrt! Brrrrrrrrrt! Brrrrrrrt!

"What's that?"

Neither Pang nor Geer bothers to answer and then the American tanks open up, .30 and .50 caliber machine guns, nearer and louder. A hollow *katush!* followed instantly by an explosion, as a tank fires its cannon.

"All right, new guy, stay behind the tanks!" Geer yells, and he and Pang break from the trees and run to unite with other soldiers, all huddling in the shadow of the tanks, moving at a fast march, wanting speed almost as much as the tankers do.

For a terrible moment Joe is not sure he can follow. The noise is like nothing he's ever imagined. Machine guns, cannon, and now mortars, ricochets zinging, and voices yelling in rage, in pain, in fear! It's a deafening howl, the noise you could imagine hearing if you pulled the cover back on hell for a minute.

Flit! Flit! Thunk!

The tree trunk nearest to Joe pops splinters from a bullet wound. Not all the German fire is stopped by the bulk of the tanks.

Pang and Geer are already dozens of yards away, paying Joe no attention.

Just say you're a coward! They'll let you go home!

No, not that. Joe's father was old, old enough to have fought with Teddy Roosevelt in Cuba. His grandfather had been a

Union Captain who'd fought at Antietam and had lost a leg to a Confederate minié ball.

Joe Pastor moves. Stiff-legged. A step. Another. A sudden, overpowering urge to be with Pang and Geer. He runs, runs down the side of the tanks, yelling as he goes, yelling to stop hearing the whizz of bullets past his ears.

He reaches Pang and Geer and, panting, trots alongside them, keeping both of them, as well as the tank, between himself and the murdering German fire.

Ka-BAM!

A tank blows up.

A jeep emblazoned with Red Cross brassards and driven by a tall colored woman, with a colored man and a colored girl so small at first Joe thinks she might be a child, goes tearing past, seemingly indifferent to the danger.

If *they're* not worried—

Something punches Joe in the arm, hard. He staggers, but keeps his feet and keeps pace with Pang and Geer.

"Hey," Pang says, glancing back. "You're hit!"

Joe blinks. Is he? Is he hit?

He takes a quick inventory and sees that the shoulder of his uniform jacket is saturated with blood.

"Oh, God!" Joe cries.

He stops, tears off his jacket, and Pang yells, "Keep cover, you fugging—"

Two machine-gun rounds plow two holes through Joe's chest. He falls.

Geer yells, "Medic! Medic!" But he does not stop. No one stops.

No one at all. They just keep moving, the tanks roaring and coughing, the soldiers tramping, and all the while the forest firebreak is a tornado of flying steel.

Joe lies on his side, watching it all. When he breathes it is shallow. He can't catch his breath. Each inhalation seems shallower than the one before it, and each breath makes a wet gurgling sound.

Joe feels no pain. He feels as if his entire body has been hit by an electric power line and he is stunned, paralyzed, his brain moving through molasses, his hands not doing what he wants them to do.

The tanks rattle on and the last of the infantry goes with them. A relative quiet descends.

I'm wounded. I'm hurt.

But I'm okay. I'm okay. I'm hit, but I'm okay.

The next inhalation is more wet than raspy. Through the fog of his shock Joe begins to feel something, something that is like pain, but like pain he's watching someone else endure. He feels disconnected from the body gasping for air, the body with lungs flooded with his own blood.

A face swims into sight, swirling and weird, like a hallucination.

"I'm here, soldier," the black face says. "Deacon! Plasma!"

"My name is Joe," he tries to say, but it's nothing but a grunt and a wet gargle. Incoherent.

"Don't talk, just lie back, soldier," the black face says—a woman too. Huh. She's doing something fussy with her hands. He glimpses big steel scissors chopping through his uniform and thinks, *What will I do now?*

He does not feel the needle prick in the crook of his elbow.

"Pump it. He's about drained out."

Then Deacon, holding the plasma high with one hand while feeling Joe's neck with the other, says, "I'm not getting pulse. What's his BP?"

Frangie looks at the blood pressure cuff, knowing what she will see. The systolic pressure is seventy and dropping. She does not bother to tell Deacon.

She stands up and her knees crack. "Tag him."

21

FRANGIE MARR—HÜRTGEN FOREST, NAZI GERMANY

"I'm here, soldier."

The soldier is nineteen years old. A piece of wood, fresh so it still oozes sap, a piece of a tree, a chunk of wood the size of a child's forearm, protrudes from his belly. Deacon holds his flashlight beam on the injury with one hand, and keeps a bag of plasma elevated with the other.

A second, smaller splinter, this one the size of a man's thumb, protrudes from the base of the injured soldier's neck.

A third splinter, this only the size of a pencil, protrudes from his left eye socket, just below the eyeball. The splinter forces the eye to bulge out.

Blood seeps. Blood gushes.

The soldier screams.

Deacon's light wavers and for a moment the only thing Frangie can see is the soldier's screaming mouth.

BOOOM!

BOOOM! BOOOM! BOOOM! BOOOM!

The barrage intensifies, shells going off so fast they almost sound like machine guns, exploding like flashbulbs illuminating a nightmare scene for milliseconds at a time. A terrified face; a soldier running; a big tree branch falling; a soldier writhing.

Each highlighted for just the duration of an explosion.

Hell by strobe light.

German 88s screech into the trees, explode, and spray shattered wood in every direction. It's a deliberate German tactic. Frangie has had to remove two splinters from herself, smaller thankfully, and in less vital locations, but exceedingly painful. The wood shrapnel lacerates flesh, and shreds veins and arteries, leaving medics to try and find those bits of tattered, slimy tubes in the midst of raw hamburger.

Months have passed. Spring has given way to summer and now a cold, drenching, muddy autumn. The skies darken too soon, and too often never brighten as rain comes again and again, turning the earth to mud—mud over pine needles. Mud beneath the slicked leaves of deciduous trees; mud caked on trucks and tanks and jeeps; mud permeating boots and uniforms; mud in hair; mud in teeth; mud that at times seems like a living, malicious beast clawing at feet and legs, pulling on soldiers as if determined to drag them down to hell itself.

Frangie feels the creeping need to itch. She, like almost everyone, has lice. Lice in the hair on her head, lice in her crotch, her armpits, lice making a home of her entire body.

She has managed maybe two hot meals in the last week, otherwise reduced to C rations. It's so cold at night that C rations freeze, but fires are an impossibility, so GIs thaw their C-rats over tin cans filled with gasoline-saturated sand and secreted at the bottom of water-sloshing foxholes.

Frangie hates every iteration of C rations. She hates the original three varieties: Meat Stew with Beans, Meat with

Vegetable Hash, and Meat Stew with Vegetables. She hates the newer meals: Meat and Spaghetti in Tomato Sauce, Chopped Ham, Egg, and Potato, Meat and Noodles, Pork and Rice, Frankfurters and Beans, Pork and Beans, and above all, Ham and Lima Beans.

The army has blessedly stopped sending the dreaded Meat Hash and the godawful Mutton Stew with Vegetables meals. Unfortunately they have not sent Chicken and Vegetables, which Frangie is convinced will be bad, but will at least be a new kind of bad.

This is the only joy in the Hürtgen forest: daydreams of food.

There are days when she is sure she would kill a German herself if she could just eat some of his rations. Everyone says the Krauts still get actual bread, bread that comes in loaves as opposed to the canned atrocity the US Army supplies.

And God only knows what sins she might commit in exchange for a plate of catfish and fried okra, or even just good old red beans and rice with cornbread so hot from the oven that you couldn't hold it.

A fresh peach? Or a strawberry and rhubarb pie? Or a bowl of ice cream churned in the kitchen with fresh cream and ice and rock salt?

Iced tea with a sprig of mint?

Her aunt's blackstrap pecan pie?

Her other aunt's Thanksgiving turkey?

Don't think about it. Tend to this poor man.

How?

He has a log in his belly, he's a goner, done for, like so many others, like so, so many others. His blood loosens the consistency of the mud around him.

Mud-blood soup. That's the meal the Hürtgen serves.

Frangie scratches furiously at her head. Her fingernails come away red from flea and lice bites. Some hair comes too: her hair is falling out. Not all at once, just a little here, a little there, a generalized thinning so her scalp could be seen if the sun ever rose. Even at noon, even when it isn't raining, the Hürtgen is always dark.

In every direction are the trees. They are close-packed, and in better times must have made for lovely, shaded walks beneath a canopy of leaves and needles.

But there are no leaves on these trees. They look like fish bones picked clean, a stumpy trunk sprouting blackened branches that stick straight out, horizontal, and often almost to the ground so that in many places just walking ahead means bending or breaking branches. The Toothpick Forest some called it now.

D-Day had been terrible, and the painfully slow and bloody slog through the bocage country was terrible as well. But that had been followed by the advance to Paris which had been relatively easy for Frangie's unit, and the drive from there to the German border had been hard, but progress had been steady. People had started betting pools on when the war would end, with most folks guessing before Christmas.

The Krauts were beaten, everyone said.

The war would soon be over, everyone said.

And then, the Hürtgen.

"I'm here, soldier." She's left the previous patient floating away on a morphine cloud. He will never come down off that cloud.

"Doc. Doc. I . . ." He's a mid-twenties buck sergeant named Oglebee, one of the infantry detachment assigned to the battalion. He's seated, leaning back against a tree trunk. His hands are open on the ground. His Thompson is on the ground beside him, raindrops making a dull musical note as they plop on the magazine.

"Tell me where you're hit," Frangie says as she motions Deacon over with the flashlight; he'd been praying over the man with the splinters.

"I'm not hit, Doc. I just gotta, it's all, you know, I can't is it, I can't. I can't. I can't."

"Come on, Sarge, screw your head back on." It's not her first case of combat fatigue, the favorite euphemism for complete mental breakdown.

"I shit myself." Oglebee starts to cry.

"Yeah, I noticed," Frangie says, straining for a note of humor in hopes he will respond.

"I'm done. I'm done."

"Nah, you just need to—"

He lunges for his Thompson, knocking her sprawling in the mud. It's an awkward weapon for what he has in mind. A .45 slug makes a big hole.

Deacon has come over. "Sarge, you don't want to be doing that. You know you'll get a general court. You'll serve out the war in a military prison."

Oglebee looks at him and suddenly a great big grin splits his face. "That sounds pretty damn good to me," he says. He flips the selector to single fire and upends the Thompson so it's aimed straight down at his foot.

Frangie grabs the barrel. She does not wrestle for control. In a soft voice she says, "Here, not there." She guides the muzzle away from the top of Oglebee's foot where the bullet will smash through a hundred small, delicate bones, permanently crippling him. She positions it to one side, aimed at the meat of the side of his foot. It will hurt like hell, but he may walk again.

"Thanks, Doc," Oglebee whispers.

Frangie tugs Deacon's shirt and they get up and walk away just as the barrage starts up again.

Amid the earth-pounding explosions Frangie hears the single round and hears Oglebee's cry of pain.

"I got him," Deacon says. "You get some sleep, Doc. You look like something that ought to be scraped up off the road."

The battalion's tanks are all dug in now, meaning, as Frangie had learned, that tanks are driven into excavated trenches so that only the turrets show. The accompanying infantry and support troops are in holes. And they are all wrapped up in, trapped in, buried alive in what the Germans called the Hürtgenwald, just over the border from Belgium and Luxembourg into Germany.

No one in the Hürtgenwald, on either side, believes the war will be over by Christmas.

In addition to being cold, wet and claustrophobic, the terrain is also steep, sometimes so steep that a GI trying to ascend a hill has to pull himself hand over hand, using the trees as grips and footholds. Hand over hand up steeply-canted ground that is all slick, wet pine needles and mud and branches as machine guns rattle and mortars fall.

But it is the tree bursts of the 88s that are the special terror of the Hürtgen. The Germans have learned to set their fuses for air bursts, up in the treetops. That way the explosions shower wooden spears down on men and women cowering in watery foxholes, like an ancient barrage of arrows in some long-ago battle where soldiers had shields.

Except these soldiers do not have shields, and their foxholes do not protect them from this injury and death from above. There is no cover in the Hürtgen. There is no hole you can hide in.

You cannot see the enemy in the Hürtgen. You cannot see much of anything besides tree trunks, so visibility is measured in a few yards. Half the patrols that are sent out become lost, turned around and baffled by the mists, the fogs, the smoke, and the endless sameness of the trees.

Just the day before, Frangie had treated a German soldier who had become so lost he lined up for chow at a US field kitchen before realizing he was at an American mess tent. One of the GIs had shot him, but only in the rear end. Frangie had bandaged and sent him on to battalion aid.

"Hey, Morton," Frangie says, crouching over a woman shivering like she's in the worst of a plague fever.

"D-d-d-doc."

Frangie pulls out a cigarette, lights it and places it in the wounded GI's mouth. She sucks too hard, chokes, and blood comes faster from her neck wound.

She will not survive. Frangie will not tell her this. She's dead, but only Frangie knows it.

The cigarette calms her, a little at least. She takes another drag and looks at Frangie through eyes that seem to be looking up from the bottom of a well.

Ah, Frangie is wrong: *she knows.*

"We're getting you out to battalion aid as soon as Manning's back with the jeep," Frangie tells PFC Morton.

"Okay, Doc." She's passive, docile. The fever ague has burned itself out. "I'm cold is all."

"I'm going to give you a little happy juice, okay?"

"Okay, Doc."

She stabs the needle into her exposed upper arm and squeezes morphine into her.

"You rest easy, Private. We're going to transport you in just a few minutes."

Frangie has stopped thinking of statements like that as lies. They are medicine, of a sort. Death might be inevitable, but hope is a gift she can give, though with each lie she feels a part of herself wither.

The last word so many men and women in the Hürtgen hear is a lie. It feels wrong. It feels disrespectful. A person should know when they are soon to meet their maker.

But no, that's nonsense. Injured soldiers are problems to be managed, and a lie makes the managing easier.

Suddenly the air is torn again by the shrieks of incoming artillery. Now, in a heartbeat, she must make the decision: stay with the doomed woman to the end and likely be killed herself? Or run for cover on the grounds that she is more useful to more people alive?

"Hang tight," Frangie says.

Then she dives into the nearest hole along with Deacon. It turns out to be a foxhole inhabited by a pair of cousins from Annapolis, Maryland, named Jessie and James, Jessie being a rather chubby young woman while her male cousin, James, is so thin he's invisible standing sideways.

"Sorry!" Frangie cries as the treetops explode again.

"Any time, Doc," Jessie says.

The four of them are so tight in the hole that none of them can really cower as effectively as they'd like. The cousins have made a sort of shelf that allows them to just barely squeeze beneath six inches of dirt piled on a mat made of twigs and leaves. Useless except against the weakest of splinters, but a frightened soldier will take any small advantage.

This is barrage number what? Frangie wonders. Fifteen? Twenty? One thousand? It's been like this forever. Splinter wounds. Shrapnel wounds. Concussion. Battle fatigue. Trench foot. The eternal dysentery. She's a doctor on rounds that never end. When she sleeps it's in snatches of an hour. Or a standing nap, as she's come to think of them, when she simply goes blank and weaves back and forth, eyes closed, until someone or something snaps her out of it.

Now, leaning against Jessie and James and Deacon, despite the mad destruction all around, she almost falls asleep again. Splinters patter on her helmet like deadly raindrops. Deacon yelps as a small shard stabs his shoulder.

The barrage ends—for the moment. The Germans have developed the trick of pausing a barrage just long enough for GIs to start thinking it's safe, and then dropping artillery on them as they emerge from their holes.

The lieutenant is yelling just that. "Stay in your holes! Stay in your holes!"

But that does not apply to medics. Frangie crawls to the man with the splinter wounds. He's dead, finished off by a mercifully quick shard of steel shrapnel through his head.

She listens for cries of pain. "Anyone hurt?" she yells.

A voice calls back, "I pissed myself, does that count?"

She goes back to the Jessie and James hole where James informs her that his feet are mostly all better now. James had suffered a very common injury: trench foot, the nasty result of feet too long in cold and wet.

"Glad to hear it," Frangie says. "In future be careful to care for your feet, I do not have time to be dealing with every—"

"Medic! Medic! Doc!"

Now the cry goes up and again Jessie, James and Deacon all unite to propel her up and out of the hole, with Deacon scrambling up after her. They run toward the cries and flop down beside a fighting hole in which a corporal is bellowing in pain. They make to pull him up, but he starts screaming that the pain is too great.

So Frangie drops down beside him and quickly discovers that he has scalded his leg with spilled coffee.

Now Frangie does her best impersonation of an exploding 88. "This is why you're screaming like a baby? What is the matter with you? You have me running over here because you're too clumsy to hold onto your coffee?"

Days pass in rain-filled holes. Nights pass the same way, but with extra fear, because the night-time is when the German patrols come out. Frangie and Deacon move from hole to hole, from tank to truck to half-track. They bandage and medicate, splint and transfuse, and load soldier after soldier onto the hood of Manning's jeep for transport to the rear. And they nag. Nagging is a big part of the job. Mostly Frangie nags them to change their socks and dry their feet, because the old World War I plague of trench foot is back with a vengeance, here, just a few miles from the caved-in remains of those same World War I trenches.

The advance through the Hürtgen, so far as Frangie can tell, is not advancing. All that's happening is that GIs are breaking down under the constant artillery and gunfire and cold and wet. And every now and then, everything goes suddenly nuts.

One of the white soldiers from the infantry down the line had come running, stark naked, through the battalion's position, waving a white T-shirt in surrender the day before. He had come running right down the firebreak, which is all that separates them from the Germans. The only reason the Germans hadn't shot the poor man was that they were too busy laughing. Frangie and Manning had tackled the fellow and both had smelled alcohol on him. The man was incoherent, hysterical and thrashing about like a wild animal. Manning had applied some special field medicine: a pile-driver punch to the man's belly, and then she and Frangie had dragged him away to safety.

"We're going over to the attack," Manning says breathlessly. She's just come back from the field hospital with a jeepload of supplies and the latest gossip.

"I thought this already was an attack," Frangie mutters.

"Who says we're attacking?" Deacon demands.

"Says me, who overheard the colonel telling the captain, that's who." Manning then shares out her loot from the rear-area trip: cigarettes, a nice, new, as-yet-unstained stretcher, and a bar of actual Belgian chocolate, very different from the army-issued version in that it did not break teeth or give you the runs.

They share half the chocolate between the three of them, with Frangie pocketing the rest for her patients. The chocolate is impossibly smooth, sinfully rich, a glorious moment of pure pleasure. It's almost as if God has reached down from heaven to say, "I know this is all terrible, but on the other hand . . . *chocolate!*"

An hour later the official word comes: they are digging out the tanks. The white infantry is coming to guard their flank. And together they are going to drive straight up the firebreak and pivot left into what the brass said was a weakly-held sector of the German line.

The firebreak is about wide enough for two tanks running side by side, with the far side of that firebreak held by the Germans. It is along this firebreak that the tank battalion has stayed for days. The Germans attacked twice and were repulsed twice. The Americans attacked once and were driven back. Frangie imagines she can hear the *ding-ding-ding* of a bell signaling the next round in this endless, brutal prize fight.

Looking up through the Toothpick Forest, Frangie sees rain clouds above the jagged black dagger points. Which means that the planes will not be coming to help with the attack. Bad weather is the Krauts' friend.

The attack is scheduled for midmorning to confuse the Germans who've become accustomed to dawn attacks. The morning is spent backing the Shermans out of their dugouts, running ammo, and in Frangie's case, dealing with sprains, bruises and mangled fingers.

The Germans hear the Shermans and have a good idea what's coming, so they launch a heavy artillery barrage. They hit no tanks, but do destroy a half-track, kill two men and wound a third who is tended by another medic, leaving Frangie free to think way too much about the coming attack.

Frangie, Deacon and Manning sit in the jeep, well behind the tanks which now idle at the edge of the trees, ready to burst suddenly out into the firebreak, guns blazing. Frangie glances at her watch: H-hour in thirty minutes. First . . .

A small spotter plane, a fragile J-3, drifts lazily above at tree-top height as its pilot radios information back to the artillery far behind the line. Germans fire up at the plane, but they too are limited by the terrain—no sooner do they see the plane than it is screened by tree trunks. By now the artillery has its fire mission: coordinates, types of ordnance, number of rounds. The spotter plane is there to assist with accuracy.

The first round from a 155 millimeter "Long Tom" whistles overhead and drops in a fiery crash in the woods on the far side of the firebreak.

Thirty seconds later a second round, and this one lands right in the first row of trees.

Up in the J-3 a pilot calls on his radio, signaling that the second shot was on target, and what happens next is simply stunning.

Frangie has been on the receiving end of German artillery and it is accurate and shattering. But it has never had the sheer intensity of what is now unleashed from the distant sky-pointing muzzles of 105 howitzers and 155 Long Toms. The woods opposite boil with fire and smoke. Entire trees go twirling through the air. Great gouts of dirt fly skyward. And it goes on and on, an ancient god's temper tantrum, a pounding, beating assault, an annihilation.

When at last the shells stop falling, Frangie hears the German cries, the counterpart of "Medic!"

Out of nowhere the captain walks by Frangie's jeep, yelling to a radio operator hurrying to keep pace.

"Ask 'em when the hell we are jumping off! The goddamned Krauts are on their asses, we should go now! Now!"

They do not go *now*, *now*. They wait as the minutes tick slowly by, minutes during which the Germans can be heard just across the firebreak in woods identical to those sheltering Frangie.

The Germans are recovering. Quickly.

The minutes drag by, and with every lost minute the Germans unpack another crate of *Panzerfausts*, redig a collapsed fighting hole, evacuate their wounded and replace them with fresh troops.

Frangie feels something change. There's a fresh, chilly breeze, portending another bout of rain. She glances at the soldiers closest to her: Sergeant Frankie Wallace in command of the tank named Firecracker. She winks down at Frangie. Frangie lets her gaze drift to Firecracker's bow gunner, P.D., his head up through his hatch. He does not wink. She cannot hear over the rough idle of the Sherman, but she can see that his teeth are chattering.

Finally, long after the dust has settled on the German positions, the signal comes. The Shermans lurch forward, crashing into view, a line of half a dozen tanks. They advance in neat order and pivot right as white infantry drifts out of the woods to walk in their lee.

It is a terrifying spectacle for Frangie. She has never gotten out of her head Sergeant Moore's wisdom that the Krauts will attack a tank before anything else. The Germans have heard the Shermans. They've had far too long to recover and prepare, and here are the tanks passing right before them, as exposed as floats at a parade, their weakly-armored flanks in direct line of sight for the Germans.

Not that the tanks are trying to sneak by. Their machine guns hurl tracer rounds into the bushes and trees, their cannon erupt at intervals, firing at point-blank range. But despite the suppressing fire the first *Panzerfaust* explodes against a turret. The commander buttons up, but then reemerges moments later: his tank is unharmed. The other tanks veer their machine guns toward the source of the *Panzerfaust*, but the Germans have long since learned to fire and move, fire and move.

A second *Panzerfaust* comes streaking and misses; a third hits a tank in the treads and it veers out of control, practically running over its own infantry, who scramble to avoid being crushed.

Five tanks now.

An 88 fires from concealment, point-blank, right from the tree line down the line, and a Sherman blows up, fire shooting from every porthole and seam.

"All right, Manning, let's go," Frangie says.

"Make sure your red cross is clean and shiny!" Manning yells as she guns the engine and the jeep goes tearing out of the cover of the forest, bumps out into the firebreak and turns a hard, two-wheel right. Because the infantry occupies the safer ground to the right side of the tanks, Manning drives along the left of the Shermans, between the Germans and the tanks.

Machine guns blaze on both sides now, tracers crisscrossing over Frangie's head.

The exploded tank goes *pop-pop-pop* as machine-gun rounds inside cook off from the heat and the slugs ricochet around inside, making mincemeat of anything made of flesh and blood. At any moment one of the tank's own high explosive rounds will reach the necessary heat and blow the tank apart like a firecracker in a beer bottle.

"There's a man down!" Deacon yells, pointing ahead, like a hunting dog on the scent. Manning brakes and Frangie and Deacon jump out. There is indeed a man, or what's left of him. He appears unhurt from the waist up, but everything below is smoking meat. A white infantryman has broken both cover and the rules to run out and throw dirt on the man's still-burning clothing.

"We got him, go!" Frangie yells to the white soldier.

The wounded man gasps, mouth working like a beached fish. He's trying to speak but he can't form words. His breath is short, sharp inhalations and quick moans, but he's trying to get at something in the breast pocket of his tanker's jacket.

"Lie still, soldier, we've got you."

But the man keeps clawing at his uniform, eyes bulging with some desperate need.

Frangie cuts away the edges of burned uniform to find the line of damage, to see just how much is lost. "Deacon, look in his jacket!"

Deacon fumbles and pulls out a rosary. "This?"

The man shakes his head.

Deacon pulls out a letter. From the letter falls a photograph of two little girls with their parents. The wounded man takes it reverently and presses it to his chest.

Manning cries out, "Shit!"

Frangie looks up to see blood pouring down the side of her neck. "Deacon!" He's already leaping toward Manning as Frangie fights down nausea. The wounded man is more charcoal than flesh below the waist. His thighs have melted and then resolidified, as a wax nightmare version. His flesh is so hot that raindrops hiss and steam when they land.

"I'm going to give you something for the pain," Frangie says and stabs a morphine syrette into him.

"My. Babies." He holds the picture for her to see.

"They're beautiful little girls," Frangie says.

"My. Babies."

"You'll be with them soon. Million dollar wound. You're going home, soldier."

His body jerks violently, as if the top half is trying to shake itself free of the destroyed bottom half. Shock. She would elevate his legs if he had legs. When the spasm passes the soldier grows sleepy. His eyelids droop.

"How's Manning?" Frangie yells.

The battle is not going to plan. A second Sherman explodes

and the flaming wreckage is blocking the path. Oily smoke rolls over Frangie and she's glad for the foul-smelling reek as it might conceal her for a while at least.

Deacon does not answer.

"I'm cold, I'm cold. Funny, huh?" the burned man says.

"Yeah, kind of," Frangie says, frantically digging out plasma. It won't save the man: it's just all she knows to do for him.

Deacon, in a shaky voice, says, "Manning's okay. Took a piece of her earlobe is all!"

Thunk-thunk-thunk-thunk!

Machine-gun rounds pierce the jeep, passing right through one door and out through the other. Manning, thankfully, is on the ground with Deacon bent over her.

And some force seizes control of Frangie Marr, some force she can only stand back and watch in horrified amazement. Because this thing inside her, this boiling rage made out of blood and lice and hunger and fear propels her to her feet. She strides past the jeep. Well out beyond any tanks. Face to face with the Germans in the forest.

"You fugging Nazi bastards!" she shouts. She pulls off her helmet and bangs her fist on the Red Cross brassard. "Red fugging Cross. Do you see a gun on me? Do you see a machine gun on my jeep? You want us to start shooting *your* medics?"

She plops the helmet back on her head and marches back, fully expecting to feel a punch to the spine followed a split second later by the crack of a rifle.

The battle rages on.

Her jeep is not hit again.

22

"The replacement?" Richlin asks Geer.

"Pang owes me fifty bucks."

"Anyone remember his name? I don't have any paperwork on him."

"It was something normal. Like Bill or Joe or something," Geer says. The back, rear of his uniform is red with blood.

Rio nods at the area. "You get shot in the ass, Geer?"

"I got shot in the side, not in the ass, and I will punch the first one of your sons of bitches who says different."

The squad is in a state of collapse, sprawled in pine needles and mud, some already snoring, others cleaning their rifles, others still doing inexplicable things like Jenou, who is, bizarrely, writing furiously in a little notebook she keeps.

"You need to go seek some, uh, medical attention? In the rear?" Rio asks, then grins, betraying the pun.

"Very funny," Geer says and scowls at Pang who laughs. "No, my rear does not require me to go to the rear, fugging comedians. It's just a graze, but it sure does bleed, and stings too. Doc says it'll heal up. Says I should try to take it easy, stay off my feet, maybe try a restricted diet. Because he's a fugging comedian too."

Rio grins. From day one at basic training she has not liked

Geer, not liked his rude bigotry, or his occasional bullying of replacements—not that Jenou is really any kinder—or, for that matter, anyone in the squad. Replacements come, replacements die. It's best not to get close to anyone until they've survived a week. At least.

No, Rio has never liked Geer, but she has come to rely on him. A loud-mouthed redneck he might be, but he can fight, and in Rio's world there are only three things she needs from any member of her squad: that they fight. That they fight. And that they fight.

Geer *fights*.

More surprising still, he and Pang seem to have become partners in a way. Geer could have fobbed off the BAR, which Pang feeds, but he's kept the machine gun and his ammo carrier. They call each other "Jappo" and "Hillbilly" respectively, but they seem to get along. Pang too *fights*.

The tanks have gone on ahead with fresh infantry, but word is they've stalled. And since there's a chance of a counterattack, Rio is trying to decide whether to bully her squad into digging in here, or figure they'll be pushed back to their start point and can reoccupy their old holes.

"Take five more minutes," she says. "Then I want to see entrenching tools in action."

The counterattack is surprisingly feeble and they are able to drive it off with three wounded and two dead in the platoon, with one of the injuries being Dick "Lazarus" Ostrowiz who manages a much-envied wound, a shoulder wound that will hurt like hell, take forever to heal, and require his evacuation up the chain, to battalion aid, to the field hospital and eventually, back to the States.

Ostrowiz, high on morphine, chuckles to himself as he is loaded into an ambulance and driven off.

Rio is once again short-handed. Geer, Jack, Jenou, Pang, Beebee, Milkmaid Molina, Jenny Dial, and Rudy J. "Private Sweetheart" Chester. Three short of a full squad. Meaning they'll be sending her more replacements, replacements who'll be wounded or run away or die so quickly there's little point in learning their names.

In this moment of relative calm, with holes dug and no artillery dropping—for the moment—Rio performs one of her most necessary duties.

"All right, people: twinkle toes!"

Universal groans.

The single biggest crippler of American soldiers in the Hürtgen is trench foot. It doesn't kill, but it sends a lot of soldiers to the rear and can be a sort of million dollar wound. So Rio regularly performs what the platoon refers to as a "twinkle toe" inspection in which every member of the squad must remove boots and socks and show their feet. The nights are more wintry with each passing day, with temperatures dropping to freezing. Cold plus wet equals trench foot.

"How long since you changed socks, Dial?"

"Um . . . I uh . . ."

"Use a rag or some underwear and wipe out the insides of your boots, Dial, then dry those socks and put on fresh," Rio says. "You have some powder?"

"I used it on . . ." She looks uncomfortable.

"Your bra. I understand, Dial, but there's no such thing as trench breast, so save your powder for your feet. Beebee! Dial needs talcum."

She moves on. Geer has already taken off his boots and set them in the air to dry, at least until the rain returns. His feet look fine, as do Jenou's and Jack's and Pang's. They've all seen actual cases of severe trench foot and they know they don't want it.

"Private Sweetheart?" Rio asks when she reaches Chester. "Why do you not have a spare pair of socks?"

He shrugs. "I lost them in a card game."

"A card game with who?"

Chester glances toward Cat Preeling's squad, similarly laid out nearby.

"Dammit, Sweetheart, don't you have more sense than to play poker with Preeling? Have you ever met *anyone* who's beat her?" She raises her voice to a yell, but one that carries a tone of amused exasperation. "*Cat!*"

Through the air comes a pair of balled-up socks, which Pang snags in midair and then tosses to Chester.

Cat yells, "But he owes me two packs of smokes for that!"

"Yes, he does," Rio agrees. "Fair is fair."

"Speaking of fair," Jenou says, "when are we getting some time off the line? I never thought I'd say these words, but I would really like a walk through the delousing tent. My fleas and my lice are battling for control and I'm losing."

"Preaching to the choir," Rio says fervently, scratching her armpit.

Lieutenant Horne strides toward them with Stick in tow. Horne has a determined look. Stick looks grim.

"That's not good news coming," Jack says.

"Is it ever?" Rio mutters.

Cat and the new sergeant of Fourth Squad are summoned and Horne leads them to a well-sheltered spot back in the trees. He takes a knee, but none of his sergeants copy the stance.

"All right, men," Horne says. "The colonel wants a platoon-strength recon tonight to—"

Groans.

"—to push off to our northeast. There's a road the tanks want to use, but Jerry's been busy over there so we need to assess the condition of the road."

"I can tell you the condition, sir," Cat says. "They've cut down trees to block the road, and they've mined the woods on either side."

Horne looks up, angry. "Have you been there?"

"No, but I've seen—"

"Then best to remain silent, however hard that is for someone of your sex."

"Yes, sir," Cat says, and smiles her wry, downturned smile for Rio's benefit.

"They're giving us some engineers to help assess conditions. Now, if it so happens that the road is not in the condition Preeling thinks it is, then you are to advance along the road until you encounter resistance, radio back, and hold position."

Rio starts to speak then sees that Stick has it. "Sir, the Krauts can lie low in the trees, wait for us to pass by and then cut us off."

"You will patrol through the trees either side of the road," Horne says as if he can't believe Stick is arguing with him.

"Sir, in the dark? Through woods that may be mined?"

Horne stands up. "I have assured the colonel that *my* platoon will handle the job."

Stick, Cat, Rio and probably even the new sergeant, Pablo Mercer, have noticed that: a) no mention is made of Captain Passey, meaning that he probably opposed the idea; and b) Horne keeps saying, *you* and not *we*.

"Who all is coming, sir?" Rio asks. She implies nothing by her tone. At least nothing she can be court-martialed for.

"Alpha, Bravo and Charlie squads, HQ squad stays behind to remain in radio contact and coordinate."

Rio nods and works mightily to avoid a sneer. Once again, Horne will be far from the action. She meets Stick's eye and sees confirmation there: Stick is to lead the bulk of the platoon while Horne sits by his radio waiting for news.

They are three squads with a nominal strength of thirty-six soldiers and an actual strength of twenty-seven. The Hürtgen has been deadly and no platoon anywhere in the Hürtgen is near nominal strength. Some platoons have been so badly mauled that their half dozen or so survivors are added to a different platoon entirely.

The first mile is a relatively relaxed walk since they are passing through American-held and engineer-cleared areas. But after that they are twenty-nine people walking in almost pitch-black while trying to spot wires and fresh-turned earth—things that are almost impossible to see in bright daylight.

"Where the hell are the sappers?' Jack asks, using the British word for combat engineers.

"Yeah, you noticed that," Geer says sourly.

"Beebee, you have that chain?" Rio asks.

Beebee unwraps a twelve-foot length of heavy chain from around his neck. The chain is bright metal. He fills a musette bag with rocks and dirt then uses a strap buckle to attach the heavy bag to the chain.

"All right, people, this is slow enough, so no dawdling. Geer will heave the chain. It should catch any wires. And it may set off any antipersonnel mines. But stay on the path! Geer."

Geer heaves the musette bag and the chain trails behind it. The bag goes fifteen feet, trailing the chain snake. Nothing. They advance. Heave. Nothing. Advance. Heave. Nothing. Advance.

This goes on until Geer has been worn out and is swapped for Chester, who is then swapped for Cat, who then swaps for one of her people. Ten feet every two minutes. 528 heaves for a mile.

Jack says, "Three hundred feet an hour. That's not exactly a quick march."

"You in a hurry?" Rio asks him.

He grins. "No hurry whatsoev—"

The musette bag blows up. It has landed on a mine.

"Definitely no hurry," Jack says fervently.

Rio knows they are in a sort of legal gray zone. They are carrying out orders, just doing it so slowly that the objective might never be reached. Preparing a new weight for the chain wastes five minutes and Stick comes walking up the line, shaking his head.

"I know what you two are doing. But Horne isn't having it. I reported our position and . . ." He shrugs.

"These woods are mined, Stick," Cat protests. "We just set off a Bouncing Betty that would have cost some poor SOB his family jewels."

"I know," Stick says grimly.

"What does Horne expect us to do? You see any engineers?"

"I can't see my hand in front of my face, Cat," he says, raising his voice which is a sure sign Stick does not like the orders he's transmitting. "But we have two miles just to reach the road and at this rate we'll get there around noon tomorrow!"

A compromise is reached. The three squads will advance with one GI on point. That GI will drag the chain behind him to snag any wires or mines his feet don't. No one will spend more than ten minutes walking point.

It's a grim lottery. It is also not something you ask unless you're willing to do it yourself, so Rio takes the first ten minutes and extends it to fifteen, just to drive home the point. She walks carefully, but at a normal pace. Cat takes the next round and her chain, dragging behind, sets off a booby trap that sprays her with dirt, but only flecks the back of her thigh with a piece of shrapnel.

Rio assigns Pang to be next and he does the job, stopping the instant the second hand on his watch shows ten minutes. One of Cat's veterans is next. But from here on it will be up to the greenhorns—they've risked enough useful soldiers.

But one of Mercer's privates refuses and won't budge. Then one of Cat's.

"You want us to shoot 'em?" Cat asks Stick sarcastically.

Rio says, "Listen, if we cut straight east here we're in Kraut territory, right? Any place they are, there will be fewer mines, right?"

"Yeah, and a lot more bullets," Mercer says, speaking up for the first time in this group.

"Not if they don't hear us," Rio says. "They sure as hell won't see us. If they're spread as thin as we are we can maybe just sneak past, and we cut a couple miles off the march."

Rio has learned a phrase from one of the war movies shown by the USO. A submarine movie had used the term *Rig for silent running*. Now she is inspecting her people as they rig for silent running, making double sure that clips do not rattle in ammo pouches, that canteens do not bounce, that anyone who stumbles does it without the obligatory curse.

"Not a word," she says. "And I will personally shoot anyone stupid enough to light a cigarette."

They pivot east and walk in a long single file toward the German positions. Twenty-nine pairs of boots crunch on wet pine needles. Twenty-nine pairs of eyes are trained on the ground, which is as invisible as the dark side of the moon.

The sergeants know that Rio has exaggerated just a bit: there is still the possibility of mines and booby traps, even close to German lines. Only when they are through the German front line can they relax at all, and even then there may well be mine fields, though they'd most likely be antitank mines, which are not set off by even a very large soldier.

But Rio cannot betray her uncertainty, so she walks point again, violating the rules and the logic that says she is more valuable than one of her privates. All well and good, but which of her greenhorns is going to keep up the necessary pace? And who but an experienced veteran will even spare a thought for non-mine threats?

She makes a fist, but the dark is so total that Jack plows into her.

"Krauts," Rio says in a voiceless whisper. She licks a finger and holds it up to judge the breeze. She has neither seen nor heard Germans, but the smell of bitter tobacco and pickled cabbage is on the slight breeze. She makes sure Jack is looking at her and makes a you-and-me gesture. Geer is with them now and she says, "Keep moving. Send word back to Cat and Mercer."

She and Jack crouch low and creep away into the forest. She'd rather have not brought Jack on this recon, she'd rather have a second Thompson than his rifle, but he was next up and she is loath to ever be accused of protecting either him or Jenou. Favoritism has no place here.

Rio places each step carefully, feeling for wires or sudden depressions or twigs that might snap loudly. Careful, but not slow. Cautious, but not paralyzed with fear. She motions for Jack to stay in her footprints.

Her finger is on the Thompson's trigger, safety off. She reminds herself of the location of her grenades and wishes she'd thought to swap the smoke grenade for the high explosive grenades, which are more useful at night, but too late now.

I still make mistakes. How am I supposed to tell my people what to do?

She sniffs the breeze, nods, and motions for even slower, even more silent movements. Then . . . low voices. Low voices speaking German.

Rio lies flat on the ground and Jack joins her. Faces so close they're breathing each other's exhalations, Rio says in a voice inaudible at a distance of more than half a foot, "I'm going closer."

"I'm going with you."

"Stay here. I want to see if it's an MG or just riflemen."

Jack's face is barely visible, even inches from her own. But she can guess at the stubborn expression. She crawls on hands and knees, the Thompson resting across her back. Each movement must be carefully managed so as not to snag on a branch or a root.

Closer. Closer. Two voices. An older man and a younger. Both smoking the putrid weeds that pass for tobacco in war-strained Germany.

Closer. Now she can hear them breathing. There cannot be more than ten feet separating Rio from the Germans, but she sees nothing. Not even shadows.

"*Ich muss scheissen,*" the older voice says.

Jack's hand grabs Rio's boot. She is irritated but not surprised to find that he has disobeyed and followed her. He crawls up beside her and says, "Latrine run."

Rio hears the German climbing heavily up out of his fighting hole. Footsteps on leaves, fading. A sound of a belt being unhitched. Trousers dropping. A sigh.

Jack jerks his head to indicate that they should crawl back now. Rio considers crawling further and perhaps cutting the younger German's throat, but that would raise the alarm. She follows Jack back to relative safety, then hurries to catch up with the platoon. She finds Stick.

"We're through their front line," she says.

"For what that's worth," Stick says.

Rio knows what he means: the Germans put a thin line up front, the real heavy-duty line further back, so they are likely between two lines of Germans. The question is whether the Germans have their own patrols out. The answer is certainly yes, but are they patrolling the gap between their lines?

They move quickly after that and in the early morning hours long before sunrise they find the road and then the engineers. Both of them. They had started out as a squad and been ambushed.

"FUBAR," Cat says in a whispered conference.

"FUBAR," Stick agrees. "Krauts'll be—"

The night erupts in machine-gun fire.

"Down, down!" Rio yells as a mortar explodes nearby.

Jenny Dial panics and starts to run. She is cut down by machine-gun fire.

The experienced Germans are not using tracer rounds, so in the darkness it is not possible to see where they are, only hear them. "That way!" Rio yells, chopping her hand toward tall, looming trees.

Jack and Jenou are firing from the ditch, Geer and Pang are setting up their BAR; Chester is flat on the road, hands over his head. Milkmaid Molina is firing her rifle. Dial is wounded, yelling in pain, not dead.

Rio fights down her panic, ignores the insane pounding in her chest, tries to read the terrain, tries to make sense of where they are, but it is pitch-black and there are machine-gun bullets pinging madly.

The Germans have two MGs and a mortar. At least.

Ahead, the German machine guns, and the secondary German line. Behind, only the relatively thin German front line.

"Chester! Crawl over here to the ditch!" Rio yells.

Where is Dial? Rio can hear her, but where is she? And where is Beebee?

The heavens choose this moment to begin dropping hailstones the size of peas, ice bullets bouncing everywhere making a clattering noise as counterpoint to the chattering machine guns.

Stick's BAR gunner opens up, but he's firing blind, spraying the woods in the vain hope of a lucky shot.

There are two paths: retreat or advance.

But retreat where? Go running and stumbling back into German foxholes? Or charge into invisible machine-gun nests? And then what?

Rudy J. Chester crawls beside Rio.

"Start shooting, goddammit," she snaps at him.

"I can't, Sarge, I can't! I dropped my gun!"

Rio hears Stick's voice raised high. "Richlin! Preeling! We're pulling back! On my signal, Alpha squad first, everyone else covering fire!"

It is the only sensible move. But withdrawing in order from a hot gun battle is one of the hardest maneuvers for any military unit.

"I see muzzle flash!" Geer shouts and turns his BAR.

"Shit!" Stick yells. "Horne says stay put!"

"Horne can fug himself!" Sergeant Mercer yells.

A mortar shell explodes and Mercer yells, "Goddammit!"

A voice Rio does not recognize shouts, "Sergeant Richlin! You're in charge."

There's a terrible catch in that voice. Rio feels goosebumps tickle her skin. She feels a twisting, turning inside her.

Stick?

"Is Stick hurt?" Her voice is the voice of a frightened little girl. She hears it. Everyone does.

"No," comes the flat reply. "Not hurt."

Stick is dead. Dain Sticklin. Dead.

Rio is paralyzed.

Not Stick. Not Stick!

"What do we do?" comes Cat's voice through the incessant rattle of machine guns.

"Stick said pull out," Rio manages to say through the lump in her throat.

Jesus, not Stick!

"Pang is hit!" Geer cries. "Medic!"

There is no medic with this patrol. Geer stops firing and tears at Pang's buttons, saying, "Come on, Jappo, come on, don't fugging die on me!"

"Geer! Keep firing that goddamn BAR!" Rio yells.

Pull out. Stay put. Rio's decision, now. Horne may hang her out to dry if she pulls back. And if she doesn't?

"Mercer! Leave the wounded and pull back behind us! Then you, Cat!"

In the dark, being murdered. They are being killed by people they can't see. Suddenly Beebee is there, right beside her. Has he been there all along?

"Jenou! Get up there and feed Stick's BAR!"

She hears gurgling from Pang. No time for Pang. No time for anything but saving the ones who can still be saved.

Mercer's squad—just five soldiers now—comes running by, hunched over.

"All right, Cat!" Rio says.

But the Germans aren't having it. Fire erupts suddenly on their right flank, across their direction of escape.

Cat drops beside Rio. "I got three dead and I'm leaving a wounded man, Richlin."

"Geer! Enfilade those fuggers on our right flank!"

"They're cutting us off," Cat says. "Everyone here will be dead in ten minutes!"

My God: do I have to surrender?

"Listen up, Cat. When I say go, you go."

"What are you doing, Rio?"

"I'm going to back those bastards off our flank."

"You'll get yourself killed!"

Rio doesn't bother to argue. Cat says, "I'm going with you."

"No, we need at least one experienced NCO to . . ."

"Fug you, Rio, I'm going with you!"

"Geer, get Stafford, Castain, Beebee and Molina out of here when we go."

"I'm not leaving Pang!"

"You cannot carry him!" But she knows there's no point arguing. Not now. Rank means nothing now. "Cat?"

"Yep."

"On one. Three. Two."

Rio and Cat jump to their feet. Each is armed with a Thompson. Each runs, fingers squeezing triggers, firing almost blind at nothing but muzzle flashes that shift location after each fusillade.

The machine gun ahead now turns its fire toward the chattering Thompsons, but as they do the remains of the platoon outrun a wedge of advancing Germans. They reach trees again and in a move that does Rio and Cat proud, they turn and fire from cover on the exposed Germans, snarling and cursing.

"Die, motherfuggers!"

"Come on, you Kraut bastards!"

Cat falls to the ground and trips Rio just as a stream of lead passes that would have cut her in half.

"Shit, Rio, I'm hit," Cat says.

"Bad?"

"My leg."

Rio has just ordered Geer to abandon a wounded Pang. She should abandon Cat. Instead she lays her Thompson on Cat's chest, gets behind her on hands and knees, grabs handfuls of uniform and pulls.

Cat is hurt, but she still has her Tommy gun and she fires despite being on her back. The file of Germans that had been sent to cut off the platoon withdraws, but keeps up a steady rate of disciplined fire.

The only way out is through a hundred-yard gap between the firing Americans in the trees and the firing Germans.

It is flatly impossible.

"Cat."

"Yeah."

"I think we may have to surrender."

But just then the firing coming from the Americans increases, and from the woods comes Geer with his BAR firing from his hip, and Jack is just behind him.

Rio and Cat join in and for a blessed moment the German machine gun is silent.

"Run!" Rio yells, and they all race pell-mell for the woods, with renewed fire zinging at their heels.

23

"You *what*?" Lieutenant Horne is livid.

"I pulled out," Rio says.

"Were you not aware, Sergeant, that I had ordered Sticklin to stay put?"

"It was a bit confusing," Rio says, sidestepping the question.

"Did you or did you not know that I had ordered Sticklin to stand fast?"

If she lies and she's caught there will be no help for her. But she can only be caught in the lie if survivors of the ambush come forward to challenge her. She is not one hundred percent sure, but she believes they will not.

"No, sir. Last thing I heard was Stick saying withdraw."

"You're a damned liar, Sergeant, and if you weren't a woman I'd have you up before a general court martial! Cowardice! Cowardice in the face of the enemy."

"Sir, you were not there." She says it levelly, uninflected, implying nothing.

"I was in command via radio, and I thought I had competent NCOs, not a pair of . . . of . . . women!"

Rio says nothing. But she looks plenty. She stares directly into his angry eyes, unflinching. After an uncomfortably long time she says, "Sir, we started out with twenty-nine GIs. We came home with sixteen. If we'd stayed no one would have come home. And you'd be explaining to the captain and the colonel how you happened to not be there when your entire platoon was wiped out."

Silence returns. She watches the calculations being done behind his eyes. He's furious, and he's a coward, but he's not entirely stupid. He knows she's right. She's helped save his career by getting out with anyone.

"I'd bust you down to private right now if I had a single NCO to replace you with."

"I would very much appreciate being a private, sir. Stafford is ready to step up, he's a damned good soldier. And if not him then I'm sure the Repple Depple can send us a three-striper."

He snarls so ferociously she nearly recoils. "No time, sadly, *Sergeant*. We're moving out."

"Moving out?" She laughs in disbelief. "We just got our asses kicked. And we've been on the line since—"

"I don't give a shit. We got orders for all hands on deck. They're rounding up cooks and typists and giving them M1s. The Krauts are attacking in force northwest of us."

"We are not the whole army. My people are beat! We lost Stick, who was the glue that held us all together. My people are exhausted and feeling about as low as you can get."

Horne looks down at the desk, smiling nastily at her upset. "Yes, shame about Sticklin. Good man. And now, guess what, Richlin? You *are* Sticklin. You're the new platoon sergeant, God help us." He spits on the dirt. "Like I said, I'm a bit short of NCOs.

Now get your *exhausted* people saddled up and ready to go in fifteen minutes. Trucks are coming. Dismissed."

Rio storms from the tent, fists clenched, lips so tight they disappear. She's supposed to take over for Stick? Run the platoon for that weak, lying coward Horne? With who? Cat is on her way to the field hospital, supposedly fine, but out of the war. Mercer was last seen sobbing helplessly into his helmet. And Geer . . .

She slows as she approaches Geer. He sits in a camp chair, bending over Pang. He carried Pang all through the awful miles. His uniform is saturated with Pang's blood. Pang's rifle lies across his chest like a holy object. His chest does not rise or fall.

"Listen, Richlin," Geer says without looking up. "Can you, um, can you uh, you know, get me Pang's address stateside? I need to write to his folks." The last few words come out strangled.

"That's not your duty, Geer, that's the chaplain and—"

"No." He struggles to control his facial muscles. "No. I'm going to write them."

"Okay, Geer," Rio says. "I'll get the address."

"Thanks, Rio."

Has Geer ever used her first name before?

"Listen, Geer, I hate to do this. But the yellow bastard made me platoon sergeant. So the squad is yours."

Geer nods, still looking down at Pang, who looks peaceful. He might almost be asleep but for the waxy stillness of his flesh. "You'll do fine, Richlin."

Coming from Geer it is a profound compliment. "I suppose we're never going to like each other much, Geer, but I'm damned glad I have you to take over the squad."

Geer stands up. Slaps his hands against his sides as if marking the end of something. "Who do you think I should make my ASL?"

"That's on you, Geer. Whoever it is will be *your* assistant squad leader, not mine."

"Think people will follow a limey?"

"Jack? If I was you, that's who I'd pick."

"Don't worry, I'll try to keep your backup boyfriend alive."

"Fug you, Geer." Rio laughs and hopes the dirt on her face will hide any blush.

Geer gives her a sidelong look. Then, having seen something in her face, he groans. "Are you kidding me? Are we moving up again?"

"Heading north. Some kind of Kraut attack. You round up anyone and everyone, regardless of MOS, regardless of whatever they have to say. Cooks, clerks, pharmacists, I don't care: get them."

"What in hell is a dead Jap doing here?"

Rio and Geer both turn. A soldier with a clipboard. He's a good-looking young man with spectacles and a very clean uniform.

"What are you?" Geer demands.

"I'm attached to graves registration, we're—"

"Well, you just got unattached, Four Eyes, you just joined Fifth Platoon. I am Luther Geer, your new lord and master."

"You can't—"

Geer cuffs him on the side of his head, knocking the man's glasses askew. He bends down and whispers, "Sorry, Pang. Gotta borrow this." He lifts Pang's M1 and shoves it into the clerk's chest. "Welcome to hell, little buddy."

The trucks do not show up on time of course, and Rio uses the time to pick a replacement for Cat. She calls together the ragtag remnants of Cat's squad and says, "Any of you people want to be squad leader?"

When almost every eye turns in one direction, she has her pick. "There you go . . . How do you say that?" She points at his name patch which reads Dubois. She's new to the platoon, but she was a corporal and had been at Anzio before being wounded.

"Doo-boyce, Sarge," she says.

"Where you from, Dubois?"

"I was born in Montana, but I was living in Oregon, working as a copy editor at the local paper."

"Well, your people seem to trust you, so I'm going to trust you. We are taking a ride, a long one. Get your people squared away, and grab anyone you see who is not attached, find 'em a rifle and hogtie them if you need to."

"Will do." Then, in a lower voice she says, "We know you were with Stick from the beginning, Sarge. We're all sorry as hell. He was good people."

Rio nods, unable suddenly to trust herself to speak.

He was good people. Past tense.

Sergeant Mercer has pulled himself together, but his squad looks spooked. Rio catches the eye of the squad's ASL, a woman named Pettyfer.

"I have no time for bullshit, so give it to me straight: is Mercer okay?"

Pettyfer glances in Mercer's direction. He has his back turned and is loading a clip. The rest of his squad looks past him at Rio and their corporal. "I don't know, Richlin, to be honest."

Rio pulls her a short distance away. "You got the word, obviously. I don't know where we're going except someone, somewhere up the line screwed up. So maybe it's all a big hurry-up-and-wait, and maybe it's right into some new shitstorm. If Mercer goes batty, you take charge."

"Aw, jeez, no!"

"Hey. You think I want this job? Do what has to be done."

It is three hours before the trucks come rattling into camp, and when they arrive they do not look good. Bullet holes pucker door panels. The canvas covers are ripped by shrapnel. One of the canvas covers has been burned, so now it's just blackened tatters. And the drivers are so far gone that as soon as they come to a complete stop they fall asleep on their steering wheels.

The dispirited, mud-caked, stinking, hungry and in too many cases battle-stunned troops climb wearily into the trucks. Rio finds herself for the first time in charge of people she does not know. Her squad is almost a family, but a platoon—even a much diminished platoon—is an *organization*.

Things, Rio thinks, *are not going according to plan.*

Someone with stars on his shoulders, Bradley or Ike himself maybe, *somebody*, had taken his eye off the ball. And now the much-battered 119th Division is on its way to die for their mistake.

Platoon Sergeant Richlin sits on the hard wood bench, scratches at her lice, wedges herself in so as not to be bounced off, takes a drink from her canteen, tilts her helmet forward and goes instantly to sleep.

After an unknown number of hours she wakes to find that

they are still in the forest, though whether it is the same forest or a different one she cannot tell. A narrow river chuckles contentedly beside the road. The hills on either side are steep and growing steeper.

The road itself is busy in both directions. Long columns of wounded GIs pass going the other way. And once again, refugees are on the move, forced off the road into the woods where they pass slowly, ghosts with backs bent beneath household belongings, or pushing wheelbarrows with old people propped in undignified positions, and children left to cling to their mother's hem.

The road takes a turn, still following the river, and ahead is a town dominated by three impressive buildings. First, perched in splendid isolation atop an absurdly steep ridge, sits an abbey that from Rio's limited view looks ancient and vaguely reddish. She is sure there's a word for the style of architecture, and once upon a time she might have asked Stick, who seemed to know most things.

The town proper is dominated by a church with twin stone towers topped by diamond-shaped gray slate roofs. The church is up a moderate slope from this building, a castle, an impressive whitewashed affair with a very Sleeping Beauty sort of round tower on one end. The abbey overlooks everything, the church overlooks the castle, the castle overlooks the town, the town is built alongside the river, and everything but the abbey is sandwiched into a heavily-forested ravine of almost comical steepness.

Rio hears heavy firing up on the ridge, machine guns and small arms and the occasional thump of a mortar.

We'll be climbing that slope unless I miss my guess.

The truck stops beside the river in an open, cobblestoned square. Now, for the first time, Rio notices that there are only four trucks.

"Everyone stay put," Rio says and climbs down. She walks the length of the truck to the driver, a man she guesses may be twenty-five, but who is so whiskered, so slack of jaw and blank of expression he looks like a much older man.

"When does the rest of the column get here?" Rio asks.

"This is the column," the driver says. "Now fug off 'cause I'm going to sleep."

To Rio's amazement he does just that, and right then, collapsing onto his seat and snoring before he is fully prone.

"Get the people assembled, Richlin." It is Lieutenant Horne.

"What are my orders, sir?" Rio asks.

Horne points with a cigarette up the slope. "Up there. The Krauts have tanks, we got tanks, and our tanks are getting their asses kicked. Fritz has this place surrounded."

Rio takes that in. "We're surrounded in a ravine with only one road out? When does the rest of the division get here?"

"They don't. It's just Fifth Platoon. The brass are running around like chickens with their heads cut off, throwing units into the line. Captain Passey and the rest of the company are elsewhere. Just you and me, Richlin." He grins and winks as if it's all some kind of joke. "So, like I said: climb that ridge. Report to whoever is in command up there."

"And you, sir?"

Horne points at the castle. "That's the HQ. I'll be there

getting the lay of the land. You can have my radio operator."

"Food?" Rio asks, increasingly furious.

"You see a field kitchen?"

"My people are supposed to climb that?" Rio points at the ridge. "With no rest, no hot food, and go right into it?"

"Shouldn't be a problem for you, Richlin. You're the tough-as-nails soldier girl, aren't you? The lady warrior with the Silver Star?"

He gloats at her, gloats as if this is a game and he's just scored points. Her choice right then is to either follow orders or tell the supercilious fool what she thinks of him. What's he going to do, court-martial her?

Well, she realizes, yes: that's what he's itching to do.

She turns her back on him without a salute or a word and stalks to the back of the truck. "All right, grab your gear." She raises her voice to a shout and says, "Fifth Platoon, saddle up!"

"What are we doing?" Jenou asks as she climbs down, blinking sleep out of her bloodshot eyes.

Rio raises her eyes to the slope.

Jenou turns to look. "What, now? Right *now*?"

Sergeants Mercer and Geer join her in a huddle, smoking and shooting dirty looks at Horne who is striding away toward the castle with his gloomy sergeant, Billy Banion, in tow.

"We've got two squads, barely," Rio says. "No kitchen, no supply line we can count on, and the people already here, most of 'em, came straight from the Hürtgen, just like us. Basically, we're at the bottom of a steep *V*. If the Krauts get the tops of the ridges they can drop plunging fire all day long. If they take the road north, we're cut off, maybe already."

"What's the good news?" Geer asks sourly.

"The good news? We have a river. Plenty of drinking water," Rio says.

"Fugging perfect," Geer says. "Light pack?"

Rio shakes her head. "Everything the people can carry. Ammo and food. Mercer? You've got a bazooka team in your squad. They any good?"

Mercer shakes his head. "Not so far."

"Everyone's GI insurance paid up?" Geer says. it's an old joke by now and no one laughs.

They must cross a stone bridge and on the other side Rio has everyone top off their canteens in the river and drink their fill. The face of the ridge is right there, right before them, five hundred near-vertical meters of dense fir forest. The trees here still have branches and graying pine needles, unlike the charred toothpick trees of the Hürtgen.

Counting the various random noncombat soldiers they've managed to dragoon, they are twenty-four GIs not counting Geer, Mercer, Rio and Horne, not even half a platoon.

"All right," Rio says, grabbing a tree trunk. "Follow me."

PART FOUR
THE BATTLE OF
THE BULGE

"Haven't you heard? They've got us surrounded—the poor bastards."

—Unknown American soldier at the Battle of the Bulge

LETTERS SENT

Dear Mr. and Mrs. Pang,

My name is Luther Geer. I was with your son when he died.

I have to tell you something about him and me. I didn't like Pang at first. But we were together in Italy and now France and Germany and what happened is that over a long time of being in this squad together I got so I liked him.

He was a good soldier. He was brave as hell any GI I have met. I hope you are very proud of him because you should be.

Maybe after the war I could come and see you and tell you more. I'm not one for letter writing so much as talking.

Anyway. I called him Jappo and he called me Hillbilly. Maybe you wouldn't guess it from that but Pang was my friend. And I am sorry as I can be that he is gone.

Sincerely,

Cpl. Luther Geer

Dear Mr. and Mrs. Sticklin,

I hope you don't mind me writing despite us not knowing each other, but I knew your son Dain well. We were together all the way from basic training.

Right from the start Stick—that's what everyone calls him— stood out. Before any of us in that group were even close to being real soldiers, Stick already was. He worked hard at it and he was very good at his job. I guess I can't even begin to count how many long conversations I had with Stick in camps and foxholes and boats and trucks. I admired and envied how much he knew about history and different places and why the world is like it is.

Dain Sticklin was everything you could ever want in a friend or a sergeant. If I ever felt like I had a big brother, it was Stick. Losing him was like a knife in my heart. But I know your pain and sorrow must be deeper and more terrible still.

I've taken over Stick's platoon now, but I feel in my heart that any time I don't know how to handle something I can just ask myself what he would have done and get the right answer.

I guess you don't need me to tell you but you raised a very fine young man. We all miss him terribly.

Sgt. Rio Richlin

Dear Pastor M'Dale,

I am writing you because I guess I need to say something that I can't say to anyone here.

There is so much pain here and so much death. None of it is like folks back home think, none of it is like what they see in movies. We are cold all the time. Filthy and wet all the time. Hungry too.

I look around me and I don't even see human beings anymore. I see walking sacks of blood and organs waiting to be ripped open, to have all that is inside them shown to the world. They are so brave and so determined and it doesn't matter because they just die. Especially the replacements who so often die within a few hours of getting to the front. The veterans don't even learn their names *because when a replacement dies, you don't want to know that they have kids or a widowed mother or hopes or dreams or hobbies.*

I keep telling myself I am doing a lot of good. I know that I have saved some people who would be dead otherwise. But even then it can be so hard. I send soldiers to the aid station minus a leg or an arm or scarred for life. Some GIs shoot themselves in the foot just to avoid something far worse.

But it's not even just the blood, it's what I see happening to the men and women here. They grow cynical, harsh, indifferent. Some have it worse still and lose their minds altogether. Grown men and women just rocking back and forth and sobbing.

It's seeping into me too, I know it. How many times can you see a human being die and feel his heart stop without losing your own mind? And I ask myself why. Sometimes I blaspheme, Pastor, because I do not know how God lets this happen. How does God let this happen? These GIs live like pigs in their own filth and spill their intestines into mud. How does God let fine young boys and girls be slaughtered, butchered, blown apart, burned to charcoal? Can you tell me that? Because I would really, really like to know that.

Sorry if I sound crazy, maybe I am. I had a man who worked with me, we called him Deacon, who was a conscientious objector. He was a good and brave man. A believer in the grace of Jesus Christ. And he just shot himself in the head because he just couldn't go on. I didn't see it coming. I didn't realize how it was for him.

I should probably tear up this letter. You'll think I've gone round the bend. But I am going to send it if only to remind you to pray for me. Please. Pray hard.

Frangie

Dear Rainy,

What is this I hear about you becoming an officer? You've gone over to the enemy! My baby sis a lousy brass hat! My God, before I know it you'll be a general.

Okay, more seriously, congratulations! I mean it!!! I could have exploded with pride when I heard about you. I would never want to compare myself to you, but I have to tell you that I too, yes your goofy brother, am now a platoon sergeant and I am busy all day long spitting nails and chewing on barbed wire as marine platoon leaders are supposed to do.

I am extremely safe sitting here on this godforsaken piece of coral with about three lousy palm trees. I of course can't name the island without bringing on the censors, but it doesn't matter because they're all the same. Nothing to do but knock coconuts out of trees and play cards with the guys.

I still don't exactly know what you are doing, although I hear from the folks that you disappeared for a while. But whatever it is, take good care of yourself. You and I have a lot to talk about when this is over, and I picture dragging the lawn chairs up onto the roof, having a beer or maybe six, and shooting the breeze. Wouldn't that be swell?

So be careful and cautious and take care of yourself, little sister.

I mean, little sister . . . SIR!

Aryeh

(I'm saluting right now.)

24

RAINY SCHULTERMAN AND RIO RICHLIN—CLERVAUX, LUXEMBOURG

Rainy is in uniform once again, with boots and a helmet with the small vertical chevron of a first lieutenant on the front. And for the first time in a very long time she has an M1 carbine slung over her shoulder. This battle is not one of wits, but hot lead.

GIs to her left and right form a row of fighting holes and log shelters. Behind this line is a second line made of supplies and trash, crates of ammo, empty C ration cans, a dead radio, abandoned packs and musette bags.

Behind that second line are interspersed pockets of mortar men firing *ka-toonk!* and pockets of GIs recovering, cigarettes dangling from snoring mouths.

Last, and below the ridge crest on a piece of terrain that is merely steep instead of being nearly vertical, an aid tent has been set up.

Way off to the left on a lower slope of the ridge Shermans blast away.

And where Rainy stands, out of the direct line of fire, is a sad-looking tent with a couple of camp chairs no one can use since the angle topples them over. There's an MP at the tent flap.

"Here to see the captain," Rainy says, and is waved inside just as rain starts falling. Inside the tent is steamy and crowded. There's a foldable map table with a map Rainy suspects is inaccurate, open and marked with grease pencil.

"Captain Mackie," Rainy says, and salutes. "I'm Lieutenant Schulterman."

Mackie is under thirty, olive-skinned, stiff as a board, and at first meeting Rainy suspects she might be a martinet. The captain is turned sideways to Rainy at first, but when she turns and Rainy can see her more clearly by the light of a single kerosene lantern, she sees mud-caked boots, mud splatters all up the legs of her trousers, and she sees that the left sleeve of her uniform blouse has been crudely hacked away to make room for a blood-soaked bandage.

So, maybe not a martinet: maybe a soldier.

"Lieutenant Schulterman," Mackie says. Her voice is clipped, but not tense. "What can I do for you?"

Rainy says, "Damned if I know, Captain. I'm not sure how I ended up here to tell you the truth. There's a bit of a . . ." She's about to say *panic*, but chooses a different word. ". . . a bit of confusion going on. I've been sent to assess the situation here."

"Ah. Spying for the brass? Well, I'll tell you, Schulterman, I got people from three different divisions," Mackie says. "We're in a box and holding lines we cannot hold for much longer. That's the situation. And no offense, Lieutenant, but about the last thing I need right now is another G2 officer."

"Sorry, Captain," Rainy says. A captain on the front line of a hot fight wants combat officers, not intelligence officers.

Mackie slices the air horizontally with stiff fingers. "Okay, look, you want to be useful? I could use some information. Grab some coffee and let's talk."

Rainy takes a cup of coffee proffered by an aide, and Mackie and a male lieutenant lead her to the map table. "I haven't had a chance to be briefed by the colonel lately. He probably has the straight poop, but all I know is I'm supposed to hold this ridge."

Rainy sets her cup down and leans over the map. "I'll give you what I have. That's the Second SS Panzer Division shooting at you, it's an old-line division. France in 1940. Poland. The Balkans. Fought the Russians at Kursk. An old-line division, but mostly green troops now, despite that. They were almost wiped out in the Falaise pocket after D-Day, so this is a lot of replacements."

Mackie takes this in and nods. "A full panzer division? Great. So what's the overview?"

Rainy shrugs. "I can give you the official version, which is that this is a German probe, a diversion. Officially the Krauts don't have enough divisions to do anything more than launch harassing attacks."

"And the *unofficial* version?"

The unofficial version is made up of hints and guesses, rumor and scuttlebutt Rainy has picked up hanging around HQ. Her natural tendency to secrecy suggests she say nothing more. But Mackie is in a spot, and she doesn't strike Rainy as the sort of officer to berate her for passing along her own judgments.

"Well," Rainy says, sighing, "some few of us think Adolf has been playing possum with us, preserving his strength, building up new units for an all-or-nothing breakout."

"Based on?"

"Based on we've seen panzer units pulled back for no good reason out of the east. We've seen front line units starved of supplies we know the Krauts have. Also too much radio chatter coming from Jerry. And finally, it makes a demented kind of sense: Adolf has nothing left to stop the Russians, so his best bet is to get us and the Brits to sue for peace. I think he's trying to cut us in two and push to Antwerp."

"With how much?"

"Officially? Maybe two or three divisions."

"And?"

Rainy shrugs. "Some of us, including my colonel, think they may have thirteen infantry divisions and six or even seven panzer divisions."

"Jesus H. That's not a diversion," Mackie says. "That's a desperate, all-out, everything-but-the-kitchen-sink attack."

"If it's any comfort, some of the top brass think if it is an all-out attack, it will actually be an opportunity. If the Germans are heading for Antwerp we have a shot at hitting their flanks and cutting them off."

"Not such an opportunity for the GIs who have to do the dirty work," Mackie says.

The tent flap opens, and a dirty, sweat-stained woman sergeant whose ripe smell precedes her enters, snaps a salute and freezes stiff, staring at Mackie. Glancing at Rainy. Then back at Mackie.

"Small war, Richlin?" Mackie says.

"You're a . . ." Rio Richlin waves in the direction of Mackie's shoulders.

"I had a choice," Mackie says, returning the salute and then shaking Rio's hand with genuine pleasure. "Either stay stateside and keep training idiot recruits, or take the ninety-day wonder route and join the war as an officer. You look like shit, Richlin."

To Rainy's utter astonishment, Rio blushes and stammers and looks down, appalled at the state of her uniform, until Mackie takes pity on her. "This isn't basic training, Richlin, and this is not an inspection. Take it easy. What are you doing here?"

"They threw us on trucks and here I am. I have a rump platoon, two dozen people, most of them still green."

"Where's your lieutenant?"

"He's checking out the big picture down at the castle," Rio says.

Mackie makes a snorting sound. "Colonel Fuller will make short work of that nonsense. Fuller likes fighters! Well, good to see you, Richlin. Go see Lieutenant Dubrowski. He's West Point, but he's a good officer. Dismissed. And, Richlin?"

"Yes?"

"It's Diane."

For a moment it almost seems as if the filth-covered killer with the *koummya* might start to cry. "Diane," Rio says, and flees.

"As for you, Schulterman," Mackie says, "I'm going to see if I can't get you some POWs to interrogate. I don't suppose you speak German?"

Outside the tent Rainy and Rio hold each other at arm's length and look each other up and down.

"Old home week," Rainy says. "I haven't seen you since our days of debauchery in England."

"Yeah, when you managed to talk me into coming to this little holiday in Europe."

Rainy nods. "I know it's been tough. I see some of the after-battle reports."

"And now you're an officer too," Rio accuses her. "First my old drill sergeant and now you. Traitors, both of you."

"What was that about, *Diane*?"

Rio grins. "I never knew her first name. I asked her once and she said it was Sergeant." She shakes her head. "You have no idea how much that woman used to terrify me. Mackie is who I wanted to . . . she's a good soldier."

"Who you wanted to be when you grew up?"

"Go ahead, laugh. But I guess it's true. Jed Cole and Mackie. *Diane* Mackie."

"How's Jenou? And you haven't heard anything from Marr, have you?"

"Marr could be ten feet away and I wouldn't know, I just got here. And Jenou is fine, she can still count to twenty on her fingers and toes." Rio sighs. "Well, I have orders to go shoot some Krauts."

"Take care of yourself, Rio," Rainy says in an echo of the friends-more-than-soldiers voice from their days in Britain.

"You too, Rainy."

They separate, and Rainy turns and calls after Rio, "Hey, if you happen to come up with any Kraut prisoners . . ."

"I'll look you up."

Rainy watches Richlin saunter away toward a gaggle of soldiers slumped against tree trunks, talking, cajoling, kicking the occasional boot sole.

I wonder if I talked her into her own death?

25

The crossroads, like every crossroads in Belgium, Luxembourg and western Germany, is a tangle of vehicles, with divisions trying to go two different ways. It takes hours to sort it out, hours during which Frangie lies comatose in the seat of her jeep with Manning—bandaged ear and all—equally asleep, leaning against and drooling on Frangie's shoulder.

BLAM!

Frangie's eyes are instantly open. She jerks upright. Looks frantically left, right, a smoking truck at the head of the column.

BLAM!

A second vehicle, this one at the rear of the column, blows up.

And now, emerging from the tree line across an empty field, come the beasts, the German tanks.

"*Tigers!*"

It's over before Frangie can rub the sleep from her eyes. More and more German tanks rumble from the woods, and advance on the stalled column at point-blank range. They cannot possibly miss.

There is only one Sherman in the column. It traverses its guns . . . and stops. The barrel lowers in submission. A few dozen GIs bolt, heading toward the woods behind them, but the Tigers' machine guns discourage that move.

"What's happening?" Manning asks.

"Nothing good," Frangie mutters.

The Tigers stop at a distance of less than a hundred yards. The barrels of their big guns are trained on the vehicles; the machine guns are leveled at the soldiers.

And now, to Frangie's shock, she sees an artillery captain walking toward the Germans with a white rag stuck on the end of his rifle. He's waving the white flag.

"We're surrendering," Frangie says in an appalled whisper.

The captain with the flag walks to one of the lead tanks. Its commander is a handsome blond man with a confident leer. Frangie squints hard and says, "It's an SS division."

"A Kraut's a Kraut," Manning says, and spits.

Frangie knows better, but stays silent. Wehrmacht—German army units—can be brutal, but they are not usually as utterly sadistic and cruel as the SS.

The captain and the SS colonel speak briefly. Then the captain comes walking back. He is followed by a file of SS *Panzergrenadiers*.

"Men . . ." the captain starts to say before being rudely cut off by an SS lieutenant who begins shouting orders in heavily-accented English.

"You are now prisoners of the Reich. You will be well-treated if you immediately obey all orders. If you do not, you will be shot!"

They are ordered to stack weapons and line up. Frangie has no weapons so she grabs her bag and she and Manning fall into line, two black faces among mostly white ones, a consequence of the chaos of the battlefield.

The SS lieutenant spots them, approaches, stops and actually pushes his face forward to sniff them. He steps back. "You smell no different," he says, and seems disturbed by this.

"I think we all stink, if—"

The blow hits Frangie before she notes his hand move. It is a backhanded swing that connects with her cheek and causes her to stagger.

"Hey!" Manning yells.

The officer snaps his fingers and a *Panzergrenadier* shoots Manning twice in the chest. She's dead before she hits the ground.

"No!" Frangie yells.

Other soldiers surge forward as if they might do something, but more *Panzergrenadiers* are leveling more weapons and just waiting for the word. One of them slams the stock of his machine pistol into Frangie's stomach and swings it sideways to catch the side of her head as she falls.

When Frangie returns to consciousness she is moving. She feels movement even before she opens her eyes. But she feels too that her own feet are being dragged, that strong arms are under her shoulders.

She pries open a bloody eye. She does not know the soldier bearing her weight; he's a white man for one thing, and instinctively she pulls away.

"No, no, missy, make sure your knees work first," he says kindly.

It's good advice. It's a few minutes before she is confident that she can walk. "Thanks."

He releases her. "I put a bandage on the side of your head, but I'm a gunner not a medic."

He's a bespectacled, early twenties white boy with brown

eyes and a mouth permanently quirked so that he always looks amused. Frangie didn't see quite what he—or any of them—should find amusing. They are in a column of several dozen soldiers being marched along in the freezing cold, with snow in their faces, as SS swagger alongside, occasionally punching or kicking a straggler.

Manning is dead.

Deacon is dead.

"I'm Frank Pepper," the white man says, holding out his hand. "From Memphis, Tennessee."

Frangie shakes his hand, frowning as she does it, because it is one thing for a white man from California or New York to shake her hand, but it's a whole different thing for a southern white boy.

"Frangie Marr. Tulsa."

"Oklahoma, huh? Cowboys and such?"

"No."

Manning. Dead.

Deacon. Dead.

"Maybe you can tell I just got here," Pepper says. "One day in the damn war and I'm a prisoner. That beats all." He shakes his head, regretful but philosophical.

"Well, thanks for helping me."

"You're thinking it's funny a southern boy helping you out."

"I guess I am," Frangie admits.

He leans close and whispers, "I'm not exactly a soldier. I'm a musician. Stand-up bass." He mimes plucking a bass. "Blues, jazz, boogie-woogie, if you're going to play music—real music—it's Nigra music."

"You play with colored musicians?"

He looks around absurdly, as though the SS will be upset by this. And perhaps, Frangie thinks, they would be. These are, after all, committed, indoctrinated Nazis for the most part. And the similarities between Nazis and white-sheeted night riders with ropes are obvious.

"I can sit in with colored players, they don't mind so long as you can lay down a rhythm. Guess who I played with? Albert Ammons! It was just one set, but man, what that fat ole colored boy does with the ivories!"

The SS guards are now veering them into a snow-covered field where they are told to wait, standing.

"Probably bringing up some trucks to take us to the POW camp," Pepper says. "Fine with me! My dogs are killing me!"

There is a low barbed-wire fence and they are made to climb over it, ripping uniform trousers and tripping the clumsy or the exhausted. The field is surrounded on three sides by forest, stark, leafless trees with branches silvered by snow. Some SS men head across the snow to the borders of the field.

Frangie does a quick count, something like seventy-five or eighty-odd GIs stand shivering and breathing steam.

"Yeah, I reckon we're going to Germany," Pepper says. "And probably not a phonograph or a radio anywhere. At least it's got to be warmer than this."

But Frangie is not sure. Her stomach is twisting in knots. There's something in the air, on the faces of the SS, in this place.

They're going to kill us.

The thought comes fully-formed and undeniable. It is a truth

Frangie feels deep down, down beyond the reach of Pepper's optimistic chatter.

She wants to tell him, wants to say the words, but saying them will make them real, and she wants desperately to believe that her instincts are wrong.

A German staff car and a covered truck push through the barbed wire and stop at the edge of the road.

"Our Father . . ." Frangie whispers.

"What?" Pepper looks at her, baffled then, slowly, alarmed.

". . . Who art in Heaven . . ."

"Are you . . ."

". . . hallowed be Thy name, Thy kingdom come . . ."

Pepper says, "They aren't gonna . . ."

". . . Thy will be done . . ." The words catch in Frangie's throat. *No, no, not Thy will, I want to live. I don't want to die. I don't want to die.* ". . . on Earth as it is in Heaven. Give us this day our daily bread . . ."

The canvas at the back of the German truck rises suddenly. Frangie sees SS soldiers hunched over a machine gun. Her breathing is sharp gasps. Her heart hammers. *No, no, no!*

". . . and forgive us our trespasses as we forgive . . ."

B-r-r-r-r-r-t!

Soldiers scream and twist and fall.

B-r-r-r-r-r-t!

Americans try to run and are cut down.

B-r-r-r-r-r-t!

The cries go up. *Mom! Jesus! No! God save me!*

B-r-r-r-r-r-t!

Men and women stagger. Blood explodes as mist from punctured bodies.

Pepper turns terrified eyes to Frangie and a bullet hits him in the hip. He falls. Frangie, even now on automatic, a medic first and last, drops to her knees to help him as all around people fall.

B-r-r-r-r-r-t! B-r-r-r-r-r-t! B-r-r-r-r-r-t!

An officer in the squad car has his pistol out and shoots crawling, wounded soldiers with no more concern than if he'd been shooting rabbits.

B-r-r-r-r-r-t! B-r-r-r-r-r-t! B-r-r-r-r-r-t!

Frangie feels a sharp blow against her knee and falls.

It stops. The machine gun falls silent.

The pitiful, fearful, pain-wracked cries of the wounded do not. Men and women are crawling across the snow leaving blood trails behind.

Frangie hears shouted orders in German. SS soldiers advance across the field, their tall boots crunching snow, chatting among themselves. Laughing.

Laughing as they stand in front of a crawling man, kick him onto his back and shoot him in the face.

Laughing as a wounded woman breaks for the woods and they shoot her in the back.

Laughing as they step on a writhing man's stomach and bounce on him, forcing fountains of blood from his mouth before shooting him.

Frangie is half beneath Pepper, who still breathes, Frangie can feel the rise and fall of his breath.

"Play dead!" she says in a terse whisper.

But Pepper isn't listening. Is he even conscious?

A dead woman is curled beside Frangie's head. Frangie can hear the trickle of her blood dripping on snow.

Boots in the snow.

Frangie does not move her eyes. She does not breathe.

Bang!

Pepper's body jerks.

Bang!

The dead woman's face explodes outward, showering Frangie with gore.

Not a breath!

Not a blink!

The boots move away.

Frangie lies amid the now-silent dead for an eternity as snow falls and Pepper's blood freezes into a red icicle that hangs from his mouth. His brown eyes are open, staring.

Numb in body and mind, Frangie pushes her way out from under Pepper. She rolls the dead woman aside. She vomits onto the ground and begins to sob. She cries like a child, without thought, without self-consciousness. She bawls like a baby.

She crawls on hands and knees toward the trees. The roads belong to the Germans now.

There's a slight hill and she tops it then rolls down the other side. Only then does she get to her feet and start to run.

26

"Lieutenant Dubrowski?"

The lieutenant is crouched behind a well dug-in machine-gun team. He's as young as second lieutenants usually are, maybe twenty-four, maybe not. "See that big rock?" Dubrowski points. "Go left of that about two bumps." The machine gunner adjusts and opens fire, the machine gun slurping the ammo belt like spaghetti. Dubrowski turns to Rio. "Yeah?"

Rio does not salute—officers on the front lines don't appreciate being conveniently identified for the Germans. "Sergeant Richlin, sir. Sergeant Mackie . . . sorry, I mean Captain Mackie sent us up here."

"What do you got?"

"Half a platoon of beat-down GIs needing a shower and a shave and about a week of sleep."

Dubrowski looks past her at the platoon gathered below his ridge-topping position. "They look like a scary bunch. Can any of 'em shoot?"

Rio shrugs. "Maybe half are complete greenhorns, but I have a dozen good people." Then, feeling she was being unfair, she adds, "And most of the rest will come along in time."

"Uh huh," Dubrowski says. He grins and Rio likes him

immediately, on instinct. This is not Lieutenant Horne. This officer hasn't shaved in a long time or changed his uniform, nor, from the look of his sunken black eyes, has he slept. He's in, and obviously has for some time been in, the line of fire, right alongside his people.

Dubrowski squat-walks away from the MG, then rises to a full six feet and strides into the middle of Fifth Platoon. The first thing he says is, "You are all out of uniform: where the hell are your neckties?"

There follow five long seconds of baffled stares, then Dubrowski slaps a soldier on the shoulder and says, "Sorry, I couldn't resist. You are about as sorry-looking a bunch of GIs as I have ever seen. Hell, you look as bad as my own people. Damned if we couldn't kill the Krauts with our stink alone!"

That last bit he says loudly enough to be overheard by some of those *own people*, one of whom says over his shoulder, "Still waiting on a bottle of perfume from Paris, Dub!"

"Perfume? Hell, Castro, you need a sandblaster," Dubrowski yells back, and winks at Rio. "Welcome to Clervaux, ladies and gentlemen. Sergeant Richlin tells me you've been in it, and now you're in it again. Let me tell you how it lays out."

He quickly sketches the position. Clervaux—and more important, the road running through it—is at the bottom of a bowl. A mish-mash of American units is on the lip of the bowl. The Krauts are outside the bowl trying to get to the lip so they can, in his words, "Drop 88s and mortars like a goddamn New Orleans rainstorm on the town and push us the fug out and take the goddamn road, which they need for their fugging tanks."

"Where do you want us, sir?" Rio asks. Most soldiers curse more or less constantly, but Rio had somehow expected something different from a West Pointer.

Dubrowski considers. Then he pulls Rio aside to speak privately. "Tell you what I need, Sergeant, you tell me if you can do it. What I'd like is to form a sort of flying squad I can deploy to harass the damn panzers they got trying to come up along a forest track."

"A bazooka team?"

Dubrowski nods. "If the panzers break through they can drive straight toward the main road, pivot into town and all of us up here will be cut off and spend the rest of the war in a POW camp."

"We haven't done much tank-killing, Lieutenant."

"I have a PFC you can have, good with a bazooka." Raising his voice, "Castro! Send word to Mazur to get his ass over here!" Then again to Rio, "He's a Polack like me, but fresh off the boat Polack, barely speaks English. But goddamn he hates Krauts. Take Mazur, pick your best squad, see what you can do."

Rio has several conflicting reactions. She can barely keep her eyes open, she aches everywhere, her stomach is rumbling and she knows her people are at least as badly off.

On the other hand, as she sees it the situation is desperate, she does not want to be a POW, and her chain-of-command now runs through Dubrowski to Mackie. And Rio would chop off her own arm rather than disappoint Mackie.

"Yes, sir," Rio says.

Mazur comes at a run, carrying a bazooka. He's a small man, barely over the legal minimum for enlistment, but wide and built like an upside-down triangle, with almost comically bulky shoulders.

"Mazur. Welcome aboard," Rio says. "Okay, here's how this goes. I am forming a flying squad to go see if we can't annoy some panzers. Stafford, you'll be my ASL. Sorry, Geer, Beebee can be your number two, I need Stafford."

So much easier not to think about Jack when I call him Stafford.

Geer shakes his head and sighs, not thrilled to trade Jack for Beebee.

"Castain, Molina, Jeffords and . . ." Rio hesitates. She needs a beast-of-burden, someone big and strong enough to carry bazooka rounds. She sighs. ". . . and you, Private Sweetheart. You're all with me. Everyone else with Geer. Geer? Go report to the lieutenant."

Geer says, "You should take me with you."

Rio nods. "Yeah, I probably should, Geer, but I need someone back here who knows what's going on."

The words *in case I don't come back* are unspoken but understood.

Rio squats with Dubrowski again, going carefully over the maps. "There's a trail right here." Dubrowski stabs the map with a finger. "Don't know how far it goes, but it might get you as far as this." Another finger stab. "Our guys are holding over here so you need to watch out for friendly fire."

"Mines?"

"The area was swept for mines when it was ours, but Fritz is a busy little fellow, so . . ."

"Swell."

They have seven rounds of standard antitank, armor-piercing bazooka rockets and three smoke rounds. As they set off, Rio asks Mazur, "Is it worth carrying the smoke rounds?"

Mazur grins revealing several missing teeth. "Oh, I love Willy Pete, Sarge. You light a panzer up with Willy and it blinds them. It gets mighty warm inside a tank that's burning and the Krauts bail out."

"You've killed tanks?"

Mazur holds up two fingers and a stub of a middle finger. He laughs. "Two and a half, see? Hah! Killed two, crippled one."

His English is almost perfect, obviously Dubrowski had been teasing. "What happened to the finger?"

"Damn dago sniper in Italy."

Jack walks point with Corporal Jeffords, a lanky Arkansan chewing and spitting tobacco behind him scanning for mines. Molina is just behind Rio, and Rudy J. Chester brings up the rear, gasping beneath the weight of his gear plus two musette bags stuffed with bazooka rounds.

Jenou drops back a bit to match strides with Rio. "Do we know something about killing tanks?"

"Not yet."

"At least we're heading downhill," Jenou says.

"Sorry to drag you into this, Jen." Rio is about to add something about being desperate for veterans, but she checks herself and says, "I need you."

"Well, isn't that nice?" Jenou says, intending to sound sarcastic, but the truth is she's oddly touched and sounds like it. Jenou has barely spoken to Rio since Stick's death. "You doing okay?"

"Like Christmas morning finding a stocking full of gifts," Rio says.

"Speaking of which, it'll be Christmas soon. I guess that's good what with everyone saying the war will be over by Christmas." Jenou fumbles in her bag and pulls out something that looks like a big, metal Tootsie Pop. "Beebee scrounged this. It's a British thing called a 'sticky bomb.' You take it out of its shell and it's basically a grenade with glue on it. You're supposed to throw it at tanks. I have two. I'll hold onto them for you."

"Why are they for me and not for you?"

"You're the hero, Rio, not me."

"No?"

Jenou shakes her head. "You know, when we started out I was just looking for a guy and a way out of Gedwell Falls. I have a feeling *that* Jenou is dead. Dead and buried."

"We've all changed," Rio says.

Jenou nods. "That's true. You used to just be my flat-chested best friend who broke out in hives at the thought of kissing a boy."

Rio glances back to see who might be overhearing this exchange. Milkmaid Molina is nearest. Her face is blank, but it's the careful sort of blank that indicates that yes, she heard, all right.

"At first I was not real happy with how you were changing and that took my mind off thinking about myself and whether I was turning into someone different." Jenou trips on a root, takes two wild balancing steps and catches herself.

"So?" Rio prods.

"So, like I said, that Jenou, the empty-headed little flirt died somewhere back along the way. Italy, I guess. Yeah, that's when I started to feel like . . . I don't know. Not like me."

Rio grabs Jenou's arm and pulls her off the trail. "Keep going, Molina, we'll catch up."

"Is this a rest stop?" Chester asks hopefully.

Something in Rio's snarl convinces him to keep moving.

"Are you okay, Jen? We never got much of a chance to talk about what's going on with your folks."

"I blame the Krauts—they keep interrupting. Anyway, to be honest, Rio, it's a relief. It was getting me down thinking of going back there, back to . . . them . . . when this is all over."

"What are you going to do?"

"Well . . . there's this GI Bill thing, you know, where the government will pay for college?" Jenou winces as if expecting ridicule.

"Jenou Castain, college co-ed?" Rio smiles crookedly.

"You think I'm not clever enough."

"Oh bullshit, Jen, you're smart enough to do whatever you want." She frowns. "Which is what, exactly?"

They start walking again, a few dozen paces behind Chester.

"Well," Jenou says, "I've been sort of noodling around with this journal . . . anyway, I thought maybe I'd study English and think about writing."

Rio is silent for a while until Jenou says, "Yeah, but it's probably a silly pipe dream."

"I think it would be wonderful. You've always had a way with words. I'd be proud of you," Rio says. "All, right, Molina? Take point. Stafford to the rear."

"How about you, Rio? Afterward, I mean? You still think

349

there's any potential in the handsome Mr. Braxton?"

Rio accelerates her pace and says, "I have to get back up front."
She ignores Jenou's drawled, "Uh-huh," and catches up to Molina.

"All right, Molina, we may be getting close, so use all your
senses, right? Listen. And smell too."

"All I smell is *me*," Molina mutters.

The trail is one person wide, sometimes just a single step wide
so that they have to walk heel-toe, which is awkward when you're
carrying weight. Snow comes drifting down through the trees,
fat flakes of it. They've been traveling steadily downhill and Rio
worries about the return climb if snow starts to fall in earnest.

All conversation has stopped. They move slowly, with all the
stealth they can manage while following a goat trail through
trees with branches that reach out to snag them as they pass. It is
getting on to afternoon and Rio considers ordering a meal break.
But Germans have noses, too, and the smell of C rations could
give them away.

Molina stops suddenly and takes a knee.

"What?" Rio asks voicelessly.

Molina points through the tree trunks, through the bushes,
to a sliver of unpaved dirt road. Rio unfolds her map and tries to
connect wavy lines on paper to the forest around her. Down there
a road. Off to the right, a stream. "Yep," she says. She waves her
squad forward and motions them to gather around.

"Okay, listen up. We have to leave the trail here and go down
this slope then follow the stream. Our guys are here." She points
at the map and as if on cue they hear the chatter of a .50 caliber.
"Krauts here. They'll have patrols out. Do not start shooting

unless I tell you or you have no choice. Right? Panzers are bunched up along this track trying to break through. I doubt they'll be expecting us, but keep your eyes open."

Now Rio takes point, with Jack just behind her. They no longer look for mines—the shadows in the forest are lengthening and the snow, falling faster now, will conceal wires or fresh-turned dirt.

She takes careful, silent but swift steps, moving with feline grace, her Thompson leveled at her waist. From time to time she stops to listen and to sniff the breeze. She looks for movement, any movement, listens for the snap of a branch underfoot, inhales any scent suggestive of German tobacco or food.

Step step step. Pause. Step step step step. Pause.

It is an excruciatingly slow way to advance, but advance they do. They reach a small trickling stream, barely enough to submerge their canteens in. But the tiny stream has cut a deep ravine, almost head high, and Rio leads them along the stream, stepping into, out of, and back into freezing water.

The temperature is dropping fast. Snow accumulates, just a dusting, but the start of worse to come. The squad breathes steam. Feet already cold are growing numb.

"Bridge," Rio says, stopping and chopping her hand forward to indicate the direction. "It looks like something Kraut engineers threw up over this stream."

In the most basic sense this stream, this ravine, delineates the line between the American Shermans dug in on the western side, and the panzers on the other side. The sound of machine-gun fire is sporadic, along with the higher-pitched sound of rifles. From time to time they've heard a tank firing followed by an explosion.

Rio now leads them up the bank, crawling on their bellies. Rio's seen nothing, but her predator's senses have warned her with a prickling on the back of her neck that Germans are nearby.

Crawl. Crawl. Pause. Crawl. And a brief snatch of spoken German, coming from way too close. In those bushes? Molina crawls beside her and points to their right. Sure enough: movement in the form of a gray uniform. A German patrol.

Rio motions everyone to lie flat. They lie still for twenty minutes as the German patrol passes within a hundred feet. And then . . .

BOOOOOM!

The first round elicits a yelp from Molina, but that sound is obliterated by a catastrophic artillery barrage that lacerates the area where Rio believes the American tanks are dug in. It is presumably German artillery, but given how frequently artillery hits the wrong target, it could be American. Either way the sound of destruction is an opportunity.

"Let's move out!"

At a crouching trot they move more quickly now, artillery exploding well to their left, the ongoing battle of the ridge blazing away behind, to the right and many hundreds of feet up from where Rio's squad is.

Suddenly through the trees ahead, Rio spots a German truck. And then, ahead of the truck, a tank.

"Mazur! What do you make of it?"

The Polish-American bazooka man peers into the forest and whistles softly. "That is a *Jagdpanzer,* a tank-killer."

"Looks strange."

"No turret. It's got a big old cannon, but it has limited movement unless you move the whole vehicle."

"How would you go at it?"

Mazur considers. He'd seemed at first like a bit of a fire-breather, but now that it's time for the show he is cool and professional, and Rio finds herself warming to him.

"Well, Sarge, they'll have most of their people over on this side of the road. If there was a way to get to the other side . . ."

Getting to the other side is flatly insane. The only way is by crawling under the bridge, and there are Germans thick on both ends of the bridge. Can she get Jenou, Jack, Molina, Jeffords, Chester, Mazur and herself under the bridge? She briefly considers a diversion, but an experienced German commander will smell that in a second.

Seven people beneath a guarded bridge? Easier with fewer.

"Here's the plan," Rio says. "Mazur, Stafford and I try for the bridge. The rest of you go along the left bank and see if you can find a place to enfilade that bridge. Castain? You got Molina, Jeffords and Chester."

Jenou looks appalled, and it occurs to Rio that this will be Jenou's first time really in charge of anything but herself. But Jenou nods worried acceptance.

Rio takes a bag of bazooka rounds from Chester and leads the way into icy water that deepens with each step so that soon it spills over the top of her boots. The artillery barrage creates crashing, ground-pounding noise and the falling snow obscures sight: it's the best chance they have.

But as they come to within twenty yards of the bridge, Rio spots a German sentry squatting beneath the bridge to relieve himself. He has his back to them and appears to be reading a letter as he defecates.

A veteran, Rio notes sourly. Only an experienced soldier has the sangfroid and cool calculation of risks required to calmly take a dump with artillery landing just beyond shrapnel range.

Rio hands her Thompson to Jack. He looks very unhappy, like he might object to Rio's plan, but he subsides and accepts her submachine gun.

Rio moves quickly now, too close to avoid being seen if the German turns around, but knowing that he can't possibly hear her and, given the situation, isn't likely to smell her.

He never turns around as her *koummya* goes around his throat. She draws it back hard, needing it to slice straight through his voice box to silence any cry. He does not cry out. He twists and falls on his back. His throat is a grisly red smile.

They reach the far side of the road unobserved, then creep in a water-filled ditch alongside the road. From here they see more vehicles, all with engines running, with tank commanders sitting tall in their hatches.

They are just waiting for the artillery barrage to stop before giving the command to attack. Just above them, so close they can smell its exhaust, is the first *Jagdpanzer*. Behind it a standard Panzer Mark IV. If they take out one or both they will block the bridge and at least delay the attack. With enough delay the artillery-plastered American defenders may have time to stiffen their lines.

"All right, Mazur," Rio says.

"I'm going to put some WP on that *Jagdpanzer* first. Then a HEAT round on that second panzer. Might get in a third round, depending. Then we skedaddle."

"Is that American for run like hell?" Jack asks.

Rio has her Thompson again. Jack acts as loader for the bazooka. Mazur shoulders the long steel tube and Jack slides a rocket into the tube.

"Watch the backfire, Tommy," Mazur says to Jack.

Careful aim. They are side-on to the *Jagdpanzer*.

Whooosh!

BAM!

The round hits squarely on the side armor of the tank. It makes a small explosion, just enough to expose the white phosphorous to oxygen. The tank's commander immediately yells orders as dense white smoke billows around him. The order is apparently to button up because the commander drops down into his vehicle and pulls the hatch after him.

Jack has already reloaded and Mazur now aims at the Panzer Mark IV. It's at an angle to them. The rocket flies, hits, and bounces away to explode in the trees beyond.

They hear shouted orders in German and Rio knows what they will be: infantry is being ordered forward to protect the precious tanks.

"Try again!" Rio says.

Jack and Mazur reload. Aim. The sound of hobnail boots running, underbrush crashing and . . .

Whooosh!

BOOOM!

The rocket hits the bogie wheels on the tank's right side and the tread spools off.

"Skedaddle!" Rio yells.

Jack grabs the ammo, Mazur grabs the bazooka, and they run back toward the bridge. No longer worried about stealth, they run, leap the German whose throat Rio cut, splash through the water and stop suddenly, almost face to face with two German soldiers.

Brrrt! Brrrt! Brrrt!

Rio's Thompson blazes and the Germans fall. But now every German infantry soldier within hearing knows where they are. They dive into the woods as a file of *Panzergrenadiers* splashes across the stream, racing to cut them off.

From the woods comes the chatter of small arms and for a moment Rio thinks they've been flanked. But no, it's Jenou and the others firing to discourage the Germans.

The Germans are discouraged just long enough for Rio to gather her lost sheep and go hell-for-leather back up the hill. They are walking back toward American lines and the possibility that they'll be shot as Germans, so Rio yells the password again and again and they pass through the lines and collapse on the ground.

Rio is laughing aloud.

Jenou looks to Jack. "What the hell?"

Jack laughs. "I think our sergeant just discovered a new hobby: killing tanks."

27

FRANGIE MARR AND RAINY SCHULTERMAN—BASTOGNE, BELGIUM

SCHULTERMAN: Frangie, I'm happy to see you well.

MARR: I don't know how well I am, but I'm happy to see you! And a first lieutenant besides! Watch out or they'll make you a general.

SCHULTERMAN: Fat chance. Okay, for the record this conversation is being recorded. I am Lieutenant Elisheva Schulterman, speaking with Sergeant Frangie—what's your legal name?

MARR: Francine.

SCHULTERMAN: Francine. Francine Marr, sergeant, medical corps. So, Frangie, for the record, tell me what happened at Malmédy.

MARR: They massacred us. That's what happened. We were ambushed and surrounded and we were taken prisoner. The SS—

SCHULTERMAN: Do you happen to know what unit?

MARR: No. But I heard someone talking about an SS officer named Peiper. I think the Peiper person was in charge.

SCHULTERMAN: Yes. General Joachim Peiper. He's notorious for what he—and others like him—did in Poland and Russia. Please continue.

MARR: There's not much to say. They marched us into a field. They drove a truck in, opened the flap and started machine gunning.

SCHULTERMAN: No warning or explanation?

MARR: What explanation could they have for murdering POWs in cold blood?

The interview lasts half an hour, during which Frangie goes from rage to sorrow to depression. Rainy switches off the recorder. They are across from each other in a small room that smells of plaster dust and mildew. There is a wooden table between them, a nice table, not military issue.

Rainy excuses herself for a moment. She goes directly to Herkemeier who is waiting for her.

"She confirms the other accounts," Rainy says.

Herkemeier nods. "This is bad. It'll scare the hell out of some GIs, stiffen the spines of others, but mostly it will mean revenge. After word gets around about Malmédy, no German prisoner—certainly no SS—will be safe."

"I can't spare too much pity," Rainy says.

"It's not a question of pity, Rainy. Soldiers fight soldiers. Eventually the two sides really come to hate each other—but as *soldiers*. This? This is different. There aren't many rules in war, but one of them is that you care for your prisoners."

Rainy sighs. "We need to minimize the damage then. Make sure this ends up being seen as a purely SS thing. If our people are going to be looking for revenge, we can at least focus the worst of it on the worst of them."

Herkemeier makes a face like he's just bitten into a bad peach. "We'll need some friendly Germans when this is all over. So in the end we're going to lie about how deeply the Wehrmacht is involved in atrocities, and pin it all on the SS. We'll most likely whitewash the Wehrmacht and the German people too. Political necessity."

"I have to get back," Rainy says, squirming at talk of politics. "I'm borrowing this." She goes behind Herkemeier's desk, slides open a drawer and takes out a bottle of German schnapps. She leaves quickly, not angry at Herkemeier, angry at the fact that he's *right*. She forces herself to calm down before opening the door to the interrogation room.

Frangie has a coffee mug before her. Rainy takes it, pours the last inch of coffee into a trash can, then pours an inch of schnapps for Frangie. Frangie sniffs at it. Says, "Smells like chewing gum," and then downs the shot in one gulp.

"Listen, Frangie," Rainy says. "GIs who deal with this kind of thing often experience severe guilt. You know? They ask themselves, 'Why me? Why did I live?'"

"Oh, I've already done plenty of that," Frangie says. She hates to admit it, but the alcohol burning a hole in her stomach has settled her nerves. "I'm not a combat soldier who lost some buddies, Rainy, I'm a medic. All I see of this war is wounds and death. Folks crying. Folks screaming. Folks begging for Jesus to save them. You can't—"

Suddenly she cannot speak. Her throat is choked, her eyes swim with tears.

Rainy waits, watching Frangie try to master herself, try to push a million pounds of pain down, down, down inside herself. Where it will fester and eat at her. Where it may become a poison that will destroy her.

She reaches across and lays a hand on Frangie's hand.

They sit that way in silence for many minutes. Outwardly silent, as Frangie tries to get control of emotions that roll through her like a series of waves, cresting, waning, crashing in again.

"I forgot what I was going to say," Frangie says at last. "Anyway. I should be getting back."

"Back to where?"

"Back to my battalion."

"Frangie."

"What?" A slow, terrible dawning, and a second, more anxious, "What?"

"The battalion suffered seventy percent casualties. They're off the line, and basically, sparing you the army jargon, the remains will be folded into some other group."

Frangie hears nothing after "seventy percent."

Rainy pours her another shot of schnapps.

"Listen, Frangie, there are two ways this goes now. Either you get sent to the rear to see if another colored unit can take you, and of course they will, but it may be a while. You could probably get some time off, some Paris time even. Or you could get shipped back to Blighty and be assigned to a hospital."

Frangie nods dully. "Or?"

Rainy sighs. "You should go—"

"Or?" Frangie demands angrily.

"Or you could sit tight here, because Bastogne is in big trouble now and is going to be in worse trouble soon. We'll need medics, whatever color they are." She leans across the table a little and squeezes Frangie's hand. "You've done enough. You've done more than enough. You've had your war. Let me get you out of Bastogne while I can. Go back to England, finish your time there. And when it's all over, go home with your head held high."

Frangie snorts dismissively. "My head held high? Until I run into my first white person and have to step off into the gutter."

Rainy, confused, asks, "Is that a metaphor?"

"A metaphor?" Frangie looks at Rainy with disbelief. "You really don't know, do you? In the south—maybe other places too, I don't know—but in the south if a colored person is on a sidewalk and a white person's coming toward them, the colored person steps aside. Into the street if necessary."

"You mean . . . that's expected?"

"Expected? Yes, you could say it's expected. Just like it's expected that I will sit in the colored section at a movie theater, or never drink from a 'whites only' drinking fountain, or—"

"But how do people know which is a white drinking fountain?"

"There's a sign."

"A sign."

"Yes, a sign that says, 'Colored Only,' or, 'Whites Only,' or 'No Dogs or Negroes.' And it's not like a suggestion; if you don't go along you wake up to find a cross burning on your lawn. And sometimes, if the white folks get drunk enough, there's a lynching."

"But that's crazy."

Frangie smiles at her friend. "You want to know the funny thing, Rainy?"

"Funny would be good."

"The funny thing," Frangie says, leaning forward and lowering her voice in volume if not intensity, "is that all my life I thought it was normal. I thought it's just the way things are. I thought, well ... yes, it's a white person's world and ... and I never even thought about it being wrong. I read a story in ... I don't know, one of the colored papers ... anyway, about this colored vet, wounded, heading home to see his folks. And he was made to move out of the white seats to make room for German prisoners being sent to a POW camp in Kansas. See, Germans are white. Doesn't matter that they're the enemy, they're white."

Rainy takes this in. How had she not known this? How had she never asked herself what life was like for Negroes? She feels obscurely guilty, despite the fact that Jews are themselves treated as second-class citizens. Yet, she is white, and while she can't join a country club or attend some universities because of her ethnic background, she is still undeniably white and has never confronted such a thing as a 'Jews Only' section.

She comes close to telling Frangie some of what she has learned and come to suspect about what Germans are doing to Jews. But her innate reserve stops her. Anyway, how would it help? She sees more than enough rage in Frangie's eyes, she doesn't need more.

"I don't think I ever understood that," Rainy admits.

Frangie slumps in her seat. Already small she becomes smaller still. "In 1921 white folks burned down Greenwood. That's a neighborhood in Tulsa. Used to be called the Colored Wall Street. White folks burned it down. They actually got hold of planes and threw gas bombs down on colored homes."

"That really happened?" Rainy asks skeptically.

"My mother . . ." Frangie stops, but only long enough to master her voice which still comes out as a low, grating sound unlike anything Rainy has ever heard from Frangie. "Some white men took her. And they used her."

Silence stretches again. Rainy feels something inside her resist. Deny. But that's madness; obviously Frangie is telling the truth. Yet at the same time, Rainy can't believe it, doesn't want to believe it. She wants her moral lines neat and clean and clear. She doesn't want to know that in her own country there are men and women every inch the moral equivalent of the Nazis.

If there is one true thing that can be said about Rainy Schulterman it is that she keeps her own counsel and shares only the minimum. If there is a second true thing about Rainy Schulterman it is that she goes where the facts lead her.

"I didn't know," Rainy says. She drums her fingers on the desk and says again, "I didn't know. I never knew. I never really . . ." Her head shakes, slightly at first, but more vigorously, more angrily. "I didn't know. How? How do I not know that? How do I not know?"

Rainy gets to her feet and paces, followed by Frangie's eyes. Despite herself, Frangie is almost amused by Rainy's reaction.

When the four of them—Rio, Jenou, Frangie and Rainy—had been together in Britain it had immediately become clear that Rainy was the clever, informed one, the one who understood the war and the history and the politics and so on. Rainy was undeniably very smart, but there were some very big holes in what she knew of the world, especially the world closer to home.

"How do you people fight for us? For our country?" Rainy demands suddenly.

"We don't," Frangie says. "We fight for *our* country. And mostly we do just the same as all the white GIs; we fight to stay alive and keep our brothers and sisters alive."

Rainy sits. This time she pours herself a schnapps as well as one for Frangie.

Frangie raises her glass and says, "There's a special Jewish toast, isn't there? I heard it once."

"Did it sound like someone clearing their throat? Was it *l'chaim*?"

"Why yes, that is it. What does it mean?"

"To life," Rainy says and clinks her mug against Frangie's.

"*L'chaim*," Frangie says. Then, "I pronounced that wrong, didn't I?"

"Oh absolutely," Rainy says, laughing. Then falling serious again she says, "This can't go on."

"Do you mean this battle? This war? Or what's going on back home to colored folks?"

"Yes," Rainy says.

28

RIO RICHLIN—CLERVAUX, LUXEMBOURG

Rio leans back against the cool stone of the castle wall and lets her eyes close. She knows how this will play out. She doesn't need to see it.

"Lieutenant Horne, I'm ordering Richlin to try and break out with as many of her people as she can," Mackie says.

The inside of the castle is chaos and blood. Blood fills and freezes in the cracks between cobblestones. The dead are lined up in a row in the courtyard. The air smells of smoke and Rio's eyes sting. The town is lost.

"I'll lead that breakout," Horne says.

Mackie shakes her head. "No. Richlin's the—"

"She's my sergeant!" Horne protests angrily.

Mackie turns on him the gaze that had once reduced Rio to a puddle on the barracks floor. "Lieutenant, I have rank, and I have Colonel Fuller's approval."

"But . . . I can't be taken prisoner! How will that look?"

"The same as it'll look for me," Mackie says grimly. "I'm sticking it out. And so are you. Richlin?"

Rio opens her eyes. "Right here, Captain."

"You have your orders." She hands Rio a small packet. "Letters from the colonel and a few pieces of mail. Get them to the general if you can."

Rio comes away from the wall and executes a more careful, more exact salute than she has in a while. "Thank you, Captain."

Mackie shakes Rio's hand. "Good luck. You'll need it."

Rio turns and trots down the circular stairway, down the tower and out into the courtyard without so much as a glance at Lieutenant Horne.

Her platoon—scarcely more than a squad now—gathers around. "Okay, here's the deal. Captain Mackie has asked me—some others too, but that's their problem. Anyway, we are to try to break out and get some documents to HQ. Wherever the hell that may be at this moment. We go as soon as it's dark."

"What are the odds?" Rudy J. Chester asks. The question is on every face.

"Bad. People who stay here will probably survive and be taken prisoner. Those who come with me have a higher chance of dying, a lower chance of being a POW. This is volunteers only."

She is down to fifteen people not including herself.

Jenou raises a hand.

"All right, Castain."

"I was just raising my hand to go to the bathroom," Jenou says, breaking the unbearable tension.

In the end seven volunteer to go with her—not surprisingly they are almost all members of her old squad, the soldiers who know her best: Jenou, Geer, Jack, Beebee, Molina, Mazur the mad bazooka man, and Rudy J. Chester. Rio solemnly shakes hands with all of those who will stay behind and accepts various letters home.

"I'm just tired," Jenny Dial says by way of apology.

"You've done enough, Dial. You fought your war, and you'll fight some more before surrender."

Dial looks like she might start crying.

"This is hard," Rio says to all of them. "This is a hard day. But if everyone keeps their head we'll be okay. All right, back to work. People coming with me, I want to see light packs—food, water, socks, ammo. Wrap everything for quiet. We move out in an hour."

But they almost don't get the chance. The American lines are crumbling. The castle itself is on fire in parts, and the whole town is layered in smoke. But a desperate sally by defending troops buys Rio just enough time.

She leads her people down dark, cobbled streets illuminated by fire and obscured by smoke. She's studied the maps carefully, but they don't really offer much guidance. What she knows is that she has to get across the river, run into the woods and hope that somehow advancing Germans don't see them.

The river banks are covered in snow—snow that leaves big fat footprints. Rio has them walk backward down the short slope, leaving footprints pointed the wrong way. She steps into the water and has to stifle a yelp: the water is freezing cold and the current is strong.

Rio makes a chopping gesture, showing where she thinks they can land on the other side. They are able to keep their feet only for a few steps before letting the water rise to their necks and abandoning themselves to the current.

They dog paddle and float and finally climb up the other side, ice crystals already forming on their sodden uniforms. Chester drops to his knees, but Rio grabs the collar of his uniform and drags him back up. And now they climb, hand over hand, grabbing tree trunks to lever themselves up another few feet.

Rio squats and raises a fist. A German patrol is sauntering along, obviously unconcerned since their forces are already pushing into the town. They pass and Rio leads the way forward, peering into near-total darkness to find the ravine she'd used to come down this same slope. But there are no landmarks in the forest, and she sits everyone down for a few minutes as she doubles back and forth before practically falling into the ravine.

"Okay, let's go."

They descend into the cut and start climbing again.

Three times they stop and listen as German voices and footsteps are heard. And it is becoming clear that more and more German troops are being moved down toward the town.

Rio is surprised that she is able to locate the hole she'd fallen in the day before, but there'd been a fallen tree nearby and that fixed the location. They crawl down into the hole.

"Molina. Find a branch and try to hide our tracks," Rio says in a terse whisper. "Geer in the entryway. Everyone else: sack out. We may be here a while."

By now they are all veterans and if any one order is instantly followed it is the order to sleep. Frightened as they each are, they are even more exhausted.

Molina spends a half hour crawling in the snow with a leafless branch confusing their tracks. Fresh snow falls and soon all sign of their passage will be invisible even in daylight.

When Molina crawls back in she's shivering so hard she can't speak. Jenou and Chester make her the filling in a human sandwich, holding her between them until her core body temperature can rise to something just short of corpse.

Mazur, carefully-shielding his flashlight so only a dim and narrow beam emerges, plays the light around the room. And it is definitely a room of some sort, made by human hands. But it has been a very long time since any human has been here. The ground shows evidence of animal burrows, mostly in the form of animal excrement that adds an extra pungency to the funk of eight unwashed bodies in a hole no larger than a child's bedroom.

Geer trades the door position with Chester, then digs out a hole in the dirt floor. "Richlin, I'm thinking we can put a spirit stove in a hole and have at least a little light. No smoke, no smell, at least not enough for the Krauts to find us."

The light is indeed dim. Rio vetoes the notion of making a small pot of coffee—the Krauts might not smell a spirit stove, but they're quite likely to notice the smell of coffee wafting up from the middle of the woods.

Molina snores in a corner beneath the few warm things anyone can spare for her. Jenou writes in her journal for a few minutes then passes out. Geer lies back and is out before he reaches full horizontal. Jack takes the burning cigarette from Mazur's slack mouth and sits beside Rio, alone near the entrance.

He holds a flask out for her.

"Bless you," Rio says fervently and takes a swig of the cognac.

"What do you make of our chances?" Jack asks.

Rio scratches her armpit and her neck, considering. "Well,

Stafford, we know where we are, but we don't know where the Krauts are. Or where our lines are. So I'd say our chances are not good."

"Ah. Yes." He is silent, but Rio senses he has something to say.

"Spit it out, Stafford."

He winces. "Just for the duration of this conversation, do you suppose I could call you Rio and you could call me Jack?"

Rio shifts uncomfortably, having the feeling that this is going to be a difficult talk. She is in a strange fugue state, simultaneously tinglingly alert, and desperately weary.

"Sure, Jack."

"Well, it's like this, Rio. I was wondering what you intended to do after this is all over."

Rio shrugs. "I don't know. I don't know anything. Every day that passes I know less and less about the world later, after, that whole world . . . and I know more and more about this." She indicates the room with a wave that widens to encompass the whole war. "It's like my head will only hold so much and all of this has kind of shoved all of that other stuff out of my brain."

"I suppose what I really mean is . . ." He draws a deep breath. ". . . whether you plan on marrying that pilot."

Rio's eyes have closed and she pries one open to look at him. Some other time, some other place, she might have been missishly coy, might have told him it was none of his business. But coyness is one of those things her brain no longer contains. And if she were Diane Mackie, she might have managed to be so stern, so unapproachably, perfectly military that Jack would not have dared even bring this up. This is a personal conversation at the worst possible time and in the worst possible place.

One thing she does know, and it makes her heart sink: Jack isn't asking because he's interested in Strand; he's asking whether Rio will be free of romantic obligations.

"I don't know about Strand," she says. "He's . . ." She hesitates, feeling that she is somehow betraying Strand even by having this conversation. But again, with her future about evenly divided between death and a POW camp, she doesn't really care. "I suppose it comes down to the fact that Strand . . . Captain Braxton . . . well, he lost his nerve."

Jack frowns. "What does that mean?"

"He's AWOL in Paris. And last I was with him, he wasn't intending to go back."

"He deserted?"

That word still burns when Rio thinks it. She can't yet bring herself to apply that terrible word to Strand. All combat soldiers have bad times when they can't take it, have to be pulled off the line. Front line soldiers do, from time to time, just walk away. But they almost all return, and their brothers and sisters don't hold it against them because everyone knows it could be them next.

But true desertion is a different story. There are deserters, even from front line units, thousands of them, but no one has a kind thing to say about those who save themselves at the expense of others who must do their dying for them.

"I'm sorry," Jack says.

"Mmm. Are you?"

Jack says nothing.

"Look, Jack, I know what you're asking."

"Do you?"

"I'm your sergeant. I'm the one who has to send you out on patrol, maybe get you killed. I can't . . . I mean, I don't know, Jack, I don't really know how to be 'Sarge' and 'Rio.' And until this is over I have to be 'Sarge.'"

Jack nods. "The truth is, Rio, I'm afraid I've fallen—"

"No!" Rio snaps and places a hand on his arm. Then, more gently, "No, Jack. No."

He subsides, seeming smaller. "A man facing death wants hope, Rio. Or Sarge. Am I a complete ass to even hope?"

She squeezes his arm. "Hope is good. Now, get some damn sleep, Stafford."

"Right, Sarge."

Rio relieves Chester at the entryway, her sleepiness banished for the moment. She can shut Jack down, but she knows what he meant to say, what he may even sincerely feel.

It seems crazy, sitting in a stinking hole in a Luxembourg forest, to even daydream about *after*. Just a month before "after" had seemed imminent. People talked about the war being over by Christmas. Well, Christmas was less than two weeks away, and it sure didn't seem likely.

And yet her mind returned unbidden to thoughts of after. Thoughts of Gedwell Falls. Her mother's arms and emotion. Her father's handshake and repressed tears. Parades? Would there be parades like there had been after that last war? Would anyone feel like celebrating?

At times in the past Rio had pictured a nice little cottage. She knew just the street she wanted to live on. At times she walked through her imaginary cottage trying to picture the furniture she would like, the curtains she would pick out, the rugs . . . But it never quite worked, and the imaginary cottage had become less and less detailed and specific over time, rather than the reverse.

She imagined herself at home, timing her dinner preparations for the moment when Strand would return from his job—whatever that was.

Kiss kiss, what's for dinner, sweetheart?

Oh, you know how I love your meatloaf!

And what would she do with the rest of her day? Tidy up? Do laundry? Care for their children, help them with their homework, make their school lunches, attend PTA meetings and . . .

The little underground chamber seems to shrink by the minute. She has to steady herself with slow, deep breaths.

What would Mackie—Captain *Diane* Mackie—do after? Did she have a home? A husband? My God, did she have children? That is a startling thought.

What about Jedron Cole? What would he be doing after? Rio grins at the memory of his gap-toothed smile.

She indulges in a fantasy of locating him after the war, taking him out for beer and giving him a gift of a box of cigars. He had been her sergeant, and she had admired him, but she'd had no notion of the weight of responsibility he had carried.

Thank you, Jedron Cole. Thank God for you.

She imagined Cole asking her what she was doing, now with the war over.

Cooking dinner, Jed. I'm cooking dinner. And I'm baking a pie!

Suddenly she hears movement outside, at least two pairs of boots trampling snow and bushes. She pulls back and goes person to person warning them to be completely silent. Geer pushes dirt over the spirit stove, plunging them into absolute darkness, with only a hint of gray coming down through the hole. Outside, day has come but there is no sunlight peeking through the eternal clouds.

Slowly, moving inch by inch, Rio pushes forward. She gathers snow and packs it onto her mesh-covered helmet. Slowly . . . slowly . . . pushes her head out of the hole. The Germans are behind her and she turns with infinite slowness to see two soldiers apparently brewing tea or coffee and having a snack.

Pickets—a Kraut outpost.

There is no longer any sound of gunfire from Clervaux. The town is taken, the Americans there either dead or being rounded up and marched to a POW camp.

Rio retreats into the hole and in a voiceless whisper says, "Listen up. They've got pickets out." For Chester and Molina's benefit she explains. "If they've got a thin line of pickets out we should be able to move come dark."

Hours pass. Hours during which they must dig themselves a small slit trench and add to the stink of the chamber. Hours during which they take painstaking care to silently open cans of C rations. Hours during which they sleep.

At last, darkness falls. Rio slithers out to find there are still two German soldiers, though probably not the same two. Being good, disciplined German soldiers they've dug themselves a hole—a hole that had they dug another few feet would have had them breaking through into the roof of the chamber.

Rio sees their helmets, both aimed away, downhill. She hears one man's heavy, regular breathing.

She loosens her *koummya* in its scabbard. Crawl. Stop. Listen. Crawl. Stop. Listen.

She's close enough to smell them and is grateful to realize that if the wind was blowing the other direction it would be them smelling her.

Crawl. Stop. Listen.

Crawl. Stop. Listen. Slow breathing. Draw *koummya*. Test grip. She wipes her hand dry on the side of her leg. Takes the *koummya* again.

Crawl.

Two feet. He must smell her or hear her or sense her at any moment and one gunshot will alert the Germans and dash any hope of escape.

Crawl.

And . . .

And . . .

Lunge!

She hurls herself forward, lands hard on her chest, but with her left grabbing the rim of the German helmet, yanking it hard and stabbing the point of the *koummya* into his throat.

She pulls the knife out and feels his blood cover her hand.

She swings her legs over the side of the foxhole and drops in as the second German snaps awake, holds up his hands to block the blow that's coming and cries out in pain as the *koummya* stabs through his upraised palm.

They are in a space no more roomy than a phone booth, with a dying, gurgling German tangled around their legs. The second German starts to yell but Rio punches him in the nose which turns his cry into a grunt.

She stabs at him, but he's fully awake and parries her thrust, taking another cut in the process.

He's bigger than she is. Stronger. And he's no raw recruit. He reaches for his rifle, but it's out of reach, so he fumbles for his own knife and Rio stabs again, the blow again deflected from its intended target—his throat—and stabbing a bare inch into his collarbone.

She has mere seconds before his greater strength and her own desperate need for silence defeat her. She collapses, literally sitting on the dying German at her feet and stabs upward.

The *koummya* goes deep into the German's crotch and she levers herself up to clamp her hand over the scream that rises within him, while simultaneously digging the *koummya* deeper, deeper, working the blade back and forth to cut up whatever internal organs the blade can reach.

The German bucks, flails, punches madly, catching Rio a stunning hit on the side of her head. She lets go of the *koummya* and the German now scrambles frantically to escape the hole. He's halfway up and out, but the *koummya* sticks from the bottom of his uniform trousers like a horrifying Popsicle stick.

Rio makes a mad grab for the *koummya*, pulls it out making a slurping sound, then grabs his uniform and pulls him back down. And now the *koummya* goes around his throat and she pulls back hard.

She sits panting in the foxhole, recovering as the two Germans bleed and die at her feet. Then she crawls back to the hole and gathers her freezing, weary flock.

29

Private Martha Swann is a draftee. She is eighteen, five feet six inches tall, a redhead, pale, with distinctly green eyes.

Exactly twenty-one weeks earlier Martha received her notice from the draft board in Chicago, Illinois. She reported, was sent to basic training, tossed on a boat, landed in Britain, spent days in the Repple Depple, and was shipped forward.

And then, before she'd even seen her own assigned unit, it had started: the brutal fight that would come to be known as the Battle of the Bulge.

Martha is from an academic family. Her father is a professor of Oriental Languages at the University of Chicago and her mother is a secretary in the dean's office. She herself has never had much interest in either of her parents' work, though she is bookish in her own way, reading voraciously, everything by the greats like Dickens and Tolstoy, but especially more modern, more exciting works by Agatha Christie and Dashiell Hammett and Raymond Chandler, who she loves to distraction. She loves mysteries, the more hard-boiled the better. She enjoys nothing more than a scene involving some cheap hood with a gat in his hand being slapped down by Chandler's great detective, Phillip Marlowe.

But prior to basic training she had never even seen an actual gun, let alone fired one. When she reads tales of action and derring-do, Martha never sees herself as the hero. She is not even in her imagination the hero's girlfriend or moll. She sees herself as one of the anonymous passers-by, one of the minor characters perhaps glimpsed on a street corner or sitting at the counter of a diner. She is by nature an observer, not a participant. She attends university football games dutifully, attends drama club productions a bit more enthusiastically, cheers on the lacrosse team, but always from the sidelines.

Martha is happy in the role of observer. Happiest when she is almost invisible, like one of those secondary characters Marlowe might describe as, "A sweet little package, but not one I had time for."

Her father did all he could—going hat-in-hand to an alderman to see whether he could get his daughter a draft deferment. The war would soon be over, after all. People said by Christmas. But the alderman had either been powerless or unwilling. And the truth is that Martha did not hate the idea of being drafted because—so she thought—it would be fascinating to observe the process, to be able to see it up close. To watch the war and take mental notes.

The first time her training sergeant had punched her in the belly with the butt of an M1 she had experienced the shattering and disorienting realization that she was not to be an observer. She was to be a *participant*.

After that she had done her best—she is not rebellious by nature, and is smart and willing—and by the time the army deemed her ready for war she had qualified with all infantry weapons, could perform basic first aid, and knew how to march in formation.

That last, she suspected, would not be of much use here in the eternal, dense, dark, frightening forests of northern Europe.

She'd been taken in the night to a freezing mud-and-snow-slush tent camp where she had spent the next day writing letters home and reading before being called out by a young PFC with the unlikely name of Benjamin Barry Bassingthwaite.

"But everyone calls me Beebee. Hell, even I call me Beebee."

He's in a jeep. The back is loaded with musette bags stuffed with who-knows-what, some crates of C rations, and what looks like a half dozen bazooka rounds.

"I'm Martha Swann."

"Let's go, Swann. Have any idea how to fire a fifty?"

She almost says, "A what?" before realizing he means the .50 caliber machine gun mounted on the jeep. It rests atop a short pole mount, with the long barrel pointed forward over her head. "I've never . . ."

"Well, let's hope it doesn't come up."

He grinds the gears, drops the clutch and the jeep goes bouncing and careening away, out of the camp, and down a wooded lane. The sun is down and the wind is up and Martha is freezing within seconds.

"Cold?" Beebee yells.

"Yes!"

"Nah." Beebee laughs. "You're not cold. But you will be."

How Beebee is steering is a mystery to Martha. He has not

turned on his lights. It is pitch-black, but for some faint starlight. And now snow begins to fall in fat flakes. From time to time a tendril of a bush will slap her shoulder as they race along. Her face is numb. Her ears ache. Her nose is streaming and burning.

In the not-very-distant distance Martha hears artillery, an ominous rumble. Beebee pulls the jeep off whatever faint trail they've been bouncing along and plunges into the untracked woods. But not for long. He careens to a stop and kills the engine.

A shape appears, illuminated only by the glow of a cigarette.

"That you, Beebee?" a woman's voice asks.

"Yep. And I brought a replacement for you, Castain."

"Fug the replacement, did you bring coffee?"

"I got what I could. It's in the back."

The woman says, "Hey, Chester! Help us move this gear."

Martha is given a box of C rations to carry and four of them, Corporal Castain, PFC Beebee, Private Chester and Martha tramp into the woods bearing gifts.

They come to a fallen tree and Martha is told to drop her box.

"All right, come with me, whoever you are," Castain says.

"Martha Swann."

"No one cares," Castain says. She leads the way and Martha hurries to keep up. "You'll spend the night in Mazur's hole. He dug it well."

"Mazur?"

"Pity about him, he was hell with a bazooka."

"Is he . . ."

"Nah. But he won't be running any foot races any time soon." Castain chuckles.

She follows Castain through near pitch-darkness made even more opaque by snow falling thick and hard. Her boots crunch on frost, feet plunging three inches, six inches, sudden drops into holes that trip her up. She spits snow out of her mouth and wipes it from her eyes. Tears stream from her eyes, not tears of sadness but cold, tears sliding down to freeze on her cheeks.

Martha is from Chicago. She has spent hours out in Chicago winters riding her sled down the hill, or entering into snowball fights with other kids in the neighborhood. This is as cold as a Chicago January, certainly no more than a dozen degrees Fahrenheit, but the difference here is that there is no fireplace-warmed parlor, and no hot cocoa by that fire while the family's maid, Wilma, lays a plaid blanket on her lap and clucks, "You'll catch your death!"

There is no escape from this cold. No respite. She is in the forest, a place infinitely stranger to her than the streets of the city.

She looks up and suddenly realizes to her utter horror that she has lost Castain.

She spins, breath coming in throat-rasping, freezing gasps of steam. Trees. Nothing but the shadows of trees against snow. She knows she must not call out—Castain has urged silence. But she is lost! Lost in the middle of a forest with nothing at all to guide her. The panic grows swiftly and—

BOOOM!

Bright yellow flame sears her eyeballs and stuns her ears.

BOOOM!

This explosion is above her, over her head! She drops to

the ground babbling incoherently, random disconnected words as . . .

BOOOM! BOOOM!

Something falls on her and in unreasoning terror she rolls over to beat at it before realizing it is just a thumb-thick branch.

BOOOM!

A hand grabs the collar of her coat and yanks her to her feet. "Move!" Castain shoves her in the back, propelling her forward as—

BOOOM!

Castain yanks her back, twists her to the right and says, "Get in!"

There is a hole at Martha's feet and she slides down into it, with Castain bundled in that same slide and—

BOOOM!

In the hole now and Martha realizes she has wet her underwear. Her teeth chatter. She thrusts her hands under her armpits and bows her head trying to get her freezing, running nose into the scarf at her neck.

BOOOM! BOOOM! BOOOM!

The flash of explosions shows her Castain's face for the first time and Martha the careful observer sees a certain prettiness barely evident beneath dirt and a scarf wrapped around much of her head.

They huddle in the hole as Martha realizes that water is seeping into her boots. How can water even be liquid at this temperature?

BOOOM! BOOOM! BOOOM!

The sides of the hole bounce against her, bruising her as the

88s thunder and pound. Dirt and wood shards clatter down on Martha's helmet and she realizes she is crying, not just runny eyes, crying, wracking sobs that join the shaking of chills.

"I want to go home!" Martha cries out, a child's cry.

And suddenly, as if on cue, the artillery stops.

Martha's first instinct as the lull extends is to climb out, to escape this vile pit of fear and wet. But Castain holds her down.

"Uh-uh. Give it a minute."

Sure enough, after a several-minute pause, a half dozen more 88s comes screaming in. One blows a tree clear out of the ground and it falls tearing through the branches of other trees, scattering snow everywhere.

Castain lifts her head and peeks out. "Goddammit, I guess the fugging tree couldn't fall the other way. Could've been good cover. All right, kid. I gotta go. Oh, yeah: the call sign is 'Hair.' The response is 'Brush.'"

Castain levers herself up and out of the hole.

"I don't . . . You can't . . . I don't even know where the Germans are!"

"Oh, they're over that way," Castain says, waving negligently. "Most likely they'll be along shortly."

"But what am I supposed to do?"

"Shoot the fuggers, what do you think?"

Alone.

Martha Swann is completely alone.

She has no watch, no way to keep track of time. Minutes might be hours, but more likely, she realizes, time is passing with extreme subjective slowness. Snow falls into the foxhole and with freezing feet she tamps it down into the slush, hoping it will freeze solid and she can stand on it. She can no longer feel her toes, her nose, her ears or fingers.

The forest at night makes strange sounds, dripping, rubbing, soft clattering. Each sound might be a German.

How many times has she read some novel where the author talks about a character's heart being in their throat? It no longer seems like such a cliché. She can barely swallow.

A sound. A furtive, cautious, creeping sound.

"Hair!" she calls out in a tremulous tone.

"Shut the fug up," comes a terse whisper. Then, a bolt of fire, a loud crack and the sound of running, falling . . .

"Hah! Got him!" a male voice says, coming from the blackness to her left.

Had someone just shot a German?

She hears crawling and scuffling and low, distinctly Anglo-Saxon curses. Then, "Hah! It's a baby deer! Meat!"

BOOOM! BOOOM! BOOOM!

The artillery comes again and again Martha rocks back and forth in the bottom of her hole until it ends. She no longer cares that she is weeping. She no longer cares that she has peed herself.

And then, a female voice, strong and confident, yells, "Here they come!"

And instantly from ahead comes the rattle of small arms fire. Someone to Martha's right fires and the female voice yells, "Wait till you have a target!"

Then all at once it seems everyone has a target, the night lights up with muzzle flash to her left, to her right, and dead ahead. She forces herself to stand on legs that want so badly to collapse. She looks out and sees right there, right there, a gray uniform.

The German fires his rifle.

Martha sees the flash. Hears the bullet strike packed snow behind her head.

And something . . . snaps.

Freezing, weeping, snot running down her lip, Martha Swann grabs her rifle and does not return fire, instead she climbs out of the hole as the German fires again and misses again.

Then he turns and begins to run away as a now-screaming Martha chases him.

A shot rings out. The German falls and through the veil of bloody rage that has seized Martha's mind she sees Rudy J. Chester. He says, "Get back in your hole, you idiot!"

But there's a certain laughing admiration in that "idiot."

It's a small probing attack, nothing more, and the Germans are driven off.

Martha crawls back to her hole, slides in, and falls instantly asleep.

Rio had made a hole in the ground the only way now possible: by clearing away the snow to reach the soil beneath and then setting off a grenade.

The ground is frozen. The grenade shatters the top layer and allows her to insert the blade of her entrenching tool. But the ground is frozen at least a foot down, and once she manages to dig and hack her way past the frost she all-too-soon found water.

One of the first things Rio had done after leaping at the opportunity to add Frangie to her rump platoon had been to ask Frangie to do a twinkle toe inspection.

Now Frangie slides down into Rio's foxhole. Both are wrapped in every stitch of clothing they own. GIs have taken to stripping dead Americans and sometimes dead Germans of boots, coats, hats, sweaters, gloves, and above all, socks. There are any number of frozen dead Germans in the woods, but very few wearing overcoats at this point. Rio has a gray wool scarf wrapped around her head and tied at the back like some bargain-basement pirate, with her helmet shoved down over it. Frangie has a wool watch cap pulled low and her clean socks stuffed up under the watch cap to cover her ears. Her helmet unfortunately pushes the socks down, exposing the tops of her ears to cold.

Or more cold. Because no part of either woman was anything but cold. Cold was everywhere. Cold was in everything. Cold was inside them, no longer kept at bay, it had infiltrated them, lurked inside them now, weakening muscles, bringing on debilitating shivers, spreading a leaden lethargy.

Hungry. Lonely. Scared. But above all, cold.

Rio sometimes wonders how anyone holds out. Every now and then the Germans—who during daylight are within sight across a snow-covered field—would warm up their loudspeakers and shout, "Surrender, Americans! Warm beds and hot meals await you!" And sometimes when Rio looked into the whiskered or just filthy faces of her soldiers she wondered if they might not have been tempted . . . but for one word.

Malmédy.

The word, which had been unknown a day before, is now on every American GI's lips.

Malmédy.

GIs had fought before this. GIs had hated before this. But the American army after Malmédy, after the deliberate murder of American prisoners, was an army stripped of doubt, stripped of ambivalence. The American army after Malmédy had a single unifying goal almost as powerful as the goal of getting home alive: killing SS. An army that had thought the war almost over, an army ready to go home as soon as possible, had become an army of hunters.

Rudy J. Chester comes stumbling in at the head of a three-person patrol composed of himself, Beebee and the new replacement who had run screaming at the Germans the night before.

"Hey, Sarge! We got a prisoner!"

"I'll leave you to it," Frangie says. "But you need to put the fear of God into Molina or she's gonna lose some toes."

Rio gives the medic a boost up and out and Chester drops and sits at the edge of the hole, legs dangling. He has a piece of rope tied around the neck of a German soldier.

"Good work, Chester," Rio says.

"What are you going to do with him?" Chester seems possessive of his prize.

"G2 says we send all prisoners to them for questioning," Rio says. "Castain?"

"F-u-u-u-g!" comes the groan from the next hole, some seventy-five feet away. Their line is thin—very thin, with far too much space between foxholes.

Jenou crawl-walks over. "What?"

"Prisoner."

Jenou's eyes travel from Rio to the German to Chester. "Ah," she says.

"Take him down the hill to company," Rio says. "Take um . . . take Beebee, maybe he'll see something to scrounge. I'll expect you back before nightfall."

It is all coded speech and coded looks. A little show for the benefit of some of the newer, greener troops, those whose notions of right and wrong had been formed in churches and synagogues and conversations around the dinner table, and has not yet been mangled and twisted and rearranged by too much experience of war.

The prisoner is SS, and while the American GIs have forgotten the names of a hundred Italian villages, and a hundred more French and Belgian towns, one place name is burned deep into the minds of every American soldier, never to be forgotten, never to be forgiven.

Malmédy.

Jenou locates Beebee who, after walking the early morning patrol with Chester, is attempting to hide in his foxhole and sleep. But Jenou pokes him with the butt of her carbine.

"Come on, Beeb. Let's go for a nice walk in the woods."

They slog along, taking turns holding the German's rope.

"*Kamerad? Amis?*" the German says from time to time in a pleading voice.

"We taking him to company?" Beebee asks.

Jenou gives him a look and Beebee falls silent. The German senses something very wrong and starts again. "*Kamerad? Kamerad. Amis!* No Hitler! America *Deutschland* yes? *Kamerad?*"

"All right, far enough," Jenou says. She stops and uses the muzzle of her carbine to push the German back against a tree. She reaches into her coat and pulls out a cigarette, which she gives to the German.

Now he knows.

His hands shake so badly he drops the cigarette, bends to pick it up, and nearly falls over when he stands.

"*Nein nein nein,*" he pleads as Jenou lights her Zippo and holds the flame to his cigarette. He reaches into his coat and comes out with an oilskin packet. Letters fall from his shaking fingers as he seeks for and finds a photograph. He holds it up for Jenou to see.

"*Mein Name ist Heinrich, ja? Heinrich Weber.*" He beats on his chest. His name is Heinrich. "*Meine Kinder.*" He points at the picture of a handsome, severe woman, posed with a younger version of the prisoner and two children, a sly-eyed girl of maybe seven, and a little boy held in the prisoner's arms. "*Das ist Helga und kleiner Fritz.*"

Helga. And little Fritz.

"*Kamerad,*" the man pleads. Whether he has chosen to drop or his strength has simply given way, he falls to his knees. He clutches his hands in prayer around the picture, holding it up as he says over and over again, "*Meine Kinder. Meine Kinder. Bitte!*"

My children, my children.

Please.

"Malmédy," Jenou says and shoots him once through the neck.

Heinrich Weber lies dead in the snow. Jenou retrieves his packet of photographs, reassembles them in the envelope. She and Beebee quickly strip the body of useful clothing, leaving him naked but for his shirt and underpants. Jenou stuffs the envelope under his uniform shirt.

"Richlin says we have a couple hours," Jenou says. "Let's get to company and see if we can find a hot meal."

30

FRANGIE MARR—ELSENBORN RIDGE, BELGIUM

Day follows day with deadly routine. The Americans sit in their foxholes freezing. Sometimes they go on patrols to locate the Germans and make sure they're still where they are supposed to be. Other times the Germans patrol, to make sure the Americans are where they are supposed to be.

Almost daily the Germans launch a probing attack, which is repulsed.

And after each patrol, after each attack, Frangie counts the cost. Bullet wounds. Shrapnel wounds. Splinter wounds. Self-inflicted wounds. Friendly fire wounds. Trench foot. Frostbite.

Her life is snow and blood.

Her life is screams and groans and final, rattling breaths.

But more and more it is the minds of the GIs that are the greater problem. Sergeant Geer is found shivering uncontrollably in the woods surrounded by frozen Germans. As tough as Geer is, no one can take it day after day after day. The cold, the cold, the cold. The fear. The numbing loss of hope, the loss even of memories of what the world once was.

Every few days she takes one or two of the worst off back down to the aid station where they can sit in a tent with a stove and let warmth torture them with pins and needles. Thawing out has become a vital tool in Frangie's medical bag: a GI who gets half a day to thaw out is good for more days at the front.

There is one army doctor and a Belgian nun with nurse's training at the nearest aid station. The nun is in her thirties or forties, it's impossible to tell in a world where everyone wears any scrap of clothing they can find. The doctor is a gaunt, gray-faced Maine Yankee whose eyes are as hollow as any front line soldier's. Every time Frangie comes, he is on duty. Has he ever slept?

"What you got, Marr?"

"Bullet to the right thigh, through and through, but I think it may have clipped the bone. And a combat fatigue."

The wounded man smokes a cigarette, takes it out of his mouth to yell, "God DAMN that hurts!"

The combat fatigue soldier sits on the dirt floor rocking back and forth chanting, "Ring around the rosy," over and over.

Is it any surprise that soldiers are going mad? In a mad world what choice did they have?

With a Belgian stretcher bearer, Frangie has manhandled the injured man off the jeep and into the tent. The Belgian is originally from the Congo, a black African with whom Frangie would love to talk, some other time, in some other universe.

The locals, the Belgian people, have been magnificent. They open their homes. They empty their larders. They bring blankets and coats and socks they can scarcely have afforded to part with. There are Belgian doctors and nurses and volunteers working without break, all up and down the Bulge. Many GIs had complained about the French. None has a word to say against the Belgians.

Everyone knows the Americans can't hold out much longer.

And everyone tells themselves, "Not today."

"I need morphine," Frangie says.

The doctor shakes his head. "I'm using brandy for amputations now." He is outraged at this, not at Frangie, at the army, at the world. Brandy is not morphine. It's little better than aspirin.

Frangie has just two ampoules of morphine left. They are in her armpit to keep them from freezing. She has a bottle of plasma stuffed down the front of her trousers for the same reason.

The Americans down south in Bastogne, and up here at the Elsenborn Ridge at the northern edge of the Bulge, have run out of almost everything: medicine, food, cigarettes, ammunition. The howitzers and Long Toms still fire rounds toward the Germans, but even Frangie has noticed that the rate of fire is diminishing day by day.

How soon until the big guns fall silent? How soon until the men and women in holes squeeze their triggers and hear nothing but *click*?

"Gauze?" Frangie asks.

The doctor jerks his head toward a pile of gray rags. Many bear faded blood stains. Bandages now are whatever rags Belgian housewives boil for them.

Frangie knows better than to ask after sulfa, let alone the new and exciting penicillin. They've been out of those forever.

Outside the tent Frangie looks up at the sky. Gray. Gray and more gray. Until the weather changes there can be no airdrops of supplies, and the roads are closed, with nothing coming in.

She stumbles toward the smell of food. There's a field kitchen, but all it serves are C rations warmed up over wood fires. They are burning the pews of the village church, carried to them, donated by the Belgian priest and a parishioner with a donkey cart but no donkey.

She makes the mistake of glancing left. There is the pile of unburied dead, frozen, GI and Kraut, their faces the awful maroon that so often results from freezing. A smaller pile is made of nothing but limbs. Arms and legs. Both gruesome piles are dusted with snow.

Frangie eats with mechanical indifference, pushing fuel in, stoking the failing fire inside her. The first time she'd sat at the rough table outside the field tent she'd earned dirty looks and cruel words from some soldiers. What the hell was a Nigra doing eating with decent white folks?

But no one has the energy for that now. And everyone, even the greenest yahoo from Alabama, has come to realize the sacred importance of anyone, man, woman, white or black, with a red cross on their helmet.

Frangie trudges back to her jeep. Despite the desperate lack of fuel, she'd left the engine running—a stopped engine was a dead engine in this cold. But now it has stopped and when she tries to start it the ignition makes one sluggish grunt and no more.

It is a mile and a half back to the front and she walks it on numb feet. She's already lost a little toe to frostbite. She'd borrowed Rio's *koummya* to chop it off.

One foot in front of the next. That was it. That is what her brain thought of. One foot and then the next. There was no point in thinking of anything else. The world of warmth and clean clothing and warm beds was a lie, a fantasy. It was a fragment of dream she remembered but knew was unreal.

This was real. These blackened, denuded trees, like black javelins stabbed into the earth, they were real. The sound of artillery was real. The sudden gust that passed through her layers as easily as a knife's blade and spread goosebumps over her flesh was real.

She trips and falls.

She lies there in the snow and thinks, *Just stay . . . just stay . . .* Her eyes close.

Enough.

Sleep.

If she lays here, in an hour she will be dead.

But after twenty minutes there comes the sound of wheels on snow. The squeal of brakes. The sound of boots on snow.

Hands touch her, grab her clothing and she thinks, *Ah, I'm dead and being stripped . . .*

"Marr! Hey!" A hand slaps the side of her face.

Frangie opens her eyes and sees dark brown eyes beneath a helmet marked with a first lieutenant's rectangle.

"Come on, let's go," the woman says, and Frangie thinks, *I know her.*

"What the hell are you doing, Marr?" Rainy asks as she and her driver bundle a nearly-frozen Frangie into the passenger seat.

"Let me go," Frangie says, though her words are indecipherable.

"Hey," Rainy says, taking Frangie's face in her two hands. "You giving up?"

Frangie nods. Yes. Yes, she is giving up and letting go of life and will she hopes and believes fly to the arms of Jesus in a warm, warm heaven . . .

"Hey!" Rainy shakes Frangie's face. "Before you give up, look up."

Rainy takes Frangie's head and forces her to look up. And there Frangie sees something impossible. A field of blue. And in that field of blue great white flowers blossom.

"S'that real?" Frangie asks.

Rainy grins. "Blue skies, Marr. Blue skies and parachutes."

The great white flowers drift down beyond the trees, each slowing the weight of boxes of food and ammunition.

The weather has cleared. The C-47s are dropping supplies.

On the roads leading to Bastogne and the Elsenborn, all over the Bulge, the Americans suddenly find that they have fighters roaring overhead to lacerate the Germans with missiles and bombs and bullets.

"You hear about General McAuliffe?" Rainy asks, trying to keep her engaged and awake.

Frangie shakes her head.

"He's the 101st's commander. The Krauts sent him a message under a white flag. Said we should surrender to avoid loss of life."

Despite herself Frangie finds a tiny glimmer of interest. "What'd he say?"

"He sent back a one-word message: Nuts."

The fighters roar. The parachutes fall, bringing food and medicine and ammunition. The Americans, down to little more than bayonets and beans, once more will have the tools of victory. Food, medicine, bullets, mortar shells, artillery rounds, and a sky full of P-47s and P-38s.

From the eternal forest comes the savage roar of soldiers who understand now that they may go on freezing, may go on fighting and maybe dying, but who now understand as well . . . that they will *win*.

PART FIVE
THE CAMPS

"All the Dachaus must remain standing. The Dachaus, the Belsens, the Buchenwalds, the Auschwitzes—all of them. They must remain standing because they are a monument to a moment in time when some men decided to turn the Earth into a graveyard. Into it they shoveled all of their reason, their logic, their knowledge, but worst of all, their conscience. And the moment we forget this, the moment we cease to be haunted by its remembrance, then we become the gravediggers."

—Rod Serling

31

"I need a driver and some muscle," Rainy says.

Rio looks up from the letter she's reading. She is sitting at a table, out of doors, outside the mess tent, in a world that is chilly but not freezing. In front of her is a tray, half-eaten: a mound of scrambled eggs, two fat sausages, a short stack of pancakes, coffee and strawberry ice cream.

Actual ice cream.

Rio wears a reasonably clean uniform and—for the first time in recent memory—is not being tortured by lice. This had required shaving her head bald before taking a walk through the delousing tent, and all she has now is a bare half-inch of dark bristle.

"Why are you looking at me, Captain Schulterman?" Rio says it with a certain playful lilt. Rio is not in Rainy's chain-of-command, not even close, after all. But when she looks up and meets Rainy's gaze, Rio drops the playfulness. She glances at Jenou, scribbling away in her journal with one hand, spearing a sausage on a fork with the other.

"What?" Jenou says.

"Captain wants us to take a ride with her," Rio says. To Rainy she says, "What's up?"

Rainy's face is stone. Her eyes are hard. "I've been interviewing some POWs and DPs. I'm hearing . . . things. I have to go check it out."

"And you need some rip-snorting killers with you?"

Rainy shakes her head, but says, "Maybe. I'm not sure." She jerks her head. "Jeep's over there. Finish your meal." She walks away on stiff legs and Rio exchanges a look with Jenou. They stand up, grab their weapons, and leave the food.

This in itself is astounding. Hot food: *left on a tray*! Just a few months earlier either woman would have personally shot any officer crazy enough to try and separate them from actual, cooked, hot food.

But that was winter, and it is now April. Spring. The Soviet Red Army is already in the Berlin suburbs. German troops are streaming west, trying to surrender to the Americans and British, and not the Red Army: no German expects even the slightest mercy from the Russians.

The American and British armies are deep inside Germany proper, but Berlin is to be left to the Red Army. The Americans are securing the southwest, driving toward Bavarian Germany and Austria beyond.

The roads are often jammed with refugees, great masses of displaced persons, called DPs, often in rags, carrying their few possessions. But they set out in the jeep, Rainy in the back with Jenou, Rio riding shotgun and Corporal Rudy J. Chester— no longer "Private Sweetheart" but a bona fide hardcore soldier with a Bronze Star and a Purple Heart—drives.

Every GI has remarked on just how undamaged most of Germany is. Yes, Berlin is a smoking pile of rocks, and some of the other cities are similarly annihilated. Hamburg was burned to the ground in 1943 by a vengeful Royal Air Force. And just two months had passed since the RAF and USAAF had turned Dresden into a torch so hot that stone melted and Germans untouched by the flames and the smoke suffocated in their cellars as the firestorm consumed all oxygen.

But the farms and villages and small towns were in far better shape than the Belgian countryside, or French Normandy or parts of Holland. And if one tenth of the stories about Poland and Russia were true they had endured still worse. But Germany?

Germany, outside of a dozen big cities, was as bucolic and serene as Rio's own Sonoma County.

"What are we looking for?" Chester asks.

Rio turns to Rainy, who says, "I don't know for sure. A camp of some sort, a string of camps around a central facility."

"Like refugee camps?" Chester asks.

"No," says Captain Schulterman.

"What is that smell?" Jenou asks, wrinkling her nose.

They drive on, veering around three cows being tended by a small boy with a stick.

"Must be those cows," Jenou says doubtfully.

Rio smells it too. And as a woman raised around cows, she knows this smell is nothing to do with cattle. There is something wrong with this smell, this stink that carries sense memories of corpses within it. It's a smell that even Rio, who has spent days within arm's reach of rotting corpses, feels seeping into her, unsettling her.

She looks back at Rainy and for the first time in a long while is afraid, because Rainy's face shows that she smells it too, and she, unlike Rio, guesses at what it might be. The G2 officer's face is as blank as a marble statue, like her cheeks and mouth have never moved. But her eyes . . .

Suddenly a creature lurches onto the road. Chester slams on the brakes and the jeep skids to a stop. Rio swings her Thompson up to firing position and trains it on . . . on . . .

He is naked but for a scrap of what must once have been a shirt. His penis and testicles are visible between legs so thin that at first Rio believes he's been skinned, down to the bone. His knees are huge knobs. His thighs are gone, just nothing, just human leather over sticks.

The man raises an arm so emaciated that the two bones of his forearm are clearly visible. Skin sags where muscle had once been. The shirt is open revealing ribs and collarbones. His head is a skull with eyes so deep they are invisible.

The four Americans sit frozen in the jeep.

The man, the walking skeleton, the stick figure collapses, falls to his knees and tries to clasp his hands as if in prayer. But his strength is gone and he falls onto his face. His bare buttocks are empty sacks of flesh, all fat long-since gone.

Rio forces herself out of the jeep, advancing as she unlimbers her canteen. She turns him over, shocked at the feel of his body. He cannot weigh seventy pounds. He might as well be a child.

The man whispers something, words, maybe, but no language

404

Rio knows. She kneels and holds her canteen to his cracked lips. He seems almost to smile as the thin trickle of water trickles down his throat.

He speaks again.

"I don't understand," Rio says.

"*Zenen ir faktish*," Rainy says, standing behind Rio now. "It's Yiddish. He's asking if you're real." Rainy kneels, takes off her helmet and sets it on the road. She speaks in the same language, the never-quite-learned and largely forgotten language of her mother and father.

"We are real," Rainy says in Yiddish. "Americans."

The man looks at her with eyes terribly large in his fleshless skull. As he looks at Rainy, his breathing stops. And slowly the faint spark in his eyes goes out.

Chester is there now, and Jenou. "I'll help you move him out of the road," Chester says.

Rio shakes her head. "He weighs nothing." She slides her hands beneath him and stands up. He is a broken doll in her arms. They leave his body by the side of the road for graves registration, and without a word between them drive on, guided by the terrible stink of filth and death.

They pass another body, also no more than bones in rags.

And then, a barbed-wire fence and a gate that stands open. A guardhouse is unoccupied. Beyond that gate men in rags, men with sunken cheeks, with every bone visible, men so emaciated they surely must be the fantasies of sick minds.

"What is this place?" Jenou asks in a voice Rio has never heard before, the voice of a frightened child, an angry, disbelieving child.

No one answers.

They drive into the camp and the specters, the human wreckage, stagger and drift toward them, ghosts of men on toothpick legs, men with flesh scarred by sores and wounds, men trying to speak and unable to raise their voices above a whisper.

Rainy, her voice unreal, like it's someone else using her mouth, says, "Chester, go back to company. We need food and medicos. Go." Chester does not argue or delay. He drives off in a cloud of dust.

"We will bring doctors and food," Rainy says, raising her voice and speaking Yiddish. Not all the men speak Yiddish, not all are Jews. Some are Poles, Russians, Hungarians, Belgians, French . . . The Jews translate for some of the others.

"Germans?" Rainy asks.

One of the men, marginally less starved than some, says in accented English, "All gone. They are run away. Will you look?"

"Look?"

He raises a hand and points. The mere effort of raising his hand seems to exhaust him. But he wobbles on, leading them as more walking skeletons come wandering to join them.

The camp is wooden huts in a row. Rainy now walks in front with their guide as Rio and Jenou refuse to look at each other and find their trigger fingers tightening.

They are shown the first hut. The reek inside is overpowering. Men lie naked or nearly naked on crude wooden shelves. Some are dead. Some are alive. Some who are alive will soon be dead.

Rainy speaks to them. *We are Americans. We will not let the Nazis come back. We will feed you. We will care for you.*

We are Americans.

We will not hurt you.

We are Americans.

"And I am a Jew," Rainy says.

They reach out for her, bony fingers at the end of fleshless arms, they reach out to touch her, needing to believe that she is real.

Their fingers are parchment. Their touch infinitely gentle.

The dead are everywhere. Stacks of dead bodies by the side of the path, lines of dead laid out, all emaciated, all in the final stages of starvation and disease. All with bullet holes in the backs of their heads, or in their chests, or in their faces. Some have not been shot but bludgeoned, beaten to death with sticks or rifle butts until jaws crumpled and skulls collapsed like dropped eggs.

"Come and see," their guide whispers, and they follow him, with dread poisoning their muscles, dragging at them, warning them no, no, no more.

Don't look.

Don't see.

They come to a shed not much bigger than the outbuilding behind Rio's barn back in Gedwell Falls. The door is open.

No, don't look, a voice in Rio's mind begs.

Don't look!

Don't see!

But one by one, Rainy first, then Rio, then Jenou, they look inside. The dead are crammed in, stacks of them, tumbled piles of men with sunken eyes. All are naked and have had lime scattered over them. For the smell. It does not work. The smell is indescribable, and each of the women knows that this smell will never leave them. A million showers will not rid them of this smell.

Their guide leads on, shuffling on bare feet, and they follow, a new smell coming to them now, the smell of cooked meat.

The guide stops and inclines his head slightly. He does not need to point. They cannot help but see.

A wide trench has been scraped from the soil. Segments of steel train tracks have been laid out in a crude grid over charred wood. A barbecue pit.

Bodies, half-burned, lie stacked atop the grill. Heat still comes from it. Accusing faces stare up at them.

"What is this place?" Jenou asks, her voice strained, stretched to breaking. Her eyes swim with tears, and only upon seeing her friend does Rio realize that tears are falling freely down her own cheeks as well.

"One of the outer camps of a larger camp complex, called Buchenwald," Rainy says. "It's a slave labor camp where Jews are worked and tortured and starved to death. There are more. Many more, all across Germany and we think in Nazi-occupied Poland as well."

"But . . ." Jenou looked pleadingly at Rainy. "It doesn't even make sense. It's insane. It's madness!"

"No," Rainy says quietly. "It's evil."

32

"Walter! I mean, Sergeant Green!"

"Miss Frangie?" Walter Green grins hugely. It almost seems for a moment that he will run to her and give her a hug. Almost. They are both part of a column moving through southern Germany, but because it's a column of more than one unit and quite long, neither knew the other was in it.

The column is stalled—as it often is—by things sinister like mines or snipers, or by more mundane obstacles, often cattle or sheep, or mechanical breakdown. And often by refugees whose children beg food and cigarettes from the GIs, who with few exceptions give all they have.

When the column stops soldiers pile off their trucks and tanks and pee in the woods or ditches, hurriedly brew up coffee, or try to write letters. You can write a letter while perched on the back of a Sherman, but as Frangie has learned, the results will not be legible. Exhibit A: the ripped, pierced, scribbled-upon piece of paper in her hand.

She shoves the mangled letter into her pocket and straightens her uniform. She resists the mad urge to smell her armpits to see whether she is merely offensive or extremely offensive, then reminds herself that she had a shower just three days ago, and she has a moderately fresh uniform without major parasitic infestation, so . . . So, she probably looks about as good as a tiny black woman wearing a green uniform and a helmet is capable of looking.

Walter for his part looks quite . . . and Frangie stops herself right there, because it is in no way proper for a good Christian woman to be thinking the thought that slips into her head upon seeing him. Especially since her reaction had been rather less thought and rather more physical. In fact, her specific first thought was that she'd like to kiss him, to kiss him from the sheer joy of seeing him alive and well.

And also, would he take his glasses off if he kissed her?

What if she took them off *for* him?

Well, that would be wrong. That would be forward to the point of . . . of . . . well, not being the sort of thing a decent woman would do.

He stands before her, grinning, and she grins back. They each perform a surreptitious glance around to see who is watching— no one—before he takes her hand and squeezes it.

And she squeezes back.

And then they each let go, but very slowly, with fingertips trailing fingertips.

"I didn't know you were in this column," Frangie says.

"No. Me neither. About you, I mean. Do you even have a unit or do you just sort of wander around Germany healing the sick?"

She laughs. "I have a unit and a captain and everything. Now, if you were to ask me what we are *doing* here, that I couldn't say."

They hear the sounds of engines firing up again. The column will be moving shortly.

"You have a jeep?" Walter asks.

"Nope, I am hitching a ride with Sergeant Moore." She cranks a thumb toward the nearest Sherman, and Moore, who sits astride his big cannon smoking.

"I have a jeep," Walter says. "And we're going the same direction . . ."

"Is this a date?" Frangie asks, then gasps in horror at her own forwardness.

Walter, however, seems charmed. "Miss Frangie Marr, would you do me the honor of accompanying me on a ride in the German countryside? We can take a picnic."

"C rations and canteen water?"

"Nothing but the best for you," Walter says.

They walk forward up the line of vehicles and find the jeep. Walter yells for his corporal who comes running from the woods, pulling his trousers up as he runs.

"I'm afraid Corporal Penn has the trots," Walter says. "We may have to make frequent stops."

Frangie climbs into the back seat as the driver slides behind the wheel. Walter seems momentarily frozen—he would ordinarily ride shotgun. But then it will be much harder to talk with Frangie. On the other hand, sitting with her in the back will be obvious. His people will look and will know that their sergeant has a personal interest in the medic. They may even decide that Sergeant Walter "Professor" Green—known affectionately by his troops as "Shucks" for his most extreme curse word, and in less affectionate moments as "Sergeant YMCA" for his insistence on physical fitness—is actually human.

"We're not even in the same unit," Walter mutters before climbing into the back. It's hard to read much emotion from the back of a person's head, but Frangie is pretty sure that Corporal Penn is simultaneously amazed and appalled.

They set off down a road that was probably very nice before being torn up by the tanks of two armies, but is still smoother than the forest tracks Frangie has been accustomed to.

They chat in voices meant not to be overheard by Corporal Penn, who will dutifully report every last word to the rest of Green's platoon.

Walter lives in a town called Davenport.

"Like a sofa?"

"Well . . . yes." He frowns. "It's a nice little city, actually, right on the river."

"The river?"

"The Mississippi." He smiles wistfully. "Yes, I think after this war Davenport will really take off. It's right across the river from Rock Island and they have a college over there. Lutherans. I don't suppose you're . . ." He trails off.

"No," she says, "I'm not Lutheran."

"But they take everyone. They don't just . . . and there's a seminary, but mostly it's a college. Where anyone. Could. Um. Get a." Walter is having a hard time finishing his thought, because he's only just realized that he is essentially talking as if Frangie might be living in Davenport, Iowa. "So, um . . . Anyway, I hear it's a good school. For. College."

"Is that where you went to college, Walter?"

"No, I went to Iowa State, over in Ames."

He's staring fixedly ahead, and Frangie is both enjoying his embarrassment and feeling a giddy, stomach-churning, blood-pumping sort of . . . what? Anticipation?

"You think I should go to college?"

He turns to her, brow furrowed. "Well, you have to if you want to go on to medical school."

"And you think I should . . ."

"Well, you said you . . ."

"Not all men think women should do things like that."

"Who wouldn't want to be married to a doctor?" At which point Sergeant Walter Green emits a sound a bit like a startled goat. His eyes widen behind his spectacles. "I . . . I didn't . . . Just that . . ." He takes off his glasses and runs his hand over his face then back over his head. It's quite chilly, springtime chilly, but beads of sweat appear on his forehead.

He has asked nothing. And his current state of mental collapse leaves Frangie wondering if he might have a stroke if he ever does get around to asking.

But she is not one to talk because her own brain feels like a milkshake machine on the highest setting. And she is acutely aware that the back of Corporal Penn's head is straining every nerve to anticipate her reaction. Her reaction is what set off the milkshake machine, because her immediate, instinctive reaction had come in the form of a single unspoken word.

Yes.

She must choose her next words carefully. "Davenport,

Iowa sounds very nice. Perhaps I will get a chance to see it someday."

The back of Corporal Penn's head likes that. And Walter Green appears to have suffered the stroke she'd worried about.

The column passes an intersection where they come across a smaller detachment of troops, a deuce-and-a-half, an ambulance, and a jeep. The smaller detachment waits, soldiers standing around, smoking. A woman captain stands a little apart.

"I know her!" Frangie says. "Can you pull over?"

Captain Rainy Schulterman does not smile as Frangie climbs out of the jeep, and for a moment Frangie wonders if she is committing some grave act of military discourtesy. She salutes and Rainy returns the gesture automatically.

"Good," Rainy says. "We could use another medic."

"Captain?"

"You're coming with me," Rainy says. "Grab your gear. Sergeant Green? Would you pass word to Sergeant Marr's CO that I am authorized to take whatever resources I need on direct orders from General Patton, and I am taking Marr."

Rainy's eyes are inhuman, cold, and her voice is impersonal. She strikes Frangie as a person straining to control herself.

"What's going on? Where are we going, Captain Schulterman?"

"I don't know yet. We're on our way to a camp. We found one a couple weeks ago, and Generals Patton and Bradley and Ike himself toured it. Now I've been assigned full time to the job of locating them."

All of it said as if Rainy is an automaton. She seems to be vibrating with repressed energy. Her face is carefully blank, but when Frangie looks down she sees that Rainy's right hand is clenched in a fist.

She says goodbye to Walter with a handshake that goes on longer than such things usually do, and climbs into Rainy's jeep, sitting behind her.

They drive off.

After less than a mile they come to a train.

The train is stopped on the tracks. It is a long line of run-down railroad cars, some enclosed, some with only sides and no roof.

They are not the first Americans on the scene. GIs, some white, some colored, stand staring, or walk away with ashen faces. Frangie sees more than one GI crying.

A terrible smell is carried on the breeze.

The jeep stops and Rainy and Frangie climb out. They walk toward the train, toward the smell, past GIs with faces twisted into masks of grief and horror.

And rage.

Some of the doors have been opened and inside the cars Frangie sees what at first she takes for dead livestock. But no, there are rags.

And that is a human foot sticking out.

And a hand.

A shaved head.

A leg so starved that she can name each of the bones visible through papery skin.

"Those are people," Frangie says. "Oh my God, Rainy, those are people!"

Frangie breaks into a run, toward the nearest car. Its door is wide open. The dead are stacked inside. Stacked so that some fell out when the door opened. Starved, sick, tortured bodies and . . .

Oh, Jesus, some are alive!

She sees feeble movement here and there, a pitiful few still living, men and women buried beneath the dead, human beings trying to crawl like worms out of a pile of corpses.

Frangie stares in horror and sees a skull open its eyes. She goes to her, holds out a trembling hand, not knowing what to do . . . there's nothing in her training to explain what she should do when she finds a teenage girl buried beneath a pile of dead.

The living skull tries to speak, but cannot, so she simply looks with imploring eyes at Frangie. Frangie takes out her canteen and trickles water into the girl's mouth. Another medic, a white man, appears beside her. She sees the caduceus on his uniform, a doctor.

"Just a little," he says. "Too much and it kills them."

His words are cool and calm and dispassionate. His face is not. Tears run down his cheeks.

He helps Frangie to move the bodies, the pathetically light bodies, the beaten, starved and finally shot, bodies. They lift the girl down with infinite care and lay her on Frangie's jacket on the ground.

"What is . . . why are they . . .?"

Rainy, standing over them, says, "It's happening all over Germany and Poland. The SS know we're coming. They try to hide it. They move the people out of the camps and send them to camps further from the line. Covering up. Hiding their handiwork."

There is an eerie singsong in Rainy's voice, an unworldly sound.

Frangie looks up at her. "But why? Who are these people?"

Rainy looks back at her from a million miles away. "Jews."

Rainy leaves Frangie to care for the few who still live. They would almost certainly die within days. Tuberculosis and starvation and beatings and unending terror are not easily cured with fresh water and C rations.

Ahead, down the length of the train, Rainy sees a commotion. A group of GIs has found some Germans.

The GIs, all enlisted, turn hard, solemn faces to Rainy. One, a staff sergeant, says, "Nazi bastards want to surrender."

They have four Germans, three enlisted men, one an officer, though he has evidently torn his insignia of rank as well as the twin lightning flashes of the SS from his uniform.

"Get them into the woods," Rainy says.

The sergeant nods. "You heard the captain."

The GIs march the prisoners into the woods, being none-too-gentle as they encourage speed with kicks and blows from the butts of their M1s.

"This will do," Rainy says. "Line them up. I'm going to question them."

The four Germans are shoved into a line. Some are terrified, others belligerent. They are all men, and all SS. Rainy passes around cigarettes for them. She speaks to them in German.

"I have some questions," she says.

"We do not answer—" a belligerent, pig-eyed sergeant says.

BANG!

The Walther in Rainy's hand bucks. The bullet goes through the man's left eye and he drops.

She goes to the next man who has stained his trousers. "Where are you based?"

"*Konzentrationslager, Dachau*," he says. Concentration Camp Dachau.

"Where you murder people."

"I . . . I . . . I follow orders, I am nobody, I am just a soldier."

"No," Rainy says in her dangerous singsong, "I know soldiers. You are no soldier."

"A soldier follows orders!" This outburst from the officer, who judging by age and arrogance Rainy guesses is at least the equivalent of a major.

"Orders to murder innocent men and women and children."

"But they are only Jews!" the officer protests.

One of the enlisted men bolts, running through the woods. The GI sergeant looks quizzically at Rainy who says, "Prisoners attempting to escape . . ."

The sergeant grins, takes the M1 from one of his men, aims carefully, and fires a bullet into the German's back. He falls.

"Only Jews," Rainy repeats.

"Yes, of course, only Jews. And some Poles and homosexuals and other antisocial elements, but mostly Jews."

Rainy forms a ghastly smile. She steps very close to the officer. "Any of you boys have a smoke grenade?"

There is an intake of breath as the GIs realize what she's asking. A smoke grenade is handed to her.

"Only Jews," she says. "Only Jews." She unbuttons the fly on his trousers. She stuffs the smoke grenade in, without pulling the pin, and then carefully rebuttons his trousers.

All the while the officer protests and demands and squirms against the rope holding his hands tied behind his back.

Rainy steps back.

She pulls something from her coat. It's an envelope that has been reopened and folded closed. She shakes out something delicate and holds up a gold chain with a tiny Star of David dangling.

"My mother sent it to me for my birthday."

The SS officer sees the Star of David. His eyes go wide. Now the SS officer realizes what she is doing. And now he is no longer arrogant or demanding. He pleads, he talks about his family, he says, "Fug Hitler, it's all over, the war is lost, we must unite against the Russian hordes of Asian mongrel peoples who will—"

Rainy fires once.

The bullet hits the grenade before spraying lead shrapnel through his groin. He falls to his knees roaring in pain, but the bullet wound will not kill him, and he knows it.

The Willy Pete, the white phosphorous, ignites.

He screams as the fire grows in his crotch and his upper thighs and smoke pours from him as his uniform burns and he writhes and bucks and screams and screams.

The remaining prisoner collapses, hands folded in prayer, begging. One of the remaining GIs says, "Malmédy, motherfugger," and shoots him in the face.

It takes a while for the SS officer to lose consciousness as the white phosphorous burns him like so much kindling.

Rainy puts the necklace in her pocket. She takes out a cigarette and barely manages to put it to her lips. Her fingers will not manage the Zippo. So she takes the cigarette, leans down, and lights it on the human fire at her feet.

"Any of you boys have a problem with any of this?" Rainy asks.

Four helmeted heads shake as one.

The sergeant says, "Nothing happened here, Captain. Not a single goddamned thing."

PART SIX
VICTORY

"Remember that all through history, there have been tyrants and murderers, and for a time, they seem invincible. But in the end, they always fall."

—*Gandhi*

LETTERS SENT

Dear Mr. and Mrs. Marr,

I am sorry to be writing you out of the blue like this. I am Master Sergeant Walter Green, US Army. I have had occasion to meet and I believe become friends with your daughter Sergeant Frangie Marr.

I am writing to ask your permission to court Frangie.

Of course this would only happen when the war is over. But I hope once that happy day comes to spend some time with Frangie. My intentions are only of the most honorable nature.

I am a little older than your daughter, being twenty-six on my last birthday. I have a degree in engineering from Iowa State University. My family—mother, father, and seven brothers and sisters, all younger—lives in Iowa, which is not so very far away from Tulsa. I am a healthy, God-fearing man. I do not smoke or drink or gamble. I believe I will easily find employment as I have numerous contacts with local businesses who assure me they could use a man with my qualifications.

I would do all in my power to make your daughter happy, and to be completely honest, I cannot imagine being happy myself unless it is with Frangie.

But I will not proceed in pressing my case unless I can do so with your blessing.

Sincerely,
Walter Green

Dear Miss Castain:

It is with regret that I must inform you that we cannot publish your short story, "On the Line with the Soldier Girls." It simply does not meet our editorial needs at this time.

However, I believe you have talent and you may yet become a published author. I urge you to continue writing.

Sincerely,

Wilmer Cutler

Associate Editor, The New Yorker magazine

My Dear Daughter,

My sweetest of hearts, I am so terribly sorry to tell you that Daddy has passed away. It was his kidneys, although the doctors say if it wasn't that it would have been his lungs.

We will bury him tomorrow.

I don't have words for this, Frangie. My heart is filled with grief. He could be difficult at times, but I loved your father with all my heart and soul and I am destroyed.

I don't know how to make this easier for you. I thought maybe I wouldn't tell you because I know you have so very much to cope with already. But in the end I thought you must be told. I wish there was another way.

I will write to Harder as well. I suppose he will be relieved.

Come home safely to me, Frangie. Obal and I need you.

Your loving mother

33

RIO RICHLIN—BAVARIA, GERMANY

The village is called . . . well, the fact is Rio has forgotten what the village is called. It is yet another village in Germany, much like the last half dozen villages—neat, orderly, prosperous, and full of resentful, frightened German civilians.

Rio and her platoon—now nearly at full strength—is to enter the village, secure the roads, power stations, railroad sidings, bridges, etc. and make sure the village is safe for the military police and the occupying authorities.

The village is in marshy territory watered by a sluggish river. Cows and sheep can be seen in wonderfully green fields where they are guarded against refugees by civilians with knobby sticks and pitchforks. Most of the DPs are former slave laborers trying to walk home from Germany, to find a way back to France, Belgium, Ukraine, Poland, Netherlands and many more nations. Others are concentration camp survivors. Some are people in search of family. Some simply need to get away from the sporadic fighting that continues on the Western Front. And, increasingly, the DPs are Germans fleeing from the Soviets and carrying with them dark tales of mass rape and summary executions at the hands of the Red Army.

But whoever they are, wherever they are from, and wherever

they are going, the DPs are like swarms of locusts, desperately needing food and water. The occupation authority does what it can, but with a rail system ripped by Allied air attacks, with cities in flame, and with Nazi dead-enders still fighting in pockets of resistance, there is little anyone can do.

As they approach, with Martha Swann walking point for Geer's squad, they are blocked by a stand-off between a farmer and his teenage son, both armed with farm implements, and two hundred or so ragged, desperate DPs. The farmer is swinging a hoe back and forth, standing literally between the DPs and four pigs in a pen.

Rio pushes through the DPs. "Anyone here speak English?"

Of course the answer is no, but some of the DPs have a few words, and Mazur is able to identify the language they are speaking as Polish, which makes these DPs long-time slaves of the Nazis.

Rio levels her Thompson at the German farmer. "You or the pigs?" she asks. "I shoot you. Bang bang. Or I shoot the pigs. Bang bang." She emphasizes her point with hand gestures and in the end fires a quick burst into three of the pigs. She points at the last pig and gestures for the farmer to get himself and his surviving pig into the barn.

The DPs fall on the dead animals and the butchery begins, which effectively gets the crowd out of the way so the platoon can march through.

Geer's squad, formerly Rio's, which now consists of Jack Stafford, Jenou Castain, Beebee, Milkmaid Molina, Martha Swann, Rudy J. Chester, and a handful of greenhorns who probably have names, but whose names are not yet important to anyone but themselves, leads the way into the village.

It is a particularly picturesque village, bordering on becoming a town, with a central square ringed by sagging, half-timbered buildings that must be centuries old. There is a church, but it's nothing special in the jaded estimation of GIs who'd by now seen a dozen major cathedrals.

Rio soon sees the signs of looting. Doors have been kicked in, windows smashed, and everything from personal items of clothing, to random bits of furniture, to store mannequins have been strewn in the main street.

"Dammit!" Beebee cries. "The place has been gone over!"

There is a fine line between occupation and looting, and the Americans have long since crossed that line. GIs have abandoned any sense of limitations when it comes to stealing. And Rio, like most noncoms and indeed officers, has prudently chosen to draw the line not at theft but at the harming of civilians.

In brief the rule is: take what you want, leave the civilians alone. Unless there is the slightest resistance, in which case: shoot the Hitler-loving bastards.

But lately the villages and towns the Americans reach have been looted by retreating Wehrmacht and especially SS. They pass a civilian, face black with blood, hanging from a lamppost. A sign around his neck says, *Verräter*. Traitor. It is not Rio's first lynched German: the pathological murderers of the *Sicherheitsdienst* and the Gestapo, both now in flight toward the Alps, are punishing Germans for any sign of disloyalty, even as they flee in hopes of saving their own lives.

A second civilian lies swinging gently against the second story of a four-story building. The placement of the rope indicates that she was pushed out of an upper story window and had her neck snapped before her feet could reach the ground. She has no sign.

"Geer, hold up!" Rio calls out and trots ahead to join him. "Where the hell is the *Bürgermeister*?"

A *Bürgermeister* is a mayor and the usual routine had been for a nervous, fidgety old man with a sash of office or some such thing to come forward behind a white flag to greet the occupiers.

Geer nods. "Yeah. Quiet. Not the good kind of quiet."

Rio nods at the town hall, a rococo structure of white plaster and green-painted cornices. "There. The church. And . . ." She looks around.

"That hotel over there," Geer says. "Anyway, that's where I'd put snipers. We can call up a tank and blow shit out of 'em, see who comes running out."

Rio sighs. "Captain was very clear: minimal necessary damage. I'll get Mangan's squad to check the church, and Big Pete can do the town hall. You check out the hotel."

"Yep. Stafford! Castain! Beebee! See if you can get around the back of the hotel."

The three set off at a loping run, down a back alley they hope will get them there.

Geer sighs. "For what it's worth," the newly-minted sergeant says, "the army can take its stripes and stick 'em where the sun don't—"

Bam!

A single, small explosion.

"Cover!" Rio yells, and everyone finds a doorway, a shattered storefront or a tight alleyway to hide in. The new kids cower nervously behind cover. The veterans light cigarettes or take the opportunity for a pee.

"Come on, Geer," Rio says. The two of them check their weapons automatically and by mutual consent take the street just to the right of the one Jack and Jenou had taken. They run crouching, boots on cobbles, breathing hard.

Crack!

A single rifle shot and the wall next to Geer emits a puff of dust where the bullet whizzed by.

"See him?"

"No," Rio admits. "But we'll have defilade if we go through this house." She kicks the wooden door, which is sturdy and locked. "Open or you get a grenade!"

Maybe the occupants speak English, or maybe they merely understood the tone, but the door opens and Rio and Geer push through.

"*Raus!* Everybody *raus!*" Rio finds the back wall of the house and guesses it shares a wall with the house behind. She fires a quick warning burst into the wall, enough hopefully to convince any civilians on the other side to run. They blow the wall with a rifle grenade and push through a dust cloud and debris into a bedroom. Then through to the street beyond.

Rio eases the window shade up, unhinges and pushes out the shutter. The view opens onto a street, and, to the right, a widening space, not quite a square, but a wedge of space between two streets.

And lying in the street, face down, is Jack Stafford.

"Jack!" Rio cries.

"No!" Jack yells. "Stay back!"

He is on his back, clutching his stomach. The side of his uniform is red.

Rio bolts for the door but Geer tackles her and swings her back out of sight.

"What the fug are you doing, Richlin? You know he's bait!"

But Rio is not rational, not even thinking, just feeling her heart tearing in two. She struggles but Geer is stronger and he keeps his arms wrapped around her. She reaches her *koummya* and draws it, the blade suddenly at Geer's throat.

"Richlin. It's me. It's me!"

The wild panic in Rio's eyes fades. She draws a sobbing breath and drops the *koummya* to the floor.

Geer releases her, bends down to retrieve the knife and carefully slides it back into its scabbard.

"Jack! Hang on!"

"No, Rio, no!" Jack yells in a voice strained by pain and fear.

She glances across the street and sees Jenou and Molina in a doorway. They look pale and frightened.

"I can get him," Rio says to Geer. "Give me covering fire, I'll grab him and—"

"Goddammit, Richlin, no! No! You know better. That sniper is sitting up there waiting for one of us to show our heads. You'd be dead before you got halfway to him!"

Crack!

Jack's leg jerks from the impact and he bellows in pain.

"You know the routine," Geer says intently. "He's gonna keep Jack screaming until we break and go for him."

Rio manages a tight nod.

Jenou yells, "What do we do, Rio?"

"Stay put!" Rio cries.

What do we do, Rio?

"I'm going to bazooka this Nazi son of a bitch!" Rio says. Then, "Castain, stay put! Molina, go back, tell them to send up the bazooka team."

No answer. She looks outside again and both Jenou and Molina are gone.

"Shit!" Geer says. "They're going to try and encircle him."

"We need to put some covering fire on the bastard," Rio says, and leans out of the window just long enough to fire a burst from her Thompson at what she suspects is the right building.

Crack!

The sniper hits the place where Rio had been half a second earlier.

Rio jerks her thumb upward and she and Geer go pounding up the stairs to find an elderly couple cowering in their bed, covers pulled up as some kind of symbolic protection.

Rio goes to the bedroom window and carefully cracks the shutter. She peers through the narrow gap and this time she is almost certain that she sees movement in a window on the hotel's third and top floor.

"Give me your M1," she says.

"Screw you, Richlin, I have it." He crouches, takes careful aim, and fires once. The sniper is momentarily visible, recoiling. "Yeah, that's him. Top floor, far left."

Rio peeks and can just barely see Jack lying on the cobbles. His belly is blood from side to side. His left leg bleeds too.

And she has nothing. No plan. No sudden rush of courage. Jack is bait in a trap. Anyone trying to help him will be shot. She feels a strange disconnection, as if her brain simply does not want to face the facts. But at the same time another part of her brain is spinning madly, going around and around in circles, trying everything, knowing it's useless, but powerless to stop herself.

Suddenly she's on her rear end. Her legs have simply collapsed. She sits with her Thompson on her lap, gazing down at it through a blur.

Geer squats beside her. "It's okay, Rio. Just stay put. I'll take care of it."

"I'm . . . something is . . . Jesus, Luther, I . . ." She tries to stand but her legs, the legs that carried her through Sicily and Italy, France and Belgium and Germany, don't have any strength left in them. She is dimly aware of tears running down her cheeks. "I . . . I don't know . . ."

Jack!

Geer takes her shoulder and pushes her back until she is looking at him. "Richlin . . . Rio . . . You're not fighting this war alone."

Suddenly there comes the sound of a grenade, instantly followed by rapid M1 carbine fire. It lasts only a few seconds.

Then the voice of Jenou Castain cries, "All clear!"

Now Rio's legs work again and she bolts from the room, practically tumbles down the steps and bursts out of the door and onto the street. She runs for Jack who already has a medic hunched over him.

"Jack!"

"Hey there, Rio," he says, managing what might be a smile, quickly wiped away by a grimace of pain. He's white, so white he might be made of snow.

"Morphine will hit in a second," the medic says. "Don't sweat it, Stafford, you just got a second navel is all."

"Jack, are you all right? Don't die on me!"

She is back on the beach in Tunisia, trying to keep the blood inside Kerwin Cassel.

She is in that terrible street in Italy, looking down at the body of Tilo Suarez.

She is watching Camacho suddenly stop running.

She is hearing those terrible words announcing the death of Dain Sticklin: *Sergeant Richlin! You're in charge.*

How many? It is her job to keep them alive, and yet . . .

Jack's smile now is hazy and his eyes are veiled as the morphine courses through his veins. "Hey . . . tears?"

Rio brushes them away. "I got some dust in my eye."

He winks in slow motion. "Uh-huh."

Stretcher bearers are coming and Rio makes eye contact with the medic who, out of Jack's sight, makes a back-and-forth hand gesture meant to convey that it could go either way.

BAM!

A muted explosion from inside the hotel.

Rio lays a hand on Jack's cheek. "I have to . . ."

"Mmm," he says and drifts off to sleep.

Rio swallows hard and starts toward the hotel, following half a dozen of her people, all rushing pell-mell.

Jenou is behind the hotel's polished wood front desk. An explosion has occurred. Molina is wincing and holding her arm, cursing freely as blood seeps between her fingers.

Jenou is on the floor.

For a time Rio ceases to exist. Her lean, strong, scarred body still breathes, but her thoughts have stopped. She does not know where she is. Does not wonder. Does nothing. But breathe.

She has no control over her body, but slumps on cobblestones, arms limp, palms upturned.

Geer wraps a blanket over her shoulders, but her gaze never flickers to awareness. Beebee brings her a canteen cup of hot tea and presses it to her lips. She is a person in a coma. Gone. No longer there.

Only slowly, gradually, does the girl from Gedwell Falls return to her body.

Only slowly, gradually, does she remember where she is.

And why.

But after a time that seems forever to her, but is only hours to the world around her, Sergeant Rio Richlin stands up.

INTERSTITIAL
107TH EVAC HOSPITAL, WÜRZBURG, GERMANY—APRIL 1945

Oh my goodness, did Jenou Castain die? Did our reluctant warrior with the perfect figure and the gorgeous blonde hair die?

No, Gentle Reader, I did not die.

But given my stupidity, I probably deserved to. I can only say I was somewhat keyed-up, having just managed to kill the sniper, and in my exuberance I did the stupid thing. Like an idiot greenhorn I reached for a souvenir in that hotel-the brass bell they used to summon bellboys-and I even had a split second to see the wire before the booby trap went off.

Thank God Kraut grenades are lousy. A decent American grenade would have killed me for sure.

Anyway, that ended my war with a bang. They got the medics and the stretcher bearers to me pretty quick. I never did lose consciousness, not then at least, and I seem to recall doing some impressive caterwauling and cursing and flailing around like a great baby.

Rio lost her mind for a while, poor kid, thinking she'd gotten me and Jack both killed. Way, way back when we began this journey I told you, Gentle Reader, that sooner

or later, man or woman, veteran or greenhorn, we all cry.
Well, I was starting to think Rio was the exception, that
she had no breaking point. It was almost reassuring
to see that she did. Tough, scary, knife-toting, Kraut-
killing Rio Richlin: human.

And after a while Rio was beside me.

She caught up to us on the way to the field hospital.
Me on one side of the ambulance, Jack on the other side,
blessedly unconscious. Both of us with swaying bags of
plasma suspended over our heads. Rio in between, getting
in the way of the docs.

Of course she blamed herself. Rio does that. If she
were writing this tale instead of me it would be titled,
"Things I Screwed Up," by Rio Richlin.

Anyway, I took shrapnel of both the metal and the
wooden variety. I lost most of one breast. I'll have a
nice scar on one side of my face. Maybe I'll lose the limp
over time. And I'll get a Purple Heart. Yippee.

A few days after I blew myself up, Hitler shot himself
in the head in Berlin, the smoking, ruined capital of
the Third Reich.

The Thousand Year Reich, old Adolf called it. Well,
Adolf: not quite a thousand years. More like twelve.

Burn in hell, Adolf. Burn forever in hell.

VE Day-Victory in Europe-came, and I guess, Gentle
Reader, you might think we all had a big party. I suppose
some GIs did celebrate, but no one I knew did. Here at the
hospital we pulled out our smuggled booze and drank

quiet toasts. But they were not toasts to victory. We drank to our friends and comrades-in-arms, the men and women who would never go home. And by the end of that we were pretty damned drunk.

And that's my war, Gentle Reader. My war and Rio's and Frangie's and Rainy's and all the others who I've written about here in these feverish scrawlings.

It only remains to go home. I only wish I had one.

I don't exactly know what I'll do with all these typed pages. Maybe I'll see if someone wants to publish them. And maybe I'll tell more of the story, because the damned thing about wars is they don't just end with a snap of the fingers, or even a bullet in the head.

This war has killed ... who even knows? Millions. Isn't that enough? Do we need to know just how many millions? Millions dead. Millions wounded. Millions without homes, sick and starved and cold and alone, being eaten from within by grief and guilt and fear.

I somehow thought if I wrote it all down it would be out of my head and on paper. I felt maybe I could capture it all, make it into something I could hold and move and stick in a box like Sergeant Cole used to tell us. But that's not going to be how it works. My body will carry scars. And my mind will carry memories burned deeper than scars.

But after what Rainy told me about Oradour, and after Malmédy, and especially after what I saw at Buchenwald and what Frangie told me about Dachau, I know I won't feel guilty about killing Krauts. If ever anyone needed to be killed, it's those Nazi bastards.

I hear stories here in the hospital, from GIs who've been in places I have not. They talk in hushed tones of German cities turned into little more than stone quarries, with desperate Germans—old men and children—sifting through the wreckage. German women selling their bodies for a candy bar. German mothers selling their daughters for a loaf of bread.

How many of those women were at Nazi rallies screaming their lungs out, yelling, "Heil Hitler?" How many husbands and fathers cheered as the mad bastard in Berlin ranted about Jews and Slavs and homosexuals and Gypsies and all his other scapegoats?

If you don't want your cities burned down around your ears and your daughters whoring for GIs, don't start wars.

Already I see articles in the Stars and Stripes and in magazines about the possibility of war starting between us and the Soviets. I guess all good things come in threes, right? World War I, World War II, hey, we can't stop there, can we?

Well, not me. This soldier girl has had all the . . .

Sorry for the interruption, Gentle Reader, but Rio just showed up here with orders for me not to go back with the other evacuees from the hospital, but to travel back with the 119th! I've got to be ready in twenty minutes, so I am going to quickly wrap this up and pack my bag.

I am going back with Rio and Geer and Beebee and the other slobs I've spent almost three years with. Not Jack, though, Jack–or "Gimpy Jack" as we now call him just to irritate him–is already on his his home, back in Britain.

I'll miss that man. Rio will miss him more, but despite my prodding she never did get to the point of telling Jack she's crazy for him. She's his sergeant, and from Rio's point of view, that's the end of the story. Stubborn girl.

But like I said, I'll miss him too. Him and Cat Preeling, who is already back in the States having been discharged with the classic million dollar wound. And Geer and Beebee and Milkmaid and Sweetheart and Sergeant Cole and Mackie. And the ones who didn't make it. I'll miss them all, even the ones I hated half the time. Personal dislikes don't mean much stacked against the fact that the fellow you think you can't put up with is standing right next to you in a freezing wet hole waiting for the next 88. If you wore the uniform, you are my brother or sister. And that is forever.

Hey! I just looked at my orders. They seem to have originated with a certain Captain Elisheva Schulterman, approved by some brigadier general no less, named Herkemeier.

Well, Rainy's another one I will have to find a way to keep track of. In fact – all right, all right, Rio is nagging me.

I was going to say that in fact, while the war may be over, it won't quite be over for us. And I guess that means this story isn't over. Maybe down the road . . .

But hell, Gentle Reader, for now at least I must end this. Rio will be threatening me with that damned knife of hers if I don't get moving.

So here are my final words of wisdom. This has been the greatest thing I have ever done or will ever do. I suppose society will try hard to put all us uppity soldier girls back in a box with a nice pink bow on it. And I don't know what happens next. I don't know what the world is going to think of me. I don't know what I'm going to do. And that really should scare me.

But Gentle Reader, we soldier girls have been to Kasserine, to Sicily, to Salerno, to the river and Monte Cassino. We've been to Omaha Beach and the bocage, to the Hürtgen and the Bulge. We've been to the camps.

Try putting us in a box. Try.

We won't scare so easy. Right now, getting ready to leave this hospital, this continent, this war, I'm not feeling afraid for the future. Hell, I am now Sergeant Jenou Castain: so of course, I fear nothing.

Except when Rio shoots me that look and starts loosening her koummya in its scabbard.

PART SEVEN
AFTER

"*The world breaks everyone, and afterward, some are strong at the broken places.*"

—Ernest Hemingway

34

"Frangie? Frangie?"

Frangie hears the voice and recognizes it immediately. It's the voice she's heard since she was a baby in her mother's womb.

Dorothy Marr looks older, wearier, worn down, but nevertheless radiant. She runs through the crowd of people getting off the bus. Frangie drops her duffel bag and throws her arms around her mother.

Obal, who has grown at least two feet so he now towers over Frangie, stands awkwardly trying to disguise the tears. Frangie frees a hand and draws him into the embrace.

It goes on for a while. It's an embrace full of pain and sadness, of things learned and regretted. But above all it is relief. Frangie is alive and Obal, their mother, and Frangie herself now drain away three years of fear and worry with a hug.

The white passengers got off first, and are greeting their own families. The colored families are on one side of the terminal, the white on the other. The bathrooms are clearly marked for white men, white women, colored men, colored women.

It's a long walk from the bus terminal to home—not for Frangie who is used to very long walks, but for her mother who seems to tire easily.

The first part of the walk is through a white neighborhood. American flags fly from porch flagpoles. Patriotic bunting can be seen here and there. Weeks have gone by since the war ended in Europe—it's just as complicated a task getting millions of soldiers home as it was getting them to Europe in the first place. Although now there is a definite lack of shooting, and the troop ship had plowed straight across the Atlantic with never an evasive maneuver to avoid mines or torpedoes.

"How have you been, Obal?" Frangie asks.

"Me? I'm fine aside from missing the whole war!"

Frangie smiles tolerantly. "You didn't miss much."

"You have to tell me everything!" he enthuses.

And Frangie thinks, *No, Obal, I don't have to. And anyway, I couldn't. What words would I use to tell you about soldiers torn and burned? How would I describe the stink of Dachau?*

"I'll tell you the important stuff, how about that?"

Obal snorts dismissively and Frangie smiles at their mother. "Not everything has to be told all at once."

They walk down the sidewalk, arm in arm, until a white man comes in the opposite direction. Then they part to make way, but the white man snorts. "I ain't walking between you Nigras! Get out of the way!"

So Frangie steps down into the gutter to let him pass.

"Do you mind very much if I make a stop on the way home?" Frangie asks her mother and Obal.

"Stop?"

"I want to see Daddy's grave."

Her mother nods and her brother looks away to conceal emotions he doesn't think are manly.

"Of course, baby."

"And then," Frangie announces, "we are going to write to Harder and tell him that this is *his* home and *his* family."

That night as she lies in her own bed with actual sheets and not even a few lice, it occurs to Frangie that she did not ask, or beg, or even suggest that Harder is now to be welcomed back: she ordered it.

She holds that thought in one hand.

In the other hand she holds the recent memory of her mother and brother and herself, stepping into the gutter.

She recalls the faces—the black faces—of men and women with bodies torn apart in defense of America. Some she lost. Some she saved. And not one of those black men and women should ever have to step into a gutter for anyone.

A different fight is coming.

"We'll win this one too," she whispers just before sleep—sleep without reveille, without artillery, without desperate cries of pain—takes her.

Rio Richlin, wearing a new uniform with her brand-new, bright, golden staff sergeant's stripes on the shoulder, pushes the wheelchair down the familiar street.

"You shoulda warned them," Jenou says.

"When? Transport opens up, you grab it," Rio says. "I just hope we don't give anyone a heart attack."

They'd made it as far as Monterey, California, before being told there was nothing available to take them north. But Rio had managed to convince a civilian truck driver who said he was going within a mile or so of Gedwell Falls and would be happy . . . honored . . . and so on.

Rio and Jenou's return to Gedwell Falls is in the back of a pickup truck, with Jenou's wheelchair wedged in by sacks of fertilizer.

"Hail the conquering heroes!" Jenou cries, following it with a sardonic grin as the truck rattles up the highway and passing motorists stare.

They spend the time remembering truck rides past. So many, many rides in the backs of deuce-and-a-halfs.

They cover the last few blocks on foot (and wheel), passing places they'd both known all their lives. Very little has changed. Even the cars are the same—Detroit is shifting back from tanks to cars, but it will take a while for new models to appear.

They walk and roll through the town square. Rio looks too long at the bandstand where Strand first asked her out. She doesn't know what has become of him and she fears running into his family or friends. What can she say? That Strand broke?

Civilians will never understand. To them a young man who flew mission after brutal, deadly mission over Italy and Germany, and broke in the end, is a coward.

But everyone breaks. Rio herself had finally broken when she saw Jack and then Jenou. Everyone, sooner or later, snaps. What matters is what happens next. Had Strand found his courage and returned to his unit?

But then they are on her block. And Rio sees her house. The gold star for her sister Rachel still hangs with sad pride in the window. A gold star for Rachel, and a blue one for Rio.

"I'll just go knock," Rio says, heart in her throat. She climbs the porch stairs, leaving Jenou on the walkway. She starts to knock, but that seems crazy: this is home. This is her home.

She opens the door and yells, "Anybody home?"

"So, Captain, what the hell are you going to do now?" Newly-minted Brigadier General Herkemeier is grinning—not something he typically does much of. And instead of his habit of obsessively straightening his trouser creases he now obsessively touches the star on his shoulder.

Rainy smiles back at him. She has not gone home, she is still in Germany, wrapping up prisoner interrogations and filing reports. VE Day has come and gone and she's been waiting on orders to take transport for the Pacific. She's fantasized about walking in unannounced on Aryeh somewhere out in the Pacific and acting like it's no big deal.

Plus, if she's in uniform she can make him salute her. She loves her big brother. She idolizes her big brother. But over the years he has at times behaved like . . . a big brother. So just a teensy, tiny bit of revenge . . .

"I assumed I'd be taking a crash course in Japanese," Rainy says.

Herkemeier sits forward suddenly. "Good God, you don't know! Where have you been all morning?"

"Sleeping after staying up half the night going over—"

"Rainy. The air corps has dropped some kind of new bomb on a Japanese city called Hiroshima. It's called an atom bomb. One bomb annihilated the entire city."

"Good lord!"

"Even the Japs can't take that kind of punishment. It's a matter of weeks, maybe even days."

"Huh." Rainy frowns and sinks back into her seat. This leaves her with no idea at all what comes next.

"Listen, Rainy," Herkemeier says, tugging at the crease in his trousers. "You know the army will be drawn down fast. I will happily move heaven and earth to keep you, but the truth is we are shifting to an army of occupation. And the word is that Army Intelligence will be cut way back."

"But we'll still need intel!"

"Oh, spies are always with us. There were spies in the Old Testament. Joshua had spies! But the whole spying business is going to be turned over to a civilian agency built on the OSS—the Office of Strategic Services. Bill Donovan's outfit."

"Wild Bill?"

"Have you ever met him?" Herkemeier asks a bit too casually.

"No," Rainy says and her radar is definitely alert.

"Well, he's really only a civilian, poor fellow, but he's likely to be running the espionage world. And . . ."

"Do not tease me, Jon."

He laughs. "He wants to meet you."

35

"I can't believe you guys came," Frangie says.

"Like we would miss this?" Jenou says.

"But the airfare and the time . . ." Frangie protests.

At age thirty-nine, Frangie Marr is still tiny. A bit rounder
than she had once been, but giving birth to three children will
do things to a woman's body. The black robe and mortarboard
hat are not exactly flattering, but they have certainly raised grins
from her old army buddies.

"Airfare," Rio snorts dismissively. "Jenou's richer than God
and I just grabbed a MAC flight."

"MAC?"

"Military Airlift Command for you civilians," Rio says. She's
also in her very late thirties, but her uniform is stiff on her rigid
body. Her chest is a whole Technicolor billboard of medals,
including the one she earned in Korea in 1953, the one with the
upside-down gold star and star-spangled blue ribbon, the Medal
of Honor, which all by itself causes full generals to fawn and eat
themselves up with envy.

Lieutenant Colonel Rio Richlin, MOH, West Point class of

1950, still manages to look too young for her rank, still has a faint dusting of freckles, and she can still laugh and even, on occasion, giggle.

"What, no *koummya*?" Frangie teases.

Rio grins. "It's hanging up over my fireplace. I'm supposed to set a good example. No unnecessary adornments."

"She doesn't need a knife to scare people anymore," Jenou says. "She has rank. She can bully anyone from major on down. Probably has lieutenants polishing her car daily."

"Oh, Jenou, you are so unfair," Rio says, winking at Frangie. "I only get my car waxed twice a week. Not daily."

"Oh, look!" Jenou points. "My God, is that Cat?"

Cat is across the room, standing and chatting with another woman, obviously a close friend.

"Is that her sister . . . roommate . . . ?" Rio squints to see better—she's been told she needs glasses. She has thus far refused.

Frangie shoots a wry look to Jenou who rolls her eyes and stage whispers, "No, Rio still doesn't know. You can take the girl out of the country . . ."

"Know what?" Rio demands.

"Rio, Cat's a lesbian," Frangie says. "You know: she likes girls."

Rio stands gaping for about two minutes. Then, "Oh. Wow." She raises an intimidating eyebrow. "And I'm the last to find out?"

"Oh, absolutely," Jenou says and Frangie nods. "You never noticed that Cat wasn't interested in guys?"

"I thought she was . . . well . . . I . . . I thought she was just, I don't know . . . shy."

"Shy. Cat *Preeling* we're talking about." Jenou nods. "Shy. Or

". . . or maybe she likes girls and you are, despite the foo-fah all over your chest . . ." she waves indicating medals and ribbons, ". . . still a Gedwell Falls girl."

"Well," Rio says tolerantly, "I won't deny that. Let's go say hi. I've missed the hell out of that soldier. I wonder what she's been up to?"

But then it's time and Frangie has to rush to her seat in the front row.

Jenou winces as she wedges her stiff leg under the seat in front of her. Rio sits the same way she does everything now: like she's made out of steel and bends only under great pressure.

"I'm sending you my new book," Jenou whispers to Rio.

"Another one?"

"Hey, property in Beverly Hills is not cheap."

"Mmm, right, not to mention the salaries of all your lithe young pool lads."

Jenou sighs. "Well, what's a twice-divorced, beat-up old soldier girl going to do for fun without pool lads to watch?"

A black woman doctor is up front now giving an inspirational speech. Both Jenou and Rio are relieved to be seated toward the back. They lower their whispers a decibel or two.

"How about you, Rio? Last I heard you weren't dating."

"No. Not since Strand and I divorced."

"Since before Korea?" Jenou shook her head. "I told you that wouldn't work, honey. He was never going to be able to live his life with you. You're . . . you know. You."

Rio turns her eyes sideways to look at her friend. "I felt like I owed him a try."

"Duty. Of course." Jenou rolls her eyes with a deliberate lack of subtlety, like some silent movie star.

Rio draws Jenou's attention downward to see the raised middle finger discreetly by her leg. Both women grin hugely as a way to avoid giggling like misbehaving children in church.

The speeches end and it is time now for the moment.

"Oh my God, I'm going to cry," Jenou says.

"Don't start that or . . . Just don't."

But there are tears in both their eyes when Francine "Frangie" Marr of Tulsa, Oklahoma walks up onto the stage to receive the piece of paper that now, finally, after time out to have children, after delays getting through college, after the grueling years of medical school, finally means that she is now . . .

"Doctor Francine Marr," the presenter says. Frangie doesn't quite skip across the stage, but she sure looks like she wants to.

Just a few rows ahead of Jenou and Rio is a gray-at-the-temples Walter Green, and Walter Jr., age fourteen, George Green, age twelve, and Alicia Green, age ten. They all stand and applaud wildly, as does an absurdly tall Obal Marr, who helps his arthritis-crippled mother to stand as well and see her daughter's impossible dream become reality. Harder stands beside his wife and his own two children.

It is not until they begin to file out of the auditorium that Rio spots the woman standing at the back.

Rainy Schulterman wears clothing just short of expensive, in the most conservative of styles, in the least noticeable of colors.

"Rainy!" Rio cries. "I haven't seen you since . . . well, *since*. What the heck are you doing with yourself? Come on, we're going to see if anyone serves beer here in Iowa. We're supposed to meet up at Walter and Frangie's house in an hour."

Rainy shakes hands with the soldier and the best-selling author. "I couldn't miss Marr graduating. I always felt a bit guilty about browbeating her into staying in after the Silver Star. Wanted to see how it all came out."

"Ah," Rio says. "Not worried about guilting *me* into it, just Marr."

Rainy smiles. "Who guilted you into West Point? And Korea?"

"What are you doing nowadays?" Jenou asks.

Rainy shrugs and sighs and makes a little smile. "I'm just a lowly bureaucrat, I'm afraid. I work for the Department of Commerce as a very junior foreign trade attaché."

Rio might still be sufficiently naive not to know that Cat is a lesbian, but she's not naive enough to buy this story. For one thing, Rio's car is not the only dull, four-door government sedan parked outside. And Rainy's driver does not look like the sort of fellow employed by the Commerce Department.

But Rainy sticks to her story with all the tenacity and subtle lies one might expect of the Deputy Director of Central Intelligence.

Even after beer DDCI Schulterman will talk only of her work as a special trade envoy to various countries she manages to avoid naming. The one personal detail Rainy will divulge is the name of her husband: Halev.

"Kids?" Rio asks, when they are seated on the screened porch of Frangie and Walter's pleasant if chaotic home.

"No," Rainy says. "You?"

Rio shakes her head. "I think Frangie has the nurturing

personality." She smiles at young Alicia who leans against the door jamb eyeing the three of them.

The girl takes the smile as an invitation—she's already at age ten as tall as Frangie—and she comes over.

"My mommy says you were in the war and were really brave."

"Does she?" Rio says. "And what does she say about herself in the war?"

"Oh, she wasn't really in the war," Alicia says waving a dismissive hand. "She just took care of people who got hurt. She was only a medic."

"Only a medic?" Rio says. "Well, you may not know it, and I guess your mom is too modest to tell you, but I have known a lot of brave soldiers. Your mother was as brave as any of them. Come here. Sit down. Let me tell you about your mother."

Later, after the party breaks up and the last goodbyes are said, Rainy Schulterman is driven to Chicago where she will catch a flight back to Washington. She has her burly driver up front, and her assistant beside her.

"I want you to get me some information on a British subject," Rainy says. "Jack . . . which may be a nickname for John . . . Stafford."

"That's a pretty common name," her assistant mutters.

"Well, cross-reference with service in the US Army. There can't be more than one Jack Stafford in both sets of data. Besides," she says, "we are the CIA, after all."

OBITUARIES

Diane Scott (neé Mackie), who was one of the first generation of women to serve in the armed forces, has died after a brief illness. Scott began as an enlisted soldier before earning a commission and serving with great distinction in World War II in Europe.

Mackie is survived by her two grown children, daughter Jennifer Ann, and her son Frank, and seven grandchildren.

Services will be held . . .

Jenou Castain has died peacefully at her home in Beverly Hills, age seventy-one. Castain was one of the original "soldier girls" and served with distinction during the Second World War, where she was awarded the Purple Heart for wounds sustained in Germany. After the war Castain became the best-selling author of seventeen novels and one memoir.

Castain is survived by four ex-husbands. She leaves her considerable fortune to her long-time friend Alberto Diaz and to the Soldier Girls' Retirement Home in Petaluma, California.

Services will be held . . .

Luther Geer, decorated World War II veteran, shoe store owner and social activist who successfully lobbied Congress for the

Manzanar Japanese-American War Memorial, has died at the age of sixty-nine. Geer earned a Bronze Star for bravery. He leaves behind his beloved wife, Ellie, and their nine children, twenty-two grandchildren and three great-grandchildren.

Elisheva "Rainy" Schulterman has died of undisclosed causes. Her age is not given. Schulterman served with distinction in the US Army in World War II. After the war she took a job with the US Commerce Department, later moving to the State Department.

Schulterman is survived by her husband, Halev Leventhal. Attempts to garner additional details about her life were answered by Mr. Leventhal with the following statement. "Rainy would roll over in her grave if I told you anything. I will only say that a great many people owe their lives and liberty to my brilliant, beautiful and so very deeply loved wife."

Services will be held . . .

Catherine "Cat" Preeling-Tomás, who was one of the original "soldier girls", has died at age seventy-six, after a long illness. Preeling-Tomás is survived by her wife, Mary, by their adoptive children Ling Ju and Carlos, and by their three grandchildren.

Preeling-Tomás worked for twenty-eight years as an English teacher at Wilberforce Middle School before retiring. She is also known for her social activism, in particular her work for peace and for gay and lesbian rights.

Services will be held . . .

Dr. Francine Marr, known to her many patients as "Doc Frangie," has died peacefully in her home at age eighty-one. Marr kept her last name but enjoyed a fifty-two-year marriage with businessman Walter Green, who passed some years ago. Marr served as a combat medic in World War II, one of the famed "soldier girls." She earned a Silver Star for bravery under fire, as well as the Purple Heart. She is survived by her three children, eight grandchildren, and three great-grandchildren.

Services will be held . . .

General Rio Richlin, US Army retired, has died at age eighty-six, after a long illness. Richlin was one of the historic "soldier girls," immortalized in a war memoir by author and close personal friend, Jenou Castain. General Richlin rose from a private to a two-star general, with distinguished service in World War II Europe and later in Korea. She earned the Silver Star and the Purple Heart in World War II, as well as the Medal of Honor, the nation's highest recognition, for actions at the Chosin Reservoir in Korea.

Richlin is survived by her husband, Jack Stafford, a retired real estate salesman and decorated veteran.

Services will be held . . .

EPILOGUE

"Sarge! We got mail."

Sergeant Elizabeth Marr-Green, often called MG, which stood for both Marr-Green and, conveniently, machine gun, tosses her iPod aside and bounds toward the door.

The sun outside is blinding. It often is. Sometimes it's bright sunshine and staggering heat, sometimes it's bright sunshine and bone-snapping cold. And other times it rains and is cold. At FOB Castor the weather is described, almost 365 days a year, as bad.

But MG's corporal, Paul Cofield, has a canvas bag of mail—actual snail-mail letters and bundles from home.

"Package for you, top," Cofield says, handing her a carefully wrapped parcel. "Letter too. Same address. Hope it's cookies."

"Like I'd give you any of my cookies, Cofield," Elizabeth says. Frowning at the return address, she carries the mail back inside her hooch and sits down on her cot. It's no one she knows, though she has the vague sense that there is something distantly familiar about the name.

She whips out her K-Bar knife and slices neatly through string and brown paper. There's a lacquered box inside, maybe eighteen, twenty inches long. She pauses, frowning even more intently, and opens the letter.

Dear Elizabeth,

I doubt very much you will remember me as we met only once, briefly, at your grandmother's funeral. But I have often thought of you since. I knew your grandmother very well. We served together in World War II. She was a very great woman, your grandmother.

Anyway, as I write this the doctors tell me I have less than a week left. I've left most everything to Jack—that's my husband— and his family. We never had children of our own, and when you're contemplating the end you want to pass something along.

In the box you will find something that served me very well when I held your rank as a sergeant. May it serve you as well.

Rio Richlin

Major General, US Army, Retired

PS: You'll want to oil the scabbard from time to time.

Ten minutes later Elizabeth emerges into the glare again.

"Whoa, Sarge, what do you have there?"

"What, this?" Elizabeth pats the knife strapped to her thigh. "Well, I just googled it and I believe it's called a *koummya*."

"Badass, top."

"Yep. Okay!" She claps her hands loudly and insistently. "Enough playtime, boys and girls, these holes aren't gonna dig themselves. I want to see some shovel work, people!"

"Fugging sergeants," Cofield says under his breath. "They're all the same."

AUTHOR'S NOTE

I confronted a surprising problem in writing this last book of the trilogy. The events from D-Day onward are much better known to people from books, movies and TV than earlier battles in North Africa and Italy. As a result some stories are tied in readers' minds directly to specific individuals, real soldiers who did terribly brave things. It felt wrong repurposing their personal stories, so I've tried to avoid that. I've also been at pains to avoid my fictional 119th Division seeming to take the place of real units, many of which suffered catastrophically. My goal has been to insert my characters without attempting to replace the real-life Americans who died at Omaha Beach, in the bocage, in the Hürtgen or in the Bulge.

That said, I've stuck as close as I know how to the actual events of World War II.

Rainy's mission is invented, but the massacre at Oradour-sur-Glane happened: 642 French civilians, of whom 205 were children, were mercilessly gunned down by the SS. And yes, the SS officer responsible, Adolf Diekmann, was killed a few days later in Normandy, though the details of *how* have never been satisfactorily determined . . .

After the war, French general Charles de Gaulle decreed that the burned and shattered village should be preserved as the SS left it. You can visit it, as I did. It is the most deeply moving war memorial I've ever seen.

The Hürtgen forest happened as well, a stupid waste of thousands of American lives. First-person accounts generally agree that nothing in the European theater of war was more terrible. Even German soldiers who'd been in the hell of the Eastern Front often agreed that the Hürtgen was worse.

Some have slighted the American soldier, alleging that they could not fight without the masses of weapons and equipment provided by the productive power of American industry. But the battles of the Hürtgen forest and the Bulge were not contests of machine against machine, but of soldier against soldier in pitiless conditions. The American soldier, outgunned, outnumbered, cut off and surrounded, held on against everything Hitler had to throw at them.

Malmédy happened as well, which set off a wave of pitiless brutality from both sides, as all the rules of war were cast aside.

The liberation of Buchenwald began at the Ohrdruf satellite camp, where SS guards did in fact build a sort of macabre grill and attempt to hide the evidence of their atrocities before fleeing. The Dachau death train also happened.

The aftermath was where I felt free at last to depart from actual history. I don't know what effect women serving in combat would have had on the politics of the United States. I know that after World War II was over, women were quickly pushed out of the jobs they had held while the men fought. The 1950s were a period of genteel but steady suppression of women, and the beginning of more women pushing back. I have to believe that feminists would have made short work of it with a nation of female war veterans marching in their ranks.

I do know that the Civil Rights Movement took inspiration from the courage and sacrifice of black soldiers. I suspect the Women's Rights Movement would have been similarly inspired.

I just used the word *sacrifice*. I don't usually like the word because it is so overused, but what word better suits the reality? American soldiers lost their lives fighting to defend the simple ideas that gave birth to the United States of America: that we are all created equal, that simply by virtue of our membership in the human race we are entitled to life, liberty and the pursuit of happiness.

More than 400,000 Americans were killed in World War II. Nearly 700,000 were wounded. Millions worked and trained and risked and did what needed to be done. They saved the world.

Race hatred, religious bigotry, contempt for anyone different, bitterness, resentment and spite fed the greatest, most terrible war in human history and left sixty million dead. No German at the start of the Nazi regime pictured Dachau or Buchenwald or Oradour. But by their moral cowardice they made those crimes against humanity inevitable.

We, the heirs of the American soldiers who lie in their thousands beneath shining white crosses and Stars of David in military cemeteries in Europe, we who have benefited so wonderfully from their pain and courage and sacrifice, have only to be vigilant, to be strong in the right, and to say with one voice: never again.

Michael Grant

ACKNOWLEDGMENTS

An undertaking as complex as the Front Lines trilogy is not the work of one writer alone. I may be the guy in the foxhole (so to speak) but I have my own sergeants, officers, and thankfully, support troops.

So, some thanks are in order: to Kelsey Horton and Mabel Hsu for their editorial support; to Jill Amack and Kathryn Silsand, the copy editors who saved me so much embarrassment; David Curtis, Joel Tippie, and Amy Ryan, who designed the book; Tina Cameron in production; Bess Braswell, the marketing director; and the hardest-working woman in publicity, Ro Romanello.

Above all, of course, is Katherine Tegen, my editor, publisher and friend. None of this happens without Tegen.

Outside of HarperCollins, I'd like to thank Stella Paskins, my UK editor, and their equivalents to the above-listed.

And of course, Steve Sheppard at Cowan, DeBaets, Abrahams and same, who is my lawyer, my pal, the guy you talk to about rights for this or any of my books, and the guy assigned to talking me down off ledges.

IMAGE LIST

Omaha Beach, D-day

Omaha Beach (Wiki Commons)

LST (Landing Ship Tank)
unloading a truck at Omaha Beach

LST (Wiki Commons)

The ill-fated Sherman-DD with its
flotation skirt not inflated

Sherman-DD (Wiki Commons)

P-51 "Mustang," the Cadillac of
the Air. Widely considered the best
fighter plane of WW2.

P-51 (Wiki Commons)

The odd-looking but deadly P-38 "Lightning"

P-38 (Wiki Commons)

Panzerfausts, the basic German infantry anti-tank weapon

P-51 (Author photo)

American soldiers at the Battle of the Bulge

Battle of the Bulge (Wiki Commons)

Oradour-sur-Glane today. General and future president Charles DeGaulle ordered it to be left as a permanent memorial.

Oradour-sur-Glane (Author photo)

SS-Sturmbannführer Adolf Diekmann, responsible for the Oradour massacre

Adolf Diekmann (Author photo)

The Hürtgen Forest

Hürtgen Forest (Wiki Commons)

Clervaux Castle (Luxembourg) today

Clervaux Castle (Author photo)

P-38 Lightning, a deadly American
ground-attack fighter

P-38 (Creative Commons)

P-47 Thunderbolt, a workhorse of
ground attack

P-47 (Creative Commons)

American combat medics at work

American combat medics (Wiki Commons)

Sten gun, British commando
sub-machine gun

Sten gun (Author photo)

Omaha Beach today

Omaha Beach (Author photo)

The German city of Dresden
after Allied bombing Public
Domain, US Army

Dresden (Wiki Commons)

Generals Eisenhower, Patton, and
Bradley view remains at Ohrdruf, a
satellite of Buchen-wald.
Public domain, US Army

Generals Eisenhower, Patton, and Bradley (Wiki Commons)

US military cemetery, Belgium

US military cemetery (Author photo)

BIBLIOGRAPHY

Note: The list of sources is partial at best. I have no practical way to keep track of the many videos and photos I took in. Even as to books I am certain to have missed a few, and books that helped me here may have been cited in earlier bibliographies in the Front Lines series.

Astor, Gerald. *The Bloody Forest.* Novato, CA: Presidio Press, 2000.

Atkinson, Rick. *The Guns at Last Light* (The Liberation Trilogy Book 3). New York: Henry Holt & Co., 2013.

Beevor, Antony. *Ardennes 1944: The Battle of the Bulge.* New York: Viking, 2015.

D-Day: The Battle for Normandy. New York: Viking, 2009.

Bérubé, Allan. *Coming Out Under Fire: The History of Gay Men and Women in World War II.* Chapel Hill, NC: University of North Carolina Press, 2nd ed., 2010.

Bowman, Martin W. *Mighty Eighth at War: USAAF 8th Air Force Bombers Versus the Luftwaffe 1943–1945.* Barnsley, UK: Pen and Sword, 2010.

Daugherty, James Harden. *The Buffalo Saga.* XLibris Corp., 2009.

Farmer, Sarah. *Martyred Village: Commemorating the 1944 Massacre at Oradour-sur-Glane.* Berkeley, CA: University of California Press, 2000.

Franklin, Robert. *Medic!* Lincoln, NE: University of Nebraska Press, 2006.

Friedrich, Jörg. *The Fire—The Bombing of Germany.* New York: Columbia University Press, 2006.

Gellhorn, Martha. *The Face of War.* New York: Atlantic Monthly Press, 1994.

Gildea, Robert. *Fighters in the Shadows: A New History of the French Resistance.* Cambridge, MA: Belknap Press, 2015.

Graves, Donald E. *Blood and Steel 3: The Wehrmacht Archive: The Ardennes Offensive, December 1944 to January 1945.* Barnsley, UK: Frontline Books, 2015.

Hackett, David A. *The Buchenwald Report.* New York: Basic Books, 1995.

Hansen, Randall. *Fire and Fury: The Allied Bombing of Germany, 1942–1945.* New York: NAL, 2010.

Hébras, Robert. *Oradour-sur-Glane—Le Drame Heure par Heure.* Nieul-lès-Saintes, France: Les Productions de Pertuis, 2001.

Heslop, Richard. *Xavier: A British Secret Agent with the French Resistance.* London, UK: Biteback Publishing, 2014.

McLachlan, Ian. *Eighth Air Force Bomber Stories—A New Selection.* Stroud, UK: Sutton Publishing, 2004.

McManus, John C. *Hell Before Their Very Eyes: American Soldiers Liberate Concentration Camps in Germany, April 1945.* Baltimore, MD: Johns Hopkins University Press, 2015.

Miller, Edward G. *A Dark and Bloody Ground.* College Station, TX: Texas A&M University Press, 1995.

Neitzel, Sonke, and Harald Welzer. *Soldaten: On Fighting, Killing, and Dying, The Secret WWII Transcripts of German POWS.* New York: Alfred A. Knopf, 2012.

Phillips, Robert F. *To Save Bastogne.* New York: Henry Holt & Co., 1983.

Rottman, Gordon L. *World War II Infantry Assault Tactics.* Oxford, UK: Osprey, 2008.

Stone, Dan. *The Liberation of the Camps: The End of the Holocaust and Its Aftermath.* New Haven, CT: Yale University Press, 2015.

Todorov, Tzvetan. *A French Tragedy—Scenes of Civil War, Summer 1944.* Hanover, NH: Dartmouth College Press, 1996.

Urban, Mark. *The Tank War.* Boston, MA: Little, Brown, 2013.

Wieviorka, Olivier. *The French Resistance.* Cambridge, MA: Belknap Press, 2016.

Yeide, Harry. *The Longest Battle: September 1944–February 1945: From Aachen to the Roer and Across.* Minneapolis, MN: Zenith Press, 2005.

Museums and Memorials:
The Imperial War Museum, London, UK
Oradour-sur-Glane, Village Martyr, Oradour, France
Bastogne War Museum, Bastogne, Belgium
Museum of the Battle of the Bulge, Clervaux, Luxembourg
Buchenwald Concentration Camp, Weimar, Germany

Please visit *www.frontlinesbook.com* for additional stories as well as videos, photos, etc.